P9-DEW-034

BEFORE HELL BROKE LOOSE

"The President already informed the attorney general that no Justice or ATF tactical units would assault the Sawtooth stronghold. Because the Old Glory Ranch is heavily fortified, its occupants well armed and determined, the President is convinced it'll turn out to be another Waco—or worse. And he doesn't want the heat."

"Who would?" Price remarked.

"He asked if elements of the Stony Man covert force could actually take the ranch," Brognola said. "I gave him your analysis, Yakov, that it's possible because we have the layout of the grounds and the building interiors from our informant."

"I also said the chances of success were only fifty-fifty," Yakov added, his light blue eyes flashing. "I hope you told him that, as well."

DON PENDLETON'S
MACK BOLAN.
STONY MAN™
MESSAGE TO AMERICA

A GOLD EAGLE BOOK FROM
WORLDWIDE.

TORONTO • NEW YORK • LONDON
AMSTERDAM • PARIS • SYDNEY • HAMBURG
STOCKHOLM • ATHENS • TOKYO • MILAN
MADRID • WARSAW • BUDAPEST • AUCKLAND

If you purchased this book without a cover you should be aware that this book is stolen property. It was reported as "unsold and destroyed" to the publisher, and neither the author nor the publisher has received any payment for this "stripped book."

First edition July 1998

ISBN 0-373-61919-7

MESSAGE TO AMERICA

Copyright © 1998 by Worldwide Library.

All rights reserved. Except for use in any review, the reproduction or utilization of this work in whole or in part in any form by any electronic, mechanical or other means, now known or hereafter invented, including xerography, photocopying and recording, or in any information storage or retrieval system, is forbidden without the written permission of the publisher, Worldwide Library, 225 Duncan Mill Road, Don Mills, Ontario, Canada M3B 3K9.

All characters in this book have no existence outside the imagination of the author and have no relation whatsoever to anyone bearing the same name or names. They are not even distantly inspired by any individual known or unknown to the author, and all incidents are pure invention.

® and TM are trademarks of Harlequin Enterprises Limited. Trademarks indicated with ® are registered in the United States Patent and Trademark Office, the Canadian Trade Marks Office and in other countries.

Printed in U.S.A.

MESSAGE TO AMERICA

PART ONE

СТАРУХА
(starookha)

CHAPTER ONE

Riga, Latvia
Maritime Fishing Docks
3:30 a.m. Local Time

David McCarter stamped his rubber-booted feet on the pier's wet planking, trying to drive the chill from his toes. Through the wide gaps between the boards, he could see the Daugava River, black and swirling below. The stink of rotting fish that rose from the water obliterated the salt tang of the Baltic Sea, which was less than a mile downstream; it made McCarter remember the old joke about sausage, that anyone who'd seen it made would never eat it. He dragged on the loosely packed, harsh Belomor cigarette he was smoking and wondered to bloody hell if he was ever going to be able to face another plate of fish and chips.

The barrel-chested man at McCarter's side nudged him with a half-full Kuban vodka bottle. Gary Manning was dressed like McCarter, in a baggy khaki pea coat with the collar turned up, worn wool pants, blue watch cap, rubber boots and crusty knit gloves with the fingertips hacked off. Under the glare of the pier's lamppost, dew glistened on the naps of their caps and coats; it dripped from the lines and cables of the trawlers and tugboats tied up along the quay.

The lateness of the hour meant nothing to the Riga trawl fleet, which worked around the clock during fishing season. A nearly constant stream of small, diesel-powered trucks rumbled back and forth in front of the two men, towing fish carts between trawlers and the processing plants, moving pieces of heavy equipment and supplies to and from the boats. Marine engines idled, rivet guns whacked, hoists and chains clanked and creaked, providing a background din that would hide both automatic-weapons fire and screams. McCarter and Manning blended into the general chaos like barnacles on a piling. They might have been a pair of trawler crewmen returning to their ship after a night on the town, or boat refitters on a midshift booze break.

Might have been.

Beneath their loose-fitting coats, they wore combat harnesses loaded with fragmentation, CS gas and stun grenades, and high-capacity 9 mm semiautomatic handguns and extra magazines rode in shoulder leather. The canvas tool bags at their feet held gas masks and silencer-equipped, German-made machine pistols. In addition, Manning's gear bag contained blocks of Semtex plastic explosive and a complete demolition man's tool kit. McCarter and Manning were two-fifths of Phoenix Force, a supersecret U.S. covert-action team, operating under direct but untraceable order of the President. If they were caught this night, the Latvian police would regard them as international terrorists. The U.S. State Department would provide no explanation for their presence in-country; the executive branch would not intervene, publicly or privately, on their behalf. If they were captured alive, the warriors of Phoenix Force would be left to twist in the wind.

McCarter and Manning's immediate concern wasn't the police, but a lanky, bearded man in black oilskins pushing a two-wheeled metal cart toward them. The guy's eyes lit up when he saw the Kuban bottle. McCarter lowered the bottle and flicked away his cigarette as the man approached them.

"*Yey,*" the sailor said, licking his lips, "*da-vai gla-tok!*"

McCarter recognized the language as Russian, not Latvian. Either the man was an expatriate sailor, one of the many who had settled here prior to the Soviet breakup, or he was posing as one. If he was with the opposition, he could have been a military black marketeer or a thug from one of the many ruthless subsets of Russian mafia. While McCarter watched the man's eyes and hands, Manning scanned the dock in both directions, looking for signs of trouble. Even if the sailor was just thirsty, there was always the chance he would make a fuss when he discovered the liquor was actually water and they were only pretending to be boozing.

A fuss was something they didn't need just now.

The earpiece hidden under McCarter's watch cap crackled. "Hawk here. I have him."

Hidden atop the superstructure of the rusting trawler moored across the pier from them, Thomas Jackson "Hawk" Hawkins, had an easy seventy-yard head shot with a suppressor-equipped, Leupold-scoped Remington Model 700 sniper rifle. McCarter knew Hawkins wouldn't risk giving away his own position and the team's presence unless everything came unglued. Despite the silencer, a close-range, cat-astrophic brain shot with a .308 Winchester bullet would be hard to conceal, what with the partial va-porization of the skull and its contents and the cut-string drop of the corpse.

McCarter shrugged his left arm, as if shaking out a mild cramp. Cold steel slid down the inside of the former SAS man's sleeve. The tips of his fingers stopped the fall of the unsheathed Devil Dart. A fur-ther twitch would drop the knurled handle of the bead-blasted killing spike into his fist. Scuffles and fights on the docks were not uncommon, but they in-variably drew spectators. McCarter's attack, if that proved necessary, would be quick and final, a single thrust under the bearded chin to skewer the tongue against the soft palate and drive the triangular point deep into the man's brain.

Manning heard Hawkins's words through his own earpiece and moved accordingly, shifting his burly, six-foot frame to shield the action from view as much as possible. Knowing Hawkins's fire lane to the target and McCarter's striking range, he gave them both plenty of room to work. No matter how the Russian met his death, Manning was ready to lunge forward and catch the falling body. In the blink of an eye, he could tumble it over the pier's railing.

The Russian repeated his request, holding out his hand. He didn't know how close he was to having already enjoyed his last drink.

"*P-yei svo-evo,*" McCarter said. "Drink your own." He chugged the last of the contents and tossed the bottle over his shoulder into the river. Then he added, "*Ee-de...v Rossiyu.*" "Go back to Russia."

"Svoloch! Basran!" the sailor cursed as he turned away.

Manning leaned close and whispered, "What did he say?"

"You don't want to know, mate," McCarter assured him. Resting his elbows against the pier's railing, the Phoenix Force team leader resheathed the Devil Dart, then checked his watch. The real-time satellite window was closing; in another twenty minutes they would lose the scrambled uplink to the Stony Man Farm command center. It was time to get the show on the road. He spoke a few words into the minimicrophone hidden by the raised collar of his jacket, giving the green light to the other two members of the Phoenix team, Rafael Encizo and Calvin James. Then he lit up another of the toxic Russian cigarettes.

Behind him, eighty yards farther down the dock, the 155-foot trawler, *Varuskya Liset,* rested at her moorings. A trio of short, burly men armed with Soviet assault rifles stood atop her gangway. They held their shoulder-slung AKS-74s down low but not completely out of sight.

They weren't protecting a cargo of Arctic cod with 5.45 mm automatic weapons.

They guarded something more precious than gold, something every jumped-up, pot-metal, Third World president-for-life wanted. The power to inflict megadeath.

When the Belomor was half-smoked, McCarter nodded to Manning and they picked up their satchels and started down the dock like a pair of well-lubricated sailors in no particular hurry to get back to work. Their zigzag route took them closer and closer to the *Varuskya Liset*—absolute ground zero.

Stony Man Farm, Virginia
8:34 p.m. EDT

AT THE SOUND OF THE BEEP, Aaron "the Bear" Kurtzman removed his mug from the computer lab's microwave oven. Steam snaked up from the cup, carrying with it the bitter smell of reboiled coffee. He took a sip and made a face. He couldn't remember how many times he'd reheated it, but five dark brown rings around the inside of the cup's rim indicated recent lowerings of the waterline.

Kurtzman dumped the undrinkable brew down the sink. There wasn't time to build a fresh pot of the black-as-tar, supercaffeinated java that he preferred, and that everyone else on the Stony Man Farm electronic-Intel squad either doctored with milk and sugar—or avoided like the plague. He snatched a pair of blueberry danishes from the covered tray beside the microwave, figuring a sugar lift, though brief, was better than no lift at all.

He pivoted his wheelchair and propelled himself back up the shallow ramp to his workstation. Like the rest of the crew, he had been working at his computer terminal virtually nonstop for eighteen hours. The strain was beginning to show in annoying little ways. His fingers cramped as they gripped the wheels' rims, and when he blinked his eyes, they burned against the insides of his lids like they'd been sandblasted. From the elevated dais supporting his massive, horseshoe-shaped desk, he surveyed the bank of wall screens that displayed what his people had on their workstation monitors, then he checked each team member in turn.

Dr. Huntington Wethers sat hunched over his computer console, grinding the stem of his unlit pipe between his teeth. He was eavesdropping on Latvian police, emergency and military radio transmissions in and around Riga. The audio signals were being simultaneously translated into English text at a CIA intercept station inside the city. The African American former cybernetics professor scanned the scrolling lines of type for aid calls from the commercial fishing pier, reports of shots fired, explosions, requests for ambulances—anything that indicated Phoenix Force's primary line of retreat might be in jeopardy, or that they might soon be under assault from local authorities. In either case, Wethers would reroute and supervise the covert-action squad's withdrawal.

At her computer station, red-haired, compactly built Carmen Delahunt was taking her third turn with the voluminous Justice Department and Interpol files on the international arms merchant, Sergio Ishmael Eshamani. Despite weeks of effort, the Stony Man team had come up empty in a critical area of the investigation. In such a situation, lab procedure called for each team member to review all the basic material, the rationale being that if five keenly trained minds tackled the same problem, one of them would be bound to find the end of the ball of string—in this case, the buyer and/or final destination of the Riga nuclear contraband. The Eshamani records went back almost twenty years, to when he had been a lackey for the Middle Eastern sales force of an Italian small-arms manufacturer. As Delahunt's fingers rattled the computer keys, her lips moved silently. Kurtzman didn't have to be much of lip-reader to realize she was swearing under her breath.

At the center workstation, Akira Tokaido kept track of Phoenix Force's on-site radio transmissions and monitored the city of Riga from a weather satellite camera. His CD player and headset lay abandoned at the far end of the desk, along with a litter of classic punk and grunge-rock CDs. He was in constant, nervous motion, adjusting the gain and filter array to get the clearest audio and video signals, drumming his fingers impatiently on the edge of the keyboard, occasionally brushing his palm across his hair. There had been no transmissions from McCarter and the others for several minutes, not since he had given the go signal.

From the back of the room, Barbara Price stared up at the wall screen display of broken cloud cover over Riga. The honey blonde was the only member of the team who looked cool and collected. The calm she projected was a function of one of her previous incarnations: model and cover girl. Price had learned to control her facial expression no matter what she was feeling. Kurtzman knew that inside the beautiful, serene shell, Stony Man Farm's mission controller was wound as tight as a ten-dollar watch.

Kurtzman folded a danish once and took half of it in a huge bite. It tasted like sugar-iced cardboard. His stomach growled ominously as he swallowed. Indigestion came with the territory at this stage of a mission. The Bear and his crew had done everything humanly possible to ensure the success of the job at hand. There had been weeks of preplanning, of triple fail-safing the escape routes, of identifying and either eliminating or compensating for the operation's weak points. But in every mission, there was a point when the Farm's planners and thinkers had to wait, reduced to mere spectators while the odds played out and the Phoenix warriors took their turn at bat.

A brief, terrible vision filled Kurtzman's mind: the weather satellite wall monitor flaring suddenly from a central bright pinpoint of red to full-screen crimson, the Riga radio signals lost in a howl of static.

Detonation.

He forced the image from his mind. Everyone in the room was fighting the same dread. As lab-section chief, he felt compelled to break the heavy silence, to focus on something constructive while they sat on their hands.

"Carmen, are you making any progress over there?" he asked.

"You tell me," she said. "I've been going through Eshamani's known client list again. Running over ground we've already covered, trying to see if we've missed anything. Do you want the high points?"

"Go ahead," Kurtzman said.

"We've agreed that only a small segment of his market is going to be interested in a chunk of high-grade nuclear material or a functional nuclear weapon. We've ruled out the U.S. and South American drug gangs who've been buying Soviet-manufactured autoweapons and conventional explosives from him. For small-scale, purely economic warfare, even the light artillery, and the ground-to-air and ground-to-ground, wire-guided missiles in his east European inventory are overkill. The client in this case has got to have big-time political motives."

"Assuming that whoever's buying the goods isn't

interested in a quick resale to another party," Tokaido added without taking his eyes from his monitor's screen.

"Eshamani's too sharp a dealer for that," Kurtzman countered. "You can be sure his price on this stuff is so high that a second middleman couldn't make a decent profit."

Dr. Wethers swiveled his chair and glanced up at the dais. "So that still leaves us chasing every two-bit terrorist group and Third World dictator on the planet," he said.

"Not quite," Delahunt said. "To make a big bang from scratch, you need highly skilled people and a well-equipped research facility. Which means major, long-term capital investment. Which means a governmental or quasigovernmental entity."

"But that assumes," Barbara Price said as she walked up the wheelchair ramp, "as in the previous Eshamani operation, we're simply dealing with the sale of weapons-grade nuclear material. Or even system subcomponents, like a target assembly scavenged from a Soviet weapon scheduled for destruction. Given the situation in the former republics, the number of functional nukes still in the field and the deteriorating security, we can't rely on Eshamani staying at the bits-and-pieces level of nuclear tech. The market for an operational device is too huge and too profitable. It includes all the groups or governments who lack the expertise to construct their own nukes, or who don't want to pay for the R and D, or who want something they know will work the first time."

"Your basic, off-the-rack, ready to wear nuclear holocaust," Delahunt said.

"And the worst of all possibilities," Dr. Wethers added grimly, "a buyer who intends to let it rip."

Delahunt typed in a command, and the rows of names, dates and numbers vanished from her wall screen, replaced by moving images. The recent surveillance video showed an impeccably dressed Sergio Ishmael Eshamani strolling on the Champs-Elysées. The short, stoutly built man was dwarfed by leggy Parisian high-fashion models clinging to either elbow, while stone-faced bodyguards brought up the front and rear of the formation.

As the video loop recycled, Delahunt zoomed in tight on the arms dealer from the shoulders up. Eshamani's most startling feature was his head, which he shaved to minimize the effect of an extreme case of pattern baldness. What hair he had grew black and thick in oddly shaped and widely spaced islands—the pair of blotches atop his high forehead reminded Kurtzman of the horn buds of a young goat. If the top of Eshamani's head was thin in the hair department, his cheeks, chin and neck more than made up for it: they were shadowed by a dark beard so heavy that he had it scraped off three times a day.

Though Eshamani and his various enterprises had been under CIA and Justice Department surveillance for nearly two decades, it wasn't until recently, when he began moving large quantities of liberated Soviet war matériel, that his operation had become a priority concern of the U.S. government. Even though the level of scrutiny had increased, there had been no direct proof, only strong suspicions of his entry into the illicit nuclear trade. Then, six weeks earlier, Justice had received a tip from an unnamed overseas source that linked a Panamanian-registry cargo ship to the in-progress transfer of Soviet-manufactured cesium to Libya.

Operating on secret orders from the President, relayed through Hal Brognola, the White House liaison to Stony Man, Phoenix Force had intercepted the suspect vessel in international waters off the Canary Islands. During an intense close-quarters firefight, the Phoenix team had killed eighteen of the twenty-man crew; only the captain and first mate survived the assault. A search of the hold turned up four pounds of high-grade fissionable material, still in its Russian-marked, lead-lined safety container. Before Gary Manning set off the explosive charges that blew the bottom out of the ship, scuttling it in two hundred fathoms of water, Rafael Encizo sent out a garbled distress call in Spanish. When rescuers arrived at the scene three hours later, other than debris that had drifted over a wide area, there was no sign of the cargo ship or its crew. All were presumed lost in an unexplained accident at sea.

For the first five days of around-the-clock interrogation by Phoenix Force, the captain and his first mate had refused to confirm what the Stony Man cyber squad had already uncovered from its review of satellite and radio intelligence: there had been contact between the Panamanian cargo ship and an unidentified small fishing trawler in the North Atlantic. On the sixth day, the mate gave up the nationality, port and name of the trawler. A further check showed that the *Varuskya Liset* was owned by a relative of a high-ranking Russian military officer. The officer had known connections to the Chechen mafia and to Sergio Ishmael Eshamani, as well as access to nuclear stockpiles.

The Panamanian cargo ship, on the other hand, had no link, direct or indirect, to the arms merchant. It turned out to be the leased property of the Libyan government. Which led Kurtzman and the others to conclude that the Soviet cesium had already been bought and paid for. Because the ship had gone down, Libya had lost its entire investment, on the order of tens of millions of dollars—something that had to have strained the relationship between buyer and middleman. Accordingly Stony Man considered it unlikely that Libya was the customer for the Riga material. As the ship had sunk without witnesses, apparently by accident, Eshamani could not know the jeopardy his operation was in.

Phoenix Force's recovery of the cesium had fanned the White House's fear that Eshamani planned to establish a global pipeline for Soviet nuclear contraband. That was something the President wanted stopped at all costs, the buyers and sellers neutralized, any nukes or material seized or destroyed. Surveillance in and around Riga in the past twenty-four hours had confirmed the presence of the Russian brigadier general, of Eshamani and of two teams of heavily armed thugs guarding the vessel in question. One of the security squads belonged to the international arms dealer. Because of weather conditions, another high-seas boarding had been ruled too risky. Instead, a surgical strike, performed dockside by a small team of experts, offered the best odds of success.

There was, of course, an enormous potential downside. If the ship held an operational device and things went sour, a city of a million souls could be ransomed. Or destroyed.

That the President had fully committed to the plan was a measure of his supreme confidence in Phoenix Force and the Stony Man personnel. Kurtzman glanced at the wall clock set to Riga time. Any second now the Phoenix warriors would be breaching the trawler's perimeter.

Very soon they would know which end of the tiger they had hold of.

Riga Fishing Docks
3:41 a.m. Local Time

TEN FEET BELOW the surface of the water, Rafael Encizo swam against an onrushing wall of darkness and cold. He maintained his bearing in the current by skimming the heel of his gloved right hand against the steel skin of the *Varuskya Liset.* When he reached the end of the hull, he turned, following the curve of the stern into a pool of bright light.

The aft superstructure of the trawler carried a huge gantry and reel; directly below it, the deck was cut by a broad ramp that sloped down into the water. The ramp allowed the trawl net's load to be dragged up on deck. Hovering over Encizo's head, backlit by the bank of floodlights illuminating the boat's net bay, was the underside of a twelve-foot Zodiac that was tethered to the foot of the ramp.

Encizo unslung his Barnett RC-150 crossbow. With the armed, cocked weapon in firing position, he dropped half of the lead weights belted to his waist and slowly rose to the surface.

When the Chechen mafia soldier guarding the ramp saw Encizo's black neoprene-hooded head, black-smeared face and the short black bow of the Barnett break the surface, he half turned, the pistol grip of his AKS-74 in his fist. For an instant, he squinted against the floodlights' glare. Was he looking at a tangled mass of oily debris? Or was it a threat? The shock of realization sent adrenaline coursing through his veins, but it was too late.

Before the hardman could bring his shoulder-slung assault rifle to bear, the crossbow thwanged, salt mist spraying from its bowstring. The sixteen-inch metal bolt covered the distance in a tenth of a second. Its modified broad-head point sliced into the middle of the Chechen's throat an inch above the top edge of his body armor. Because of the relative positions of the bowman and target, the bolt's entry angle was steeply upward. Four razor-sharp blades transected the Chechen's windpipe and larynx, and the point of the broad-head buried itself into the front of the vertebra that supported the base of his skull.

The soldier staggered back a step, hunching his shoulders and gagging. He released the autorifle, letting it drop on its sling, and clawed for the fletched end of the bolt shaft protruding from his throat. A second passed, then the shaft came away in his fist as the explosive-tipped broad-head detonated with a muffled cough. A tiny pop that turned a maybe into a sure kill.

For the briefest instant, hot explosive gases ballooned the flesh of the Chechen's neck and face, making his eyes bulge enormously. The small, shaped charge neatly separated his skull from the knobby column of his spine. The quartet of surgical steel razors fractured away from the broad-head's core, blowing ragged rents in the sides of his neck. The soldier's knees buckled, and his eyes became twin blood-laced zeros. As he rolled down the grade to the edge of the water, his semidetached head flopped through nearly 360 degrees of arc.

Encizo rose from the water and quickly recocked and rebolted his weapon with another of the minifrag broad-heads designed by Gary Manning and Stony Man Farm's armorer, John "Cowboy" Kissinger, for perimeter penetration.

Calvin James surfaced on the other side of Zodiac. The tall African American unplugged the barrel of his silenced Heckler & Koch MP-5 KA, cleared its action and covered Encizo while he kicked off his fins and pulled off his face mask and snorkel. As James removed his own headgear, the corner of his mouth and the pencil-thin mustache above it twisted in an expression of disgust. The sulphurous, carrion stink of fish guts and spilled diesel in the net bay was awesome. He stepped out of his fins and moved to Encizo's side.

They advanced uphill with Encizo facing front, covering the lip of the ramp with the Barnett, and James walking backward behind him, sweeping the H&K over the gantry area that looked down on them. As they neared the top of the ramp, they dropped to their stomachs and peered over the edge. The main deck of the *Varuskya Liset* was bathed in hard white light. Beyond the base of the crane, which stood about thirty feet across the deck from the start of the ramp, was a low metal structure that sheltered the fish-sorting and processing area. The shelter had two doors on each side and no door on the end that faced them. Each of the entrances was guarded by an armed and armored Chechen soldier. Beyond the processing shed, a four-story-tall radar mast dominated the deck.

In front of the mast, one story above the deck, was the captain's cabin, and stacked on top of that was the ship's bridge.

Encizo and James ducked back below the lip of the ramp when a fifth man moved into view atop the processing shed.

"Counting the guys on the gangway, I make it eight," James whispered. "But there could be more, out of sight up in the bridge."

Encizo nodded, checking the dial of a small instrument strapped to his wrist. He showed the radiation reading to James, then enabled the communications device at his belt. He folded down the microphone of the headset hidden under his diving hood and spoke softly into it. "Bud, this is Bud Light. We are home and have a signature. Repeat, heat is confirmed."

McCarter's terse reply crackled into both of their headsets. "Bud Light proceed."

Encizo stripped off the tight-fitting neoprene hood; now that he was out of the frigid water, it was slow-cooking his head. The communications headset came off with it. He slicked back his grizzled black hair with a hand, and replaced the earpiece and mike.

An untrained observer viewing his face under the black camouflage war paint might have thought it calm, the eyes relaxed to the point of almost appearing sleepy. It was a dangerous illusion, based on faulty but lingering stereotypes of race and intellect. The Cuban's square, Indian features and the smoothness and economy of his movements belied a brain that routinely planned its attacks five moves ahead and a body that was capable of blinding speed and power. Beneath the seemingly calm exterior, Rafael

Encizo was revving at seven grand, his brain and body redlined.

"The roof guy first?" James asked.

"Take him," Encizo said as he unplugged the barrel of his silenced Beretta 93-R autopistol. He checked the weapon's action, then reholstered it in shoulder leather. In the imminent close-quarters battle belowdecks, the high-capacity 93-R would be his mainstay; it was his weapon of last resort if more firepower was needed above deck.

Encizo didn't have to warn his partner about ricochets in an all-steel environment. James knew that, silenced guns and subsonic ammo notwithstanding, a slug whining off the superstructure would alert the enemy, and probably get some if not all of them killed. As he peeked over the lip of the ramp, the man atop the shelter turned away and walked toward the bow, continuing his tour of the shelter's roof perimeter. James thumbed the fire-selector switch to single shot and settled into a prone shooting position on the metal ramp. Through the steel against his belly, he could feel a pulse, not his own, but the slow, throbbing beat of a pile driver at work farther down the pier. It rattled his guts.

James braced his elbows on the edge of the ramp, lined up the H&K's open sights with the roofline and flipped off the safety. His breathing fell into the pile driver's slow and solid rhythm.

The roof guard strolled back to the aft end of the shelter. He paused and surveyed the stern of the ship. He was looking right at James, apparently without seeing him, when the former SEAL squeezed off a round. The H&K phutted, ejecting a single spent case. The 9 mm hollowpoint slug caught the soldier under the nose, and the impact snapped back his head. For a moment, his chin pointed at the sky, then he fell over in slow motion, dropping to his side. He hit the roof on the pile driver's down beat.

No one rushed away from the sides of the shelter to check on him.

Encizo touched James's arm, and they rose and crossed to the crane on the run, pausing at the doorless end of the processing shed. James immediately bellied down on the deck and crept forward to take a low peek around the right-hand corner of the building. He quickly pulled back. With hand signals, he told Encizo that the closest of the two guards was standing away from structure, over by the gunwale.

Standing upright, Encizo edged around the corner with the butt of the crossbow's skeleton stock firmly planted against his shoulder. The Chechen had his back to the shelter. He was relieving himself over the side through the hawsehole, a man-size opening in the gunwale that allowed access to a mooring cleat. As the soldier zipped himself up and turned back to face the shed, Encizo fired the bow.

The bolt zipped across the deck, striking two inches above the man's chin. Its razor tip shattered his bottom front teeth and speared into his mouth. The stunning force of the hit sent him stumbling backward, legs tangling over the cleat. As he toppled through the hawsehole, the broad-head detonated. It made a sound like a soggy, air-filled paper bag slammed against an open palm. Blood mist twinkled in the light for an instant, then it was gone.

Before the soles of the man's shoes dropped out of sight, James was up, dashing along the side of the shelter. When the second man stuck his head out of the doorway, the muzzle of James's H&K was less than a yard away. The soldier caught the rush of movement out of the corner of his eye; it was the last thing he saw before the hollowpoint slug slammed his temple. James snatched hold of the falling corpse by the vest and eased it down on the deck.

The inside of the shelter was all business: grim gray steel walls, well-worn stainless-steel-clad cleaning tables and open hatches that led to the refrigeration holds. Encizo looked over the edge of a hatch as he knelt behind one of the tables. There were no fish down there, only a big-time stink and three feet of the concentrated salt brine used to lower the freezing temperature of the catch. The men guarding the dock side of the shelter were out on the deck, in plain view of the three thugs covering the gangway. None of them could be safely taken out until the bow of the boat had been swept. Everything had to be done in order, by the numbers. The battle plan depended on Phoenix Force clearing and controlling the top deck without alerting the men on the decks below—it was the only way a force of five could dissect a force of twenty or more and survive. Encizo hand-signaled for James to stay put and exited by the door he had entered.

The Cuban moved along the superstructure to the captain's cabin, where a set of steep stairs led up to the bridge. As he climbed the steps, he leaned out and looked into the dark cabin, noting the empty bunk. He padded silently across the cabin's roof, which was also the rear deck of the bridge. The inside of the pilothouse was lit up like Christmas. Through the window set in the back door, he could see a short corridor that opened onto the bridge proper, and two men inside. One was seated on an upholstered bench behind the ship's wheel; the other stood facing his shipmate with his back to the front windows and his arms folded across his chest. Neither had body armor, but both were wearing automatic pistols in ballistic nylon hip holsters.

Encizo took out the Beretta with his left hand and thumbed off the safety. With the crossbow in his right fist, he slipped through the door, low and cat quick. Before either sailor realized what was happening, he was in their midst. As he fired the 9 mm pistol point-blank into the seated man's forehead, the other man had the presence of mind to reach, not for the pistol on his hip—which he could never have gotten out of its holster—but for the wooden handle hanging from a chain above his head. The ship's horn.

The Barnett's bowstring twanged as Encizo sent a bolt into the center of the sailor's unprotected chest. In this case, the explosive feature of the broad-head was pure overkill: its stainless-steel razors had already cut an *X* through the middle of the man's heart, stopping it cold. The dead sailor's fingers brushed the horn's knob but didn't get a grip as he crumpled to the floor. Encizo stopped the swinging handle with the Barnett's cocking stirrup. Close, he thought.

Encizo checked the other rooms in the bridge and, finding no one, moved back onto the rear deck. He slipped into a prone position with the rearmed crossbow and looked down onto the deck. The men guarding the top of the gangway stood clumped in front of the gate; the other two soldiers leaned against the shelter's outside wall. They were all chatting back and forth, occasionally laughing.

The Cuban gritted his teeth. The shot angles were

much steeper and tighter than he liked. The closest targets, the men by the gangway, stood almost directly under him; that, coupled with the body armor they were wearing, meant he had to hit a softball-sized bull's-eye on top of their heads. If the broadhead didn't strike square, it could glance off the thick bone of a skull. He considered using the Beretta because it had better penetration power, but decided against it. If the target moved and he missed with a 9 mm slug, it would clang on the deck like a dinner bell. At least with the Barnett, a shot outside the ten-ring might not alert the men inside the ship.

He pulled back from the edge of the roof and spoke into his headset mike. "The summit is clear," he said. "I have position."

CALVIN JAMES ACKNOWLEDGED Encizo's transmission, then took a deep breath and slowly let it out. It was up to him now. He rechecked the action of the H&K, making sure its fire-selector switch was set on single shot. As much as he would've liked to, he couldn't come charging out of the shelter firing on full auto. James was a gifted marksman and athlete, but he knew the limits of what was physically possible. Shooting full auto on the run against multiple moving targets, although safer for him, would almost guarantee a miss—and a ricochet. Single shot, target by target, was the only route under the circumstances. Like a shadow, he glided across the shelter's work area, pausing near the sternmost door, which was secured open with a nylon cord and metal hook.

He put his back against the cold steel wall. He shut his eyes and relaxed, letting the tension drain from his shoulders, arms, hands, fingertips. He rotated his head, stretching the tightness from his neck. He had to be loose in order to be smooth; he had to be smooth in order to be quick; he had to be quick in order to survive. Once he took that first step out of the shelter, secrecy went bye-bye and the level of risk skyrocketed, not just for Phoenix Force, but for the still sleeping population of Riga.

All hits, he told himself. No misses.

He reached down to his belt and activated his communications device. In a whisper he said, "Bud, this is Bud Light. I am go. Repeat, go. Counting down from fifteen...fourteen...thirteen..."

AT JAMES'S SIGNAL, McCarter gave Manning a nudge and they started weaving toward the entrance to the ship's gangway. As they set foot on the ramp, the three Chechen guards leaned out and shouted down at them to clear off.

McCarter took the lead up the gangway, keeping James's count in his head as he climbed. Six...five...

A guard yelled through a cupped hand for them to turn back, that they were boarding the wrong ship. He punctuated the warning by showing them his Soviet-made autorifle.

McCarter didn't stop climbing, with Manning on his heels. Four...three...

The Chechens braced themselves and took aim. Thirty feet of steeply angled gangway separated McCarter and Manning from the muzzles of the trio of AKMs.

Two...one.

JAMES DUCKED OUT of the shelter with the H&K in his left hand. Barely clear of the doorway, he already had the back of the first Chechen's head in the ring-and-post front sight. He punched a round into the base of the man's neck. As the corpse crumpled to the deck, it exposed the other shelter guard to point-blank fire. The side of his face bathed in his comrade's blood, the second hardman managed to turn toward his attacker, but his autorifle remained frozen in his hands, aimed uselessly at the deck. James looked right into the man's eyes as he tightened down on the machine pistol's trigger. With the ultimate defeat bearing down on him, there was no remorse in the Chechen soldier's face, only glaring hate.

The second *zip-thwack* of the H&K attracted the gangway crew's full attention. With a grunt of surprise, the man nearest James spun away from the ramp, swinging his AKM sights around as he pivoted. The soldiers behind him swiveled, as well, both of them stepping away from the gunwale to get a clear firing lane.

From the moment he popped out of the shelter doorway, time for James had dropped into crawl mode. Things appeared to be happening at quarter speed, allowing his brain to vacuum up the tiniest details. From experience, he knew the sensation wasn't real; time was moving along at its normal, brisk clip. The only difference between Calvin James the instant before he made his exit and Calvin James now was that he had surrendered control of his body, action and reaction, to his subconscious mind, to years of training and instinct.

As the gangway crew drew down on him, he dropped to a knee to present them with a smaller target, and he had the machine pistol's folding stock snug against his shoulder. A split second before he cut loose on the closest man's forehead, the rearmost of the soldiers twisted suddenly out of line, sprawling sideways. James glimpsed a feathered shaft protruding from one side of the man's neck, and peeking out the other, the front half of a wetly gleaming broadhead. The short fuse of the C-4 charge ignited on impact. James touched off the H&K, instinctively averting his eyes as the mined arrow tip exploded, sending tiny bits of tempered steel shrapnel flying in all directions. Even as he protected himself, he swung the H&K's muzzle on the third hardman.

He only looked away for an instant. But an instant was too long.

When James looked back, the dead men were falling. The head-shot Chechen slumped, loose limbed, to the deck. His crossbow-shot comrade toppled so hard against the middle guy's back that it pushed him out of James's sights.

The surviving Chechen grinned at James over the muzzle of his AKM.

Even as James tucked and rolled, he knew it was all over.

CHAPTER TWO

The two opposing sets of security teams eyed each other like packs of junkyard dogs separated by a hurricane fence. The threat of instantaneous, limitless violence hung heavy in the air, along with the smell of boiled fish and cabbage.

Sergio Eshamani stood with his back against the galley's steel-clad service counter, his hands thrust into the pockets of his belted, black kid leather trench coat. He was bracketed by eight male members of the Salvatore Lovecchio clan. The sober faces of the Sicilians bore the scars of what—and who—they had done. Their hands were not in their pockets, nor were they on pistol grips of the compact, 9 mm Beretta 12S submachine guns and Smith & Wesson 12-gauge pump-action room brooms that hung from their shoulders on leather slings.

The stare-down game with the Chechens on the other side of the room reflected the Sicilians' pride in their work, their unflinching loyalty, their absolute fearlessness. Nobody, but nobody, was going to back down the Lovecchio family.

Across the galley's scarred gray linoleum floor, seven AKM-packing Chechens maintained eye contact with Eshamani's troops while their boss, Briga-

dier General Avril Krukillov, two-handed a black nylon gym bag onto the scale in the middle of the long
dining table. The contents of the bag clinked when he
set it down on the scale plate. The dial's red needle
swung up and stopped, quivering just below eighteen
kilos. Both of the gym bags on the tabletop weighed
the same, and their combined weight was about eighty
pounds.

Eighty pounds of Krugerrands.

A faint smile lit the Russian's broad, ruddy face as
he pulled a pocket calculator from inside his brown
wool overcoat.

Because of his own inherited affliction, Eshamani
tended to divide people into the haves and the have-
nots, hairwise—and Krukillov had it in spades. The
general's hairline tapered to a sharp V three inches
above the bridge of his nose. The hair itself was iron
gray, glossy, incredibly thick and straight, and styled
in an inch-long brush cut.

Krukillov tapped the current price of gold into his
calculator and came up with the value of the table's
load: close to half a million dollars.

The gold was meant to wow the Chechen thugs
who did all of the general's wet work. It had definitely
impressed them. They positively twitched, fighting
the urge to tear open the bags and sieve the bright
coins through their fingers. Krukillov was obviously
pleased, as well, but in a much more relaxed way.

Eshamani knew the general was thinking on a bigger canvas. His delight had less to do with those particular bags of pirate treasure than with the apparently
limitless horizon that stretched out before him. The
free market was indeed a glory and a marvel to be-
hold. As one of the officers entrusted with the collec-

tion of the former Soviet republics' scattered nuclear stockpiles, Krukillov supervised the transportation of said weapons to centrally located sites for dismantling and destruction. Arranging for a few weapons here and there to be misplaced was child's play for a soldier of his rank and experience. On paper the diverted nukes would never be categorized as missing; they would be in perpetual transit somewhere in the vast and complex bureaucratic system. The general didn't need a calculator to figure out how many similar deals it would take to make him unassailably rich—he could count far enough for that on the fingers of one hand.

"When do I get the rest?" Krukillov asked.

The "rest" was three million dollars, payment in full for delivery of three operational nuclear devices.

"It will be moved electronically to your Swiss account," Eshamani told him, "as soon as I verify the PAL codes."

The PAL, or Permissive Action Link, was the multiple-digit, maximum-security access code that allowed the weapons to be armed and fired. Without the correct PAL codes, the Soviet nukes were nothing but very expensive, shiny boxes for holding plutonium.

The general nodded to his security team. "Bring out the *starookhas*," he said. As four of his Chechens left the galley, he took a silver hip flask from his overcoat pocket. Unscrewing the cap, he offered the flask to Eshamani. "Pepper vodka?"

The arms merchant declined.

Krukillov raised the flask in the air and said, "To a long and profitable association." He tipped back his head as he took a long pull of the spiced liquor.

Their association had already been profitable for
Eshamani; as to its being long-term, that had never
been in the cards. Even when they had been dealing
in components destined for ongoing, secret R-and-D
programs, the end had always been in sight—and it
was mushroom shaped. Now that they had moved up
into functional weapons, the half-life of the operation
was even shorter. At some point in the very near future, after one of the buyers exploded a device, the
heat would come down heavy on them from all directions. Eshamani had no doubt that Krukillov was
already setting up a patsy to take the blame on his
end. But the final result would be the same: the pipeline would be closed. While the route was open,
Eshamani's marketing challenge was to move as
much product as quickly as he could, even if that
meant selling the stuff at bargain-basement prices.

The four Chechens returned to the galley. They
pushed two dollies, each bearing a heavy wooden
crate the size of a refrigerator. The Chechens shifted
the olive drab crates onto the floor and, on the general's command, began unscrewing the front panels.
Inside each of the heavily braced and padded crates
was a gleaming silver artillery shell with a warhead
a shade under eight inches in diameter. The noses of
the warheads bore the symbol of the three-bladed fan,
the universal radiation-hazard warning. A special security container encased two-thirds of the chest-high
shells, from the bottom to a couple of inches below
the join of the warhead and casing. The container
made it impossible for the packaged round to be
chambered into a cannon straight out of the box. Each
of the security jackets had a massive lock with a nu-
meric keypad and two heavy-duty lifting handles.

Stenciled in Russian along the locked seam were the words Do Not Open Except To Fire.

The general produced a slim folder and pushed it over to Eshamani. "This is a synopsis of the operations manual and ballistic data for the weapons system," he said. "The notations on the last pages refer to the PAL access codes—they are grouped by weapon serial number."

As he rounded the galley table, Eshamani flipped through the pamphlet. One look told him it wasn't good enough. "I need to run through a complete arming sequence right now," he told the Russian.

"You don't trust me?"

"Trust has nothing to do with it," Eshamani assured him. "At some point, I'm going to have to explain the operation of this weapon to the buyers. When that time comes, you're not going to be around to help me answer questions."

"Very well," the general conceded.

As Eshamani flattened the folder on the table, Krukillov leaned over his shoulder, gusting him with stale vodka breath. The general's stubby fingers brushed across the first set of numbers. "These digits are the code that unlocks the container." He entered the numbers into the keypad on the front of the container, and the lock sprang open with a metallic click.

The Chechen assistants lifted away the halves of the security jacket, exposing the warhead and shell casing of the 152 mm howitzer round. It was known in the arms trade as an AFAP, an Artillery Fired Atomic Projectile.

"Beautiful, isn't it?" Krukillov said, patting the warhead's nose.

From the crate, the Chechens took out a small keypad with an LCD readout. Using a short cable, they plugged the keypad into a socket that was machined flush with the warhead's steel skin.

"Do you know why we call it *starookha?*" Krukillov asked.

"'Dirty old woman'?" Eshamani said, taking his best shot at a translation.

The general's eyes glittered. "That's right. Like waking up after a night of too much vodka to find a *starookha* in your bed, this is the nastiest of surprises."

Eshamani smiled, but only barely. A two-tenths-of-a-kiloton nuke was the equivalent of four hundred thousand pounds of TNT. Equating that to drunken sex with a bag lady was a typically bleak—and unfunny—Russian joke.

"Let's go through the command sequence," the arms merchant said. He took the keypad from the Chechens.

"The first set of numbers is the handshake-engage," Krukillov said. "It allows you to proceed with the fusing and arming protocols."

As the general read off the numbers, Eshamani tapped them into the keypad and they appeared in red on the unit's LCD panel. When he hit the final key, the six numbers blinked twice, then vanished, replaced by six red asterisks. "What's happened?" Eshamani said, showing the readout to the general.

"The stars mean the handshake code has been accepted. The next set of digits encode the targeting information." The general turned back through the ops folder until he found pages of conversion tables. He showed them to Eshamani. "Refer to these tables when you set the electronic fuse timer and the altitude of the nuclear burst."

"Give me some numbers."

"We'll set the fuse for one minute, target range of ten thousand meters with no radar-homing beacon, ground-burst detonation." Krukillov showed Eshamani where each of the codes appeared on the tables. Then he said, "Obviously, while the targeting information is variable, the input order is not. The data input sequence is clearly explained in the operations manual."

Again, after Eshamani had poked in the values, stars appeared on the readout panel.

"Now what?" he asked.

"The arming code," Krukillov said. "You should note that the handshake-engage code for all *starookha* AFAPs is the same. The final, six-digit arming codes are different for each weapon."

Eshamani punched in the numbers as the general read them off. The digits blinked twice and kept on blinking. "Something's wrong," he said. "There aren't any stars."

"That's because I switched a number on you, on purpose. I wanted you to see what happens if you make a mistake. Hit the zero button six times to clear the keypad, then I'll give you the correct code."

"How many tries before the PAL locks out?" the arms merchant asked. The lockout was a security feature that kept unauthorized users from inputting random number sets until they hit the jackpot.

"You have three tries at the handshake and arming steps," the general said. "After that, the system will no longer respond to the keypad."

"Is there a way to recover from a lockout?"

"Not without dismantling the AFAP," Krukillov said. "You'd better tell your buyers to be careful. They're not going to be able to send these weapons back to the factory for retooling." The general gave Eshamani the correct arming code.

The numbers again disappeared, replaced this time not by asterisks but by six little red hammer-and-sickle symbols.

The *starookha* was combat ready.

"As I understand it," Eshamani said, "these things have to be fired from a cannon in order to detonate?"

"For all practical purposes, that's true," Krukillov said. "The electronic fuse will not operate unless the shell is spinning at about 17,000 rpm. To get that result, the round's propellant charge has to ignite and the shell has to pass through a howitzer barrel."

"How do I abort?" Eshamani said.

"Replacing the security case automatically shuts down the LCD unit and clears the arming system's input memory. There's no limit on the number of times you can abort, but if the system has already experienced lockout, putting on the security jacket will not reset the cycle."

"I'd like to test-run the second weapon, to make sure I can operate it," Eshamani said.

"No problem," Krukillov agreed, stepping out of the arms merchant's way.

Eshamani plugged the LCD unit into the other *starookha* and, referring to the ops manual, began feeding the nuclear warhead six-digit codes.

WHEN THOMAS JACKSON Hawkins heard Calvin James start the countdown through his headset, he abandoned his 7×35 mm Steiner binoculars and moved behind the sandbagged Remington 700. From his hide atop the bridge roof of the derelict trawler, Hawkins peered through the Leupold M-3A telescopic sight.

The Leupold's field of view was much narrower than the Steiner's, less than ten feet from side to side at the designated target distance. It was also slower and more awkward to shift back and forth, not just because of the weight and length of the rifle, but because of the sandbagged shooting rest he had built. Which meant Hawkins couldn't take in the whole battlefield at a glance, but was reduced to tunnel vision. Without a spotter, he had to perform all his own bullet-impact observations through the Leupold, not an easy thing to do with a heavy-caliber rifle mule-kicking your shoulder.

On the upside, Hawkins knew the plan, knew where his teammates were supposed to be and what their individual objectives were. And his position was elevated enough to control the dock side of the top deck of the *Varuskya Liset* from bow to stern.

Squeezing the sandbag under the Remington's butt, Hawkins adjusted his sight picture, framing the target zone in the lens. The zone was the gate that led from the ship to the gangway, the gate where three body-armor-clad Chechens stood guard. Hawkins had already cranked the scope's internal Bullet Drop Compensator—BDC—cam down as low as it would go. Because the shot was under one hundred yards and at a downward angle, it required an additional low hold to compensate for the bullet's natural rise once it left the barrel.

Hawkins pulled back from the scope. With his naked eye, he could see McCarter and Manning climb-

ing the gangway, ignoring the challenge from the
guards, calmly walking into the Chechens' fire lane
and three 30-round mags of 5.45 mm bullets. Though
it was a cold night, beads of sweat oozed down the
sides of Hawkins's face. He already knew he only had
time for one shot. The question was where should he
take it? There was no room for error; in fact, there
was very little room, period. A clean miss would send
a 168-grain slug crashing into the side of the captain's
cabin. A through-and-through shot to the head or neck
would also mean a ricochet.

Hawkins found the stock weld with his cheek and
set the cross hairs in the middle of the gangway opening. With a slight shift of his weight against the buttstock, he could move the aim point to any of the three
men. He let his breathing fall into the slow, even
shoot-cycle rhythm.

Because of the limited field of view through the
scope, Hawkins couldn't see James come bursting out
of the shelter, shooting the nearest guards at point-
blank range. He did see the Chechens spin away from
the gangway, turning their guns in James's direction.
Hawkins bore down, his fingertip easing back the trigger, holding it just before the break point. As he hung
there, short of snapping the .308's cap by a quarter-
ounce of finger pressure, the guard on the left and the
one on the right fell away under James's and Encizo's
fire, leaving the middle man crouched in the gangway
opening, still armed and dangerous.

With Encizo momentarily out of ammo and James
caught flat-footed, Hawkins had no choice. He
touched off the shot. The rifle butt slammed back into
his shoulder. Thanks to the J. A. Ciener suppressor,
the noise exiting the business end of the sniper rifle

was around 138 decibels, less than the noise of a .22 pistol or a rivet gun.

THE BRIGHT LIGHTS that washed the top decks of the *Varuskya Liset* made for an excellent killing ground. Captain Andrei Sarnov had a clean shot on the figure in black neoprene kneeling on the bridge's rear deck. He held the PSO-1 scope's reticle arrow point in the middle of the man's back and watched as he quickly cocked and reloaded a nasty looking skeleton-stock crossbow. Sarnov's hide and command post was in the radar mast crow's nest of a trawler moored one dock over from the *Varuskya Liset*. The four-power scope's built-in range finder made the distance across the water to the target a bit under two hundred yards. With a practiced flick of the wrist, Sarnov adjusted the BDC so he could shoot dead on.

Sarnov was furious, and wanted very much to drill the nameless bastard who was jeopardizing a year of very delicate and very dangerous work. But because he was angry and knew it, he resisted the temptation. He eased off slightly on the SVD's trigger, holding the Soviet-made semiautomatic sniper rifle on target. Due to the location of his hide and its angle of view, he couldn't see the action going down on the other side of the ship.

He was hearing about it through his headset, though.

Uri Turgenev's excited voice made the earpiece crackle. "They've taken the gangway! Two more men on board!" he said.

Turgenev was in position on the dock near the bow of the suspect trawler. In the metal cart he pushed, concealed under a tarp, was an assortment of weapons of war: a pair of AKM assault rifles, an RPG launcher and grenades.

Another man spoke to Sarnov through the earpiece. Vlad Ferdishenko, who watched over the stern of the ship and the net bay from a small truck parked on the dock, was as upset as Turgenev. "Who the hell are they?" he exclaimed.

The question had come up several times in the past few minutes, first when an astonished Sarnov had witnessed the assault along the side of the processing shelter. The simple answer was that they were professionals. Sarnov knew slick work when he saw it, and those men were good. Not only physically skilled, but disciplined, seasoned warriors.

The follow-up question was much more complicated. Who were they working for?

Sarnov ran through the list of possibilities. They could have been part of a double cross by the arms merchant Eshamani, a scheme to get a few weapons for nothing. Or they could have been hirelings in the pay of Krukillov, who intended to take Eshamani's money and give him nothing. That possibility seemed unlikely because the unidentified hit men were killing the general's own Chechen thugs left and right. When he thought about it, Sarnov couldn't see the reward being great enough for either man to take the risk. The really big money was in doing business, moving product. That narrowed down the list considerably. Sarnov was left with Western military intelligence, or freelancers from the Russian mafia, or mutinous elements of Eshamani's security force.

A woman's voice broke his train of thought. It came from beside him in the crow's nest, not through the headset.

"Shall I kill the sniper now?"

Sarnov looked over at Natasha Beloc, the lone female assigned to the Spetsnaz recovery team. Like him, she wore a one-piece, nonreflective black jumpsuit. Except for a few stray wisps, her curly blond hair was hidden under a black watch cap, her cheeks were flushed with the cold and her right eye was pressed snug into the PSO-1's rubber eyecup. The twenty-six-year-old Beloc had twice qualified for the Russian army's biathlon team. Inside of six hundred yards with the Dragunov, she was a superb, almost uncanny shot. When she said "kill," she meant just that. Her target was seventy-five yards farther away than his, across the dock from where the *Varuskya Liset* was moored. Their vantage point in the crow's nest gave her enough of a down angle on the enemy sniper's hide to score multiple torso hits.

Should she kill the sniper? Again the impulse to mark and control Sarnov's own turf was there, nagging him like a tiny splinter of wood caught under his fingernail. He needed a second to think, to weigh the actual nature of the threat and his response options.

"No," he told her. "Wait..."

The original plan had been to trap the conspirators and their nuclear contraband on board the ship. To achieve that end, Sarnov had positioned his four-person unit to control all escape attempts from the vessel. He had no intention of boarding the trawler with such a small attacking force. As top-notch as his people were, such an idea bordered on the suicidal. There were just too many guns on the other side. That the unidentified hit crew might be taking them all on, apparently confident that they could do the job, amazed Sarnov. Either they were crazy, he decided, or they were counting on some part of the ship's defensive force to back them up.

According to the plan, once the trap closed, Sarnov would alert the Riga authorities, military and civilian, who would do all the mopping up. He wasn't concerned about the danger the nukes presented to the city of Riga. Sarnov and his team had been pursuing the born-again entrepreneur Krukillov for a year. They knew exactly what type of nuclear weapons were on the ship. Their surveillance operation had documented the paperwork ''errors'' that had jumbled the transfer of a cargo of AFAPs from Latvia to a Russian disposal site. From the start, the Spetsnaz team's mission had been a clean sweep of criminals and stolen goods; simple containment and overwhelming force had been the means to that end.

And nothing had changed, except that the unidentified attacking force was lowering the odds against them, essentially doing their work for them. Sarnov could have dropped his aimpoint and stitched a line of rifle fire across the steel hull, warning the trawler's passengers of the impending attack, but there was nothing in it for him. Better to let the four crazy bastards slip unnoticed belowdecks and reduce the odds even more.

Sarnov spoke into his headset microphone. ''The plan stands,'' he said. ''Don't shoot until someone actually tries to leave the ship. Try to turn them back with autofire. If that doesn't work, or if they return fire, shoot to kill. If you see anyone moving one of the weapons on deck, terminate them at once.'' He covered his mike with his hand. ''At the first shot from their side or ours," he told Tasha, "kill the sniper."

The Spetsnaz captain found it hard not to root a little for the suicide-assault team. He was curious how far they'd get before the odds kicked in. Of course, the outcome couldn't possibly change, no matter how well they did. Sarnov checked his wristwatch. He would give them three or four minutes to work before he called the Riga equivalent of 911.

As McCARTER CHARGED up the ramp, clearing his silenced autopistol out from under the pea coat, a heavy slug freight-trained six feet above his head, slapping something soft but solid on board the trawler. In two leaping strides, he reached the gangway and found the surviving Chechen flat on the deck, blowing bloody bubbles down his chin. Hawkins had played the odds, slamming the guard in the side with a .308 bullet. Without steel inserts, body armor reduced gunshot trauma by sixty percent. In this case, body armor had saved the man's life, but it couldn't stop the slug's impact from splintering his ribs and punching them into his lung. McCarter thumbed off the Beretta's safety and inflicted one hundred percent gunshot trauma to the Chechen's brain.

Stepping clear of the tangle of corpses, the former SAS man dropped into a kneeling position, his weapon out front, then waved Manning on. Manning put his back to the superstructure and took a silenced subgun from his satchel. He passed the weapon over to McCarter, then withdrew a second H&K for himself. With the demolition kit bag in his left hand, he followed Calvin James to the bridge tower's aft entrance and the stairs that led belowdecks.

After reholstering his handgun, McCarter turned and trotted for the bow. When he arrived at the doorway set in the front of the bridge tower, Encizo was waiting there for him. The Cuban had abandoned the crossbow and was holding his Beretta 93-R in a two-handed grip. The fire-control switch was set on triburst, which meant every trigger pull sent a trio of 9 mm hollowpoints flying out the barrel.

McCarter cracked open the tower door and stole a look down the steep metal stairway.

No one was in sight.

Quickly and quietly, the two warriors descended to the landing of the second deck. The stairway continued down to the third deck, which held the trawler's refrigeration unit, the repair shop, the engine room and, at the stern of the ship, the fish holds.

The second-deck landing ended in an undogged bulkhead door.

McCarter reached for the handle with his left hand, holding the H&K ready to rip in his right. He had a fatalistic, professional soldier's view of nuclear proliferation. He knew that eventually some of it was bound to get out and get exploded, that innocent people would die by the tens of thousands, sacrificed in the name of some political cause, but he was damned to bloody hell if it was going to be on his watch. He was willing to die to prevent it from happening.

McCarter eased the door inward an inch or two. It opened onto the crew quarters. There were three banks of gray steel bunks and the walls were lined with steel lockers. The place smelled like a pit. McCarter and Encizo checked the bunks for sleeping sailors. They were all empty. At the other end of the room was another door. McCarter knew it led to the galley.

As they moved to either side of the bulkhead, McCarter and Encizo could hear voices and laughter through the wall.

McCarter folded down his headset mike. He spoke softly but distinctly. "We're in position."

"ROGER THAT," Manning said into his mike, dragging back the sleeve of his pea coat so he could read the face of his watch.

He and James were in the "wet room," which stood between the aft door of the galley and the tower's rear staircase. The wet room held the crew's foul-weather gear and fish-cleaning slickers. Everything hung neat and name tagged from hooks set high in the steel walls. Along the base of the wall, under the oilskin coats and hats, were sets of rubber boots, also name tagged. Before it ended at the galley door, the room turned a dogleg right to a set of open showers. Manning and James knelt beside the closed galley door.

"In ten, on my mark," McCarter said through his mike. There was a pause, then he said, "Mark."

"Gotcha," Manning replied. As his watch's sweep hand turned, he plucked a pair of thunder-flash concussion grenades from his combat harness and pulled the pins. He nodded to James, who took hold of the door's handle, then he released the safety clips, letting them flip off onto the floor.

THOUGH LUIGI LOVECCHIO, nephew of the head of the Sicilian clan, continued to stare stilettos across the galley, he was bored. He had already won the no-blink contest. The Chechen he had targeted was so cowed that he was willing to look anywhere but back into Lovecchio's eyes. To pass the time, the Sicilian tried listening to the discussion between his employer and the Russian. He couldn't make any sense out of it. Mostly they were just rattling off bunches of numbers. Even when they used actual words—his English wasn't all that great—it still sounded like so much double-talk to him.

When Eshamani and Krukillov moved over to the service counter, both apparently happy with the way things were going down, Lovecchio's mind began to wander a bit. He started thinking about his sixteen-year-old girlfriend in Palermo.

Because his back was turned to the aft door, he didn't see the concussion grenades fly into the middle of the room, which meant his eyes missed the direct blast of blinding light. Like everyone else in the galley, he had no protection from the thunderclap. The powerful shock wave shattered the room's light bulbs, plunging it into darkness.

The Sicilian didn't notice. It was already dark inside his skull. The head-splitting pressure of the blast in the enclosed steel room blacked him out for a second. He didn't feel his knees buckling, but he awoke with a sickening jolt as they hit the deck.

Before he could shake off the numbness in his limbs, the galley's forward door swung open. A lit flare skittered across the floor, bathing the room in hard white light.

Lovecchio knew what was coming.

He grabbed for the pistol grip of his shoulder-slung 12-gauge.

McCARTER BURST through the doorway, on the heels of the flare he had tossed. In the flickering light, most of the enemy gunners were still down, but none of them were out. As he crossed the threshold, McCarter opened fire, scything back the men nearest to him with 9 mm lead. Encizo stepped to McCarter's side, triple-thumping the scattering human forms with his Beretta 93-R.

The hardmen, still stunned by the concussion and half-blinded by the flash, tried to crawl or run away. Some realized that escape was impossible and stood their ground, raising their weapons to fight to the death. The thugs fanned away from the source of bone-shattering pain and sudden death, moving in all directions at once. Like predator fish attacking a panicked school of anchovies, McCarter and Encizo had to keep focused on individual targets if they wanted to hit anything.

They swung from head shot to head shot, wasting no bullets on the body armor. Blood and skull contents sprayed high onto the steel walls. Clouds of gun smoke roiled in the strobe light of full-auto muzzle-flashes. Ricochets whined around the room, and through-and-through slugs clanged against the metal, leaving bright silver pieces of flattened lead. The men caught in the Phoenix Force meat grinder screamed and cursed. Return fire from a stubby 12-gauge pump gun rocked the room, but it was aimed by a dying hand and crashed harmlessly into the ceiling.

McCarter dumped his empty magazine. As he slammed home a fresh one, a pair of panicked gunmen tried to overturn the galley's dining table. They soon discovered that it was securely bolted to the deck, which left them flat-footed and in the line of fire. The Phoenix warriors blew them apart with simultaneous 3-round bursts.

In the middle of the room, a pair of refrigerator-sized wooden crates drew hardmen like moths to a flame. It wasn't much cover, but it was the only option they had. Four thugs clawed over each other to reach it.

McCarter and Encizo stepped wide of the boxes and chopped the men down from either side, peeling them away from the cover. While they were so occupied, three of Eshamani's security men managed to slip through the door at the far end of the galley.

GARY MANNING DIDN'T hesitate when he saw the blur of movement through the galley door. He knew it wasn't a *friendly* blur, which would've shouted a warning before charging into a prearranged, close-quarters cross fire. From his position just inside the entrance to the wet room's showers, Manning cut loose with a full-auto burst at knee height, shooting the legs out from under the first two men.

Calvin James fired his H&K from a kneeling stance near the door to the stairway, hitting the third man full in the face with a 3-round burst. The Chechen went down on top of his screaming buddies, pinning them to the deck with his deadweight and twitching limbs.

A pair of single-shot whispers from James's weapon ended the shrill cries of pain in the wet room, while the sounds of the gun battle and death throes from the galley likewise lessened, then ceased.

"We're clear in here," James shouted toward the half-open doorway.

SERGIO ISHMAEL Eshamani, blood seeping from his ears, fully regained consciousness as he was dumped face-first down an emergency hatch set in the kitchen floor. He tumbled, arms flailing wildly, into the bright lights of the engine room below. The broad curve of a generator housing broke his fall after a six-foot drop. He slid belly-first over the housing's broad, green-enameled back and landed in a heap at its foot.

Behind him, Krukillov hit the housing with both feet and jumped to the deck. He immediately jerked Eshamani up by an armpit.

"Hey!" he said, giving the arms merchant a vigorous shake.

Moments before, thunder-flash grenades had landed on the galley deck less than ten feet from where Eshamani and Krukillov had been standing. When the grenades had exploded, they had knocked the arms merchant and the general sideways, blowing them off their feet, slamming them against the edge of the galley's service counter and spinning them around its corner. When they had fallen, they had toppled behind the counter, out of view.

Because of the thickness of Krukillov's skull and the layers of muscle guarding his bull neck, the blast's concussion hadn't made him black out. He had had the strength to grab the unconscious Eshamani by the back of his jacket collar and drag him along the rear of the counter into the long, narrow kitchen area, thereby saving his life.

"The Zodiac," Krukillov said, pinning the smaller man upright against the side of the humming generator. "It's our only chance."

Eshamani nodded in agreement. It was then he realized he had the AFAP ops folder crumpled up in his fist. When the grenades had gone off, slamming him senseless, he had clutched it out of reflex. He shoved the document into an inside coat pocket.

"Can you run?" the general asked.

Eshamani tested his knees. "I think so."

Only when the arms merchant started chasing the Russian through the clutter and grease of the engine room did his head clear enough for the shock to sink in. He had had close calls many times before, but they had always been of a different variety. He had nearly been *arrested,* nearly *convicted,* but he had never been nearly *killed* before. He had no doubt that the attackers intended to leave no one on board alive. And that whoever the intruders were, they had come within a gnat's eyelash of getting the job done.

Krukillov looked up from the base of the aft stairway to the landing that stood between them and the top deck. It was clear, for the moment. "There've got to be more enemy outside," the general said. "Once we reach the top deck, we've got to move fast and low. If we don't reach the net bay in short order, we're dead. When you clear the door, head for the gunwale and keep tight to it all the way down to the trawl ramp—it'll block any small-arms fire from the dock."

"Understood."

"Can you drive the boat?"

Eshamani nodded.

"When we hit the ramp, you start up the engine and get the Zodiac moving. I'll provide the covering fire."

Eshamani looked at the general's empty hands. He started to ask the obvious question, but Krukillov whirled away and began mounting the stairs two at a time. Eshamani had to strain to keep up with him. The Russian didn't hesitate at the tower door, but shoved it back and dashed out. Eshamani followed, running in a half crouch.

Out of the corner of his eye, Eshamani saw the forward gangway was blocked by a pile of dead bodies. Their mingled blood ran in a gummy, blackening river down the deck, draining toward the stern. Ahead of him, the general was sprinting toward the stern. As Krukillov reached the hawsehole that allowed access to the ship's middle mooring cleat, he lost his footing on the wide patch of gore and skidded onto his backside. As he slipped, a single, heavy-caliber rifle shot sailed through the hawse opening and banged the superstructure where his chest should have been.

Before Eshamani could reach him, the Russian had already scrambled past the hole and regained his feet. Eshamani didn't slip on the blood, but when he neared the opening he threw himself into a shallow dive that cleared the hole and slammed him belly-first on the deck. As he pushed up, he saw Krukillov bend over the two dead Chechens sprawled alongside the processing shed. He snatched up their dropped AKMs by the shoulder straps and retreated to the cover of the gunwale.

As Eshamani ran up to Krukillov, something whined high overhead, followed instantly by what had to be a gun crack. The bullet came from the water side of the trawler. Another shot rang out, then another. All of them sailed well above the *Varuskya Liset*'s superstructure, apparently aimed somewhere across the dock. "That's a Dragunov sniper rifle," Krukillov said. "We could be in a cross fire once we hit the crane deck. Don't stop for anything."

It was only thirty yards to the edge of the ramp, but it was across unprotected deck. At every stride, Eshamani expected a bullet to cut him down, but they made the protection of the net bay's ramp without drawing more fire.

The situation changed abruptly as soon as they closed on the Zodiac and came into view of the dock.

Eshamani glimpsed a small truck on the pier, a figure half-concealed behind it and the winking starburst of a muzzle-flash. Bullets spanged into the ramp beside them.

"Hurry!" Krukillov growled. He held the AKMs straight-armed out in front of him like a pair of dueling pistols and opened fire, full auto, spraying the dock and the side of the truck with 5.45 mm slugs, forcing the shooter to take cover.

Meanwhile, Eshamani jumped into the inflatable. The electric start, fifty-horsepower outboard turned over for him on the first try. As he gunned the motor in neutral, the Russian's AKMs came up empty and, discarding the guns, he hurled himself into the Zodiac's bow.

"Go! Go!" Krukillov shouted.

The arms merchant jammed the engine in gear and twisted the throttle wide-open. Only the load in the bow kept the boat from flipping as he cut the tiller arm over hard, slashing a sweeping 180-degree turn through the net bay. As they cleared the hull, something screamed past them.

The RPG slammed into the side of the trawler's net bay, blowing a huge dent in the steel. The shock of the explosion made Eshamani flinch at the tiller. The Zodiac swerved wildly, and for a moment he lost control of the boat. When he recovered, they were traveling at fifty miles per hour and headed right into the bow of another moored trawler. He veered off at the last second, barely scraping the Zodiac's rubber skin against the hull. As they roared into the darkness, rifle slugs from across the water sailed inches over Eshamani's head, sparking as they thunked against the trawler's side.

McCARTER ROLLED the limp corpse to one side and examined the body beneath. A wash of dark blood coated the man's face and matted his hair to his skull, masking the extent of the head wound he had received. McCarter checked for signs of breathing and, finding none, applied thumb pressure to the center of the eyeball.

No response.

He moved on to the next body.

It was an unpleasant job, but it had to be done, and quickly.

The four Phoenix warriors worked their way through the galley's heaped corpses, separating and turning them, making sure there were no survivors. Although it ate up seconds of precious time, they couldn't afford to have one of the bad guys "wake up" on them while their attention was fixed elsewhere. They had to secure the room before tackling the gleaming silver shells in the wooden crates.

McCarter and the others had just completed the grim task when an urgent voice boomed through their headsets. It was Stony Man Farm, via satellite, with a traffic update.

"Bud, this is Hardcase," Hunt Wethers said.

"Roger, Hardcase," McCarter replied.

"Company is on the way. Repeat, company is on the way."

CHAPTER THREE

Thomas Hawkins scanned the dock side of the *Varuskya Liset* from his hide on the roof of the derelict trawler's bridge. The bridge's roofline made it look like the turret of a medieval castle. A two-foot-high, rust-spotted metal wall ringed the roof perimeter, and the wall's top edge was cut by evenly spaced, foot-square notches. It was in one of these perfect little firing ports that he had set up his sandbags and the .308 Remington bolt-action rifle. Hawkins's primary assignment on the mission was traffic control on the pier during and after the assault. The shooting position he had picked filled that bill to a T: no one could come or go in either direction without coming under his sights.

The hide didn't do quite as good a job covering the decks of the suspect ship. Over the top of the Leupold scope, he could see the full length of the trawler, but because of his angle of view, the decks were partially hidden by the gunwale. He did have a clear sight of the top-deck access door set in the back of the bridge tower; the only other way onto the deck was through the door in the front of the tower. Anyone attempting to flee the scene would have to come from the bow of the boat and pass near the bodies heaped up in the gangway entrance.

Hawkins figured those corpses would deter anyone from trying to escape that way. The ramp down to the dock was too long and too open. The safest way off the ship, and the most likely route, would be inside the protection of the gunwale, toward the stern and the trawl ramp.

That gunwale presented a shooting problem for Hawkins because it screened practically the entire escape route. Though the top of a running man's head might be visible above the edge of the solid wall, that small target would also be moving up and down, and therefore in and out of Hawkins's view field. The only places the gunwale failed to provide complete cover were at the hawseholes. The four openings along the side of the hull were each as tall as a standing man and six feet across. Their lower thirds were partially blocked by massive metal cleats.

Hawkins had his shot lined up, his weapon securely sandbagged, when the tower door banged open. A gray-haired man in a brown overcoat crossed the deck in a full-out sprint and disappeared behind the gunwale. Hawkins recognized General Krukillov from surveillance and briefing photos. Then a second, shorter man burst out of the doorway and beelined for the same cover.

So Eshamani had slipped the noose, too, Hawkins thought. The head rats were deserting the ship. As he settled in behind his weapon, he could see the top of the general's head bobbing up and down, first vanishing then reappearing above the gunwale. The silvery brush cut rapidly closed the distance to the midship hawsehole.

Hawkins found the stock weld and peered through the Leupold's optics. He touched the tip of his finger to the trigger and applied steadily increasing pressure until he felt the resistance of the break point.

Six feet of deck wasn't much room to work a trap shot on a running man, especially with that big cleat in the way, but a tracking lead was out of the question. Hawkins only had a partial view of the moving target; if the general slowed down when he was momentarily out of sight, it would completely throw off the shot timing. Hawkins centered the cross hairs at the right edge of the hawse opening, between the point of the cleat and the gunwale—an estimated eighteen-inch span. His hold was for the chest height of a standing man or the head height of a kneeling man.

A hit was all he wanted.

And any hit would do.

Hell, even a close miss might keep the buzzards aboard long enough for McCarter and the others to mop them up.

The instant the shadowy blur appeared in the left of the hawsehole, Hawkins broke the trigger. The Remington coughed softly—and kicked like a mule. Hawkins rode the recoil wave, fighting to reacquire the target in the scope's field of view. He got the briefest glimpse of the man's legs flying up as he slid past the hawsehole.

For an instant, he thought he had scored in the ten-ring.

Then he saw the chipped paint on the metal wall where the slug had hit.

There was no blood spray.

A clean miss.

Hawkins worked the Remington's butter-smooth bolt, chambering a second round. He bore down again, but before he could lock in on the narrow bullet window, the smaller man dived headfirst past the opening.

With a curse, Hawkins grabbed the sniper rifle from its chocks and rolled to his feet. He knew his secondary position at the rear of the roof would give him a better fire lane to work the stern of the trawler.

He never got there.

As he rose, something big and bad whooshed over his head. The heavy-caliber bullet snatched off his knit hat, sending it and the communications headset flying off the bridge. Hawkins threw himself down beside the roof's decorative wall. For a second, he thought he'd been head shot. His scalp tingled all the way to the base of his neck, then it went numb. When he tested his head for blood, though, his fingertips came away dry.

Then, with an ear-ringing whap, a second slug smacked the outside of the wall. A little peak appeared in the metal on his side of the barrier, six inches beyond the end of his nose. Another sniper, he thought. Serious opposition. Whoever was shooting at him had the range and a steady hand.

He started to crawl along the wall toward the rear edge of the roof. He got about two feet when another bullet slammed the rusting metal in front of him, this time blowing right through it. The impact sprayed rust flakes in his face.

He was pinned, but good.

THERE WERE DISASTERS and then there were bloody huge disasters.

McCarter had to know which kind was bearing down on his crew. "Who's coming?" he said into his headset mike.

"Who isn't," Wethers replied. "I'm tracking top-priority emergency responses from police, fire and military units all over the city. It amounts to near total mobilization. They're en route as we speak, and from the chatter they know what to expect. They've started civil-defense procedures."

"What's the ETA?" McCarter said.

"You've got four or five minutes, tops, before they seal off the land exits to the pier."

"Roger that, Hardcase," McCarter said. He was looking at the radiation symbols on the noses of the artillery shells inside the wooden crates. "The trouble is, we've got a couple of rather large items sitting here that we can't move ashore and we can't leave as is."

"Item" was the Riga mission's code for an operational nuclear weapon. Had Phoenix Force found radioactive material or bomb components, the code designation would have been "product."

A different voice, but a very familiar one, spoke through their headsets. "Bud, can you disable the two items?" Kurtzman asked.

"Roger," Gary Manning said without hesitation.

"Then proceed and we'll update traffic and alternate routes as you work."

"We're on it, Hardcase," McCarter stated.

Gripping a lifting handle, Encizo tried to shift one of the shells in its crate. "Whew!" he said. "These babies must weight a couple of hundred pounds."

"Two and a half, actually," Manning said, taking a claw hammer from his demolition kit bag and handing it to Encizo. "Knock the crates apart as quickly as you can."

"What are we going to do with these things?" James asked as he helped Encizo clear away the hardwood bracing.

"Like McCarter said, we can't move them off the ship," Manning replied, pulling a cordless power drill from his bag. "Even if they didn't weigh so much, they're big and they're obvious. They look like what they are, 152 mm artillery shells, and they've got those radiation stickers plastered all over them. We could get them off the boat, but we'd never get them off the pier. So we've got to deal with them here."

Manning chucked a gleaming five-inch bit into the drill.

"What are you going to do with that?" James said.

"Make nuclear Swiss cheese," Manning told him. "This diamond-tipped bit cuts through stainless steel like it was butter. If anyone fires these shells after I'm through holing them, the warheads'll whistle through the air like a goddamned calliope. And they will never, ever detonate." With that, he revved the drill and started punching holes in the warhead.

"Oh, man," James said, watching bright curls of metal flying as he and Encizo attacked the other crate.

"You guys better stand back," Manning warned as he cored the first warhead with random boreholes. "I'm flying blind here. I might hit the radioactive target by accident and aerosolize some plutonium dust. You don't want to breathe that stuff—it can be bad for your health. If I had the time, I'd put on a dust mask myself."

"If you don't hurry up," McCarter told him,

"none of us is going to live long enough to get cancer."

"Don't rush him too much," James cautioned. "We don't want any mistakes."

"Hey, they aren't going to go off," Manning said as he bored a four-inch-deep hole in the second weapon's nose.

"I know, but—"

A rocking boom from the stern area of the ship cut James off in midsentence and knocked pots and pans off the galley's stove.

"Damn!" Encizo said, gripping the edge of the table to steady himself. "I thought Hardcase said we had four or five minutes."

McCarter was already on the horn to his outside man. "Hawk, this is Bud. We have someone knocking at the back door. Who the hell is it? Hawk, are you on it? Hawk, come in."

There was no reply.

"Bloody hell!" McCarter exclaimed. "Hardcase, this is Bud. We just took an incoming HE round and Hawk is off-line. Who's shooting at us?"

Dr. Wethers' reply was immediate, his voice grave. "Bud, for sure it isn't anybody wearing a white hat."

"Now what?" Encizo asked.

"Gary," McCarter said, "what else do we need to do here?"

"Chuck these babies in the drink," the Canadian replied. "The brackish water pouring into the warheads will ruin their circuitry."

"Jesus, Gary," James said incredulously, "that would contaminate the bay and the tidewater for a thousand years. It'd be a mini-Chernobyl."

"Have you got a better idea?"

"If you want to sink 'em in salt water," James said, "why not toss 'em into the fish hold?"

"He's right," Encizo cut in. "We saw lots of brine down there."

"Let's roll," McCarter urged.

Each of the warriors grabbed a lifting handle, and they lugged the awkward, heavy weapons out of the galley and up the stairs. They were all sweating by the time they reached the door to the top deck.

"Once we get out on deck," Manning said, "let's not carry these frigging ball-breakers. If we can skid them along the deck, we can move much faster and lower."

"Yeah," McCarter agreed. "If we meet resistance, return fire but keep moving to the shed. We have to destroy these weapons before we leave the ship."

McCarter and James went first, submachine guns in one hand, the lifting handle of the nuke-tipped artillery shell in the other. The underside of the shell made a loud scraping noise as they dragged it along the deck. The river of spilled blood acted as a lubricant and made the job easier. They reached the processing-shed door without drawing fire, and hauled the shell up to the edge of the fish hold.

Encizo and Manning entered the shed a moment later, both puffing from the effort. As they skidded their artillery shell over to the hold, McCarter and James tipped their weapon into the brine. It hit with a monstrous splash that sent milky water slopping up onto the floor.

The four of them quickly dumped the second weapon in after it.

Streams of air bubbles rose from the holes in the warheads as they filled up with concentrated salt solution. The sight brought a grin of satisfaction to Manning's lips. "They're only fit for the scrap heap now," he said.

A chorus of sirens punctuated the end of his sentence. Their singsong wails appeared to be coming from all directions at once.

McCarter took a look out of the doorway that faced the dock. At the entrance to the pier, scores of blue-and-white lights flashed, reflecting against the walls of the fish-packing plants.

They had waited too long to make their escape by land.

McCarter dropped his weapons on the fish-cleaning table and dumped his combat harness on the floor. "Come on," he said, "it's time to go."

"What about Hawk?" Manning said. He spoke to McCarter's back as the Phoenix Force leader exited the processing shed's water-side door.

His question hung in the air, unanswered.

HER RIGHT EYE PRESSED tight to the Dragunov scope's eyepiece, Tasha Beloc held her fire, trying to outthink her target. She knew the man had to bail off the back of the roof. With two well-placed shots, she had proved to him it was either jump for it or die where he lay. It was only a drop of three yards to the rear bridge deck. From there, a quick tuck and roll would put him in the tower or off the far side of it.

To safety and escape. But diving off the back of the roof meant that for a few seconds he would be vulnerable.

It would make a challenging shot, but it was well within her ability, and thanks to glasnost, within the ability of the SVD. Prior to the fall of the Soviet

Union, even a biathlete like herself had been unable to get such fine, Match-grade cartridges for the Dragunov. Now that the 180-grain, soft-nose Norma bullets were available, they extended the capabilities of the weapon, which had built-in limitations. Its semi-automatic action could not seat cartridges with the same precision as a bolt gun. A thin barrel made accurizing difficult, if not impossible. The standard scope was only four power, which all added up to a relatively short killing range for a sniper gun of less than six hundred yards.

Still, at under ten pounds, it was a light gun and easy for her to carry. And because she had worked with it for so many years in competition, she had supreme confidence in it, within specific limits.

A less highly skilled shooter might have used up most of the 10-round magazine, punching holes in the turret top in order to flush the target into view. Beloc knew that her best accuracy came from a cold barrel. She also knew her firing window was going to be so narrow that she'd never be able to recover from the recoil of a preliminary shot and still get her gun on target.

She relaxed and slipped into no-blink mode, the only tension in her body in the tip of her trigger finger. As she slowed her breathing, sirens howled, very near. Reinforcements from the Latvian police and military had arrived and closed off the end of the pier. He was going to jump now; she could feel it.

"Hold it," Sarnov said, putting a gentle hand on her shoulder.

Beloc immediately let up on the trigger, and as she did so, her target made his move. Through the telescopic sight, she saw the figure in black vault the turret. He was backlit for an instant, before he rolled off the far side of the tower, out of sight to the main deck below.

Beloc knew she could have killed him.

"You just saved that lucky bastard's life," she said.

"Look," the captain said, pointing at the *Varuskya Liset*'s processing shed. Four men in black had exited one of the side doors and were crossing the deck, single file. They weren't carrying nuclear artillery shells, they didn't even have side arms. The men disappeared under the cover of the gunwale, only to reappear at the hawsehole.

Beloc snugged the SVD's fiberglass stock to her cheek as she sighted in on the forehead of the man standing in the gunwale's opening.

ENCIZO, MANNING and James caught up with McCarter as he climbed over the mooring cleat. They were all fit to be tied.

"Goddammit, man," James said, "we can't just leave the kid behind."

"Even if he's dead," Manning said, "we can't go without him. We've got to find him and take him home."

McCarter half turned toward them, a sardonic smile on his face.

"What the hell are we going to do about Hawk?" Encizo demanded.

"Join him," McCarter replied. He pointed down at the man calmly treading water beside the trawler's hull, then stepped off into space.

CAPTAIN ANDREI SARNOV watched, expressionless, as the Riga police and military forensic personnel tied handkerchiefs over their faces to protect themselves from the stench in the galley. For two hours, while the land and water access to the pier was cordoned off, the blood and voided bowel contents of twenty-odd corpses had lingered in the airless, windowless steel room. The effect of so much death in so small a space was gut-turning.

Although Sarnov had a clean handkerchief in his hip pocket, he didn't take it out. As a Spetsnaz officer, he was expected to be tougher than tough. He wanted the queasy Latvians to see that his face wasn't turning green around the gills. Also, from experience, Sarnov knew that wearing a hankie over one's nose was a pointless exercise, unless it had been soaked in perfume first.

Despite the breakup of the Soviet Union and decades of ill will between the former satellites and Russia, the local civilian and military authorities treated Sarnov and the rest of the Spetsnaz unit with the utmost courtesy and respect. They knew they were an elite military force, a force whose lives were now dedicated to protecting the interests of both Latvia and Russia. The physical presence of Captain Sarnov had something to do with it, too. He commanded simply by his bearing and by the icy, all-business expression in his eyes. Eyes that had seen much in almost twenty years of service. With a glance, he had deflected questions and protests, and sent the police and army scurrying to search every inch of the ship with radiation-detection devices.

Looking at the piled bodies, Sarnov still had no clue who the hit team was or who had sent them, but he knew for sure who they weren't. There had been no backup, no double cross from any part of the trawler's security squads. All of them were dead. Only a few weapons had returned fire, and apparently unsuccessfully. The men who had executed this mission were not crazy or suicidal as he had first thought.

And they hadn't lucked out. Four men didn't luck out against a well-armed, professional opposing force of nearly thirty.

Even though the bodies had been moved from where they'd originally fallen, Sarnov could replay recent events from the direction of the blood splatters. All the gunfire had come from one end of the room, the bow end. Scorch marks on the galley floor indicated that a pair of concussion grenades had gone off prior to the attack. Those explosions had shattered the light bulbs wire-caged in the ceiling. In the confusion and darkness, a pair of men had entered by the bow door and opened fire, using a flare to light their targets. Nine-millimeter shell casings still littered the floor, making the forensic people mind where they stepped. All but three of the security men had been killed in the galley; those three lived long enough to reach the wet room, next door. Apparently Sergio Eshamani and Brigadier General Krukillov were the sole survivors of the assault.

There was no joy in Sarnov's heart as he stared at the fractured crates that had housed the weapons; instead, a sinking sensation racked his guts. He was afraid that, as the old saying went, he had won the battle but lost the war.

Then he noticed that mixed among the splinters of wood on the floor were a few tight spirals of steel. He knelt down and waved his Geiger counter over the shavings, and the machine chattered a harsh warning. The weapons' warheads had definitely been breached.

As he straightened up, a Latvian soldier rushed over to him and announced, "The ship is clean belowdecks, sir."

"You're sure?"

"We've gone over everything three times with the Geiger counters and recovered nothing more."

Sarnov muttered a curse under his breath.

"But your people have apparently found something on the top deck," the soldier continued. "They passed the word that they want you to come up and have a look."

"That's better news," the captain said. "But before we go, this room must be cleared." He put his arms in the air and started waving the body baggers toward the aft door. "Everyone must leave at once," he told them.

"Our work isn't finished in here," the head of the civilian forensics unit protested.

"For the moment it is," the Spetsnaz captain corrected him. "The galley is highly radioactive. There are plutonium fragments scattered all over the floor. Get some people in here who can clean them up, and leave your shoes in the wet room for decontamination."

Sarnov replaced his own shoes with a pair of rubber boots from the wet room, then followed the soldier up to the top deck. They passed by a police photographer who was taking flash shots of the bodies by the gangway. Beyond the corpses, Sarnov saw the twin tracks, ragged lines drawn in blood, heading toward the stern. They led through the processing shed's first doorway.

When he entered the shed, he found Turgenev, Ferdishenko and Tasha Beloc standing around an open hatch set in the floor. Turgenev had a Geiger counter in his hand, and was passing it back and forth over the opening. The counter sang like a thousand lunatic crickets.

"It shouldn't be reading this high," Turgenev said, shaking his head. "We've got a major radiation leak on our hands."

"They've breached the warheads somehow," Sarnov explained.

"How about with this?" Beloc said. She removed the cordless drill from the kit bag left behind on the table and let Turgenev scan it with his Geiger counter.

The little machine screamed.

"Those guys really did a job here," Ferdishenko said. "It took some guts to put a hand drill to a nuclear warhead."

Sarnov nodded. Whoever they were, they had guts to spare, and brains, too. Clearly they had never intended stealing the weapons for resale. Destruction had been the only thing on their minds. And they had managed to compromise the weapons and contain most of the leaking radiation in the fish hold.

Down in the milky water, Sarnov could barely make out the casings of the artillery shells. He couldn't tell how many shells had been dumped in the hold. He still had a tiny flicker of hope.

"Vlad, find some long-handled gaff hooks," he said.

Using four gaffs, the Spetsnaz team snagged one of the warheads by its drill holes and lifted it halfway out of the brine.

Sarnov stared at it. It was, he thought, ruin heaped

upon ruin. The treasure of his nation had been squandered on such devices; for the safety they promised, four generations of Soviet citizens had gone without food, without comfort or hope of same. The only satisfaction to be had, and it was slight at best, was that the West had likewise crippled itself to pay for weapons it would never use.

They lowered the shell back into the hold and fished out the second one. Salt water poured out of the randomly drilled holes as they raised the warhead into view.

Sarnov unhooked his gaff from the warhead and used it to poke around in the murky water, searching the rest of the hold from wall to wall and finding nothing. Hope died for the Spetsnaz captain.

There were only two *starookha*s on board the ship, and Krukillov had stolen three.

PART TWO

THE SAWTOOTH CONSPIRACY

CHAPTER FOUR

Los Pavos, California
3:11 a.m. PDT

Edward Kelso eased the Mustang coupe down Main Street. On both sides of the road, businesses catering to Interstate 5 traffic—fast food, gas and booze—were dark. Ahead, in the flat distance, a half-dozen stop signals blinked at him, yellow and out of sync. The town's seven-thousand-odd residents dozed peacefully amid the musty sweet stink of corporate poultry farms upwind, secure in their beds because they believed there was nothing in Los Pavos to steal.

At the mouth of an alley on Kelso's right, partially hidden beneath a crudely lettered billboard proclaiming God's Eternal Love, was a county sheriff's cruiser with its headlights and engine off. As Kelso drove past, by the harsh glare of a streetlamp he could see a head behind the wheel of the green-and-white car. It was a speed trap, manned by the town's lone night-duty policeman, a deputy sheriff.

There was no way the Mustang Kelso had stolen from the San Fernando Valley two hours earlier could have been on the deputy's hot sheet. Still, Kelso watched his rearview mirror intently, aware of the surgical gloves he wore drawing skintight across his knuckles as he squeezed the steering wheel.

No lights came on behind him. The cruiser stayed put.

He continued at a sedate pace for two more blocks, then turned right at City Hall, a thirty-foot-long, aluminum-sided trailer, and onto a wide residential street without sidewalks. After going one block, he turned right again and began paralleling, backtracking his route down Main. As he neared the end of the speed-trap alley, he cut lights and engine, coasting past the driveway and coming to a quiet stop.

This early morning was typical of the central valley in summer: sweltering, airless, pulsing with cricket song. The day to come wasn't going to get any better—just hotter. Kelso reached under the front of his bucket seat and found the grip of the .22-caliber pistol. He lifted the Walther automatic into his lap. The weapon's stubby barrel was extended by six inches of silencer. Inside the surgical gloves, Kelso's hands were slippery with sweat, not from fear, but from the sauna effect of the latex.

He took the flat tin of camouflage makeup from the passenger's seat and liberally smeared antiglare green over his wide forehead, meaty cheeks and chin. He did his bare arms, then picked up the gun. Before he opened the car door, he shut off the dome light. He rounded the rear of the Mustang on the run, his crepe-soled shoes padding soundlessly on the pavement.

The sheriff's cruiser sat in a pool of lamplight 150 feet away. Kelso zigzagged down the alley, darting from Dumpster to trash cans to parked pickup truck, the black of his T-shirt and slacks merging with the shadows. He advanced rapidly on the driver's side of the car. The window was rolled all the way down, and an elbow in a short-sleeved khaki uniform shirt stuck out over the ledge.

Kelso moved into the car's blind spot, alongside the left rear fender. He could see the deputy through the back window and the mesh screen that separated the front seat from the rear. The deputy had propped up a newspaper on the steering wheel and was reading it by the light of the streetlamp.

Kelso took three more quick steps, then poked the pistol's silenced muzzle around the doorjamb, through the open window. At the last second, out of the corner of his eye, the deputy caught the blur of movement. Startled, he glanced into the side mirror.

The firing pin snapped once, dry and crisp. The muffled shot thwacked, like a nail gun punching steel into a two-by-four. Powder grains from the muzzle blast dusted the deputy's earlobe black. As the man slumped over on the seat, Kelso leaned through the window and methodically put seven more insurance rounds into the base of his skull.

With a .22, one never knew. Even at point-blank range, the lightweight, standard-velocity slugs could glance off bone and fail to penetrate the cranial cavity. A hit gun was never used twice, either, so it was always used to the maximum. Kelso tossed the empty Walther onto the car's floorboards, grabbed the deputy by the arm and jerked him back up into a sitting position. Then he tipped the dead man's hat down over his face.

Kelso trotted back to the Mustang, heart pounding, nerve ends tingling. When it came to murder, Kelso was like a skilled plumber or carpenter. He could admire a piece of work—his own or someone else's—

for its neatness or style, but the act of killing didn't excite him anymore. His thrill came from the mission itself, the careful planning, the teamwork, the absolute commitment and, most of all, the element of personal risk.

He got back in the Mustang and started it up. The cop-killing, never a wise move, was necessary in this case; the only direct radio link between the town and the California Highway Patrol was now broken. Kelso knew a million things could still go sour this morning, things he had never even considered. The thought raised the hair on the back of his neck.

He drove the car half a block before turning on his lights. He continued until he saw his objective on the right. The 432nd National Guard Armory was a two-story brick building with barred windows. It sat in the middle of a block-long rectangle of asphalt. The street he was on ran along the back of the armory compound, beside the floodlit vehicle-storage yard that, like the entire perimeter, was bounded by a fifteen-foot-high hurricane fence topped with spirals of razor wire.

He blinked his headlights on and off as he crossed the intersection, then pulled over to the curb. On the other side of the street, a parked semitruck and trailer immediately started up and, lights off, swung into reverse. The big rig cut a wide arc, partially blocking the road as it brought its tailgate to within a few feet of the fence.

As Kelso got out of the Mustang, the trailer's rear door rolled up and three men in black clothes, their faces also covered with green camouflage makeup, jumped down and began attacking the fence wire with long-handled bolt cutters. A fourth man, the driver, hopped down from the truck's cab and took a kneeling position beside the left front fender. He shouldered an M-16 automatic rifle equipped with a silencer.

Nothing stirred in the row of squat prefab houses across the street. In Los Pavos, they were used to big trucks coming and going at all hours.

By the time Kelso jogged over to the trio working on the fence, they had created a man-size slit in the heavy wire.

No words passed between them.

None were necessary.

The powers that be had allowed Kelso to handpick his team. He had been under fire and worse, with every one of them, in Vietnam. Recently the quintet had been involved in organization "fund-raisers": the Security National Bank of Des Moines; the armored-truck job in Kansas City; the Fargo City Savings and Loan. Kelso's guys were not shy about using their weapons to get what they wanted. They knew the morning's itinerary cold; Kelso had made sure of that. He was a fanatic for detail. That was how he had earned and kept these men's respect over the years. The little things often made the difference between success and failure, living and dying.

None of them, Kelso included, had ever been convicted of a crime in the United States. Their military-service records were clean, as well. They didn't have easily traceable connections to the organization, which didn't hand out membership cards and had no mailing list. The Sawtooth Patriots didn't believe in that kind of regimentation. Ultimately that's what the battle was all about. Personal freedom. As far as Kelso was concerned, it felt great to fight for a cause again, to know that you were doing something with right on your side, something that would make a difference.

Kelso accepted a satchel from the tallest of the three men, former U.S. Army Sergeant Rudy Speck. While Tim Ringman and Neil Mallone held open the cut in the fence, he and Speck slipped through into the storage yard.

There were two rows of equipment between them and the armory building. In the first were six-by-six trucks, jeeps and howitzers. In the back was a quartet of small tanks painted desert camouflage and an equal number of armored personnel carriers.

The armory building's alarm system was external and primitive. In less than two minutes, Kelso and his tall shadow were inside, their shoe soles softly squeaking on the well-waxed linoleum of the hallway. Twin flashlight beams locked on to a small rectangular sign sticking out at right angles to the wall above a door on the left. The battalion commander's office was locked.

They kicked the door in unison, splintering it off its hinges, and headed straight for the room's side wall that was lined with tightly packed metal bookshelves. A quick search of books and notebook spines did not turn up what they were looking for. Kelso aimed his light at the unconcealed wall safe. It had to be in there. With Speck illuminating things over his shoulder, Kelso took a small wad of plastic explosive from the satchel, shaped it and stuck it along the safe's door seam. He inserted the detonator and set the timer.

The two of them knelt down in front of the commander's desk, awaiting the explosion. For an instant,

Kelso's flashlight beam swept over Speck's sweaty, green-daubed face. The man's eyes were full of glee. It was a look Kelso knew and one he understood. It brought back a sudden torrent of memories. Of 1968 and the Cambodian border. Tiger cages, heat, thirst and pain. Of a lone NVA prison-camp guard who had been obsessed with trying to crush their testicles with his rifle butt.

For hours the bastard had jabbed that metal-shod club through the bamboo bars, bashing their tailbones, knees and shins, whiling away the time until the rest of his unit returned from a foraging expedition. The cages were so narrow they could not escape the blows; they could only cover with arms and legs and take them.

Finally Kelso had had enough. It didn't matter to him that resistance meant death. The guard was no longer jerking the gun back quickly after every jab, but left it propped on the cage cross brace while he grinned in at them, considering his next lunge.

Kelso had waited for the inevitable next blow and when it came, he absorbed it. Then he struck. From a fetal position on the floor of the cage, he kicked the extended buttstock with both feet, driving it back and up over the cross brace, driving its crude, fixed-spike bayonet three inches into the middle of the guard's forehead. The guard had grimaced horribly, clutching at the gun muzzle. His knees buckled and he slumped back, dragging the rifle out of the cage. He dropped to his side, thrashing and kicking in the red dirt.

Kelso quickly reached through the bars and jerked the man's knife free. As he began to saw off the lacing that held the bars together, he looked over at Speck, naked in a separate cage. Amid a face caked with blood and filth and oozing sweat, his eyes twinkled with delight. Sergeant Rudy Speck knew he was about to be turned loose on the world. For how long, it didn't matter.

"Kill him!" Speck bellowed as Kelso stepped from the tiger cage. "Blow the mother's head off!"

That was how the other American POWs had felt, too. From their bamboo pens they cheered as Kelso grabbed the butt and pistol grip of the guard's AK-47 and used the rifle as a lever to turn the little man onto his back.

How long they were free mattered to Kelso. He knew a single rifle shot could alert the returning squad of NVA.

He threw his full body weight against the buttstock, driving the steel spike completely through the guard's head and into the ground. The little man stopped thrashing. Kelso gave the weapon a savage twist, snapping the bayonet off at the muzzle, leaving the guard pinned to the earth.

Once the other POWs were free, they didn't scatter and flee into the bush. Kelso hadn't allowed it, and he had the guard's AK. Under his direction, they took weapons from the camp cache and hidden along the main trail. When the rest of the NVA unit entered the camp, their former captives ambushed them. Afterward, also under Kelso's direction, the Americans did horrible things to the enemy survivors.

At the hollow whump of the explosion, Kelso flinched and covered, forcibly brought back to the present. Acoustic tiles blown free of the ceiling bounced off the desktop and slapped the wall behind him. Then he was up, hurrying to the safe through clouds of smoke. The safe's door hung by a single twisted hinge. Speck stepped up behind him, holding the light. Kelso elbowed the door out of the way and reached inside, removing account ledgers and sheaves of loose paper, dumping everything on the floor until he found what they had come for. The gun book, the history of every cannon on the premises, on computer diskette and in hard copy.

He quickly leafed through the pages of the notebook, checking the number of effective full charges, or EFCs, each gun had fired. EFCs were a measure of a gun's probable life span; a field howitzer was worn out after about fifteen thousand. From this information, Kelso picked the best gun of the lot. He tore out the pages of the firing tables that documented the cannon's firing history, tabulating the range to be reached from any elevation of the gun firing a specific charge and shell. The table also included the specifics of time of flight, standard fuse timing and corrections for wind and air temperature for various charge-and-shell combinations. Kelso pocketed the pages and the diskette, and dumped the notebook on the floor with the rest of the debris.

He and Speck ran side by side back down the hallway. Outside, Ringman and Mallone had completed their job. They had cut an entire section of fence free of its supporting posts and rolled it to one side. They had also lowered a pair of steel tracks from the rear of the trailer to the ground. A dozen packaged 155 mm howitzer rounds were already secured inside the trailer.

Kelso matched the serial number on the pages in his hand with one of the howitzers. Even as he was pointing out the gun, Mallone was running from the trailer with a winch cable slung over his shoulder.

They hooked the cable to the gun's trails, released the wheel brakes and winched the howitzer back through the gap in the fence, up the tracks and into the trailer.

While Ringman and Mallone battened down the gun, Kelso and Speck slid the tracks into the trailer and pulled down the trailer door. Kelso locked the two men and the howitzer inside, then ran for the front of the truck with Speck on his heels. He climbed into the passenger's side of the cab, relieved Wiley, the driver, of the silenced M-16, and passed the weapon to Speck, who took the window seat. As they rumbled down the street, Speck held the automatic rifle out the window, watching the dark line of houses for signs of life.

Kelso checked his wristwatch. The elapsed time was eight minutes. In another four minutes they would be at a dead-end side road, changing trucks, transferring their cargo. Only Kelso knew exactly what they were going to do with it. It wasn't a matter of security that kept him from telling Speck and the others, but rather a matter of need-to-know.

Of course, there was no way he could stop them from trying to guess among themselves. There were clues, all right. No one in his right mind stole something as big as an artillery field piece and then took it to another country to use it.

As Wiley steered the truck up the freeway on-ramp, Speck put the butt of his M-16 on the floor and trapped its muzzle between his knees, keeping the weapon out of sight but accessible. He turned to Kelso and gave him a wide, knowing grin.

Kelso smiled back. It came easily. Speck could strain his brain and still he would never guess. He just didn't think big enough.

CHAPTER FIVE

Cody, Wyoming
10:23 a.m. MDT

Although E. Paul Rutherford had the full use of his legs, he sat behind the K-CHAT on-air console in a wheelchair. As radio talk-show host, he had to move quickly along the control panel and back and forth to the storage cases stationed around the glassed-in room, where shelves held cassettes of commercial announcements, taped music and news programs and sound-effect selections. Standard office chairs with little swivel wheels weren't up to the task. The wheels lasted only a couple of shows before blowing out and scattering their tiny steel bearings over the floor.

The reason that E. Paul Rutherford was so hard on furniture was that, dripping wet, he weighed 450 pounds.

The console's call lights were flashing.

"Rutherford here," he said into station's boom mike, cupping one ear closed so he could properly modulate his syrupy baritone. "Welcome to K-CHAT. You're on *Truth Watch.*"

"This is Chuck from Billings," a man's gruff voice said.

"Hey, Chuck, what's on your mind today?" As he spoke, Rutherford's massive pink jowls trembled. He was mostly bald; what hair he had, he combed over from a part just above his right ear. The top of his head was the normal size for a man of five foot ten, but from the cheekbones down, he grew larger and larger, spreading out in all directions like the flanks of a mountain.

A mountain in a Brooks Brothers pinstriped suit.

"The same thing that's on my mind every day," Chuck answered. "This country is being invaded. I've seen it myself, with my own two eyes."

Rutherford checked his computer prompter, on which Polly, his producer and call screener, logged each of the incoming calls and the subjects the callers wanted to discuss. He was looking for another call to pull up, in case this one turned suddenly boring or profane. "Are we talking UFOs, green men from Mars or what, Chuck? You've got to be more specific. And get on with it, I've got a lot of people waiting to speak this morning."

"We're being infiltrated by the armies of the New World Order," Chuck said.

"Before you explain that, why don't you tell us what you do for a living?"

"What I *did* for a living, Mr. R. I'm out of work since the goddamned environmentalists and federal government conspired to shut down the copper smelter over by Big Hat."

"Sorry to hear that, Chuck. Now, tell us about this army."

"It's part of an international conspiracy to enslave the American working man. They're starting the campaign here in the West, where they have lots of room to maneuver and where the population is spread out and especially vulnerable to attack. I'm not just some nut. I've got evidence on this. I've seen the trains.''

"Okay, Chuck, I'll bite. What trains?''

"A week ago Thursday, at seven in the morning, I was hunting over in the Clark River basin and I saw a hundred-car train coming from Johnsonville. Two engines pulling a string of flatcars covered with tarps. But not all the tarps were tied down—some had come completely off. What do you think was under them, Mr. R.?''

"I haven't a clue, Chuck.''

"Russian and East German trucks. Personnel carriers. Must have been two hundred of them lined up.''

"You're sure about this?''

"I know a Commie red star when I see one.''

"Did you follow the train, Chuck? Did you see where it took all those trucks?''

"No, I didn't. Believe me, I'm sorry now that I didn't, but I was about a mile from my pickup at the time.''

"Thanks for the report, Chuck.''

"Thank you for being on the radio, Mr. R. You're our guiding light. You're helping to save America.''

"You bet.'' Rutherford glared at his wall clock; some days seemed endless. "All I can say is, signs and portents, Americans. Signs and portents. If there's anybody out there who can confirm Chuck's story, or knows where those Evil Empire trucks ended up, give us a call here at K-CHAT. Next caller, you're on *Truth Watch*.''

"This is Denver from Butte. Howdy, Mr. R.''

"Not John Denver, I hope.''

"Hardly. Denver's my first name. I didn't see that

train, but I've heard about other suspicious activity around here."

"What kind of activity?"

"Drug gangs from Los Angeles and Miami and New York City being flown into deserted air bases. I know, 'cause friends of mine have seen 'em. These drug punks are being trained as shock troops for the New World Order. The plan is to give 'em dope and guns, and once they're all doped up, they're going to do house-to-house searches all through Montana, Wyoming and Idaho. They'll seize all valuables, guns, ammo and Bibles. They'll be robbin', rapin' and killin' anyone who resists. These drug gangsters are going to be sent into combat first, like a human wave, against property owners—that way they'll soak up all the ammo the honest citizens have stored away. Then the Pakistanis'll come in and finish everyone off."

"What have the Pakistanis got to do with this?"

"Goddamned UN troops," Denver replied. "They're already here. Training up in the mountains. They're going to enforce the martial law of the New World Order."

"But why the Pakistanis?"

"Because they're not white," Denver said. "It's one of the rules of these New Order bastards. To do their dirty work, they always send in occupying troops of a different color than the general population. Whites'll go to Pakistan or Hong Kong. Africans will go to West Yellowstone. They've done psychiatric research that shows black troops have less mercy on people they're enslaving if those people are white, and vice-a-versa."

"Well, Denver, you've given us a lot to think about this morning," Rutherford said.

"I just want to say one more thing, quick, before I hang up."

"Sure, Denver."

"You aren't corrupted by money and power, like the rest of the American media. I pray you have the strength to stay that way. God bless you."

"Bless you, too," Rutherford said.

At 10:59:27, the fat man punched up his last auto-glass commercial and rolled back from the console. He locked the chair's wheels and, with a grunt, pushed up to his feet.

Rutherford's producer met him at the control-room door, clipboard in hand. It appeared she had a list of things for him to do. The slim, thirty-year-old redhead started to speak, but he cut her off before she could get out a word. "Sorry, Polly, I don't have a second to spare. I've got an early lunch over at the Irma starting in ten minutes," he told her. As he lumbered past her down the corridor, he said, "I'll be there until 3:00 p.m."

The Irma Hotel, a Cody landmark, was only a few blocks from the radio station's offices, but Rutherford hated to hurry. Hurrying made him perspire, made him short of breath and made his face even pinker than usual. He drove to the hotel restaurant in his full-size Cadillac sedan.

From the outside, the Irma wasn't much to look at, a long, boxy building. Inside, it had its own peculiar charm. It was built by Buffalo Bill Cody, the cowboy master showman of the late nineteenth century and town's namesake. Its elaborately carved cherry-wood bar had been a present to Buffalo Bill by Queen Victoria, a token of her appreciation after seeing one of his performances. There were the standard Wild West decorative touches, stuffed buffalo and moose heads. Over the cash register hung a bullet-hole silhouette portrait of Buffalo Bill, artistically rendered in several different calibers on a thin sheet of steel. The restaurant's walls were lined with dark wood-paneled booths; the high ceilings were also dark. Combined with the weak lighting, it made for a brooding, serious drinking atmosphere.

Rutherford huffed over to his usual booth, off in a particularly dimly lit corner. He moved the table over to give himself room, then slid in, his buttocks filling the booth's bench seat from one end to the other.

When the perky young waitress arrived, he waved off the menu she offered him and announced, "I'd like a large bowl of the soup of the day, followed by the Lite Eater's Cobb salad with bread sticks, and a glass of low-calorie beer."

As his appointment walked up, Rutherford was just tidying up what had once been a platter of salad greens and mixed deli meats and cheeses. He mopped up the last of the Italian dressing with the stub of a bread stick. Wiping his mouth with his napkin, he extended a hand to the FBI man.

"Always good to see you, Parker."

The agent shook hands, then, with difficulty, took a seat opposite the radio personality. He had trouble sliding in because the table was shoved so far over on his side.

When the waitress saw Rutherford's guest appear, she returned at once with her order pad.

"What are the specials today?" Rutherford asked her.

She rattled off three selections, none of which suited him.

"Why don't you have the chef chicken-fry me a nice sixteen-ounce buffalo steak, medium rare. Mushrooms and onions. Baked potato and trimmings. Steamed vegetables. Sourdough rolls."

"To drink?"

"Another low-calorie beer for me."

"And you, sir?" the waitress asked Parker.

"Too early for lunch. Just coffee, black, please."

After the waitress left with the empty dishes, the FBI agent leaned over the table and said, "You're dicking the wrong guy, Rutherford."

"A very unpleasant expression."

"You want unpleasant?" Parker said, finding the table's pedestal with the soles of both shoes. He put his hands on the table edge. "This is unpleasant...." His back braced against the booth, he shoved with hands and feet, scooting the table across the rug, burying its edge deep in Rutherford's massive gut, creasing him all the way to his rib cage.

"Do you think I'm stupid, Mr. R.?" the agent hissed.

Rutherford couldn't reply; he was too busy fighting for breath.

"You've been taking the Bureau's money for a year now. You've been playing footsy with some real bad apples. But you've given me diddly-squat."

The fat man struggled against the pressure, trying in vain to push the table back.

"Do you know how mad it makes me every time I see you smiling down from one of your *Truth Watch* billboards?" Parker said. "You've got your talk-show syndication scam in high gear, but you should never, ever forget who brought you to the party. I set you up as God's gift to the airwaves and I can take you down, pronto." He shoved harder with his feet, until he could lock his knees. The booth back behind the radio host made an ominous cracking sound.

"Okay, Okay, enough," Rutherford gasped, his face turning dark red. He waved his hands in surrender.

Parker let the table slide back a little. "I hate getting physical with you, but you don't seem to get the point. My patience, and that of the Bureau, is gone. It's time to take these scum-buckets down. You're going to get me what I need to do the job. Evidence of serious criminal activity, felonies, something I can take to a grand jury."

"Or you'll stop paying me?"

"Of course I'll stop paying you," Parker said, "but that isn't what should be keeping you up at night. What you should worry about is how your superpatriotic pals are going to take the news that their golden boy is a federal snitch."

The waitress rolled over a small trolley cart bearing Rutherford's meal. As she set out the plates, he picked up the fresh glass of beer and drained it.

"Can I get you another beer?" she asked.

"Please." He looked down at the food, then up at Parker. "Do you mind?" he asked, gesturing at the plate with his knife and fork. "It would be a shame to let it get cold."

Parker watched Rutherford attack the food, sawing off great bloody hunks of breaded, pan-fried buffalo steak, jamming them into a mouth already crammed with half-chewed vegetables, baked potato and sourdough roll.

"I'm glad I didn't put you off your feed," the FBI man said, sipping at his black coffee.

Rutherford made short work of the platter, finishing it before the waitress could return with his beverage.

"Did you save room for dessert?" she asked.

"Apple pie, I think," Rutherford said. "With double à la mode."

She wrote it down on her pad as she turned away.

"So, what's it going to be?" Parker said. "Are you going to do your duty, or are you going down?"

Rutherford drank the beer before he answered. "You seem to think I haven't been trying all these months, but I have. I've been working hard to get you what you need to make your case. I'm onto something big that's about to break—it'll blow the lid off. I can't talk about it yet, but I think you're going to be surprised at just how big it is. I think you're going to be very pleasantly surprised."

"I'll look forward to that," Parker said. "But make it sooner than later. You're not going to like later."

As Rutherford watched the FBI man leave, he automatically picked up the beer glass and tried to drink out of it.

It was empty.

And his hand was shaking.

Just when everything seemed to be going right for him, the bottom started falling out. He was caught in a bad place—between the gears of the Department of Justice and the shadowy, actively violent militia group known as the Sawtooth Patriots. His radio career needed another month, two months at most, to really take off, but even then he wouldn't be free to tell the Feds to go to hell. He was on their hook, but good.

From Parker's new, get-tough attitude, Rutherford figured more stalling was out of the question, which meant he had to produce something to keep the agent at bay. The trouble was, the people Justice wanted him to inform on weren't stupid. They didn't make mistakes, and they knew all about FBI spies, how to uncover them and how to deal with them. Parker knew damned well how good they were. He knew that Sawtooth had in its ranks alumni of earlier ultra-right-wing groups that had been targeted by Justice, including the antitax vigilantes, Posse Comitatus, and neo-Nazis from the Order—not to ever be confused with *Truth Watch*'s favorite subject, "the New World Order," which was a liberal, humanist, anti-Christian, antifamily, race-mixing, individual-crushing, abortion-and-homosexual-loving, one-world dictatorship.

The upper echelon of the Sawtooth organization trusted Rutherford, but only to a point. They encouraged him to spread their paranoid message of impending Armageddon and armed resistance over the airwaves. They had given him fifty thousand in cash that Agent Parker didn't know about, but they hadn't shared any real secrets with him yet. He had nothing to show the Feds for a year of under-the-table funding, for a year of their help in building up his career, which was intended to make him more attractive to the militia and other, similar groups.

Of course, he had heard the rumors that elements of Sawtooth had robbed banks and armored cars, that members had killed civilians who opposed the group's beliefs. Those civilians included judges, sheriffs and county prosecuting attorneys. But he had never met any of the people who had supposedly committed these crimes; he had never heard their names mentioned or a word spoken about the deeds in question by Sawtooth's leaders.

Maybe the bank jobs and the murders were as real as the supposed Pakistani troops jackbooting through downtown Jackson Hole? Rutherford shook his head, feeling suddenly weepy and sorry for himself.

How did he ever get into this crazy position?

He'd never had any choice in the matter.

He'd been doomed from the start by his genes, cursed from the moment of his conception by God. As a morbidly fat person with no education past high school, no skills except the ability to jabber convincingly in a comforting tone of voice, the FBI's offer to hook him up with a nationally known PR firm that would not only construct him a new image, but make him a household name throughout the west, was something he didn't have the willpower—or the intelligence—to pass up.

If something looked too good to be true, it probably was.

Before Special Agent Parker intervened, E. Paul Rutherford was nobody, so if Parker walked away, he'd be worse than a nobody, he'd be dead. The question was, could he get what he needed to pacify the Justice Department without tipping his hand to Sawtooth and blowing his cover?

He didn't know the answer, and that terrified him.

As the waitress cleaned up the table, she said, "Will there be anything else this afternoon?" Then she saw the expression on his face. "Are you all right, Mr. Rutherford?"

"Yes, I'm fine," he said, forcing a smile. "Bring me another low-cal beer. I've got to stick around for a while. I've got another couple of people coming by in a few minutes."

Two beers later, a pair of tall, lean men entered the

Irma and headed for Rutherford's booth. They reminded the talk-show host of those Marlborough Country ads. Both of them wore long canvas dusters, well-worn Stetson hats, jeans and cowboy boots. In the Irma, where it was like a Wild West costume party seven days a week, nobody paid them any mind.

As the man in front stepped up, he removed his aviator's sunglasses. Oswald Carmody, the commander in chief of the Sawtooth Patriots, had flint-hard gray eyes and a longish, hollow-cheeked face. He grabbed a chair from a nearby table and spun it around in front of Rutherford's booth. With the chair turned backfirst, he sat down.

The other guy Rutherford knew as Matt Cook, a member of the Sawtooth executive council. His brown beard and handlebar mustache were tinged with highlights of gray. Cook also took a chair and set it next to the booth. There was no way either of the men could have squeezed his legs under the table with Rutherford sitting on the other side. True to cowboy etiquette, they both kept their hats and coats on.

"Good show this morning," Carmody said. "People love hearing about those trainloads of Commie trucks."

"Thanks," Rutherford said. "I'm getting a little worried about Chuck's calls, though. He's been on the air a little too much lately."

"Chuck is a very committed soldier of the armed resistance."

"I know that, but we don't want anyone to think he's a plant. Can't you get somebody else to make the call in his place? Or at least have him change his voice and give another name?"

Carmody turned to Cook. "Make a note of that,"

he directed. "We'll give Chuck a vacation for a couple of weeks."

"Yes, sir," Cook said, pulling a spiral pad out of his duster's slash pocket. As he did so, his coat opened up wide.

Rutherford could see the automatic pistol hanging in a leather shoulder holster. Its walnut grip and wide blue-steel backstrap stuck straight out from under Cook's armpit. The pistol's hammer was cocked all the way back. Rutherford knew it was just the tip of the iceberg; Matt Cook was a walking arsenal. All Sawtooth members that Rutherford had met made it a practice to carry multiple handguns, three, four, even five concealed around their persons. Sometimes they packed machine pistols and stubby riot shotguns, as well.

"We want you to come out to the ranch for the weekend," Carmody said. "Bring your tape recorder."

Rutherford tried not to act stunned. The ranch was Carmody's private spread, a thousand acres of high-plains desert backed by the Sawtooth Mountain range. It was also the militia group's training center and retreat. As far as he knew, there had never been any media allowed on the ranch before, not even a tame representative like him. He suddenly saw a way out of his current predicament. Maybe a sketch of the ranch's grounds or the interiors of the buildings would satisfy Parker. Or it was always possible that he'd glimpse something incriminating on the tour. Don't act too delighted or too anxious, he told himself, just flattered that you've been asked.

"I'd enjoy that," he said.

"We'll send a car around to pick you up."

Rutherford wanted to ask Carmody why the policy about nonmembers on the ranch had been changed and what he was supposed to do with his tape recorder, but kept his mouth shut. Maybe they figured a little publicity would boost their recruitment numbers, maybe even get some spin-off groups started in other states. They would tell him in their own good time if they intended to, and if they didn't, his asking about it would be a mistake. He didn't want Carmody to think he was pumping them for information.

Cook leaned forward and said, "Say, how's that ghostwriter of yours working out? We saw him walking up the street as we drove in. Hope he's not making you bigger than life." There was unconcealed amusement in Cook's eyes as he looked over at Carmody.

Sticks and stones, Rutherford thought, sticks and stones. As for the ghostwriter thing, that was a bit of desperate inspiration. When Carmody had gotten curious about the occasional presence of Parker, Rutherford had explained that he had hired an out-of-work English literature professor to help him write his autobiography, tentatively entitled *Truth Watch*. The book's scheduled publication date coincided with the projected signing of an eight-state radio-show syndication deal that was currently in the works.

"He's slow, but he's good," Rutherford said.

"Can't wait to read it," Carmody commented.

Rutherford automatically searched the man's face for sarcasm and found none. Carmody never made fun of him; he was always respectful. Dead serious and deadpan. A straight-arrow guy, he said what he believed and believed what he said. The mind-set he projected was infectious. It really wasn't surprising that he could get other men to buy into the byzantine conspiracies of the New World Order, or to follow him into a gunfight or to commit a bank robbery. Had Rutherford been younger, leaner and meaner, had Carmody asked him nicely, he, too, might well have picked up a gun to defend individual freedom and property rights.

"You'll get one of the first copies that comes off the press, I promise," Rutherford said.

"Autographed, of course," Carmody countered.

"Of course." Things were most definitely looking up.

Rutherford caught the waitress's attention, then turned back to his companions. "Now that business is out of the way, gentlemen," he said, "what are we going to have for lunch?"

CHAPTER SIX

Thermopolis, Wyoming
4:32 p.m. MDT

The Beechcraft Kingair flew under a dress parade of broken high clouds. Carmody's view from the copilot's seat was of a jumble of deeply eroded yellow mountains, sun shafted and shadowed, that stretched from horizon to horizon. He had read somewhere that seventy or so million years ago, the awesome desert below had been a tropical paradise populated by dinosaurs.

Carmody had thought a lot about the nature of total change, and had come up with three basic requirements: it had to be the right precipitating event, it had to occur in the right place and at the right time. Since his service in Desert Shield and Storm and his discharge from the U.S. Army Reserve National Guard, he had been trying to stage-manage such a change in his own country. It was a complex and dangerous business that he privately liked to think of as "hurrying the hand of God," and its climax, Operation Firestorm, was close at hand.

The twin-engined plane banked a turn. Below, he could see the town of Thermopolis, an oasis of green trees and red, rounded knobs of rock. Afternoon winds made the air rough on the landing approach. The charter pilot compensated for the twenty-mile-per-hour cross breeze and set the Kingair down smoothly on the airstrip.

Les Johnson cracked back the headset from his right ear. "Where do you want me to park it?" he asked Carmody.

"Over by the Learjet on the service apron."

Carmody watched the pilot as he taxied the aircraft off the runway. Like most of the participants in Operation Firestorm, Johnson was a veteran. He had served three tours in Vietnam as a recon pilot, spotting targets for jet fighters and artillery from a single-engine, usually unarmed Cessna. Though his hair and the stubble of beard were grizzled, he was still as hard as nails. Unlike the rest of the personnel, Johnson was not a volunteer; he was being paid handsomely for his services.

He had been hired to provide twenty-four-hour, on-call transportation of men and matériel for a two-week period. No one had asked him how he had come up with the Beechcraft on such short notice, but it was obvious that the tail section had been recently repainted. Under close inspection, the edges of the old FAA identification numbers could been seen peeking out in places under the new ones.

It was certainly more cost-efficient to steal a plane than to buy a stolen one from someone else, especially when you were going to burn it when the job was done. By heisting the Kingair himself, Johnson had saved roughly 160 grand, and he'd had a much wider selection of aircraft to choose from.

Sawtooth had invested a considerable sum in the

background check on the ex-recon pilot, but it had been necessary. Because of what he had to know in order to do his job, he was in a position to sink the mission and get them all killed. Johnson's track record since Nam was most impressive. For many years, he had flown support missions for CIA ops in Southeast Asia and Central America. When the plug was finally pulled on the Nicaraguan Contras, he went to work for the Medellín cartel. He had logged hundreds of hours night-flying raw coca paste from Peru to processing centers in Colombia before he was busted. To make amends and stay out of prison, he had agreed to switch sides and fly guns and men into Peru for DAS, the Colombian FBI. A misunderstanding about payment had escalated into a three-day torture session in the subbasement of the Bogotá central police station.

Like the other former soldiers under Carmody's command, Johnson had plenty of reason to hate big government and its instrument of social control, big law enforcement. Unlike the rest, he had struck back. Four months earlier, he had taken out an entire Justice Department tactical unit, killing eighteen of its finest fighting men in a single, devastating, air-to-ground rocket attack. A complete professional, he had wasted no women or children, just the hotshot bastards behind the black ski masks. In that one act, he had taken cleaner, more appropriate revenge for Waco, Ruby Ridge and a host of other big-government atrocities committed against American citizens than the Oklahoma City bombers.

Again, it was the right event at the right time and place.

Carmody had nothing but contempt for the

Oklahoma bunglers. He felt the same way about the Muslim fanatics who had blown up the World Trade Center. Both groups were made up of stupid, lazy cowards. The Muslim terrorists thought they were going to kick off a planet-wide jihad with a cow-dung bomb in a rental truck. The fertilizer bomb was easy to make and plant, but it was the wrong weapon. The target was safe to hit because it was unguarded, but it was the wrong target. Predictably the explosion, when it came, brought the wrong result. Instead of sparking a world uprising, all it did was produce minor damage to a building and kill a few people. Because postexplosion there was no ripple effect, no wider consequences, the bombing was categorized as a limited act of revenge and, as such, quickly faded from the news.

The Oklahoma City dilwads had made exactly the same mistakes. They'd had big plans for what was going to happen after the bang, which was supposed to be a call to arms that would unify the American militia movement. They used cow dung explosive, also in a rental truck, and they had compounded the goof with their choice of a target. The Alfred Murrah Building was easy because it was undefended. It was also largely worthless, actually and symbolically, which was why it was such a sitting duck. Who really gave a damn about what happened in Oklahoma City? Obviously nobody. The bombing had dropped out of the national headlines even faster than the Trade Center hit.

Neither attack had changed anything in the long term. Self-limited and therefore self-defeating, both were quickly swallowed up by larger events.

Carmody had learned a couple of things from his

analysis of the prior bombings. First, pick a target that can't fall out of the news. Second, use the right weapon for the job. He had no qualms about taking out innocent civilians; indeed, their deaths by the hundreds of thousands were absolutely necessary if the desired result was to be achieved. Unlike the Trade Center or the Oklahoma City operation, Carmody's plan extended beyond zero hour of the cataclysmic event, to a chain of predictable actions and reactions.

That chain of action and response, not a smoking bomb crater, was the real goal. In carefully measured steps, it led to the horrors of Armageddon, and past them to a new and better America.

Not all these ideas were his own. He owed much to someone older, with wider experience and education. And infinitely deeper pockets.

"Stay here," Carmody told Johnson and Cook as the props stopped turning. He had to raise his voice and repeat himself to be heard over the roar of the single-engine, red-and-white plane just coming in for a landing. "I'll be back in a few minutes."

He climbed out of the Beechcraft and crossed the tarmac to the lowered steps of the Learjet. On the hull beside the open door was a black-and-silver corporate logo. That was a bitter joke. The five-million-dollar aircraft no longer belonged to Monstrel Mining and Chemical, Inc.; it was the property of the U.S. government. It had already been scheduled for confiscation by the IRS.

As Carmody mounted the stairs, a huge figure appeared above him in the doorway. Bald on top, the man wore his side and back fringe of pale blond hair down to his shoulders. He had an ugly little blue-steel machine pistol in his right fist. The bodyguard recognized Carmody and reholstered the miniUzi beneath his sports coat. He stepped aside so Carmody could enter the cabin.

Every organization has levels of responsibility and commitment. The Sawtooth Patriots was divided into four unequal parts, stacked like a pyramid. The lowest and largest level was made up of believers who bought into the end-times-are-here party line, who had guns and stored supplies, but who hadn't taken the pledge to kill for the organization. The next level up consisted of fifty foot soldiers committed to defending the group from outside attack. The third level was made up of a dozen men willing to take offensive action against an identified enemy, if so ordered. The top level, where all the command decisions were made, only had two chairs in it.

"Take a walk, Paolo," said the man sitting at the rear of the cabin. Charles Krick smiled at Carmody and waved him to a seat. Krick's designer Western wardrobe was a little too much for Carmody's taste, the hand-tooling and silver toe caps on his boots too ornate, the watchband of gold nuggets a little too flashy. The CEO of Monstrel was sharp faced, with a straight, thin nose, and he wore his white hair trimmed very short.

"What's the news?" Carmody asked.

"The tools have arrived," Krick said. "I just had confirmation from our Persian friend."

"That's a relief to hear."

"It was a near thing, too."

"How so?"

"There was a problem on the other end. Some very expensive articles were lost—not ours, though. A bloodbath, I gather. The Persian said he almost bought the farm. Apparently our goods were shipped by separate container weeks ahead in order to make the scheduled delivery date. He assured me that everything would be ready for us in two days, as promised. He'll be meeting us at the storage site to facilitate."

"What about the PAL code?"

"He's going to handle all of that in person. He insisted on it."

"As long as we get the code..."

"How's the 12-7 team doing with the trainer?" Krick asked.

"No problems there. We've been running the operation on a scale-model range."

"Too bad we couldn't have corraled a secondD-20 howitzer for you to use," Krick said.

"Yeah, it would've been nice," Carmody replied, "but the logistical problems were just too big. The risk of discovery during transport would've doubled, and firing it for practice would've alerted everybody within a hundred miles what we were up to. We'd all be dead or in federal prison by now."

"Still, I'd feel a lot more confident if I knew you had worked on a life-size howitzer."

"Don't worry about it. I know the 12-7 guys from the Gulf War. We've all gone from trainer to live fire before. We know how to make the jump. We'll hit the target."

"And the B team?" Krick asked.

"They acquired their matériel this morning. They'll be testing it, nice and loud, early tomorrow."

"Poor B team," Krick said.

"War is about sacrifice," Carmody countered.

"I hope the ranch is ready to take what's coming," the white-haired man said.

"We started installing the final grid of the defensive perimeter today. It should be completed by tonight."

"No clue as to our infiltrator?"

For months they had known they had to have a Fed, or Feds, in their midst. They hadn't discovered a security breach, nor had they received a tip from a suspicious Patriot. It was a question of inevitability; they had to have been infiltrated. Every antigovernment organization could, and would, be penetrated by Justice if it was large enough. Krick and Carmody had taken the spies as a given and worked around it.

"No," Carmody replied, "but he'll show himself soon. He has to, and when he does, I have something special planned for him."

The commander in chief of the Sawtooth Patriots rose from his seat. "I'd better get back in the air," he said. "I want to check the minefield work while it's still light." He extended his hand to Krick. "Don't worry about the mission. We're going to nail it."

"See you on the East Coast in two days," Krick said, pumping his hand.

Carmody hurried down the Lear's steps and headed for the Beechcraft, gripping the brim of his tall Stetson to keep it from blowing off in the wind. He didn't look across the runway where the field's most recent arrival sat, so he didn't see the man photographing him through a telephoto lens that poked out the copilot's window of the red-and-white Cessna.

The shutterbug was Special Agent William Parker of the FBI.

Old Glory Ranch
Highway 26, Western Wyoming
5:35 p.m. MDT

JACK HUTTON LEANED on his shovel and wiped the sweat from his face with the tail of his shirt. He had just finished digging the last spadeful of dirt from the last trench in the last grid. At the other end of the shallow ditch, the mine-laying team was working back toward the bunkhouse, placing antipersonnel and antitank mines inside the perimeter of the ranch compound's ten-foot-high hurricane fence. On either side of the crew were open trenches, each dotted with mines of various sizes and connected by bright lengths of electrical wire.

The idea for the defensive strategy had come from Oswald Carmody himself. He had sworn that the Old Glory Ranch wouldn't be another one-sided Waco. If armored personnel carriers and tanks entered the perimeter, they would pay for the trespass.

The mined grids of open ground extended from the ranch's buildings like the spokes of a wheel. They were armed by a master panel in the main house's fortified bunker-basement. Each separate minefield could be rigged to explode either by contact or by electric impulse, simply by throwing a switch. They could also be as easily deactivated. The grid system allowed the defenders to control all the approaches to their stronghold. By arming one of the minefields and disarming the bordering grids, the Patriots could move men across the mined ground and concentrate flanking fire on crippled opposition forces.

The flexibility of the system was the stone bitch, Hutton thought. On the other hand, there was no denying that it did simplify his job. Because there was no "safe way" in, no clear path over the minefields, there was nothing for him to commit to memory and then map. How the Justice Department tactical units were going to handle the assault, he didn't have a clue. That wasn't his problem, and he was glad of it. He had his hands full just getting the site-analysis information off the ranch and into the hands of the FBI.

When the mine-laying team reached the end of the trench, the Sawtooth Patriot officer in charge of the detail ordered everyone to move to cover behind the bunkhouse. The officer, former National Guard Master Sergeant Vernon Drake, spoke into his walkie-talkie. Drake was a certified pain in the ass in his neatly pressed desert-camou fatigues and matching boonie hat. "Grid N is hardwired, and we are clear," he said. "Repeat, we are all clear. Proceed with the firing check."

Hutton sat on the ground, his back up against the bunkhouse wall. Looking down the narrow walkway that separated the enlisted men's quarters from the main house, he could see the ragged, snowcapped peaks of the Sawtooth Mountains about two miles away. Out of sight, eight miles in the opposite direction, was the two-lane highway that marked the southern edge of Old Glory Ranch. He couldn't hear what was happening inside the house, but he knew what was going on because he had seen it many times before. In the bunker, the fire-control officer was working the control panel, tripping the arming switches on all the mines in the grid. A sensor attached to the last mine in each string would confirm that they were ready to rip if someone or something stepped on them. The sensor also confirmed that current was traveling through the entire grid circuit, so all the mines could be fired at once.

After about five minutes, the word came up from the bunker via Drake's walkie-talkie. "Grid N is off-line," the fire control officer said. "Repeat, Grid N is off-line. Everything checks out. Nice job, boys."

"Okay, let's get that trench filled in," Drake said. "Pronto."

"Easy for him to say," Hutton muttered as he walked along the side of the ditch.

His digging partner heard the remark. "We're almost done with this shit, so you got nothing to complain about," Bill Boggs said. "You're through working for today. You can take a shower, eat dinner, hit the rack early. Not old Boggsie—I pulled all-night guard duty at OP-3."

OP-3 was the hilltop observation post closest to the highway and farthest from the compound. The sandbagged cleft in a rock outcrop was cold and uncomfortable, and boring. Between 10:00 p.m. and dawn, you could count the traffic passing by on your fingers and toes, if you could feel them.

"Tell you what, Boggs. I'll take your watch tonight."

"You're bullshitting me."

"No, I'll do it. I don't mind. I haven't been sleeping good. Anxious about what's coming, I guess. You can pay me back some other time, or not. It doesn't matter."

"You're a pal, Hutton."

"Yeah, I know."

As Hutton and Boggs filled in the ditch, they were followed by a man with a rake, who was followed by another man with a push broom to smooth out the yellow dirt to match the rest of the compound. They had the job half-completed when the Beechcraft landed on the ranch's foot airstrip, which was on the mountain side of the property, outside the perimeter fence. Hutton leaned on his shovel and watched Carmody and Cook jump into a jeep and drive around to the front gate. The commander in chief took a quick look at the minefield, approved what he saw, then went into the main house to clean up for supper.

After the evening meal, Hutton drove down the ranch's curving dirt road and relieved the sentry at OP-3. It was around midnight when a car appeared on the highway from the south. It blinked its headlights once without slowing. Hutton blinked his flashlight twice. The car vanished over a rise in the road.

Taking his M-16 with him, Hutton deserted the observation post, skidding and sliding on the slope of loose rock. In darkness, he crossed the flat ground and its scrub-brush obstacle course, heading for the fence line. When he got close, he saw the car parked there on the shoulder of the road. When he got closer still, he could make out the shape of a man leaning against the driver's door.

"I was starting to get a little worried about you, Hutton," Agent Parker said.

"Me, too," Hutton replied. "Things are getting scary up there." He handed Parker a couple of sheets of lined notebook paper, folded into a tiny square. "I've mapped out all the defenses and given you the building floor plans, including the secret connecting passages. Also the names of some of the new personnel. It's everything I could get."

"Thanks," Parker said, pocketing the papers. "What about the artillery trainer?"

"They practiced with it for five hours today. I included a sketch of their target range, but you can't tell much from it. It looks like a high-angle-of-fire shot, though. I haven't seen anything that resembles an artillery piece. I don't think they have one yet."

"That's good news."

Hutton took a breath, then said, "When are you going to shut these bastards down?"

"Soon," Parker said. "Very soon. Stay ready and out of the line of fire."

"Right. For sure I'm keeping my head down. I'd better get back. They shoot deserters."

"Good luck."

Hutton hurried over the flat ground and scrambled up the slope to the observation post. His heart froze in his chest when he looked over the top of the sandbags and saw the post was occupied by two men. He couldn't make out their faces. He grabbed the auto-rifle's pistol grip and swung the weapon around on its shoulder sling.

"Don't do that, soldier," Carmody warned him.

"Oh, it's you, sir," Hutton said, anything but relieved.

The other figure cloaked in darkness moved forward. When Matt Cook took his weapon from him, Hutton knew it was bad.

"Where were you just now?" Carmody asked.

"Taking a whiz, sir. I didn't want to do it too close to the OP. The smell, sir."

"That's real considerate of you, Hutton." Carmody reached out and put something heavy into his hand. "Do you know what that is?"

By feel, Hutton recognized the sight tube and head strap of a cyclops night-vision device. He said nothing. He couldn't speak; his mouth was too dry.

"Who do you think you're kidding, you rat?" Carmody snarled.

CHAPTER SEVEN

Chocolate Canyon
Millard County, Utah
5:05 a.m. MDT

The tractor-trailer lumbered down the rutted dirt road. On the horizon to Edward Kelso's right, the sun was peeking up, but the air was still cold and the morning light tinged with purple. The dew that lingered on the road helped to keep the dust down. For a hundred miles in all directions, the land was open range. Highway 6, which they'd followed through most of Nevada, was fifteen miles behind them.

Kelso took a reading from his laser range finder, then pulled his head back inside the truck cab. The distance was right. Just ahead, a rise in the high-plains desert coincided with the irregularly shaped contour mark on his topo map.

Oswald Carmody had delegated all responsibility for the test firing to Kelso, a measure of the commander in chief's confidence in him, and his lack of confidence in nearly everyone else. Kelso regarded the vast majority of Sawtooth Patriots as ridiculous posers. They loved the militia movement because of its phony martial trappings: the camou uniforms, the brigade and division designations, the cute unit nick-names, the pretense of military command structure and discipline. They were believers, though. They did think the New World Order was going to eat them for lunch, and they had committed their limited abilities to the struggle against an impending, oppressive world government. But when push came to shove, the rank and file were sponges for bullets, mere cannon fodder.

Kelso, on the other hand, was a bona fide cannon shooter. He took very seriously the responsibility he'd been given. Well in advance, he had worked out all the necessary alterations to the semitrailer, making it a secure mobile firing platform for the stolen 155 mm field gun. He had picked the general area for the firing test, siting it close enough to an existing military range so the sound of repeated cannon shots wouldn't raise public alarm, but far enough away so the Lake Desert Test Center folks wouldn't run out and investigate the unscheduled bombardment.

He had also decided on the test range. The lay of the land on the surrounding plain closely matched the contours and elevations of the real target and firing position. Kelso flipped the clear plastic overlay sheet down over his topo map. The plastic overlay had many widely separated marks on it. Most of them were ringers; only three had anything to do with the actual target. At the top of the overlay, a rectangle with a dot in it indicated the howitzer's firing position, and just below that, a triangle indicated an observation post. At the bottom of the overlay was a black cross with a simple "TGT" notation, and no other grid or target references. With the plastic sheet folded down, it sat in the middle of the low rise on the topo map.

"Stop here," he told Wiley.

The driver braked the truck to a halt in the middle of the road.

"Leave it running," Kelso said. "You stay behind the wheel, everybody else out. Let's shake it."

Kelso and Speck jumped down first, followed by Mallone and Ringman, who rode in the truck cab's sleeper. While Speck passed out flags of different colors to the others, Kelso hustled out onto the rise. In the center of the flat-topped hill, he planted a red flag. At his direction, the others quickly staked out a large rectangular area with their pennants. Then they all climbed back into the truck.

Kelso slammed the passenger's side door shut. "Move," he ordered.

Wiley slipped the Kenworth into gear, and they headed away from the flagged area, up a long, straight stretch of road and a very gradual incline, toward a line of dark brown hills about five miles away.

Kelso knew he was going to make history real soon. Nuclear devices had only been detonated in anger twice before. Now one was about to go off in anger again, and it would make a similar kind of statement: don't mess with us. He was bound to become famous for being the man who pulled the lanyard. Kelso liked the idea of having his name associated with the biggest antigovernment bang ever set off in the U.S. It would be a bang heard around the world. Chunks of existing textbooks were going to have to be thrown out in order to make room for him.

Many targets had been suggested for the nuclear

strike, but in the end it had been decided that shooting the beast in the purse would hurt it the most. It was a target that wouldn't draw much sympathy from the everyday Joe. Outwardly there might be tears for the victims and their families, but inwardly, all the "sheeple," or sheep people, would be laughing with relief, maybe even glee. Only the slaves of the beast would really mourn the death and destruction. They'd be cowering under their beds because they'd know their day of judgment was at hand.

When the Kenworth closed on the dark brown hills, the entrance to the box canyon became visible among the folds of smooth rock. It was wide enough for four semis to park side by side.

Wiley feathered the brakes, slowing to a crawl. "Looks kind of soft to me," he said, referring to the dry streambed that led into Chocolate Canyon.

"No, it's fine," Kelso assured him. "I already checked it out. Pull in a hundred feet and stop."

Wiley crept the Kenworth between the canyon's two-hundred-foot-high walls, then hit the brakes.

"Okay," Kelso directed, "let's get this thing lined up."

Everyone but Wiley climbed out of the cab. Mallone and Ringman opened the rear doors of the trailer and bolted them back as Kelso scrambled up beside the gun. Speck relayed Kelso's signals to the driver as they adjusted the position of the trailer to bring the M-198 to bear on the distant target.

"That's good. Right there," Kelso said, pounding the sheet-steel wall of the trailer with his balled fist. He hit the start button on his stopwatch. "We're on the clock, boys."

They all knew their jobs inside out. Wiley left the

truck engine running and securely chocked the rig's wheels, front and back. Then he grabbed a pair of binoculars and a walkie-talkie and headed up the side of the canyon on a dead run. Mallone and Ringman climbed into the trailer and up the ladders bolted to either side of the box. Under Kelso's watchful eye, they had customized the trailer during a short stop the day before, cutting out a big section of the box's rear roof and hinging it so it could be winched open and dropped onto the roof of the truck cab. This allowed the cannon barrel to be raised to the maximum; it could also be fired through the open rear doors. Toward the center of the box, the howitzer, its tow wheels cranked up and its split-rail carriage spread as far as possible, was bolted to the trailer frame. There was room in the front of the trailer for shells and gun crew.

Kelso checked the elapsed time, then got behind the M-198's electronic sight and began laying the gun on target. The sight compensated for the lack of level in the weapon platform and for shell drift. Because they knew the distance to the stationary target and had the firing tables for the cannon, they had already calculated the charge and shell fusing.

The Sawtooth leader called out sight adjustments to Speck, who raised the eight-inch bore with a hand wheel. There was no horizontal-control officer and no vertical-control officer on this mission. It was seat-of-your-pants work. When Kelso was satisfied, Ringman and Mallone set the packaged shell in the shot guide and rammed it into the breech.

Kelso spoke into his walkie-talkie. "Wiley, are you in position?"

"Affirmative," came the reply.

"All clear!" Kelso shouted.

They bailed out of the trailer by its side door. As Kelso hopped down, he held the uncoiled lanyard in his hand.

He gave the cord a hard jerk. The cannon's lock snapped, and a 155 mm HE round boomed out of the gun. The trailer rocked from the blast, and its side walls flared with the concussion, searing clouds of propellant smoke pouring out of the open top and the doors.

There was no way they could have remained in the box for the shot.

Having to abandon ship before every shot was an annoyance that ate up time, but they wouldn't have to deal with it at H-hour. Because they still needed the trailer to transport the weapon to the real target, they couldn't cut away the walls yet. At H-hour, they'd be shooting from an open platform.

From on top of the canyon rim, Wiley reported what he saw downrange through his binoculars. From the aiming stakes, he could calculate the distance of the miss and call the observation and correction down to the trailer.

"Short, fifty right," he said. "Left four hundred."

Kelso and the others climbed back into the trailer. Ringman and Mallone cleared the breech of the shell case, while Kelso adjusted the cannon himself this time. In fifteen seconds, they had reloaded and were again bailing out of the trailer.

The rocking boom torqued the trailer on its suspension as a second HE shell screamed downrange.

Wiley was silent for a moment before offering corrections. "Short, ten right," he said. "Left eighty, add four hundred."

The gun crew scurried to relay the howitzer and reload. By the time they jumped down again, they were all sweating from the effort and the heat trapped inside the trailer.

Kelso yanked the lanyard; his men covered their ears.

The truck and trailer jolted hard against the chocks, but they held. The trailer's rivets did not. By the dozens, they popped out of the trailer skin as its weakened walls ballooned from the blast.

The third round arced just over the target, but along the imaginary observer-target line that ran through the middle of the flagged rectangle. It gave Wiley enough data to make the final correction. "Over line," he said. "Drop fifty, fire for effect."

The howitzer boomed again, sending echoes rolling over the high desert plain.

The fourth time was a charm. The HE shell landed in the dead center of the rectangle, hurling smoke, chunks of dirt and the colored pennants high into the air.

"Nailed it," Wiley announced. "End of mission."

Kelso checked his watch. Elapsed time was six minutes, well within the mission parameters. With the box cut off the trailer, they could reduce the time another minute and a half. He wanted as much time as he could get, in case it took him more than four rounds to get on the real target. On the whole, though, he was quite satisfied.

"Let's bag it," Kelso said.

They worked with speed and precision, swinging the roof section into place and battening down the gun. They had just finished unchocking the truck and trailer wheels when Wiley raced up, out of breath. He climbed into the cab and goosed the engine.

Kelso had him reverse the truck out of the wash, then cut a K-turn to head back down the road the way they had come.

Wiley slowed the Kenworth as they approached the shell craters. At Kelso's command, he stopped the truck once more. The gun crew hopped out of the cab and spent a couple of frantic minutes picking up what was left of the aiming stakes. Kelso figured why leave anything behind that would help the Feds with their investigation?

They returned to Highway 6 without drawing pursuit, aerial or ground. If anybody anywhere was asking questions about the cannon fire, they were too far away to make a difference. Kelso directed Wiley to head east, toward Salt Lake City.

"So when are you going to tell us what we're really going to shoot at?" Speck asked.

"Yeah," Wiley agreed. "It'd be nice to know who and what we're going to ice with our cannon."

"It'd be something to look forward to on the ride," Ringman added with a grin.

Kelso thought about it for a second. They were en route to the target, but they had a stop along the way to pick up the nuke. They would be spending the night at a roadside rest stop and making the hit at ten the following morning. Lots of things could go wrong with that much time left. If one of the crew turned out to be a federal plant, *everything* could go wrong. He didn't think for a minute that any of his men were double-crossers, but there was no point in taking the risk. Plus, he took no small pleasure in withholding the information, and teasing them with it.

"Come on," Mallone said, "let us in on it."

"No can do."

"Christ, Kelso…"

"Trust me," he said. "You won't be disappointed."

CHAPTER EIGHT

Kensington, London
3:05 p.m. GMT

Sergio Eshamani had spent a rough day and a half in the company of the Russian brigadier general. In that time, he had learned more than he cared to about the man. Across the living room of his Kensington town house, Avril Krukillov sat on the white leather couch with his shoes propped up on the art deco coffee table. He was drinking straight, nearly frozen Absolut vodka from a sixteen-ounce tumbler and talking a mile a minute.

No matter how much vodka the general drank, it seemed to have no effect on him. He had been drinking ever since they had made their escape from Riga. He drank on the commercial flight to London. He drank on the drive down from Heathrow. And he had been drinking steadily since they had arrived in Kensington.

His speech wasn't slurred.

His eyes weren't the least bit bloodshot.

Chalk it up to a marvelous constitution and decades of training.

The only change Eshamani had noticed over the

past several hours was that the general was repeating himself even more frequently than usual.

"How will you ever repay me for saving the glorious, fun-filled life you enjoy?" he asked yet again. "Think of all the young models you would have missed if I had left you on the galley floor pissing your pants."

"I didn't wet myself."

Krukillov leered at him over the vodka glass. "But you know you surely would have." He chuckled and took a long swallow of Absolut.

Eshamani knew by now that there wasn't any point in arguing. Even if the Russian had been sober, he was too hardheaded to listen to anyone who didn't outrank him, who couldn't stand him up against a wall and shoot him. His usefulness to the arms merchant was at an end. It was clear to Eshamani that the *Varuskya Liset* had been targeted by an official government agency, probably Russian or Latvian. If the brains behind the raiding party knew the weapons were on the ship, then they also knew who was involved in the operation. That meant the Krukillov nuclear-weapons pipeline had been permanently shut down after a single transaction.

"I assume that must've been your first time under fire," Krukillov said. "Under the circumstances, soaking your shorts is nothing to be ashamed of. I am a veteran of many pitched battles. They don't faze me anymore."

"Interesting," Eshamani said without meaning it.

"From now on, every time you mount one of your young models," the general said, "you will think of Krukillov." His eyes narrowed and his forehead wrinkled, bringing his hairline even closer to the bridge of his nose. "Under the circumstances, you should pay me what you owe me for the two *starookhas* in Riga."

The general was a fugitive from his own land. A rich fugitive, but not as rich as he might have been.

"I paid you for the one weapon that was delivered into my hands," the arms merchant said coldly.

"It was not all my fault that the other two were lost," Krukillov argued. "Security was partly your responsibility, as well. I think we can both agree that your Italian mafiosos weren't up to the task, either. A fair man would split the difference—pay me for one of the two. That way we would both assume part of the loss."

"I never took possession of the articles in question, so no more monies will be transferred. End of story."

Eshamani could see from the expression on the general's face that nothing he had said had sunk in.

"Where are all the bosomy young women of your swinging life-style?" Krukillov demanded. "I have yet to meet a single gorgeous model. I thought you would share a few of them with the man who risked his own life to save yours. I would like to start with a pair of blondes with very long legs and pillowy soft behinds."

Not in your dreams, Eshamani thought. He shared his women with no one, not even his discards. He folded his arms across his chest and ignored the request.

Although the arms merchant lamented the loss of the two nuclear artillery shells, he had covered himself against almost every eventuality. He had paid out about one and one-half million dollars to the general, and there was another quarter of a million in transportation costs for the surviving weapon and its accessories. Even so, Eshamani wasn't out of pocket, since the nukes had been ordered well in advance, and each of the three interested parties had given him two-million-dollar cash deposits pending delivery. Because one of the clients had requested delivery inside the U.S., Eshamani had had to make special arrangements to reduce the danger of discovery and confiscation. The weapon had to travel by a roundabout sea route. To make the scheduled delivery date, he'd advance-shipped the third weapon two weeks earlier. Happily that meant that, despite the loss of two-thirds of the Soviet nuclear contraband, he would still make a handsome profit from the shell's ten-million-dollar price tag.

The question gnawing at the back of his mind wasn't about money; it was whether crossing the Baltic and North Seas had done him any good. Had he thrown off the pursuit, or was he still under surveillance? The incident in Riga also made him wonder about the previous attempt to transfer Soviet nuclear material to Libya. Perhaps the Panamanian-registry freighter hadn't sunk by accident. Perhaps the same team of killers had sent it to the bottom of the Atlantic. For all Eshamani knew, he had been hunted for months. The idea was very unsettling. He walked past Krukillov to the foyer that led to the front door. A dining-room chair had been moved to the short hallway and on it sat a stocky, dark-complected Sicilian holding an AR-18S Sterling-Armalite carbine. The Sicilian rose quickly to his feet as his boss approached.

"Anything to report, Claudio?" Eshamani asked.

"The street and park are clear, boss."

Eshamani had a few men roaming outside, and

there were more hired guns stationed upstairs and at the back of the ground floor. He didn't think the assault on the *Varuskya Liset* could have been a joint East-West action. Things weren't that cozy between the intelligence services of the former sworn enemies. It was either one or the other, East or West, and most likely East. He certainly couldn't imagine Britain's MI-6 cooperating with their Russian counterparts to take him out on English soil. The Brits were way too fussy about their jurisdiction, and too much bad water had passed under the Cold War bridge. If it had been an Eastern hit team in Riga and they had followed him to London, they would be operating solo, without backup and resupply. As a naturalized British citizen, Eshamani enjoyed the full protection of British law. All he had to do was keep the bears off his back long enough for the bobbies to arrive. That's what all the Sicilians were for.

Not that he planned on sticking around Kensington much longer. He had a plane to catch and business to conclude on the other side of the Atlantic. In little more than twenty-four hours, a happy American buyer would walk away with his very own nuclear weapon and the equally happy Iranian-Italian middleman would collect an enormous paycheck.

"Claudio, have the limo brought around to the front," the arms merchant said. "It's time for us to leave. We don't want to get stuck in the afternoon traffic."

Eshamani knew that by dealing in nukes, he was asking for big trouble, and trouble in the long term. But that's what made it challenging and so exciting for him. It was the Super Bowl of arms sales. For years Eshamani had been prepared to pull a vanishing act at a moment's notice. He had false passports and cash stashed in airports and banks around the world. He could arrive in Paris as one person, and leave for Stockholm as another. A couple of jumps like that would put the hounds off his trail, and he could choose a new, more permanent identity and nationality at his leisure. Lately he was leaning toward turning Argentinian.

"You're leaving now?" Krukillov asked, lumbering to his feet.

Eshamani slipped into his Armani suit jacket. "That's correct."

"Will we meet again?"

"I wouldn't count on it. Our business is through."

"Then I must say goodbye." With that, the Russian grabbed Eshamani by the shoulders and held him in an ironlike grip while he planted a wet kiss on either cheek.

It was hard to say which Eshamani hated the most, the Russian's meaty hands crumpling his silk suit jacket or the sloppy wetness drying on his cheeks. Had he been armed at that moment, Eshamani would have put a bullet in the general's gut.

Claudio cleared his throat to get Eshamani's attention, then said, "The car's ready, boss."

"I'm ready, too." Eshamani wasn't taking any luggage with him. His apartment overlooking New York City's Central Park had a complete selection of clothes and personal effects. He patted the side of his Armani jacket and felt the crinkle of folded sheets of paper in the inside pocket.

The PAL codes.

Recipes for someone else's disaster.

He wouldn't leave home without them.

FROM THE THIRD-STORY window of the Georgian residence directly across from Eshamani's town house, Spetsnaz Captain Andrei Sarnov kept careful watch. The fronts of the stately, whitewashed blocks of homes were separated by a pair of narrow one-way streets. Between the two streets was a pocket park ringed by a wrought-iron fence, with grass, flower beds, tall trees, benches and a children's play area. Sarnov counted the visible opposition. A man in a tan overcoat leaned against the town-house doorway, while two others in sweat suits were doing circuits of the little park. A light blue four-door sedan kept circling the streets. The car also had two men inside.

A noise made Sarnov half-turn.

Behind him, nose to nose on top of the queen-size bed, the occupants of the home lay trussed up with rope and duct tape. The securely gagged man and woman were in their early sixties.

"Stay quiet," Sarnov warned them. Then he added in a much softer tone, "I assure you, you have nothing to be afraid of. No one is going to hurt you or rob you. Try to sleep, if you can. It will help make the time pass more quickly."

The Spetsnaz officer turned back to the window, picking up a pair of binoculars. He had correctly guessed that after fleeing Riga, Eshamani would head for his closest hidey-hole, London, where many of his visible assets were held. So far, things had gone smoothly. They had moved into position without incident. But Sarnov knew that could all change in an instant. He hadn't bothered to ask Her Majesty's government for permission to operate on its sovereign soil because he knew permission wouldn't have been forthcoming. He didn't need a pass to do his job. His team had a responsibility that superseded national boundaries, and they had the authority to take human lives, if necessary, in order to regain possession of the third artillery shell.

Peering through the binoculars, Sarnov saw movement on the roof of the building to the right of Eshamani's home. All the residences on the street were connected, sharing exterior walls and rooflines. Vlad Ferdishenko crossed over to the target building and quickly stepped to a tiny dormer window set in the copper-plate roof. It took him only seconds to cut the glass from the frame and drop out of sight inside.

Sarnov scanned the park. The men in sweat suits hadn't seen anything. They continued their sentry duty, walking the path in opposite directions. On a bench just off the path, Tasha Beloc sat eating some chips and reading a book. She had what looked like a CD player headset on. It wasn't. In the short dress and black tights, she looked like a schoolgirl. She wasn't.

A limousine pulled up in front of the town house.

"Tasha," Sarnov said into his headset's microphone.

"I see it," came the immediate reply.

The front door opened, and Eshamani descended the stairs to the street in a crowd of security men. If anyone had wanted to put a hole in him, there was no clear shot. A gunman opened the limo's rear door.

"Tasha," the captain said again.

"I'm on it," she said, closing her book and getting up from the bench. She moved briskly away from the Eshamani residence to a car parked on the street in front of Sarnov's station.

"Trail him, Tasha," Sarnov said. "No matter

where he goes. Use the usual reporting procedure, and we'll catch up when we can.''

She pulled out of the parking space and accelerated, making a quick tour around the park in order to catch up with the departing limousine. ''Krukillov is still inside,'' she said as she turned right and disappeared.

''Understood,'' Sarnov said. ''We'll take care of him.''

There was a lesson to be taught this afternoon. If you deal in nukes, you can't run and you can't hide. If you deal in nukes, you will die.

Sarnov set down the binoculars and checked his gun. Like all the mission's weapons, it had been supplied by the GRU officer at the Russian embassy. It was a British product, a 5.56 mm XL 70 E-3 Enfield. The bullpup-style autorifle held a 30-round mag that it could unload at 650 to 800 rounds per minute. A thick silencer tube extended by nearly a foot the stub of a barrel that protruded from the front stock. Still, the extremely short gun fit inside the wooden tool tray that was part of Sarnov's cover. He pulled an oily rag over the weapon and zipped up his light blue coveralls.

''Vlad? Uri?'' he said into his microphone. When they each responded, he gave them the attack order. Then he removed the headset and put it down on the windowsill.

''I'm leaving now,'' he told the gagged and bound Londoners. ''Don't worry. The police will be here soon to release you.''

With his tool tray in hand, he descended the stairs to the ground floor, exited the building and started to cross the park. He had gained entrance into the surveillance house by posing as a building inspector. That was how he hoped to reach Eshamani's front door.

"DO YOU LIKE the Englishwomen?" Krukillov asked the guard seated in the foyer.

The Sicilian shrugged.

"I've heard they respond with great enthusiasm to Latin men."

The bodyguard squinted at him.

"Their own men are cold and don't know how to please them."

Still the man said nothing.

"Maybe you know some Englishwomen? Maybe they would like to come over for a visit?" the Russian persisted.

The Sicilian rummaged in the handkerchief pocket of his suit jacket and produced a toothpick that he proceeded to use with great care between his top front teeth.

It was hard for Krukillov to maintain his upbeat mood. With Eshamani gone, there was no one to torment. The bodyguards had a poor command of English and no Russian at all. Teasing one of them was like teasing a very stupid dog.

Krukillov looked at his empty glass. At least there was still plenty of vodka in the house. He went into the kitchen and opened the refrigerator's freezer compartment. He took out the frozen bottle of Absolut and filled his tumbler with the syrupy liquor. After a good sip, he checked the bottom part of the fridge. The leftovers of the Indian take-out meal his host had ordered sat under a tinfoil wrapper. Krukillov helped himself to some of the tandoori chicken, washing down each bite with a slug of neat vodka.

The general had a little time to kill before he could set his own escape plans in motion. The false passport and identity cards Eshamani had arranged wouldn't be complete until the following afternoon. Then it was off to the Caribbean, where he would open bank accounts in his new name and transfer some of the Swiss funds to them. It irked him that he had been forced to leave the bags of gold in Riga. They would have made traveling much easier. Although he had things to complain about, the situation could have been worse. He could have been dead or penniless.

Something heavy thudded on the other side of the kitchen ceiling just above his head.

Something heavy enough to make the light fixture rattle.

Krukillov lowered the chicken leg from his mouth and stepped out of the kitchen. As he approached the foyer, he saw the Sicilian watchdog mounting the stairs with his AR-18S at the ready. The general peered around the corner, looking up at the bodyguard as he turned the first landing.

A flurry of silenced gunshots slammed into the Sicilian, bouncing him off the wall. He slid down the stairs on his face, ending up in a twitching heap at Krukillov's feet. Above, the landing's wallpaper was splotched with gore and pocked with 5.56 mm bullet holes.

Behind the Russian, at the other end of the foyer, someone was at the front door, turning the handle.

The guard sitting outside knew it was locked, knew he had to use his key to get in.

Krukillov snatched up the AR-18S, whirled, and

sent a 5-round burst into the door at chest height. Spent cartridge casings were still clattering across the hardwood floor as the general rushed back into the kitchen. The outline of a head appeared at the back door, but before he could fire, it was gone.

That line of retreat was no good.

He had to find a secure position quickly and defend it.

Krukillov tried a door at the far end of the kitchen and discovered that led to the daylight basement. It was a closed box, with no door to the street. He didn't like it, but he knew it would have to do. At least he could control the only way in.

He closed the door behind him and quietly descended the wooden steps. The room was so dim it took his eyes a second to adjust. The available light was filtered through a pair of draped windows set high in the walls. Krukillov unscrewed the light bulb from the ceiling fixture and picked his corner, beside the rows of Eshamani's wine racks. As the general knelt, he steeled himself for a fight to the death.

WHEN CAPTAIN SARNOV opened the waist-high iron gate on Eshamani's side of the little park, someone shouted at him.

"Hey! Hey, you!"

Sarnov turned to see one of the sweat-suit boys bearing down on him. He had his right hand behind his back, no doubt reaching for a gun. Instead of waiting for the man to come to him, the Spetsnaz captain walked back and met him halfway, in front of a bench.

"What are you doing around here?" the Sicilian demanded.

Sarnov lifted the tool tray by the handle, sliding his other hand under the oily rag. The silenced bullpup stuttered, blowing splinters and smoke out the end of the tray. The Sicilian's knees buckled, and he sat down abruptly on the bench, his head lolling over onto his shoulder.

It looked as though he was taking a nap, except for the ragged ring of holes in his chest and all the blood.

As Sarnov turned up the walk to Eshamani's front steps, the guard on the porch rose from his chair.

"Building inspector," Sarnov announced, then he opened fire, stitching a line of slugs up the Sicilian's chest to the point of his chin. The man was slumping down the wall when Sarnov reached the top step. He sat the dead guard back on the chair.

The captain had his hand on the doorknob when he smelled smoke. The heat from the second full-auto burst had set the oily rag on fire. As he ducked down to smother it, gunshots ripped through the door where his chest had just been.

Unable to kick in the door without putting himself in the line of fire, Sarnov had to kneel there and wait a few eternal seconds until Uri Turgenev and Vlad Ferdishenko could open it for him from the inside.

The first thing Sarnov saw was the lifeless body of one of the guards draped down the stairs. It was steadily leaking fluids into the Persian rugs.

"Did you get the general?" Sarnov asked.

"He wasn't upstairs," Ferdishenko said.

"And he didn't come out the back," Turgenev added.

They quickly fanned out and did a fruitless search of the ground floor. The search terminated in the kitchen.

It was Sarnov who noticed the closed door. He pointed at it with his bullpup Enfield. ''Where does that go?''

''Probably down to the basement,'' Turgenev said.

''Shut off the light,'' the captain said.

Ferdishenko killed the kitchen light and Sarnov inched the door open. It was dark down there, but not pitch-black. He inched the door closed.

''There are windows looking into the basement?'' he asked.

''Yes,'' Ferdishenko replied. ''Two in front, two in back, none on the sides. They're very narrow. I don't think he could fit through them.''

''Can you see into them well enough to shoot?''

''They've got curtains over them, but if we have a target...''

''Get outside and get into position,'' Sarnov said. ''Vlad in front. Uri take the back. Fire when you see him fire.''

Sarnov accompanied Ferdishenko to the front of the house. As the younger man went out the door, the captain bent over the dead guard on the stairs. He grabbed the corpse by the back of the shirt collar and dragged it into the kitchen. After pulling over a kitchen chair close to the basement door, he hoisted the dead man onto the seat.

Holding the corpse in place with a hand, he paused to give his men time to get into position.

After two minutes, he opened the basement door a crack, pursed his lips and made a ''shhing'' sound. Soft though it was, it was loud enough to get the general's attention. Then Sarnov drew the door back all the way, stepped behind the chair and tipped it forward, dumping the body headfirst down the dark stairs.

The thudding racket was met by a burst of autofire from the left side of the cellar. As Sarnov ducked back, he caught a glimpse of muzzle-flashes lighting up the stairwell.

Then, in stereo, came the tinkle of broken glass and the muffled, canvas-ripping sound of full-auto return fire. More glass shattered, and the general's gun rattled back briefly, then stopped.

Ferdishenko and Turgenev emptied their weapons, reloaded and emptied them again.

When they were done, it was very quiet in the basement.

Sarnov flipped the light switch on and off a couple of times before he realized the bulb was missing. He descended the stairs. There was enough light from the broken windows to see what he needed to see, anyway.

The general lay crumpled against the wall of the cellar, sprawled in a pool of mingled red wine and blood. The right half of his head had been shot away by the first salvo. The second barrage had impacted above the corpse, chewing great hunks out of the stone wall and savaging the arms merchant's extensive wine collection.

Sarnov stepped away from the spreading sheet of red.

"Captain!" Turgenev shouted from the kitchen. "Sirens!"

Sarnov heard them. They were close and getting closer. He dropped his weapon on the floor and took the cellar steps two at a time.

TASHA BELOC FIGURED the limousine was headed for Gatwick International Airport as soon as it got on the A23. When it stuck to that route, she was sure of it. Eshamani was making his break. It didn't matter whether he led them straight to the third weapon or not. If he didn't take them to it, they would kill his bodyguards, kidnap him and make him give up the name of the buyer and the intended target. Actually that way seemed preferable to her, a bit more just. Why should the thief Eshamani die quickly? What mercy did he offer the future innocent victims of the stolen nukes?

She pushed the question of justice from her mind. It didn't really matter how Eshamani died, only that it was soon.

The limousine turned off for the airport and, once there, pulled in at the British Airways passenger-loading area. Beloc double-parked six car lengths behind the limo and waited until the arms merchant and three of his henchmen got out and started for the terminal. The limo signaled a turn, squeezed into the flow of traffic and began to drive away.

Beloc couldn't afford to wait to make sure the limo was really leaving. She left her own car running and hurried into the terminal after Eshamani. She knew she was taking a big risk; an unoccupied car at Gatwick drew a lot of attention, fast. It was certain to be searched and towed away in a matter of minutes. If the airport stop was a ruse by Eshamani and he returned to the limo farther down the loading zone, she could be left without transportation.

She had no choice. She had to stay on Eshamani's tail.

Ahead the arms merchant and his three bodyguards

got into the British Airways ticket line. Beloc let a
few people move in front of her before she lined up
herself.

Above the service counter, a television monitor displayed a list of flights departing for all corners of the
world. Beloc's stomach tightened; Eshamani could
have been going anywhere. The line advanced, and
the arms merchant stepped up to the counter, surrounded by his Sicilians. Beloc leaned over the velvet
rope as the man bought tickets for himself and his
companions. The clerk handed Eshamani his fat batch
of tickets, then gave him instructions for the gate
number and departure time. Half lip-reading, half
eavesdropping, Beloc managed to pick up the details.
From them, it was easy for her to figure out the flight
number and destination.

Eshamani was going to New York, first-class.

On behalf of the Russian government, so was she.

CHAPTER NINE

Chocolate Canyon
11:15 a.m. MDT

U.S. Army Corporal Sean Smithers was not easily twitched when confronted by scary male human beings. He'd been working around guys like that for years. It wasn't so bad at his current station, but during his Ranger training at Fort Bragg, and later, on his first tour of duty in Honduras, he had been in the company of guys so tightly wound, so beyond the pale, that just turning his back on them gave him an awful sinking feeling.

In the Humvee's rearview mirror, Smithers could see the blond guy in the garish red-and-green Hawaiian shirt sitting directly behind him. The man was staring right back at him.

Smithers returned his gaze to the road ahead. As he did so, he got that same sinking feeling, as if he was turning his back on a mountain lion.

He knew he should never have tried to make conversation with the blond guy while they were loading up the Hummer. In an attempt to be funny, he had said something dumb about the gigantic black ballistic nylon backpack the guy was toting. For his trouble he'd gotten back a look that said *How do you want to die?*

The guy wasn't any bigger than Smithers—about six feet tall—so he couldn't intimidate the corporal with sheer size. It was the man's intensity that was so spooky. Smithers had never seen anybody so focused, not even at Fort Bragg. In comparison, the other three passengers seemed almost normal. None of them had introduced themselves yet, and Smithers had a feeling they would never quite get around to it. Like the blond guy, they were also in civvies; none of them wore top-security-clearance ID tags around their necks.

After his failure at making small talk, the corporal had kept his mouth shut and driven the Humvee down the long, straight, gravel road, which was what he had been ordered to do.

Two miles ahead on the desert plain, Smithers could see the first roadblock. The one-lane gravel track on either side of the "incident" had been sealed off by armed U.S. marshals and federal agents in black helmets and body armor. Between the pair of wooden barricades, it was a circus of parked official vehicles, conflicting badges and uniforms and hundreds of yards of yellow plastic hazard tape. He stopped at the barrier, and an FBI man armed with an M-16 looked in the vehicle, nodded to the white-haired guy sitting beside Smithers in the shotgun seat, then waved them on.

His passengers were definitely "somebodies," Smithers decided. At least to the Justice Department.

When they rolled up beside a broad area of desert that had been taped off, the big guy with black hair and cool blue eyes reached over from the back seat and put a hand on Corporal Smithers's shoulder. "Stop right here," he said. "This is fine."

As the white-haired passenger got out of the vehicle, a pair of men with ATF written on their chests in big white block letters walked over from the side of the road. The big black-haired guy climbed out, followed by the shortest member of the quartet, a man with brown hair worn slightly long, covering the tops of his ears. The blond guy scrambled out after them.

"We've kept everybody off the site, as requested," the stocky ATF man said to all of them. There was a look of intense displeasure on his face. It fried his cookies that his own hotshot crime-scene units hadn't been allowed first peek at the evidence.

Who were these guys? Smithers asked himself.

Three of them comprised Able Team, the domestic-action arm of Stony Man Farm, which targeted home-grown terrorism and violence. The blonde was Carl "Ironman" Lyons, a former LAPD detective. Like a tightrope walker, Lyons balanced a keenly honed strategic mind with the fighting style of a berserker. The guy with brown hair was Hermann "Gadgets" Schwarz, a master of all things electronic and mechanical. Gadgets had graduated from Vietnam with experience in demolition and booby traps, and in counterintelligence and guerrilla warfare. The guy with the white hair slicked straight back was Rosario "Politician" Blancanales. "Pol" had matriculated with honors from the same school as Schwarz; his major was psy-ops.

The fourth, the black-haired man, was a free-roving, often solo performer for the same Sensitive Operations Group. Although he had many identities, his given name was Mack Bolan. The name he had earned from his sworn enemies was "the Executioner." All four had, during long and distinguished careers, put the fear of God into hundreds of mobsters, terrorists and assassins before sending them, disassembled and screaming, into the bowels of Hell.

Although all of Smithers's passengers got out, only two of them seemed to give a damn about the shell craters on the other side of the hazard tape. Mack Bolan and Gadgets Schwarz climbed over the bright barrier and got to work at once.

As it was hot in the Humvee, Corporal Smithers climbed out, as well. He leaned against the side of the Hummer and watched the pair move across the cordoned-off desert. They stepped cautiously from crater to crater, then the Executioner selected one to dissect. He handed one of the wooden stakes he was carrying to Schwarz.

"Is that the one you'd have picked, Corporal?" Rosario Blancanales asked.

Smithers flinched. The white-haired Latin had come up beside him so quietly that the sudden question had startled him. "Uh, yes sir."

"Why's that?"

"It's a clearly defined shell crater with a shallow angle of entry, sir," Smithers said in a rush. "The big guy's already found the entrance groove where the shell penetrated the ground prior to detonation. The other guy's looking on the other edge of the crater for the mark the fuse left when it blew free of the warhead."

As the corporal finished speaking, across the desert the brown-haired guy straightened up. He had a smile on his face.

"Got it," Schwarz said to Bolan.

The Executioner didn't look up from his work. He was using a flat rock to tap in an aiming stake a foot or so back from the edge of the entrance groove. Gadgets Schwarz followed his example and used a chunk of rock to pound in a marker where the fuse had impacted. Then he placed a compass on top of his stake and lined it up with the post on the other side of the crater.

"What they've got there," Corporal Smithers said, "is a straight line leading back..." Half-turning, he saw the white-haired man was already facing the way the shell had come. Under his high-altitude suntan, Smithers's cheeks flushed with embarrassment. "But I'm not telling you anything you don't already know, am I, sir?"

Blancanales squinted up the rise in the road to the line of dark brown hills. "No, Corporal," he said. "I'm afraid not."

Bolan and Schwarz double-checked their work by locating the side spray—the chunks of rock that the explosion had thrown out of the opposite sides of the crater. After they had found and staked the middle of each fan of rubble, Schwarz stepped into the crater and likewise marked its center. With his compass in the middle of the shell pit, he measured the angle formed by the opposing stakes. When he divided that angle in half, it lined up almost exactly with the previous estimate, confirming the direction to the cannon.

A soft grunting noise from the other side of the road made Smithers turn and look over the roof of the Humvee. Ignoring the activity in the taped-off area, the big blond was doing a series of nonstop Shotokan karate katas at high speed and with almost manic intensity.

"What's with that guy, anyway?" the corporal asked.

"He's the eighth wonder of the world," Blancanales said. "That's how he relaxes."

"Why is he here? He's not even looking at the crime scene."

"He doesn't do investigative work anymore," Blancanales replied. "That's not his specialty."

Smithers could guess what his specialty was from the flurry of linked power strikes. The guy moved like a propeller that had broken free of its engine mount at maximum rpm, in wild, looping spirals. It wasn't pretty, but it wasn't meant to be. Every blow was a death strike.

Bolan and Schwarz stepped back over the tape barrier and returned to the Hummer.

"Hey, Ironman," Blancanales shouted across the road to the blond guy. "Wrap it up."

"Ironman" Lyons drew himself up and then bowed to his imaginary foe. When he stepped back to the vehicle, Smithers saw that, despite all the violent kicks and punches in the heat of the day, he was barely perspiring.

"Corporal," Bolan said, "we need to take this Hummer off-road."

"No problem, sir."

After they had all piled in the vehicle, Bolan directed him off the gravel and onto the desert scrub beside the fence of yellow tape. When they were close to the crater that had been staked out, the big guy got out and in short order had the vehicle lined up with the pair of aiming posts. He hopped back in the shotgun seat and pointed at the compass on the dash. "Keep us on that course. You can do that, can't you, soldier?"

"Yes, sir."

"I'll tell you when to stop."

As the corporal drove, his passengers spoke very little, but what they said seemed important.

"I make it at least four from the boot tracks," Schwarz said. "They staked out the target with these." He showed his partners a shred of fluorescent green pennant.

"From the shell craters," Bolan said, "it looks like they were firing HE out of a 155."

"Our boys from California have headed north and east," Blancanales said.

Smithers stole a glance into his rearview mirror. The blond guy did look a little more relaxed now. He was staring out the window with unfocused eyes. He didn't utter a word during the bumpy overland trip, but Smithers could tell he was listening to what his partners were saying.

Following the compass course, they crossed back onto the road a short distance from the brown hills. As they did, the Hummer was pointed right at the entrance to Chocolate Canyon.

"Hold it here," Bolan said, opening his door. "Let's do the rest of this on foot."

Smithers, Blancanales and Lyons watched through the dusty windshield as Bolan and Schwarz walked up the dry streambed between the cliffs.

After a few minutes of stony quiet inside the hot vehicle, Bolan and Schwarz returned.

"The tracks of a semitruck lead into the canyon about two hundred feet, then stop," Bolan said. "It looks like they've got the howitzer inside a truck trailer. That's the shooting platform they're using."

"That fits with the crime scene in California," Blancanales said.

"Except for bootprints and tire tracks, the firing position looks clean," Bolan stated.

"Counting the driver, there were five of them," Schwarz went on. "Four men crewed the gun and the fifth acted as observer, probably up on the cliff there."

"We need to talk to the Farm," Bolan concluded.

Stony Man Farm
3:05 p.m. EDT

SOMETIMES WHEN THINGS fell into place, you wished they hadn't.

Hal Brognola was on the secure, scrambled phone link to the White House. His neck and shoulders ached as if they were being drilled at very slow speed by a very dull drill bit. He'd already spent a tense half hour explaining the situation and response options to the President. In the shifting sea of related evidence, two facts stood out.

The Soviet nuclear artillery shells had been discovered in Riga, and halfway around the world, a howitzer had been stolen that could fire them.

Brognola saw it as much more than mere coincidence.

When the President asked about the discrepancy between the calibers of the Soviet and American howitzers, Brognola explained, as it had been explained to him by John "Cowboy" Kissinger, Stony Man

Farm's armorer, that 152 mm Soviet artillery shells could be fired out of 155 mm U.S. cannons.

"The Russian nukes would rattle a bit on the way out of the barrel, but otherwise they'd work just fine," Kissinger had said.

The President said that he understood, but that he was still having trouble with the direct connection between stolen nukes, stolen howitzer and the Old Glory Ranch. Brognola knew that he was being asked to sell the Chief Executive on the threat before he signed on to the plan that was intended to resolve it.

Brognola ran down the list of known facts, tying them together with means, motive and opportunity. A reliable FBI informant at the Wyoming ranch had passed on the news that the militia was running drills with an artillery trainer, a small-caliber, single-shot gun that was used to prepare soldiers to operate a real cannon's sighting and aiming systems. They already knew that the commander in chief of the Patriots and many of its recruits had recent combat experience in the field artillery units of the National Guard. Oswald Carmody and the others had participated in the one-sided artillery duels of Desert Storm that knocked out seventy enemy guns in the space of an hour. Stony Man and the Justice Department were well aware of the psy-ops campaign the group was waging in the rural West. The Sawtooth Patriots, directly and indirectly, were planting seeds of fear through radio and print media and on the Internet.

Fear of repression by armed agents of a shadowy world government.

At that point, the President brought the big Fed up short. "I don't see the motive in all this. How does the scare campaign fit in with the whole nuclear-attack scenario?'' he asked.

"The false rumors they've spread about blacked-out helicopters and United Nations troop movements on country highways are a way of controlling people's perceptions of real events that are about to take place,'' Brognola said. ''In order to precipitate the all-out government repression they've described, to fulfill their own prophecy of tanks in the barnyards and house-to-house searches of simple ranch folk, they're about to initiate the most horrible, unthinkable terrorist attack in the history of humankind. Their motive, simply put, is to use the manufactured 'truth' of their oppressive-world-government story in order to build a guerrilla army of resistance that would do battle for control of American soil.''

"You paint a very ugly picture, Hal, of some very dangerous men.''

Brognola explained the final link in the chain of circumstantial evidence that pointed to the Sawtooth Patriots: the test firing of a 155 mm howitzer in Utah earlier in the day. "I have no doubt, sir,'' Brognola told the President, ''that this weapon will be used against U.S. citizens.''

"Do you have any proof that these militia people are connected to the stolen Soviet nuclear weapons?''

"No direct proof.''

"I think you said your people destroyed two of these weapons in Latvia. Are you confident that the pipeline is sealed and that no other weapons have left the former republics?''

"The pipeline is sealed at that end,'' Brognola said. "A communiqué from British Intelligence in the last hour has confirmed the death of one of the men involved, a Russian brigadier general. He was shot by persons unknown in the basement of a London residence. The other alleged conspirator, Sergio Ishmael Eshamani, has since disappeared. We assume that by now he's switched identities. According to MI-6, the London hit looks like a professional job. There were bodies all over the place. The bottom line is, without the Russian to sneak weapons out of the system, the pipeline no longer exists. Unfortunately we have no way of knowing whether we got all the weapons he diverted. We could ask the Russians, but I doubt they'd tell us the truth, even if they untangled it from their paperwork. It would be too embarrassing for them to have to admit publicly that they can't keep track of their own goddamned nukes.''

"What do you suggest we do?''

Brognola didn't hesitate; he plunged right in. ''We have to hit the militia stronghold before dawn and deactivate it. We might get lucky and find the stolen howitzer on the premises. Even if we don't, we might find a clue as to the intended target for a conventional or nuclear artillery strike.''

"That's a lot of 'mights,' Hal.''

"I know it is, sir. That's why it's a job for us and not FBI or ATF. If we take the ranch and find nothing, it'll look like an internal conflict, a turf war among militiamen. However, and I want to stress this, I'm confident that we'll find what we're looking for.''

"So?'' AARON KURTZMAN said when Brognola returned to the farm's computer center. ''What did he say?''

The head of the Justice Department's Sensitive Operations Group took a seat beside Kurtzman, Barbara

Price and Yakov Katzenelenbogen, Stony Man's tactical adviser and the former Phoenix Force team leader. "The President said he's already informed the attorney general that no Justice or ATF tactical units would be committed in an assault on the Sawtooth stronghold. Because the Old Glory Ranch is heavily fortified and its occupants well-armed and determined, the President is convinced it'll turn out to be another Waco—or worse. And he doesn't want the heat."

"Who would?" Price said.

"He asked if elements of the Stony Man covert force could actually take the ranch," Brognola said. "I gave him your analysis, Yakov, that it's possible because we have the layout of the grounds and the building interiors from our informant, but that it would require the combined Able and Phoenix teams."

"I also said the chances of success were only fifty-fifty," the craggy-faced man added. Under heavy salt-and-pepper eyebrows, his light blue eyes flashed. "I hope you told him that, as well."

"Of course."

"And what did he say?"

"He asked me if I thought the risk should be taken. I told him that the unanimous opinion of everyone at Stony Man was that we should commit both action teams and Striker, and that we should proceed with all due haste. His reply was, 'Do it.'"

"I've got photographs from Wyoming scrolling up on the wall screen," Carmen Delahunt announced from her computer station.

The grainy color pictures showed Oswald Carmody

exiting the steps of a Learjet. The plane's corporate logo was clearly visible.

"That's the Sawtooth head guy," Kurtzman said. "Who shot the photos?"

"SAC William Parker," Brognola said. "He's been working the case on the ground. He's developed the informant inside the Old Glory Ranch."

"Monstrel?" Barbara Price said, reading the plane's black-and-silver decal. "How does that fit in?"

"Krick is the CEO of Monstrel Mining and Chemical," Hunt Wethers replied. "He's Harvard educated, well-traveled and was until recently a very rich man. For the past few years, he's been dabbling at the fringes of extreme right-wing politics on the state level. He became politically active after the federal government forced the closure of some of his most toxic mining sites. EPA investigators found they were polluting the public groundwater supplies of three states with known carcinogens."

"So Krick is Sawtooth's banker?" Delahunt asked.

"Was," Dr. Wethers said. "Monstrel is history. Krick has lost every civil lawsuit so far, and there are criminal cases pending. He's broke, but as you can see from the Lear jet, he's still keeping up a good front."

Tokaido interrupted the discussion. "We've got an incoming scramble from Utah. It's Striker."

"Put it on the speakers," Kurtzman said.

"What've you got, Striker?" Brognola asked.

The big man's voice boomed in the windowless room. "I think we found the California Guard's missing howitzer," he said. "A 155 was fired four times from a box canyon off Highway 6, then the shooters beat it. They took the cannon with them. It looks like a test run to me. They had a rectangular area staked out on the desert as a target. From that, I'd say they're after a *very* big building.''

''What about the range?'' Katz said.

''The target was five miles away and it was hit with HE direct fire. They've got the gun inside a semi-trailer—that's how they're moving it around. There were five men involved in the operation. Earwitnesses report all four shots were fired in under two minutes. From the speed these guys worked and their accuracy, there's no doubt they're a well-trained gunnery team. Unfortunately no one saw them fire and no one re-members a truck turning onto the highway after the barrage. We've got tire tracks, but they're only going to help if we find the truck. The trail here is ice cold. These people could be anywhere within a five-hundred-mile radius by now.''

''Anything else, Striker?'' Brognola said.

''Yeah, Gadgets has something he wants to say. It's important.''

''Go ahead, put him on.''

''I've been thinking about the target they drew in the dirt,'' Schwarz said. ''If they really mean to hit a building and it's as big as what they'd staked out, a few rounds of direct fire HE aren't going to do it much structural damage. Individual floors would be wrecked, but even that would be limited because of all the interior supporting walls and baffles. Heck, even a few dozen rounds of HE wouldn't do that much damage to a really solid structure. We have to assume that a building with this big a footprint is going to be solid. Our stolen M-198 howitzer can shoot four rounds per minute, max. So, to fire twenty-four rounds, not counting the time for the registration shots, would take six or seven minutes. These guys have to got to know they're not going to have that long to work.''

Brognola already knew where this was going. He dipped into his shirt pocket for his antacid tablets.

''What I think the target should be telling us,'' Gadgets went on, ''is that the shooters don't intend to use conventional artillery rounds. They're just practicing with them to get comfortable with the cannon. They're planning on firing a nuke.''

Katz nodded in agreement. ''He's right, unfortunately.''

''We have no choice but to proceed with the mission as outlined,'' Barbara Price declared.

''And hope to hell we beat them to the punch,'' Tokaido added.

''Striker,'' Brognola said, ''the Phoenix team is leaving within the half hour to join you. Move to the rendezvous point and wait for their arrival.''

CHAPTER TEN

Old Glory Ranch
3:50 p.m. MDT

From his observation post on the flank of the mountain, Oswald Carmody saw the muzzle-flash from the plain a half mile away, then a split second later, heard the faint gun crack. A two-hundred-foot-tall cirque of rock framed the downhill side of the lake below him. With a sizzling hiss, the D-20 trainer round cleared the rim of the mountain bowl and dropped with a *sploosh* into the middle of the wind-riffled, quarter-acre lake.

"Fire for effect," Carmody said into his walkie-talkie. He hit the start button on his stopwatch.

In fifteen seconds, the trainer boomed again, and again a *sploosh*.

Again, almost dead center in the lake.

Instead of a two-foot-high plume of water, Carmody visualized air hot enough to melt granite into thin soup and a concentric shock wave that would reduce blocks of skyscrapers to a single towering column of dust.

"End of mission," he said into the communications device. "Nice work, 12-7."

"Roger," came the reply. "Are we done for today?"

"Yeah, that's it. I'm coming down."

Carmody started packing his gear into a knapsack. He knew the crew was sick of practicing with the D-20 trainer, but the intensive work they'd put in had really paid off. Despite the gusting afternoon winds this day, they had laid round after round on the target. As a weapon, the trainer itself was about as deadly as a 12-gauge shotgun. Mounted on a tripod, it fired a single heavy-caliber rifle bullet from a scaled-down barrel, but it used the same sighting and elevation systems as the real D-20 cannon. The Soviet panoramic sight and clinometer systems took some getting used to, even for an experienced gun team like 12-7.

The "12-7" code name was Krick's idea.

It referred to December 7, 1941, the "day of infamy" sneak attack on Pearl Harbor.

The commander in chief of the Sawtooth Patriots shrugged on his pack and picked his way down the mountainside, skirting the larger boulders and clumps of sagebrush. The name of the gun team had been Krick's brainstorm, but the firing range was all Carmody. He had worked it out to an almost perfect one-tenth scale.

As would be the case in the real attack, the range's lake target was invisible to the howitzer crew, blocked by a tall barrier jutting up from the plain. In order to score a hit, they had to use a high angle of fire and lob the shot over the barrier. Because of air resistance and gravity, the target end of an artillery shell's trajectory was always steeper; in this case, to clear the intervening obstacles, the nuclear warhead had to fall almost straight down on the target. An attack using indirect fire required an observer to monitor the registration of the preliminary shell impacts and call in range and elevation adjustments to bring the following rounds on target. At H-hour, as in all the practice sessions, Carmody would man the observation post himself.

Calling in megadeath from a safe distance.

By the time Carmody reached the plain, the gun crew was waiting there in the jeep to pick him up.

"What do you think, Oz?" the driver asked as Carmody piled into the front passenger's seat. His name was "Skel" Peterson; he got the nickname from his extremely thin and angular face. Peterson had a quick, analytical mind and physical reflexes to match. He was also one hell of a gunner.

"Remember what we did to those Iraqi gun emplacements during Storm?" Carmody said.

"Kicked their mooshy brown butts," assistant gunner Rick Link answered from the back seat. He wore the brim of his desert-camou boonie hat tied up on one side with the chin thong, Australian style.

"Ninety percent casualties in the first hour," Bob Gabhart, the number-one cannoneer, chimed in.

"An honest-to-God sixty-minute war," said Billy Ray Ransom, the second cannoneer.

Both of the team's cannoneers had the same build: stocky, with powerful legs, arms and shoulders. They needed all those muscles to keep the heavy shells moving steadily onto the shot guide. Unlike Ransom, who had a full head of short, spiky brown hair, Gabhart was practically bald over the crest of his block-shaped skull.

"We're going to do the same thing here," Carmody said. "You guys are on the money. We can't miss."

"I'll bet we can bracket the target, and get the nuke off in three shots," Gabhart said.

"That'd be sweet," Peterson said. "Then they really wouldn't know what hit 'em."

Billy Ray Ransom laughed from the back seat. "They'd probably think the Russians MIRVed 'em until they checked the missile-defense radar. Hey, Joint Chiefs, guess what? No incoming blips from Kamchatka on this deal. Ooh-wee, they are gonna be fit to be tied."

"The Beech is coming in," Peterson said. He pointed toward the ranch compound. The twin-engined plane was making its final approach.

"That'll be the fat man," Carmody said.

"What's he here for?" Rick Link asked.

"A little psy-ops," Carmody said. "Don't worry about it, he's completely under control."

"All you got to do is feed him," Gabhart said, "and he'll follow you anywhere."

At Carmody's order, Skel Peterson headed the jeep for the airstrip. They arrived just as the lone passenger was getting out.

With great effort and painful slowness, E. Paul Rutherford descended the Beechcraft's steps. Over one shoulder was a normal-sized carry-on flight bag. Next to his tremendous bulk, it looked like a woman's purse.

"Get in," Carmody said to the talk-show host. Without being told, the gun crew bailed out to make room for Rutherford. Carmody moved over behind the wheel.

Puffing from the exertion, the fat man obeyed, planting himself in the front passenger's seat.

"How was the flight?" Carmody asked.

"Fine."

"You brought your equipment, I trust?"

"Yes, it's all packed in my case. But you didn't say what I supposed to do with it while I'm here. I don't know what you have in mind."

"Nothing too difficult," he assured the radio personality as he turned the jeep around. "Very soon people are going to want to know all about the Sawtooth Patriots. I want you to be in a position to tell them. It'll be good for you, and it'll be good for us."

"Am I going to interview you?"

"Me and the other men at the ranch. I want you to get a feel for the place, and a feel for the Patriots. You know, who they really are and what they stand for."

"Uh-huh, I can do that. And I think you're right— I think it would make an interesting series of broadcasts."

"First thing," Carmody said, "I'll take you through the main house. It's built on the site of the original ranch house, which burned down in 1968. The original house was built in 1881 by my great-grandfather."

Carmody drove through the main gate and parked by the house's massive, iron-bound front doors.

As they got out of the jeep, a strange sound echoed across the compound yard. Ghostly and shrill, it seemed to come from the general direction of the ranch's well—a cylindrical flagstone structure shaded by a steeply sloping tin roof. Under the shade of the little roof, attached to its support posts, was a wooden crank handle with a rope affixed. The rope extended straight and guitar-string taut down into the well's opening.

"What the hell was *that?*" Rutherford asked his host.

"Nothing," Carmody replied.

Another moan drifted across the courtyard.

"There it is again," the fat man said.

"I'll fix it," Carmody told him. On the way to the well, Carmody stopped to pick up a chunk of rock the size of a football. He dropped the stone down the well. A second passed, and then the stone made a thunk instead of a splash. The groaning noise abruptly ceased.

Carmody slipped free the loop of cord that held the crank locked in position and adjusted the rope, dropping it down about an inch. Then he looped the handle securely back into place.

"Come on, let's go inside," he said, walking past the fat man.

JACK HUTTON, FBI informant, saw the rock coming down at him, but there wasn't anything he could do to avoid it.

His wrists were duct-taped together in front of him; his ankles were also bound. The wad of rag that gagged his mouth was held in place by more turns of the gray plastic tape that encircled his head. Looped under his armpits was the end of the well rope. The rope kept him dangling in place and mostly submerged. It was all he could do to keep his mouth and nose above the water.

The stone hit him on the point of the right shoulder and bounced softly into the water.

Hutton bit into his gag as the pain speared through him. If he'd had any brains, he told himself, he would've moved directly under the falling rock and let it bash his head in. But he couldn't do it, he couldn't kill himself. He wanted to live, to survive long enough to see the Sawtooth Patriots go down in flames.

As the pain in his shoulder faded, the horrible sensation of all-over cold returned. Life-sucking cold. He started shaking against his bonds as if he was about to fly apart.

Then the rope dropped a little, and it was suddenly much harder for him to keep his face above the surface. For a second, he panicked, swallowing the water that seeped into his mouth. He tried to lever himself up with the toes of his shoes, but he couldn't keep his balance on the slippery stone lining of the well. He slid down again, and the rope creaked as his weight stretched it tight.

He knew this torture wasn't meant to extract information from him. Prior to his being tied up and lowered into the freezing pit, Carmody hadn't asked him one question. Evidently the commander in chief of the Patriots didn't care what he knew or what he had told the FBI.

This was torture as punishment.

Punishment for betraying the movement.

As he'd been lowered into the well, Carmody had promised to make him sorry that he'd ever been born.

In his mind, Hutton stayed strong. He was scared because he was getting so weak, the cold water sapping away all his strength, but he still had a couple of things to hold on to. He had turned informant on the Patriots because he'd learned that under the veneer of valid complaints, under their bugle-and-drum rhetoric and their paranoid claims, they were purely evil, and that what they wanted to do to America was purely evil. At least he had the satisfaction of knowing he'd given the Feds the floor plan of the ranch buildings and the details of the mining of the compound. He hoped that the Feds would use his information to storm the place and kill every one of the mothers' sons. He remembered that Parker had said the Justice Department was going to send in the troops real soon. That gave him reason to hope that maybe the cavalry would even arrive in time to rescue him.

The tightly stretched rope gave another quarter inch, and cold water came pouring through the gag and into his mouth.

He swallowed the water, choking on it, coughing and making it shoot out his nose. He had to concentrate, to focus his entire mind on maintaining his position, or he would drown like an unwanted kitten in a gunnysack.

Arlemont Shopping Plaza
Salt Lake City 4:50 p.m. MDT

"THAT'S THE PLACE," Edward Kelso said, pointing at the huge sign on steel posts that marked the entrance to the shopping center. "Pull into the drive and go around to the back."

Wiley steered the semi into the parking lot, and they rolled over a series of speed bumps until they reached the end of the line of connected, single-story retail shops. Around the corner to the left, set at the far end of the lot, was the Western Super Discount Appliance store. Wiley headed for the concrete-block structure and, when he reached it, he turned, making for the loading bays in the back.

When they pulled up, a man in a short-sleeved white shirt with a pen protector in the pocket stepped out from behind one of the warehouse's overhead sliding doors. Suspenders held up his gray slacks. He mopped his forehead with a handkerchief as the men in the truck piled out.

"You picking up the special order for Old Glory Ranch?" the appliance salesman asked.

"That's right," Kelso replied.

"I thought you weren't going to show up today," the salesman said. "It was getting to be so late."

"Not a chance of that," Kelso told him.

"Got the item right here." He pointed to a wood-braced cardboard carton about five feet high. It was already strapped to a refrigerator dolly. On the side of the carton, in big red letters, it said The Thunderbolt. Industrial Grade, Super Heavy Duty Washing Machine.

Kelso smiled when he saw that. Some joke—it would clean out the dirt, all right.

"You have to sign for it," the salesman said, handing him down a clipboard and pen.

When Kelso had done that, the salesman asked, "Can we roll it right into the back of your truck? The reason I ask, that's one heavy washing machine. I've never seen the like around here. We sell home appliances, and we don't usually handle industrial units."

"We'll take it from here," Kelso assured him.

Ringman and Mallone hopped up on the dock and rolled the box to the loading-dock steps. Speck joined them there, and the three men lowered the dolly to the ground. Wiley had already opened the trailer's side door. Once they lifted the carton inside, they securely battened it down.

"Boy, that trailer looks like it's been through a war," the salesman said to Kelso. He was staring at the black smoke and scorch marks on the edges of the roof and across the closed rear doors, and at all the popped rivets in the side walls.

"Yeah, we're kind of hard on equipment, I guess."

"I guess that's why you guys need an industrial washer."

Kelso climbed into the cab and pulled the door shut. He waved at the salesman as they pulled away from the dock.

"A two-tenths-kiloton washing machine," Speck said, slapping his thigh. "Can you beat that?"

"Hell of a spin cycle," Wiley added.

They were all still laughing as they exited the parking lot.

Old Glory Ranch
5:05 p.m. MDT

SHORTLY BEFORE the evening meal was served in the main house's dining room, Rutherford excused himself to wash up. As hungry as he was, and as good as the smells from the kitchen were—pot roast, he thought—he was always reluctant to show his true colors when dining in someone else's domain. It was one thing to look like you ate like a pig; it was another to demonstrate that vast appetite before strangers.

Especially trim and fit strangers.

When placed in an unfamiliar dining situation, instead of setting-to with his usual boundless enthusiasm, Rutherford invariably made a great show of picking at his food, pushing it around the plate while he engaged those sitting around the table in spirited conversation. He did this while seething with yearning inside, forced by his own twisted pride to watch as others gorged themselves without remorse.

He knew it was idiotic for him to pretend that he hadn't reached such monumental proportions by eating to excess. What did he expect people to believe, that one night he had gone to sleep skinny and, to his horror, awakened the next morning tipping the scales at 450 pounds? Still, he couldn't make himself act naturally.

With difficulty, Rutherford put thoughts of food and associated shame from of his mind. If he wanted to continue feeding in the fashion to which he had become accustomed, he had to pass on something of value to Agent Parker of the FBI. He had already seen much inside the ranch house that was disturbing to him.

The Sawtooth Patriots had at least two heavy-caliber machine guns that guarded the front and back of the main house. They were set in fortified emplacements behind what had once been large picture windows. The glass had been removed from the frames and replaced on the outside with two pieces of plywood that left a gap of about a foot in the middle of the frame. On the inside of the house, crudely welded panels of steel plate reduced the view to a slit just big enough for the gunner to sight through and for the machine guns to fan back and forth, covering their field of fire. The areas around the machine guns weren't just sandbagged, but were shielded with more of the half-inch steel plate. Beside the sandbags were stacked boxes of belted 7.62 mm cartridges.

At one time the main house must have had a homey, cabinlike atmosphere with its peeled-log walls, bare ceiling beams and rustic wood stove. Now

the Western decorations—saddles, blankets, antique
guns and animal heads—were overpowered by
stacked sandbags. The place looked like a bunker.
Sandbags cut the width of the hallways in half. They
were piled waist high in every corridor. The floors
were probably hardwood, but they could no longer be
seen. The Patriots had covered them with plates of
steel. At the end of the brief home tour, Carmody had
told him there was more to see under the house. Rutherford guessed that the steel plate was intended to
protect whatever was down there from direct attack.

Because he'd never seen the militia in its own environment before, the talk-show host had never had
reason to take their threats and posturing with anything but a grain of salt. Talk was talk, and it was
cheap. Before this, he had pigeonholed the Patriots as
country dimwits, harmless nutcases and the means to
a multistate syndication for his program. As he
walked through the house, unescorted, the prepara-
tions for all-out war told him how far in over his head
he really was. If there was a dimwit at Old Glory
Ranch, it was surely him.

Instead of heading for the sink and towel in his
assigned room, and the hand-washing he claimed he
needed, Rutherford made a beeline for Carmody's office. He had been allowed to take a quick look into
it on the tour, and what he had glimpsed made him
want to see more. From the doorway, he moved directly to the big worktable set up in the middle of the
room.

At first he didn't know what he was looking at.
There didn't seem to be any order to it. Layers of
printed material covered the entire table. There were
what looked like Soviet and U.S. military manuals

and a couple of Russian dictionaries, ballistic texts and complex tables of numbers and map references, all stacked amid a clutter of maps. Topographic projections, detailed street maps and highway maps.

When Rutherford looked more closely at the map titles, he saw they all covered the same geographical area.

Ogden, Utah.

The Sawtooth Patriots were planning something for Ogden, the fat man thought. That news was bound to please Parker. It looked like solid, incriminating evidence. Coupled with possession of the illegal machine guns, it was grounds for a search warrant. Even if it turned out to be nothing more than a Fourth of July parade, it would still get him off the hook with the FBI for a while.

Leaning over the table, Rutherford shifted the topmost map aside. Under it was a detailed street map with a straight line drawn across it in red felt marker. The line didn't coincide with any of the streets, but cut across them at a steep angle. At one end of the line was a big circle, and beside the circle, a symbol.

A crudely drawn death's-head.

When Rutherford saw the name of the building complex that was inside the red circle, it made his head spin and his palms begin to sweat. He steadied himself with a hand on the edge of the table. If the Sawtooth Patriots were serious, they intended to make big trouble for America. If they were serious, they were even more dangerous than the defensive fortifications of the ranch suggested.

He took a tiny point-and-shoot camera from his pocket, and with slippery, sweaty fingers, shot a series of close-up flash photos of the material on the table-top.

He was so intent on the job that he didn't see Carmody standing in the open doorway behind him.

THE COMMANDER IN CHIEF of the militia wasn't angry; in fact, he appeared quite pleased. He had reason to be, everything was falling into place. Not all of it was his doing, of course; some of it was just luck. But the most important parts were his.

Carmody knew he had a knack for twisting reality, for making people see exactly what he wanted them to see, and to see it in exactly the way he wanted them to. It was a skill that he enjoyed using and refining, if for no other reason than to find out how far he could go.

A case in point—Carmody had personally put reflective stickers on highway signs and then identified them to his rank and file as secret troop-movement markers that would direct the invading New World Order forces into America's heartland. The radio waves and the Internet throbbed for weeks with the story. Troop-transport sightings were reported. High-powered-ammunition sales skyrocketed in a three-state area.

Another case in point—he knew his enemies and their lackeys would be looking for a certain kind of information at Old Glory Ranch, based on what they surmised about the militia's aggressive intent. Like the reflective stickers he had planted along the Wyoming roadside, the information he'd left out on his worktable led nowhere.

Without making a sound, Carmody backed away from the doorway and turned down the hall.

CHAPTER ELEVEN

JFK Airport, New York
8:15 p.m. EDT

The British Airways 747 touched down on the tarmac with a jolt. As the big engines reversed, slowing the plane, Sergio Eshamani watched the runway lights whip past his window. He'd had a good rest on the flight, thanks to a sleeping pill and two shots of vintage cognac. He felt totally relaxed as the aircraft taxied to the arrival gate.

The passport he handed the immigration clerk at the checkpoint said he was Dominic Taddei, citizen of Italy. His purpose in the United States, as he explained to the man in uniform, was tourism, a well-earned vacation. The clerk accepted this story without question; he didn't bother running the passport number against the computer database, although a terminal sat right in front of him on the counter. As the clerk handed back the stamped documents, he wished Eshamani a nice vacation.

Eshamani had brought no changes of socks, but he had several changes of ID with him. He tossed the Taddei ID into the nearest trash can and left the airport terminal as Walter Bertrand Combs of Hightower, Texas. The trio of bodyguards that dogged his heels to the passenger-loading zone also had double IDs.

At the curb, a stretch limo was waiting for him. The extralong vehicle was necessary because of the number of hired gunmen who had come along for the ride. In addition to the three shooters he had brought from London, Eshamani had five more Sicilian soldiers stationed inside the limo. As the trio from London took their seats, they were handed the tools of their trade by their countrymen. The new arrivals immediately checked the silenced miniUzi machine pistols, then set the weapons down on the carpet at their feet.

There was enough 9 mm firepower in the limo to start—and win—a small war.

As the limo pulled away from the curb and into the flow of traffic, the Sicilian capo cleared his throat. He didn't look happy. "We had some bad news, boss. A phone call a couple of hours ago from London. The Kensington house was hit hard."

Eshamani straightened up in his seat.

"We lost all of our guys. The Russian bought it, too. All of them slaughtered like hogs."

In an instant, the sense of confidence and relaxation that had marked the arms merchant's arrival in the U.S. evaporated. Someone had tracked him from Riga to London, someone skilled and ruthless. Perhaps even more ruthless than he was. One thing was certain: his enemy would not be put off by a mere transatlantic hop.

As the limo pulled onto the expressway, Eshamani pressed the switch that lowered the smoked-glass window between the passenger and driver compartments.

"Lupo," he said to the driver, "it's important that we aren't being tailed."

"Gotcha, boss." The uniformed man scanned his side mirrors as he changed lanes, identifying the colors and shapes of the vehicles behind them. He accelerated to eighty miles per hour, then cut back to his original lane. Again he searched his mirrors.

"Well," Eshamani said, "are we being tailed?"

"I don't think so, boss."

"Make sure."

The limo driver nodded. Without a signal, and at the last possible second, he swerved onto an off-ramp that descended in a tight circle to the right. The passengers either grabbed hold of the straps hanging from the ceiling or held on to the edges of their seats as the heavy car skidded around the turn. Lupo braked hard at the stop sign at the bottom of the ramp and, seeing a gap in the oncoming street traffic, squealed a right turn.

He scanned his mirrors again. They rolled past two blocks of brick factories before he said, "I think we might have a shadow, boss."

Eshamani had no intention of dragging a tail to the nuclear merchandise, especially if it was connected to the people who arranged the Riga and London hits. The last thing he wanted at the secret storage site was a prolonged firefight. Even though there was considerable risk in getting rid of the pursuit on a city street, he had to take it.

"Lupo, turn off the main street," he said, "and put some distance between us and the tail. We'll need thirty seconds or so to get set up."

The driver accelerated, scanning the street ahead for a likely turnoff.

"Get your guns ready," Eshamani told the Sicilians. "When Lupo stops, pile out fast and get busy. We're going to leave the tail in no condition to follow, except maybe as a ghost."

Lupo saw his opportunity ahead and seized it. He slashed a hard right turn that sent the limo's rear wheels skidding. Then the tires bit, and they shot down the narrow alley between empty factories. They were doing one hundred miles per hour, and the alley's mouth loomed ahead when Lupo smashed on the brakes. The limo's nose dipped, and they hit the cross street with locked wheels and smoking tires. Lupo's skilled footwork had dropped their speed to forty. He stomped on the gas and cut the wheel over, screeching a wide left turn.

Tires spinning, they surged forward. Before they reached the next corner, Lupo again stepped on the brakes. The limo slewed around the left turn. The slew became a gut-wrenching, four-wheel drift that ended with the right-side wheels slammed up hard against the curb.

The limo's doors popped open, and all eight gunmen hopped out. They moved into position behind the protection of the car body, their miniUzis up and ready to rip.

They could hear the car coming, its engine racing as it approached the ambush. A gray compact sedan squealed around the corner. In the glare of the streetlight, one person was visible behind the wheel.

The Sicilians opened fire the instant the car rounded the turn, the momentum of the skidding sedan carrying it into closer range. The windshield was hit by fifty bullets in the blink of an eye; it collapsed inward over the steering wheel. The hood sprang open. Even though all the miniUzis were silenced, because there were so many of them, they still made a racket in the canyon of dark and deserted factories. Clouds of cordite smoke billowed up from behind the limo.

The sedan kept sliding toward them, and as it did, its front end turned away from the attack. The front passenger's door was pounded by such concentrated autofire that the metal buckled and the door sprang open. The front and rear tires blew out on the right side, and sparks flew as steel wheels grated over bone-dry asphalt.

The sedan ground to a stop ten feet from the side of the limo and ten feet ahead of it. Three of the Sicilians hurried out from behind cover, and sighting down their weapons, looked into the ruined front seat. One of them reached in through the blown-out passenger's window and filched something from the seat. He took it over to the limo and held it up for Eshamani to see.

It was an almost empty fifth of gin.

"Lupo needs a new pair of glasses," the gunman said. "It was a drunk driver, not a tail."

Better safe than sorry, Eshamani thought. "That was his tough luck," the arms merchant said.

"Hers, boss. It was a woman."

"Whatever. Let's get out of here."

When they were rolling again, Eshamani told Lupo, "We're going to Jersey. Get us back on the expressway. Keep your eyes open for anything else that looks suspicious."

"Just make sure it isn't a school bus full of kids," one of the Sicilians said.

"Yeah, that could take more ammo than we brought along," said the guy sitting next to him.

The laughter of the Sicilians faded quickly when they saw that their boss was not amused.

Eshamani picked a fleck of lint from the knee of the trousers of his Armani suit. He decided that maybe he was being a little bit paranoid, but after what had happened in Riga and London, he had a perfect right to be cautious. As far as he knew, he wasn't a wanted man in the U.S. yet. There was no direct connection between him and the weapon stored near Union City. The way he had it planned, there never would be. Long before the *starookha* was ever used, he'd be out of reach.

Following Eshamani's directions, Lupo drove them down to the docks along the Hudson River. They turned onto a dark, pothole-riddled street. Looming on the left, and taking up an entire block, was a boarded-up manufacturing plant, circa 1910—four stories of greasy redbrick and vandalized window-panes. Lupo parked opposite the plant, in front of one of several metal warehouses built on pilings over the river. The warehouse was shaped like a cylinder cut in half lengthwise; it looked like an aircraft hangar on stilts. The windows in the front and high along the sides of the building were painted out with white-wash. Inside the warehouse was dark; outside, a series of bright floodlights provided a theft deterrent around the entire perimeter.

As Eshamani exited the limo, he got a whiff of a garbage barge upwind, an aroma that mingled with the stink from the nearby oil refineries. He crossed quickly to the warehouse's front door, which had a sign that read International Scrap Metal, Inc. He

"GAS"
E

REE
TS!

LAY! **Details inside!**

Play the

"LAS V

3 FRE

FREE GIFTS!

1. Pull back all 3 tabs on th
   see what we have for you
   FREE!

2. Send back this card and
   never before published! '
   they are yours to keep ab

3. There's no catch. You're
   nothing — ZERO — for
   any minimum number of

4. The fact is thousands of r
   Gold Eagle Reader Servic
   they like getting the best
   and they love our discou

5. We hope that after receiv
   subscriber. But the choic
   all! So why not take us up
   You'll be glad you did!

© 1997 GOLD EAGLE

FREE!
No Obligation to Buy!
No Purchase Necessary!

Play the
"LAS VEGAS"
Game

PEEL BACK HERE ▶
PEEL BACK HERE ▶
PEEL BACK HERE ▶

YES! I have pulled back the 3 tabs. Please send me all the free books and the gift for which I qualify. I understand that I am under no obligation to purchase any books, as explained on the back and opposite page.
(U-M-B-06/98)

164 ADL CGTA

NAME _____ (PLEASE PRINT CLEARLY)

ADDRESS _____ APT.

CITY _____ STATE _____ ZIP

   GET 2 FREE BOOKS & A FREE MYSTERY GIFT!

 **GET 2 FREE BOOKS!**

 **GET 1 FREE BOOK!**

 **TRY AGAIN!**

Offer limited to one per household and not valid to current subscribers. All orders subject to approval.

PRINTED IN U.S.A.

▼ DETACH AND MAIL TODAY ▼

The Gold Eagle Reader Service™: Here's how it works:
Accepting free books places you under no obligation to buy anything. You may keep the books and gift and return the shipping statement marked "cancel". If you do not cancel, about a month later we'll send you 4 additional novels, and bill you just $16.80 — that's a saving of 15% off the cover price of all four books! And there's no extra charge for shipping! You may cancel at any time, but if you choose to continue, then every other month we'll send you 4 more books, which you may either purchase at the discount price...or return to us and cancel your subscription.

* Terms and prices subject to change without notice. Sales tax applicable in N.Y.

If offer card is missing write to: Gold Eagle Reader Service, 3010 Walden Ave., P.O. Box 1867, Buffalo, NY 14240-1867

BUSINESS REPLY MAIL
FIRST-CLASS MAIL   PERMIT NO. 717   BUFFALO, NY

POSTAGE WILL BE PAID BY ADDRESSEE

GOLD EAGLE READER SERVICE
3010 WALDEN AVE
PO BOX 1867
BUFFALO NY 14240-9952

NO POSTAGE
NECESSARY
IF MAILED
IN THE
UNITED STATES

opened the door with a key. The warehouse had been leased through one of Eshamani's assumed and discarded identities. The arms merchant stepped back and let four of his bodyguards enter first. They turned on the lights, then checked to make sure the office area was clear. Only when they gave the okay did Eshamani and the rest of his troops step inside.

The place had a thoroughly hammered look to it. The office furniture was scarred, gray military surplus; the chair backs were all split, and yellowed foam bulged from the gaping wounds. The concrete floor was stained with a miscellany of drips and blotches. An ancient adding machine under a dusty cover stood abandoned in a corner.

Eshamani pulled a clipboard from a hook by the office's rear door and hit the warehouse light switch. Again his Sicilians took the lead. Once the place was secure, they waved for their boss to enter. The warehouse proper was three stories high, from the wooden plank floor to the metal ceiling. At the river end of the building, there were enormous double sliding doors. The side of the building also had big double doors. Both sides of the warehouse were stacked with metal shipboard cargo containers. In the center of the roof, running the entire length of the building, was a crane for moving the containers onto truck trailers.

Eshamani walked down the line of stacked containers, checking their serial numbers against his list. When he found one he wanted, he examined the seals on the container's doors. They were unbroken. He put a yellow chalk mark on the door beside them. He repeated this procedure on three more of the huge metal boxes. Customs declarations had identified the contents of all four containers as ''metal scrap'' acquired in the former Soviet bloc. Indeed, that was what was inside of them.

Mostly.

Mixed in with the different job lots of steel scrap were the dismantled barrel, carriage and wheels of an otherwise fully operational 152 mm Soviet D-20 howitzer.

The fourth cargo container held a dozen rounds of Russian-made, 152 mm HE, and one *starookha.*

The following morning, Eshamani would have the warehouse crew pull the identified containers out of the stacks and move them to one side. According to their arrangement, the buyer was going to bring in his own trucks to move the contraband material. Eshamani wanted to make sure the transfer went smoothly and quickly, with emphasis on the latter.

The sooner the nuke was off his hands, the sooner he could get on with his wonderful life.

WHEN TASHA BELOC exited U.S. Customs at JFK, she was confronted with a sea of waving cardboard signs, each bearing the name of an arriving passenger. The sign with her name on it was being held by a tall man with buzz-cut, fire-engine red hair.

"Good evening, Lieutenant Beloc," he said. "I'm Leonid Sokolov, your escort from the embassy."

"Eshamani'll be coming out in a minute," she told the Russian intelligence officer. "He was behind me in the line for customs."

"We have his limousine under surveillance outside. We can wait for him there."

Beloc followed the embassy man out of the terminal and over to a late-model, medium blue Pontiac sedan. The car was running. The man sitting behind the wheel looked up as Sokolov opened the front and rear passenger's-side doors. Beloc got in front, the red-haired man in back.

There was no time for introductions.

"Here he comes," the driver said.

Eshamani exited the terminal with his three body-guards. The smiling limo driver already had the rear door open for him.

"Have you brought the weapons?" Beloc asked Sokolov.

"Under your seat."

Beloc's fingers found the butt of a pistol. She put the 10 mm Glock in her lap.

"Is this all?" she said. "I gave the embassy a complete list of what we needed."

"Everything else is in the trunk," Sokolov assured her. "Don't worry, it's all there. I saw to it myself."

Beloc cracked back the Glock's slide half an inch to make sure there was a round in the chamber. There was. Then she pressed the muzzle against the driver's rib cage.

"Out," she ordered him.

"What are you doing?" Sokolov demanded, staring at the weapon poking through the gap between the front seats.

"Out!" she repeated, jabbing hard with the pistol. "Keep your hands where I can see them."

The driver reached across his chest for the door handle; the palm of his other hand was pressed flat against the headliner.

"We're supposed to be your backup, Lieutenant," Sokolov protested as the driver quickly walked away from the car.

"My backup will arrive on the next flight from London."

The red-haired man scowled at her. "You Spetsnaz still think you run the world."

Beloc pointed the weapon at his heart. "It's pretty clear that I run this little corner of it. Now get out, or I'll kill you."

As Sokolov obeyed, the brake lights on Eshamani's limo winked off.

Beloc dropped the Pontiac into gear and pulled out into traffic four cars behind Eshamani's vehicle. She kept a safe distance from the rear of the car, even after it turned onto the expressway. She figured that Eshamani would be nervous after Latvia. She was right.

When the limo suddenly exited the expressway, she had to follow, even though there were no cars between them. She took the curve slowly until the big car cut a hard right at the bottom of the ramp, then she floored the gas pedal to maintain visual contact. She had no more than gotten into position behind Eshamani again than the limo slashed a panic turn into a narrow alley.

"Hell!" Beloc said, feathering her brakes. Either they had seen her, or they suspected they were being followed. No matter, she knew she had to pursue. There was no one behind her to take over the point. She just wished she'd had time to move some of the heavy weapons up from the trunk.

She cut the Pontiac's headlights as she swung into the alley after the limo. The big car was really moving. She put her foot down hard on the gas and fought to keep from swerving into the alley's walls as the power surge hit the rear wheels. In the distance, brake lights flared and she started gaining quickly on the limo. Then it made a hard left turn at the end of the alley and disappeared.

"Come on, come on," she said, urging the car faster. She hit her brakes 150 feet from the end of the alley. She had planned to make a smooth slide out onto the street, but as she cleared the ends of the buildings, she was hit by the glare of onrushing headlights from the right.

She squashed her brakes as the car zoomed past, missing her front bumper by inches. Instead of turning, she skidded straight across the street and halfway up the alley entrance on the other side. The female driver hadn't even seen her. As she dropped the Pontiac into reverse and began to back out, she heard the sounds of numerous silenced automatic weapons and shattering glass from around the next corner. She stopped and listened, her heart pounding high in her throat.

When she heard the limo roar off, she backed out and headed for the corner. She knew what she was going to see before she made the turn. The arms merchant had laid an ambush for her and if it hadn't been for sheer luck, she would've stumbled right into it. Beloc didn't stop at the shot-up car; there wasn't time. The limo was already turning right at the next corner, returning to the main street.

She did turn her head and look as she sped by the smoking wreck. It was a no-survivor hit. Because of the position of the shooters and the angle of the turn, the poor driver didn't have a chance. Beloc knew she wouldn't have had one, either.

Once she had the limo in sight again, she was even more cautious about maintaining her distance. The pursuit got easier when Eshamani returned to the expressway. She actually relaxed a little. She thought about what Leonid Sokolov had said about the sheer egotism of her special-forces unit. He had misunderstood her completely. She hadn't rejected his help because she thought no one but Spetsnaz could do this job. She had put him on the street because there was way too much tax-free money changing hands in the arms deal. She knew how easy it was to buy someone off, to pay someone to walk away at a critical moment. She trusted Sarnov, Turgenev and Ferdishenko with her life, no one else.

When the limo exited the expressway in Union City and headed for the river, the traffic thinned and she was forced to drop back farther or risk discovery. The big car was four blocks away when she saw the flare of its brake lights and watched it pull into the warehouse driveway. She cut her headlights again and parked on the street a long block away. After checking the magazine on the Glock, she moved closer to the limo on foot, keeping to the shadows along the building fronts.

As she approached the side of the warehouse, the interior lights went on. She didn't like stepping into the pool of light around the side doors, but she had to do it. With the Glock up and ready to shoot, she ran soundlessly across the wooden planks of the dock. No one was guarding the outside of the warehouse. She kept low and tight to the metal wall of the building.

Through the gap between the double doors, she could see into the warehouse. Sergio Eshamani stepped into view. He was looking at the stacked cargo containers and referring to a clipboard in his hand. He moved out of view. Beloc relaxed her fingers on the Glock, reset her grip, then tightened down again.

If the nuclear warhead was inside one of those containers, Spetsnaz was going to have a hell of a time finding it. If Eshamani didn't give away the exact location, they would have to open them and start searching through the contents. Unless they got lucky, it would take days, days they didn't have.

If she could have called in the U.S. authorities, the mission would have been much simpler. The problem was, her unit had been ordered to capture the weapon and return it without alerting the Americans. It was the only way her government could save face. If they turned the job over to U.S. authorities, or worse, let the Americans find the weapon on their own, it would appear that the Russians could not police their own stockpiles, that they had to rely on the Americans to do their job for them. That was not acceptable.

As Eshamani and his bodyguards moved to the front of the warehouse, she ducked away from the door and retreated to the side of a Dumpster in front of the neighboring warehouse. Kneeling there, she saw Eshamani return to his limo. He only had two gunmen with him, which meant that he had left the other six to guard the place. Clearly something important was inside.

After the limo pulled away, Beloc jogged back to the Pontiac and used its cellular phone to call the embassy. She left a coded message for Sarnov and hung up when the receptionist said the ambassador wanted to speak to her. Inside the car's trunk she found two black nylon gun cases: one long and narrow, the other short and very thick. She unzipped the long one far enough to see that it contained a Heckler & Koch MSG-90 semiautomatic sniper rifle with a Leupold scope. It was a more accurate gun than the Dragunov she was used to, and had a much better scope. The shorter case held three folding-stock 7.62 mm Valmet assault rifles with silencers and extra 30-round magazines.

Under the gun cases was a ballistic nylon duffel bag. From it she took a black jumpsuit, boots and watch cap, and quickly changed clothes. Shouldering the gun cases on their straps and lugging the gear bag, she crossed the street at its darkest point, moving to the block-long front of the deserted manufacturing plant. She stepped into the deep shadow of a truck entrance. The wooden gates leading to an interior courtyard were chained and padlocked. Putting down the war gear, she jumped up and grabbed the bottom rung of the ladder to the fire escape. The ladder groaned mightily as it swung to the ground. She held the ladder down with her boot while she picked up the bags, then climbed the fire escape carrying seventy pounds of deadweight.

Once she reached the roof, she moved to the front of the building and got into position behind the low brick wall that marked the end of the roof. She laid down an insulated blanket on the tar paper, then took the H&K sniper rifle from its case. After checking its magazine, she opened the rifle's bipods and set the weapon up on top of the low wall.

Through the Leupold, she could see the front and side of the warehouse. Even if the floodlights were cut, she could control movement along those corridors. Unfortunately, the river side of the building was out of her field of vision. There was nothing she could do about that until her backup arrived. If they didn't make it in time, she had to hope that the weapon would be moved by truck, rather than boat.

The sound of an approaching car on the street below made her pull back from the scope's rubber eyecup. She looked over the edge of the roof in time to see a very low-slung sedan glide to a stop beside the Pontiac. The doors of the car flew open, and six young men in baggy clothes jumped out with tools in their hands. They were, to say the least, organized. One of them broke the driver's window with a hammer, while another punched out the trunk lock. As the trunk and driver's door swung open, the other young men started jacking up the car, front and rear, then set about removing the tires and wheels.

Beloc was glad she hadn't left anything important behind.

Only the cell phone.

They got that, of course. Along with the battery, the radio, the tool kit and spare tire. She watched as the youth gang dropped the stripped Pontiac onto the street on its axles, then piled back into their car and glided away into the night. She thought about sending a single 7.62 mm round over their heads, just to say hello, but from what she had read about American street gangs, they would probably return fire with automatic weapons. It would make too much racket.

She didn't want the police anywhere near the warehouse.

CHAPTER TWELVE

Crowheart Creek, Wyoming
11:30 p.m. MDT

As soon as David McCarter turned onto Highway 26 out of Riverton, he pushed the Ford one-ton van's engine, suspension and steering to the limit, using both sides of the narrow two-lane road, which prompted Manning to wisecrack about his being "a graduate of the Montana School of Driving." In truth, none of McCarter's passengers was sweating the squealing tires and the sudden side-to-side shifts of momentum. The warriors of Phoenix Force knew their team leader had once been a test driver for British Leyland.

Because the Wyoming Highway Patrol was stretched so thin over so many miles of highway, their chances of being stopped for speeding were nil. It was a good thing, too. If a state trooper had happened to look inside the van, there would have been a lot of explaining to do, not just about the tactical black outfits they were all wearing, but the highly illegal weaponry that was packed in around them.

As they rolled along at eighty-five miles per hour, a country music station played softly on the radio. It was a time for private thoughts, maybe even a few private prayers. The battlefield was close, and with it, always, the chill of death.

In his headlights, McCarter saw the beige box of the Winnebago parked on the shoulder to the right. He tapped the brakes and turned onto the soft ground. During the daytime, it was a picnic spot, of sorts—a dirt parking strip, two tables, a portable toilet, some low trees, all overlooking a small but vigorously running creek. McCarter pulled in behind the conscripted war wagon and cut the motor. The inside of the Winnebago was all lit up, its rooftop generator throbbing.

The men of Phoenix Force moved quickly and silently, gathering up their weapons cases and gear bags. After locking the emptied van, McCarter knocked on the side door of the Winnebago.

When the door opened, Rosario Blancanales stood backlit in the doorway. "Come on in," he said, "we're making popcorn."

"Popcorn, hell," McCarter said as he stepped inside. "All I smell is bloody gun oil." Mack Bolan and Carl Lyons had gun parts and cleaning rags spread over the small dining table. "Cheers, mates."

The rest of Phoenix Force climbed into the RV with all their gear. The combined battle crew of nine made the Winnebago feel cramped, even claustrophobic. The blinds inside the front windshield had been pulled down all the way, and the captain's chairs in the driving compartment were turned to face the rear.

Right away, McCarter unrolled the large aerial recon photo of Old Glory Ranch that he had brought from Stony Man Farm. He tacked up the photo on the kitchen cabinets. The extreme blowup was marked with small yellow arrows that indicated items of special interest: the heavy-machine-gun emplacements, the mined areas and the three-story-high water tower with its sniper hide. Under the photo, he stuck up a floor-plan diagram of the compound's buildings and beside that, a cross-sectional sketch that showed the underground passages that connected the ranch buildings. "Can everybody see?" he asked.

There were grunts of assent all around.

"Good," McCarter said. "As I go through this, if anybody has any suggestions or questions, feel free to stop me." He tapped the photo of the compound with a finger. "What we have here, gentlemen, is a hardsite designed to withstand a long-term siege. The militiamen would love to hold a Waco-like standoff against federal law enforcement. They want the public platform that international press coverage would give them. A standoff is precisely what we don't want. Our mission is to penetrate and neutralize the compound, then to locate and remove the nuke, if it's there. If we strike out on the Soviet weapon, and we can't find the 155 mm howitzer, then we'll search the premises for anything they've left behind that might help us locate their intended target."

"What about prisoners?" James asked.

McCarter's green eyes narrowed. "We're not going in there to arrest these sods. The Sawtooth Patriots stepped over the line a long time ago. They aren't just bloody idiots in camou fatigues—they're idiots with innocent blood on their hands. They've killed police and civilians, and they're planning to waste a lot more noncombatants before they're through. If anyone inside the compound resists, kill them."

"That means kill them all," Blancanales said. "I checked the FBI psych profiles on the men we know are at the ranch. Carmody has gone through his ranks and winnowed out the wish-washy and the wannabes. The occupants of Old Glory are all hard-core, totally committed Patriots.''

"Don't call them that," Bolan said. "Ever."

"Yeah," Lyons concurred. "It makes me want to puke.''

"Militiamen, then," the white-haired Latin conceded. "These guys aren't going to surrender."

Schwarz addressed Blancanales. "You're telling us that when we come crashing in on these guys, they're so brainwashed that they'll actually think we're U.N. troops from Bangladesh and fight to the death?"

"Or maybe pull a mass murder-suicide, like Waco or Jonestown?" Hawkins added.

"That'd be real considerate of them," Manning said.

"Some of them will think we're enforcers from the New World Order," Blancanales said. "Hell, some of them think foreign troops are hiding under Detroit right now. They're all fanatics of one twisted stripe or another. That makes them unpredictable, psychologically speaking. From the layout of the ranch, the way they've fortified it, and from their rhetoric, it's safe to say they look at Old Glory as their last stand. So don't expect any white flags to pop up when the shooting starts."

McCarter tapped the aerial photograph again. "There is a fifteen-foot-high wire perimeter fence, and inside it, a stretch of open ground that surrounds the various outbuildings. From the left, we've got a bunkhouse, a connecting walkway that leads to the main house, an open area that divides the barn from the house and a water tower. Another open area divides the barn from the gasoline reservoir shed here at the top far right and the storage shed at the bottom far right. According to the FBI informant, there are upward of fifty enemy scattered through the complex. The marked machine-gun positions are all armed with M-60s. And we have a sniper hide in the catwalk around the water tower's tank. We assume the faintly visible line extending from the fence, here, to the runway is a buried utility pipe. Any questions so far?''

The Stony Man warriors all shook their heads.

''There's a major weak point in their defensive strategy,'' McCarter went on. ''Manning and I have already gone over it. They've got the whole open area inside the compound mined to keep out tanks and Bradleys, and opposition foot soldiers. According to the informant, the militiamen have rigged the mine-field in grids. Each grid can be separately armed and fired by an electrical signal from the heavily fortified command center in the basement, here.'' He pointed at the cross-sectional drawing of the main house.

''Which means all the mines in a grid are wired together,'' Gadgets Schwarz said. ''If they can blow them all at once, so can we.''

''Right,'' Manning said, ''but there's a problem. From the informant's description, the mines are controlled by a two-step switch. The first step arms them and the second one detonates. We can't blow the mines from outside the perimeter fence until the grid has been armed from the command bunker, which means we have to let them know we're coming.''

''That shoots the no-siege plan to hell,'' Hawkins said. ''If we warn these jerks, we can't stop them from retreating to the main bunker. If we don't stop them from crawling down their hidey-hole, they're going to have the standoff they want. How're we going to dig them out of there?''

"We can't chop through the floors of the main house," McCarter said. "They're sheathed in steel plate. The only way in is through these underground passages. They lead into the command center from the bunkhouse and barn. Manning says we can blow the steel connecting doors.''

"How do we get to the passages?'' Encizo asked.

McCarter nodded. "That's my next point. The other weak spots in the defense are at the bunkhouse and storage-shed ends of the compound. On every other side of the house, two machine guns share responsibility for a zone of fire. On each of these sides there's only one M-60. The plan is to split up and hit the ranch from both ends at once, but before that, we have to deal with the observation posts.'' He pointed at three symbols on the aerial recon photo some distance from the compound.

"Striker, you, Manning, Encizo and James will eliminate OP number one, then you'll close in on the bunkhouse end of the compound. Hawk and Blancanales will take OP number two. Hawk, you'll remain there and control the road leading away from the compound and support the attack with discretionary sniper fire. Gadgets, Lyons and I will take OP number three. Blancanales will peel off from Hawk and join us, then we'll work our way to the gas and storage side of the compound outside the perimeter fence.

"Once everyone is in position, Gadgets and Manning will penetrate the perimeter and rig the mine grids at opposite ends of the compound to blow on our command. When that's done, we'll break through the wire and decommission the two machine-gun

posts with LAWs. Which should prompt the militiamen to arm their minefields. Then Gadgets and Manning will blow the mine grids to give us a safe route
across the compound. By blowing up both of them at
once, we'll confuse the militiamen and, with any luck,
make them split their forces.''

"So," Encizo said, "we cross the blown minefield
and take and hold the bunkhouse. Then we access the
underground passage to blow up the doors to the command center?''

"That's the idea," McCarter said. "The faster we
move, mates, the easier this job's going to be. Any
more questions?''

There were none.

McCarter swiveled the driver's chair around and
raised the blinds that blocked the windshield. Ducking
under the RV's dash, he removed the fuses for the
brake and headlights. As he started the engine, Manning stepped up beside him. The Canadian handed
him an AN/PVS-7 cyclops night observation device.
McCarter pulled the NOD over his head and adjusted
its straps for a snug fit. He turned the NOD on, then
cut the inside lights of the Winnebago. Gunning the
engine, he shifted the automatic transmission into
Drive and steered the RV onto the dark highway.

"HOW ARE YOU FEELING NOW?" Carmody asked Jack
Hutton.

The informer sucked down the spoonful of hot
soup. Despite a half-hour-long hot shower, his whole
body was still shaking slightly. He didn't answer.

"Feel like you're ready to talk to me?''

"I would've talked to you before," Hutton said,

dipping the spoon back into the steaming bowl, "if you'd have asked me."

"Not with the same enthusiasm," Carmody said. He leaned across the dining room table. "When are the Feds coming?"

"They wouldn't tell me something like that."

"I didn't ask if they *told* you, I asked if you *knew.* If you want another swim, Hutton, I can arrange it."

The man's eyes widened in horror.

Carmody could see the guy draw into himself, like a snail pulling back into its shell. He smiled. Now that the stoolie was all toasty warm, now that he had some hope and knew what was in store for him, the threat had infinitely more power.

"Cook," Carmody said to his second-in-command, who was leaning against the dining room's knotty pine wall, "escort our little buddy here back to the well."

Hutton dropped the soup spoon as Matt Cook grabbed him by the shoulders. "No," he protested. "No, wait. The Fed said 'very soon.' He wouldn't tell me any more than that. Honest to God."

"Not tonight, not tomorrow, not next week, just soon?"

"That's the truth. I swear it."

Carmody looked the soldier in the eye. He believed him. The Feds would certainly protect themselves from a situation like this and avoid telling their inside man anything more than he needed to know. He nodded to Cook, who roughly hoisted Hutton to his feet, kicked away the chair and shoved the man toward the door.

As Cook passed, Carmody reached out and stopped

him. "Put the rope around his neck this time," he whispered.

Carmody checked his watch as he moved to the dining-room window. He looked out the view slit at the Old Glory runway. It was almost time to turn on the landing lights. Johnson would be back shortly with the Beechcraft, and the real nuclear howitzer team would be leaving the ranch, en route to its real target.

THE SENTRY at the ranch's forward observation post wasn't looking through the AN/PVS-4 NOD mounted on his M-16 when the blacked out Winnebago glided down the highway bordering the edge of the ranch property. The sentry, Ron Welch, was rubbing his face and stomping his feet, trying to stay awake. The wind sweeping over the mountains and down across the plain covered the sound of the RV's engine. Because the vehicle's brake lights had been disabled, Welch didn't notice when it stopped in the middle of the empty road, allowing three armed men to jump out before it rolled on.

It wasn't that Welch didn't take his job seriously; the trouble was he had been taking it seriously for too long. Carmody had been telling his troops for more than a week that the shit was about to hit the fan. Every day while the fire team practiced with the howitzer trainer, the rest of the Sawtooth Patriots had been running close-quarters combat drills, digging out the mine grids, filling sandbags, welding steel plate and pulling sentry duty. Welch was so bone tired that even the fear of being overrun by federal troops couldn't keep him on top of his game for more than a few minutes at a stretch.

He pushed on his eyeballs until it hurt, then he pushed harder, making starbursts appear inside his head. Then he picked up the M-16 and scanned the distant road with its night-vision device. Something moved between him and the fence. It was too small to be a man and it was moving too fast. A coyote, running full tilt.

Welch swept the NOD over the intersection of the highway and the ranch road, eight miles of dirt track that made a single S-curve around a low hill before ending at Old Glory's front gate. Nothing there.

He rested the weapon against the sandbags of the OP and took a sip of water from his canteen. He swished it around his mouth, then spit it out. What he needed was a pot of superstrong black coffee. Though he was exhausted, Welch was ready to die for what he believed in, ready to fight back against the race-mixing, white-culture-crushing, international conspiracy. Before he'd met Carmody, his anger at the unfairness of the world had been unfocused. He had wanted to strike back, but other than acts of vandalism and aggression on isolated individuals, he hadn't known how. Carmody had shown him the way, the path out of the hopeless muck of the humanist present, the path leading to a bright white future.

Far off in the night, a coyote howled. The shrill sound sliced through the singing of the wind and then it was gone. Welch shifted the M-16 back to his shoulder and, leaning against the sandbagged rim, slowly swept the terrain with the PVS-4. He felt the sandbag cold against his chest and the night-vision scope's rubber cup pressing against his eye socket. He smelled desert sage. It was the next-to-last sensation he ever had.

The last thing Ron Welch felt was the stunning impact of a 9 mm parabellum at the base of his skull. His world went white from wall to wall before it went black.

McCarter hopped down into the OP and checked the warm body for signs of life. There were none. He rejoined Lyons and Gadgets at the base of the low hill and they advanced to the rendezvous point and waited.

After a few minutes, a figure crossed the plain from the direction of the road. It was green and ghostly in their NOD goggles' fields of view. They all knew it was Blancanales by his easy, rolling gait.

"How'd it go at number two?" McCarter asked as the Latin stepped up.

"Piece of cake," Blancanales said. "Hawk's in position by now. Anybody coming down the road from the ranch is going to shake hands with Mr. LAW."

McCarter took point for the four-man column, moving in a low, fast crouch toward the lights of Old Glory Ranch in the distance.

OF THE DIVIDED STONY MAN force, Bolan and his crew had the longest march before they made enemy contact. Their first objective, a two-hundred-foot-high pile of volcanic rubble, was four miles north of the highway and a mile west of the ranch compound. Although the Executioner kept them moving at a trot, they made hardly any sound; their gear was all securely battened down and essentially noiseproof. He led Manning, James and Encizo in an arc away from the ranch and the OP, keeping the targets at a constant distance until he lined up the sentry's hilltop position with the bunkhouse end of the compound. By putting the hill between them and the Old Glory Ranch, and attacking the OP from that side, he could take it without being seen by the men in the compound.

The big guy cut the pace as he turned for the hill. Instead of moving in a straight line, he zigzagged, taking advantage of what little cover there was on the desert plain. The closer they got to the hill, the closer they were to the gun on its summit, and the easier targets they made. Bolan did his best to keep them concealed; it was his top priority. If the OP alerted the compound, their plans were scrapped, their mission scrubbed. His other concern had to do with the safety of his men in the event they were seen by the sentry. To this end, he chose a start-stop, side-to-side route to the foot of the rubble hill that was calculated to confound the shooter and, above all, spoil his first shot. He selected the route based on years of experience on the other end of a sniper rifle.

At the bottom of the hill, Bolan signaled a halt. Taking out the OP was a one-man job. His job. As the others closed ranks with him behind a boulder, he put down his MP-5 machine pistol and his drag bag, then shrugged out of his combat harness. In order to scale the side of the hill without detection, the Executioner had to dump the nonessentials. If he hung up a piece of gear on the loose slope, it could start a landslide of softball-sized rocks—something guaranteed to bring the sentry up firing. He left everything on the ground, except for a silenced Beretta 93-R in shoulder leather and a flat black Fairbairn-Sykes commando knife in a forearm sheath. He crept up the hillside like a cat, light-footed and quick. There was no way he could keep the rocks from shifting under the soles of his boots, but because he put weight on them so briefly, they hardly moved at all. Nearing the summit, he dropped to his belly and crawled the last thirty feet to the bulwark of sandbags that circled the OP.

Facing the defensive wall, the Executioner drew himself up into a coiled crouch, then he closed his eyes and listened hard. He could hear the sentry breathing on the other side of the defensive wall. He pulled the commando knife free of its sheath with his right hand and with his left picked up a chunk of rock. He chucked the rock over his shoulder, down the slope. It landed with a dry clatter somewhere in the dark.

The sentry stopped breathing.

Bolan heard the man's boots crunch on the floor of the OP as he turned to face the sound. The observer was accustomed to hearing occasional, spontaneous landslides from time to time; this noise was different. Directly above the Executioner, the guard leaned over the top of the pile of sandbags. Bolan could sense the shape of a weapon, its barrel just above his head. The barrel tracked back and forth as the sentry used the PVS-4 atop his M-16 to search the desolate hillside for movement.

He was looking too far away.

Bolan lunged up and struck hard with the commando dagger in his fist. He had intended to slide the flexible, double-edged blade through the man's throat and up into his brain for a quick, silent kill, but at the critical moment the sentry instinctively drew back from the attack. Though he only moved a couple of inches, it was enough to spoil Bolan's aim. The point of the knife caught the guard under the chin, and the powerful upward thrust sent it skewering into his mouth, just behind his lower front teeth, through the tip of his tongue and the roof of his mouth, into his nasal cavity.

The Executioner knew the instant he struck that he had missed. He threw his shoulder into the man, knocking the assault rifle away, driving himself over the barrier. The M-16 crashed to the ground as Bolan landed on top of the wounded sentry. The man couldn't scream because his mouth was held shut by the blade, but he fought hard, spraying blood from his nose and mouth, desperately clawing for his attacker's face. Bolan yanked his Beretta free and put a silent mercy bullet into the militiaman's forehead. The commando knife was driven so deep into bone, that to free it he had to put his boot on the dead man's face.

Bolan rejoined the others at the foot of the hill. They didn't ask him how it went. They didn't have to, they could see. The right arm of his black shirt glistened with blood from wrist to elbow. After pulling on his gear, Bolan looked at his watch. They had forty minutes to crawl a mile on their bellies, while towing their heavy armament behind them in padded drag bags. He hand-signaled for Manning, James and Encizo to follow him.

When they rounded the rear of the base of the hill, the compound came into view. A halo of light surrounded it. Bolan dropped into crawl mode and began to advance on the enemy position. It was a tedious and nerve-racking approach. He picked the line of least discomfort around the larger rocks and bushes, keeping to the low places in the terrain, the gullies and erosion scars. Though they could have come under fire from the compound at any moment, the Executioner knew the odds of that actually happening were slim. Because the ranch was brightly lit, so was the inside of the silver hurricane fence. The reflecting mesh would confuse the view of ground-level sentries and make it hard for them to isolate an attacking force from the terrain until that force was very close to the compound. As everything was so flat, the militiamen didn't have a good angle of fire; even the water-tower sniper would have trouble zeroing in.

They were within twenty-five yards of the fence, and one hundred yards from the bunkhouse, when Bolan stopped crawling and waved Manning forward. With a second hand signal, he told James and Encizo to spread out to firing positions on either side.

The Canadian demolition expert dumped all of his gear except the combat harness and the autopistol under his armpit. Manning removed his tool kit from the drag bag and clipped it to his chest. Then he advanced on his stomach to the wire, alone.

ON THE OTHER SIDE of the compound, Gadgets Schwarz was in the same totally vulnerable position as he crossed no-man's-land, inch by inch. The only sentries he could see inside the wire were standing by the front door of the main house, out of the wind, which was picking up. The breeze curling over the plain had already driven a tumbleweed up against the fence line. He crawled forward, into the sights of the machine gun stationed in the storage shed. The closer he got to the sagebrush, the better he felt. It was big enough and dense enough to conceal him while he did his job.

Belly down in the dirt, he quickly clipped a small hole in the wire of the fence. Inside the compound, there wasn't any brush, no cover whatsoever. He couldn't reach an arm through the fence without giving himself away, so he had to work from the outside. Whoever had planted the land mines directly in front of him had done a good job of covering up the trench and smoothing the soil, but the work had been completed very recently and there was still a difference in the moisture content of the areas of dirt that had been turned over, a difference that could be seen from his angle. It started a foot inside the fence. He looked more closely at the earth at the edge of the disturbed area. There was a definite hump in it.

Schwarz pushed a nonreflective, pencil-lead-thin probe through the hole in the fence and carefully brushed the soil away from the mine's trigger. Although he didn't uncover all of the device, from the trigger it looked like an antitank model. He couldn't tell whether it was armed or not, but he assumed it wasn't because men were moving around the compound—men who otherwise might be killed by one of their own weapons.

Having located the first mine in the string, he used his tool to etch out a short, shallow trench in the earth between the fence and the mine. The soil was loose and it only took him a minute. Then he excavated the side of the mine that faced him, digging until he found the arming sensor and the connecting wires. He hooked and drew the sensor close to the fence and clipped a set of wire leads to it from a spool in his tool kit. After covering all the wires in the shallow trench and concealing the mine, he retreated from the fence, spooling out wire from his chest pack as he went.

When he reached the fallback point, McCarter and Blancanales were each removing a LAW from their respective drag bags. They prepared the rockets for firing as Schwarz connected the wire leads to a battery-powered detonator.

HAWKINS LOCKED DOWN the bolt of his silencer-equipped, Remington 700 sniper rifle. One round of New World Order ammo coming up, he thought as he snugged up against the stock. He framed the opposition sniper in the Leupold sight's view field. Thanks to the well-lit compound, he had no trouble picking out the man on the water tower's catwalk. The militia sniper was lying prone on a padded mat on the leeward side of the tower, keeping warm, out of the breeze.

It was a nine-hundred-yard shot, into a gusting cross wind. On top of that, because of the facing, prone position, Hawkins's target was reduced to head and shoulders. That didn't leave much margin for error.

Though it was dicey, Hawkins was ready to take the shot, anyway. A near miss, which he knew he could score, might drive the guy off the tower, which would remove the threat to the attacking force.

As he dropped the Remington's safety, movement at the ranch house's front door caught his attention. He lowered the scope to center on two men. One was dragging the other by the back of his shirt. The man being dragged was bound hand and foot and gagged. Hawkins didn't like the look of that one bit. It occurred to him that the FBI's secret informant inside the militia might be in big trouble.

Hawkins's assignment was to trigger an alert inside the compound. He had full discretion as to how that panic was brought on, which meant he decided who died first. He adjusted the Leupold's BDC for the new range so he could shoot dead on the crosshairs.

The man doing the dragging was bearded, lean and muscular. The bound man, who was much smaller, struggled frantically, digging in his toes as he was hauled across the compound. As the bearded guy flung his captive up against the side of the well, he glanced over his shoulder at the house. One of the sentries standing there must have said something to him. He said something back.

Hawkins watched as the bearded man grabbed the well rope, tied a quick noose in it, then slipped it over the smaller man's head. It was clear what was about to happen when he lifted the bound man onto the lip of the well.

The roof structure of the well partially blocked Hawkins's view, preventing him from attempting a head shot on the would-be hangman. Hawkins dropped his aim point a fraction and started his trigger squeeze.

If a ruckus was what McCarter wanted, a ruckus was what he would get.

E. Paul Rutherford waited inside the door of his room until he was sure the men talking in the dining room were gone. Then, clad in slippers and a camp tent of a velour bathrobe, he made his way down the dark hall to the ranch house kitchen.

Although he preferred to take his food in restaurants because there was less effort involved, in a pinch he was perfectly willing to do for himself. Earlier in the evening, he had only picked at dinner; now he was ravenous, way too hungry to fall asleep. On top of the calories he had missed, he was frightened, and when frightened, he tended to eat even more than his normal amount. He thought of himself as a "nervous eater."

Rutherford opened the refrigerator. Bathed in the light of a single bulb were the remains of dinner's gargantuan pot roast on a covered plate. He took it and the chafing dish of vegetable accompaniment—potatoes, carrots and onions—and set it on the counter. Finding the bread box, he began to make himself a towering sandwich of half-inch thick slices of roast. When he sat down and began to have a go at it, he felt better almost immediately.

Maybe it was just low blood sugar that had him so panicky. After all, what did he *really* have to worry about? He had his roll of film, his sacrificial offering to Agent Parker and the Justice Department. Maybe the FBI would use the information to shut down the militia. God knows, they needed shutting down. He couldn't see how the destruction of the Sawtooth Patriots could harm his career at this point. He had ridden them as far as he could; the syndication deal was practically a lock. And if the FBI did nail Carmody based on his information, he could get even more money out of them in future.

Rutherford took another huge bite of sandwich and packed a pair of potatoes into his cheeks.

MATT COOK CONSIDERED himself a good soldier, a guy who could follow orders to the letter. Of course, some orders were easier to carry out than others. When his CO in Desert Storm had told him to bracket an Iraqi gun position with HE, that had been easy duty. When his CO in the Sawtooth Patriots told him to take a prisoner outside and hang him, that was easy as pie, too. The rules of engagement were the same.

War was war.

Traitors had to die.

He grabbed Jack Hutton under the armpits and hoisted him up onto the rim of the well. "You're getting a break you don't deserve," he said, looking into the man's eyes. "If it was up to me, I'd stake you out somewhere over thataway and leave you for the buzzards." He adjusted the noose, moving the knot to the side of the man's neck.

"You should've known better than to sell us out to the Feds. You should've known we'd figure it out. Did you think we were stupid or something?"

Hutton tried to speak, but could only make muffled, unintelligible sounds around the gag.

Cook took him by the shoulders and turned him around, pushing his legs out over the black emptiness of the well.

"Look down there and tell me who's the stupid one."

The informant craned his neck around so he could face his murderer, so he could show him that he wasn't sorry for what he had done. That it was worth dying for.

"Let's see how far your neck stretches, hard guy," Cook said. He uncranked about twenty feet of bucket rope and draped the slack neatly over the edge of the well. Then he locked the crank in place with the loop of cord.

As he reached out to put his hands on Hutton's trembling shoulders, bracing his legs to boost the man off the ledge and into eternity, something hit him in the stomach so hard that it knocked him away from the well. It literally blew him flat onto his butt in the dirt, and he sat there, hunched over at the waist.

The shock was so powerful that for a second he felt nothing at all, not even the hard, cold ground beneath his behind. He was instantly struck numb, from head to foot. He floated, disembodied, in a space that wasn't Wyoming, or the Old Glory Ranch.

A place between life and death.

He returned to the land of the living only with a great effort. It was then that he realized that he was opening and closing his mouth like a fish out of water, that a river of slobber was drooling down his beard, but no sound was coming out of his throat because there was no air left in his lungs. It had all been driven out by the force of the impact. He gasped for breath.

Then his hands and feet started shaking. His heels drummed in the dirt, raising a cloud of dust. A burning pain knifed through his midsection, and he knew that he had been shot. He looked down at his belly and saw the round, dark hole in his white T-shirt. Blood began to ooze from it. His heels drummed faster against the ground; he couldn't make them stop.

The pain swallowed him whole.

And he began to scream.

CHAPTER THIRTEEN

Oswald Carmody closed the door of the floor safe in his office, but didn't bother to lock it. He had already transferred the cash contents of the safe, roughly a quarter of a million dollars, to the center compartment of his nylon travel bag. The money had been contributed by many donors, but the lion's share of it had come from Charles Krick. As Carmody turned down the corridor, heading for the entrance to the command bunker, he heard terrible, shrill shrieks of pain coming from outside the building. They didn't sound human; they sounded like a gut-shot bear. It wasn't the FBI stoolie singing his last tune because Cook had gagged him before dragging him out of the main house. Carmody put down the money bag and reversed course, running through the wide living room to the front doors.

On the porch outside, he found one of the two sentries frozen in place. The other was hurrying away across the compound toward the well.

"What is it?" Carmody demanded of the man. "Who's screaming like that?"

"It's Cook," the sentry said. "All of a sudden he just went down out there, over by the well."

Carmody stepped to the edge of the porch. He

could see Cook curled on his side on the ground, kicking his legs and yelling. The stoolie sat perched on the edge of the well with a rope around his neck.

Carmody turned back to the sentry. "What happened to Cook?"

"Don't know, sir."

"Did you hear a shot?"

"No. I didn't hear nothin', sir."

"Well, goddammit, get over there and help him!"

Carmody watched the sentry lope across the compound, carrying his M-16 by the pistol grip. He was a little more than halfway to the well when his partner reached the fallen Cook. Instead of kneeling down beside the writhing man, the sentry suddenly jerked backward and down, as if flicked in the head by a giant invisible finger. Blood spray glistened in the floodlight as the sentry toppled, loose limbed, to earth.

Carmody knew goddamned well what had just happened. "Sniper!" he shouted. Then he called out over his shoulder, "Can you see him, Burke? Can you get a shot at him?"

There was no answer from the Sawtooth Patriot sniper.

As he started to run along the porch, Carmody cupped his hands and yelled through them, "Burke!"

There was still no answer.

Behind him, the surviving sentry had turned in the middle of the compound and was sprinting back for the main house.

Carmody peered around the side of the building, up at the water tower. There was no one on the catwalk, and the water tank had sprung a leak at what would have been Burke's standing chest height. With his eyes, Carmody tracked the arc made by the fine jet of water. He followed it all the way to the ground, where it splashed new mud onto the crumpled corpse of the rifleman.

"Jesus," Carmody exclaimed, turning back for the front doors, "we're under attack! Everyone to battle stations! Incoming! Incoming!"

The second sentry was within twenty feet of the front porch and safety when he, too, was sent sprawling by a silent gunshot. Hurled facedown in the dirt by a bullet to the back, he tried to crawl the rest of the way. His hands clawed at the dirt, his legs pushed at it, but like a bug impaled on a pin, his body didn't move an inch.

Carmody ignored him. The commander in chief of the Sawtooth Patriots reentered the house at a dead run, yelling a warning at the top of his lungs. All around him, militiamen moved quickly into their assigned positions. Even the men who had been sound asleep at the first shout were already up and armed. Their response to the threat was automatic, instinctive; they had been drilling for this eventuality for a long time. On the way to the bunker entrance, Carmody grabbed his money bag.

The doorway to the command center was set in the floor of a small bedroom in the middle of the ranch house. The door itself was heavy-gauge tempered steel, three inches thick, hinged on the inside. When Carmody entered the bedroom, the bunker door was open, tilted up and leaning back against an interior wall. He dashed down the flight of metal stairs that led to the underground command center.

"Is everybody here who's supposed to be here?" he asked Billy Ray Ransom.

"Yes, sir."

That meant that twenty men, including the howitzer team, were inside the bunker, leaving a force of thirty up top to defend the perimeter.

"Batten us down," Carmody said.

With the help of Peterson and Gabhart, Ransom pulled down the door and bolted it from inside. "We're sealed, sir."

"Arm the mine grids," Carmody told the man sitting at the command console. "Arm all of them."

"I'm on it, sir." The militiaman started flipping the rows of switches marked with adhesive tape, A through M.

From overhead, there came a heavy pounding. Someone was beating on the outside of the steel door.

"Who the hell is that?" Carmody said.

"It sounds like the fat man, sir," Gabhart said. "He didn't make it down before we buttoned up. Should we open the door for him?"

"No," Carmody said. "That door doesn't open for anybody. Rutherford's on his own."

"Sir, the observation posts are all off-line," said the Patriot's communications man. "There's no response to the emergency signal."

"I think we can assume they're neutralized. Either dead or captured." As Carmody spoke, the entire building rocked. Dust came raining down from the bunker's ceiling as violent explosions hit both ends of the compound simultaneously.

GARY WISEHART SCANNED the main gate of the compound over the fixed front sight of his M-60 machine gun. The five foot soldiers in the bunkhouse were crowding in behind him, peering over his shoulder, trying to see out the gun port, too.

"Jesus, back off. Give me some room to work," he told them. His voice had gone all high and shrill, but not nearly as high and shrill as Matt Cook's. From his firing position, Wisehart could see the mortally wounded Cook rolling around on the edge of the minefield.

He didn't roll for long after the mine grids were armed.

The solid whump of a detonating land mine sent a puff of smoke, dirt and Cook ten feet into the air. The screaming abruptly stopped. Then the airborne dirt, rocks and body parts rained down on the compound.

"Holy hell," Wisehart said, blinking his eyes. The informant was no longer sitting on the edge of the well; the well rope hung straight down. Wisehart shook his head. "Oh, man, that was nasty and a half."

"What happened?" said the M-60 gunner stationed behind Wisehart, on the other side of the bunkhouse. Through his own gun port, he was covering the perimeter fence between the bunkhouse and the mountains.

"Cook just bought it, big time," Wisehart said. "He sat on a mine."

Trying for a better look out the gun slit, the foot soldiers pressed in on Wisehart again. "Goddammit, you guys aren't in position," he said. "Get in position."

Reluctantly the foot soldiers drew back to the tiers of bunks and got ready to direct concentrated autofire at the bunkhouse door.

"I don't see a goddamned thing moving out

there," said the bunkhouse's third gunner, whose station was at the end of the building. "Where the hell are they?"

The third gunner was looking at the hurricane fence directly across the compound from his view slit when the wire exploded in a rocking ball of flame. From post to post, an entire thirty-foot section of fence vanished. In the bright light of the compound, something sailed through the gray smoke, through the wide break in the fence. At that moment, the machine gunner's body was supercharged by fear. The adrenaline rush made his vision so acute that he saw the flying object clearly. He saw the head of the rocket and the stabilizing fins behind it.

He saw death coming.

When the LAW rocket slammed into the plywood sheathing outside the steel-reinforced gun port, the piezo-electric crystal in its nose cap crushed, sending an electric current to the detonator. The sheet steel of the fortification became an instant liability. The cylindrically shaped, three-quarter-pound ocotol charge of the HEAT warhead blew a three-foot hole in the metal and broke free thousands upon thousands of steel splinters from the back side of the barrier. Those needles surfed on the 66 mm warhead's shock wave; tumbling, they flew through the bunkhouse interior.

That shock wave alone vaporized the machine gunner's head.

The steel splinters fanned out randomly from the entry hole, killing and maiming the men inside the bunkhouse.

MACK BOLAN HELD the bunkhouse gun port steady in the LAW's front sight and waited. Only after Manning had fired his rocket and the fence had burst into flame did Bolan press the trigger bar. The firing tube shuddered against his shoulder as the rocket launched. He glimpsed its tail fins as it vanished into the curling cloud of smoke. Then from the end of the bunkhouse came a flash and a solid bang.

On the other side of the compound, two more explosions racked the night. McCarter was right on time.

Bolan squinted to see through the tendrils of smoke. The strong breeze had already swept most of it away from the fence, and he could make out the bunkhouse. He could see that the sheet of plywood over the machine-gun port was on fire.

Bull's-eye.

"Everybody down," the Executioner said. Then, to Manning he growled, "Hit it!"

The Canadian flipped the switch on the detonator.

The entire strip of earth between the fence and the bunkhouse suddenly lifted ten feet into the air. The air itself was alive, screaming with metal fragments. They rattled against the sides of the buildings, cut slashes in the roof of the well and in the sides of the parked vehicles.

From the opposite end of compound, there was a similar rolling roar as another entire minefield went up at once. The detonation was followed by something unexpected, an explosion so violent that it rocked the ground under Bolan's stomach. An enormous red-orange fireball leaped into the sky over the far side of the compound.

The gas-storage tanks, Bolan thought.

Then all the floodlights winked off.

Everything went black, except for a raging gasoline fire.

Bolan pushed up from the dirt and sprinted for the break in the fence, his H&K subgun in his right hand. He didn't call out for the others to follow him; he knew they would be right on his heels. He scrambled over the fused ends of the wire, which were still hot from the LAW warhead, and burst through into the compound. The former minefield was a jumble of smoking, overturned earth, a field plowed by cordite.

He ran to the side of the well, and knelt there for a second until Manning, James and Encizo closed ranks. All of them looked at the well rope, which was hanging down into the hole. It swung, quivering slightly as if a heavy weight was attached to it. None of them said a word. The informant was dead. There had been no way to save him.

Bolan took off, charging straight for the burning end of the bunkhouse. The others ran for the covered walkway that connected the bunkhouse to the main house.

As he charged the building, the Executioner yanked a frag grenade from his combat harness, pulled the pin with his teeth and let off the safety spring. He was twenty feet from the LAW's entry hole when automatic gunfire came from inside the ruined gun port. Shooters from the bunkhouse were panicked, trying desperately to return fire. It was unaimed and therefore pointless. Bolan dropped into a feet-first slide and chucked the grenade through the ragged opening.

Bolan put his back to the outside wall as the explosion rocked the bunkhouse.

"THEY'RE BREAKING THROUGH!" came the strangled cry through the command center's intercom.

The communication abruptly ended as a string of explosions shook the bunker. Ceiling tiles rained down on the militiamen, and the lights flickered, then went off.

"Auxiliary power!" Carmody shouted. "Get the backup generator started."

It took a couple of minutes for the Patriots to get the gas-powered generator started. When they did, the room lights came up.

Carmody was beside himself. "How the hell did they get in so easily?"

The man behind the console answered. "It looks like they blew up several grids to open a path. We can still detonate the rest of the mines."

Through the steel reinforcing of the bunker roof, they could hear running feet and the clatter of autofire.

"What good would that do?" Carmody snapped. "They're already inside the buildings. The question is, are they in the underground passages?"

"According to the infrared detectors," the man at the console said, "they aren't down there yet."

"Don't take your eyes off the readout," Carmody said. "I want to know the instant they break the beams." He crossed the room to the CB, flicked it on and picked up the microphone.

"This is OGR," he said. "OGR calling Sky King."

CARL LYONS WAS the first one through the hole in the fence. The heat from the burning gas tank made him flinch, but it didn't slow him down. They hadn't planned on torching the gas, but shit happened when you were playing with high explosive and shrapnel.

Into the Sawtooth Patriot compound, Lyons carried a car-killer: a full-stocked 10-gauge semiautomatic shotgun with a combat sling. Its 3.5-inch Magnum shells had fifty percent more power than those of a 12-gauge and fired fifty percent more shot weight; in this case, fifty percent more stainless-steel, double-aught buck. Stony Man's armorer had expanded the weapon's tubular magazine capacity to eight rounds and customized the Countercoil recoil compensator to further reduce the violent barrel rise when the Ithaca Roadblocker was touched off.

Lyons skirted the plume of fire that had once been the gas-tank shed. The M-60 in the storage building hadn't gotten off a shot at him, and from the looks of the hole where the gun port had been, it never would. He reached the corner of the barn without being fired upon. He could see the flash hider and front sight of the machine gun sticking out of the gun slit in the back side of the barn. The M-60 didn't have an angle on him yet.

He walked along the side of the building, and as he walked, he fired the Roadblocker from the hip. Ten-gauge thunder shook the air. Double-aught buck skimmed the side of the machine gun's barrel, knocking its aim point away from Lyons. The guy behind the gun swung it right back. Lyons blasted again, and this time the full-choked pattern of stainless-steel ball bearings bent down the machine gun's front sight. The weapon jerked violently at the solid impact, then wobbled, then its muzzle tilted up in the air.

Probably knocked the guy flat on his butt, Lyons thought as he unslung his satchel charge and ignited the fuse. He wedged the explosive package through the view slit cut in the steel and let it drop. As he turned from the slit, he saw frantic movement inside the barn. Men were running, trying to beat the boom. He followed suit, breaking into a sprint.

Even though he expected the explosion, even though he was counting down the seconds in his head, the sheer force of it drove him to his knees beside the barn. A wave of heat hit his back as the wall of the three-story wooden structure cascaded into the compound. The satchel charge had blown the sheet-steel barrier out through the side of the building, shearing off the vertical supports that held up the roof. When the plate crashed to earth, the armed land mines under it started popping off, sending fragments whining through the yard.

Lyons looked back and saw half the roof coming down. The barn was collapsing in on itself in a cloud of dust. And it was starting to burn. The shingles were already on fire from the burst gas tank, while the inside of the barn was burning from the satchel explosion, the flames licking out from under the split and jumbled debris.

Over the sounds of the detonating mines and the roaring fire, he could hear the moans of the men trapped and dying under the wreckage.

As he moved on, Lyons fed the Roadblocker a pair of Magnum shells to bring the magazine up to full.

McCARTER, FOLLOWED BY Schwarz and Blancanales, reached the front of the storage shed as Lyons disappeared around the burning gas tank and headed for the far side of the barn. The former SAS man took a second to admire his own handiwork. The LAW he had fired had scored a direct hit on the shed's machine-gun post, plowing right through the middle of the gun port. The force of the shock wave had blown the shed's door off its hinges. A quick look inside the doorway told McCarter that no one had survived the shrapnel spray.

He and the others were dashing across the open ground that separated the shed from the barn when Lyons's satchel charge went off. The barn doors on their side blasted open, and six militiamen blew out, followed by a roiling cloud of smoke, dust and straw. The men were running when the explosion hit them; they were knocked into the air, off-balance, and they hit the ground hard. Behind them, the barn roof beam split as the supports on the other side dropped away and the building started caving in.

Two of the militiamen landed on their stomachs facing the Stony Man warriors. Somehow they managed to get their guns up to cover their buddies' retreat. Their fire was full auto but poorly aimed.

McCarter, Schwarz and Blancanales shot their machine pistols from solid kneeling positions. The pair of militiamen died in the dirt where they lay.

The four others didn't turn around to see what had happened. They scrambled to their feet and made a beeline for the safety of the main house. They had a long way to go and very little time to get there.

Still kneeling, McCarter and the others punched out fifty rounds of precision fire. Through-and-through body shots kicked up dirt all around the fleeing men, and they went down in a tangle of arms and legs.

Another rolling cloud of dust whooshed out of the barn doorway as the far side of the building collapsed, taking the entire roof with it. McCarter, Schwarz and

Blancanales dumped their empty mags and reloaded before moving closer to the doors.

When they looked inside the ruined barn, everything was burning. It was a funeral pyre for the Sawtooth Patriots.

"Man!" Schwarz exclaimed, shielding his face with a forearm as flames shot out of the opening.

"Bloody hell," McCarter said.

"What's wrong?" Blancanales asked him.

"We can't get to the passage, dammit," McCarter said. "The passage leading underground from the barn to the bunker. Not until that bloody bonfire cools off."

"That could take days," Schwarz said.

"Come on," McCarter urged, breaking into a trot. He peered around the corner of the burning barn and saw Lyons waiting for them at the other end. McCarter gave the Able Team leader the thumbs-up sign, and they all crossed the open ground between the barn and the main house.

"WE NEED YOU to gun it, Sky King," Carmody said into the CB's microphone. "The departure schedule has been moved up." As he released the transmit switch, another explosion rocked the room.

"What's the damage?" Carmody shouted as he regained his feet.

"They've blown up the gas tank and taken the barn and storage shed," the communications officer said. "Nobody got out alive. The guys upstairs report that it's all burning."

Les Johnson's voice crackled over the CB speakers. "You got trouble down there, OGR?"

Carmody thought for a second. What was the point

in lying to the guy? As soon as he flew over the ranch, he'd see the place was burning down around them. If Johnson was going to scrap the mission, it was better to know it now, while there was still time to figure out an alternate escape plan. "Yeah, we got trouble."

"My price just went up."

"How much?" Carmody asked, as if it mattered.

"Times two," Johnson said. "In cash, as previously agreed. Is that a go?"

"Roger, a go, Sky King. What's your ETA?"

"Touchdown in ten. Airborne again in three."

"We'll be on the runway."

As Carmody switched off, the communications officer said, "Sir, we've got company in the bunkhouse passage. The sensors just went haywire. They're coming this way."

WHILE MANNING PLANTED a C-4 charge on the bunkhouse door, James and Encizo poured autofire into the ranch house side door and windows.

Answering fire from the main house picked chunks of wood out of the wall a foot above their heads.

"Hurry up!" James said as he dropped a spent mag and slapped a fresh one into his H&K subgun.

"Duck and cover," Manning said, tripping the detonator switch.

The bunkhouse door came down in a flash. While the smoke was still thick, they charged in, spreading out as they filtered through the doorway.

Gunfire erupted from under a tier of bunks, stitching a line of slugs across the drywall. It would have cut them down if they hadn't jumped at the first gun crack.

James returned fire with his H&K, aiming at the

muzzle-flash coming from under the bed. He saturated the bunk and its mattress with a storm of 9 mm parabellum slugs.

On the other side of the room, one of the machine gunners was trying to get his M-60 disentangled from the wreckage so he could point it at them. Manning and Encizo riddled the man with a flurry of 9 mm bullets, driving him against the sheet steel of the gun port. He slumped to his backside behind the still unfired machine gun.

The LAW rocket, followed by a fragmentation grenade, had done devastating damage to the room's occupants. The walls were streaked with smoke and blood spray, and peppered by thousands of hits by oddly shaped bits of steel. Bodies and body parts lay sprawled on the floor and across the beds. None of the Patriots in the bunkhouse showed signs of life.

As the warriors finished the grim work, Bolan entered the room through the doorway they had just blown.

"We're clear in here, Striker," James said.

"A clean sweep," Encizo added.

Manning was already at the trapdoor that led down to the underground connecting passage. He put down his satchel charge and rolled the limp body of a militiaman off the handle. "Think anybody is waiting for us down there?" he said as he straightened up.

"I don't think anybody got out of this room alive," Encizo answered.

"There's only one way to tell," Bolan said. The big guy moved the machine pistol to his left hand and with his right, picked up the satchel charge Manning had brought. "Cover my back."

"Cover *our* backs," James corrected him. "This is a job for two."

Bolan nodded, then gestured at the trapdoor with his subgun. "Open it up."

The Executioner and James descended the steep concrete stairway. They could see that the passage dead-ended on the right of its intersection with the stairs. Crouching just above the bottom step, Bolan peeked low around the corner, then jerked back.

The corridor was made of concrete blocks. The floor was poured concrete. Everything was smooth and well lit. There were no side passages, no niches big enough to conceal a gunman.

Bolan looked again, pausing a little longer before he ducked back. The corridor was clear. It ended in a heavy metal door that looked like it had been scavenged from a ship. On the other side of the door, if the informant's sketch was accurate, was the command bunker. He moved up the stairs so James could have a look.

When the former SEAL drew back, Bolan said, "Cover me from the stairwell while I plant the charge." Then he turned to Manning and Encizo, who waited above the trapdoor. "When the satchel blows," he told them, "get to the bottom of the stairs and back our play."

"Gotcha," Manning said.

Bolan stepped past James, down into the corridor. He moved low and quick along the far wall.

He saw the infrared sensors too late.

He had already broken the beams with his legs.

On the other side of the metal door, he had no doubt that alarms were going off. He whirled and raced for the stairs.

"Out!" he said to James, turning and pushing the man up the steps ahead of him. "It's a trap!"

"DROP THE LID on those bastards!" Carmody snarled.

Peterson, Gabhart and Ransom struggled with a large T-shaped metal handle set high in the wall that faced the bunkhouse. The long part of the handle was connected to a heavy multistrand cable that disappeared into a hole in the concrete block. Heaving in unison, the trio pulled the handle and its cable three feet from the wall. A second later came a heavy distant crash, the sound of steel against concrete.

"Kill the lights in there," Carmody said.

When that was done, the commander in chief of the militia stepped up to the flood valve. He opened the valve, then moved to the command bunker's door. On the other side of it, the roar of rushing water was clearly audible. A river was emptying into the narrow, sealed corridor. Water started seeping around the seals at the edges of the door.

Carmody bellowed into his side of the barrier, "How do you like that, assholes?"

Which brought a rousing cheer from the men in the bunker.

CHAPTER FOURTEEN

When Les Johnson was five miles from Old Glory Ranch, he saw the leaping, flickering light from the burning gas tank and barn. He had seen lots of similar fireworks during his career, so he knew exactly what kind of party was going on down there.

A party with full metal jackets.

He had to wonder if he'd sold his services too cheaply. Maybe he should've asked for three times the money.

He put the Beechcraft Kingair's controls on autopilot, undid his shoulder belt and picked up the body armor draped over the copilot's seat. He shrugged into the vest and adjusted the steel trauma plates so they didn't gouge into his torso.

In another four, maybe five minutes, he was going to be within range of whoever was attacking the Sawtooth Patriot's compound. He was dropping into a free-fire zone like a very dumb duck. He had to land his aircraft, turn it around at the end of the strip and take off in the opposite direction.

Seven thousand feet of runway made for a hell of a long shooting gallery.

Johnson and the Beech had to run the Old Glory gauntlet twice. With enough time in between each run for the adrenaline-pumped federal shooters to reload their weapons.

As he neared the ranch, he could make out more detail. The destruction at the far end of the compound was total, the buildings leveled.

It made him start rethinking his decision.

He owed the Sawtooth Patriots absolutely nothing. They owed him exactly nothing in return. Up to this point, everything between them had been on a cash-on-the-barrelhead basis. Johnson wasn't a member of the militia. He didn't subscribe to their paranoid philosophy. He had seen too much of the world to buy into any simple explanation of everything, but he did agree with their assessment that the world was going to hell in a handbasket.

That was on a par with agreeing that the sky was blue, or that all politicians were corrupt.

When it came to politics, Johnson didn't have any. He had lost interest in the American political system twenty years ago. If he had faith in anything, it was in the power of money and in his skill as a pilot. He liked lots of money and he liked a large helping of personal risk.

But he wasn't stone crazy.

He decided to overfly the ranch once at two thousand feet, to dip a wing as he passed and see if anybody took a potshot at him.

GARY MANNING TENSED as Bolan called for a retreat. He poked the muzzle of his H&K down at the stairwell, ready to provide cover for his teammates. He saw Bolan shove James up the staircase. There was a grating sound in the floor under his feet, and something clacked. A huge, well-greased latch. Manning stared helplessly down as, with a groan and a rush of air, the three-inch-thick steel door dropped from the edge of the entryway and crashed against the fourth concrete step, sealing the stairwell from wall to wall.

"Oh, shit!" Encizo said, lowering his weapon as he looked at the barrier. "Where the hell did that come from?"

"We friggin' missed it," Manning said. "Now we've got to get the damned thing up."

The Canadian jumped down into the stairwell and tried to get his fingers under the edge of the door. Encizo hopped down beside him. Both men struggled in vain. The door had gouged so deeply into the concrete that there was nothing to get hold of.

"I hear water running down there," Encizo said. "Sounds like lots and lots of water."

"Striker!" Manning said. "What's going on?"

There was no answer.

"This thing is heavier than shit," Encizo said. "Look what it did to the steps, it turned the concrete to powder. I don't think we could raise it even if we could get a grip on it."

"Striker! James!" Manning shouted.

"EVERY MAN IS BORN TO DIE," Oswald Carmody said to the twenty Patriots assembled in the command bunker, "but very few men get to die for something they believe in. I know you'll fight on here at Old Glory until your last drop of blood is shed. You know that I'd rather stay here and fight on alongside you, that I'd rather die alongside you, but we have a larger war to win. Skel, Gabhart, Link, Billy Ray and I will be making the same sacrifice, on another battlefield, in a few hours. Maybe we'll all regroup in a much better place, if that's God's will.''

He looked from man to man. ''The longer you hold the enemy at bay, the better the chance our ultimate mission will succeed. The Sawtooth Patriots are going to remake the world, and we start today.''

The militiamen gathered around him, putting their hands on his shoulders or patting his arms. They knew all about martyrdom. It was part of their special take on history, part of their end-times philosophy. Glorious martyrdom, like Waco, like Ruby Ridge. They had known for months that it was going to happen to each of them, sooner or later. They looked almost relieved that the waiting was almost over.

Ransom handed Carmody a miner's headlight and he put it on.

At the rear of the bunker, on the side of the ranch house that faced the mountains, was a four-foot hole in the wall. The hole had been concealed, until moments before, by a pair of metal cabinets that served as gun racks. The opening led to a tunnel made of corrugated pipe, also four feet in diameter. It was a combination air intake and escape tunnel for the bunker. For obvious reasons, only a handful of the militiamen at Old Glory Ranch knew of its existence. The corrugated sewer pipe led away from the bunker at a gradual, upward angle. At a depth of five feet, it passed under the minefield to the perimeter fence. On the other side of the fence, it was buried two feet under the surface and continued at that depth across the desert to the edge of the runway, where it ended in a camouflaged exit.

Carmody switched on his headlight and entered the tunnel first. The space was so narrow he had to crawl through it on hands and knees, his machine pistol hanging on a lanyard around his neck. He pushed the money bag up the passage ahead of him. Peterson, Ransom, Gabhart and Link brought up the rear.

They passed under the minefield without incident. Once they reached the perimeter fence, the going got easier because it was level. They were somewhere in the middle of the long tunnel when the pipe suddenly jolted and an explosion echoed from behind them.

"What was that?" Link said.

"Keep moving, man," Peterson told him. "Just keep moving."

A few minutes later, they broke through the camou netting at the mouth of the tunnel and crawled out into the night. Carmody looked back at Old Glory, burning. He could see muzzle-flashes lighting up the ground floor of the main house.

"Here comes the Beech," Ransom said, pointing at the sky.

"He's off-line for the runway," Peterson said.

The wing lights on the right side of the aircraft dropped as it passed over the compound.

"He's doing a flyby!" Link said. "The bastard's not going to land!"

MACK BOLAN STOOD in the pitch darkness, listening as water poured into the concrete passage from a series of pipes concealed in the ceiling. His ears were still ringing from the clang the trapdoor made when it dropped. The water level was rising quickly above his knees. It was cold.

"Striker?" James called, sloshing through the torrent toward him.

"Here," he replied. "Against the wall, another yard or so."

James brushed his arm with a hand. "Wow, is it ever dark."

Bolan checked the luminous sweep hand of his watch. "At the rate the water's coming in, we've got about four minutes before this chamber fills up to the ceiling. Let's see if we can't move the door."

They tried shoving on the back side of barrier, but they couldn't budge it an inch.

"What are we going to do?" James asked.

Bolan could hear the man's teeth chattering. It was river water pouring in, straight from the glaciers of the Sawtooth Range. If they didn't drown in the passageway, they'd surely die of the cold. At that moment, though, their odds of drowning looked real good.

"Manning!" Bolan shouted into the trapdoor.

The answer was muffled, but affirmative.

"You and Encizo get clear of the bunkhouse. Do it now!" Bolan said. He pressed his ear to the steel to make sure he could hear the reply.

"Roger, Striker," came the response. "We're gone."

Bolan shrugged out of the satchel charge's canvas strap. Then he dumped his combat harness. "Feel like a swim?" he asked James.

"We're going to swim out of here?"

"Not exactly, but we're going to have to hold our breath awhile under water."

"I can do almost two minutes, no sweat."

"That ought to do it." Bolan fumbled with his harness until he found the slim flashlight clipped there. He turned it on and played the narrow beam down the corridor. Water had climbed up all but three of the stairs, and was now almost completely filling the passage. Only about six inches of air space remained.

"When I give the word," the Executioner said, "we're going to dive in and swim to the sealed door at the other end of the corridor. We're going to stay under water until the satchel charge blows. Let's hope the concussion doesn't knock us both out."

James started filling his lungs, stretching them so they would hold more air.

With the flash between his teeth, Bolan primed the explosive package and propped it against the bottom edge of the barrier. "Let's go," he said to James. "Follow the wall." Then he dived into the water.

James knifed in after him. He lost the glow of the flashlight almost immediately and, as Bolan had suggested, found the wall with his hand and swam along it until he reached the end. Bolan waited for him there, hanging on to the door handle. James gripped the handle, too. Both men braced themselves for the explosion.

There was a bright flash of light, and a sudden, awful pressure that slammed their chests and eardrums. They didn't black out. Lungs screaming for air, they swam back down the passage to the stairwell. Both of them were thinking the same thought as they pulled themselves up the stairs: don't let the trapdoor still be there.

It wasn't.

As they scrambled up through the smoke, Manning and Encizo were there to help them out.

"Man, what a bang!" Manning said.

The bunkhouse was now open to the stars, the wind gusting through the nonexistent back wall sending bedding and personal items across the compound. The rising water helped to focus the explosion by confining the area it had to expand in. The stairwell acted like a concrete-barreled cannon, blowing the barrier up and out through the bunkhouse roof and taking out the side of the building in the process.

Sounds of full-auto gunfire from the main house mixed with the roar of a twin-engined aircraft turning for a landing approach.

"Somebody's trying to make a getaway," Encizo said.

"Not if I have anything to say about it," Bolan told him.

Dripping wet, the Executioner crossed the ruined room and tried to pull out an M-60 from under the rubble and overturned bunks. When he couldn't shift it, he turned to Manning and said, "Give me a hand here."

BEFORE HE CROSSED the threshold of the main house, Lyons thumbed in a pair of ear protectors. He put the sole of his boot to the side door in a powerful snap-kick that splintered away the lock. Something moved to his right as he entered. A muzzle-flash came from behind a couch. The wind made by flying lead brushed his face.

The house was full of rats.

Lyons detonated the Roadblocker into the front of the sofa. The couch jolted onto its back legs as an enormous hole opened up in the back cushion. Though Lyons was ten feet away, the muzzle blast of the Magnum shell set the plaid fabric on fire. He jerked the smoking sofa away from the wall. Behind it lay a headless man. Lyons took a second and smothered the flames with a pillow. He had no choice in the matter; they couldn't let the main house burn, not until they'd searched it.

As he straightened up, somebody else shot at him. He saw a man duck back into the doorway at the far end of the room. At some point, it must have been a family room or den. Now it was all sandbags and steel plate; in an emplacement on the right stood an abandoned M-60.

Lyons put his back to the wall beside the doorway and sucked in a quick breath. There were only two ways of doing anything: Ironman's and everyone else's. He didn't sneak a peek around the corner to see what he was up against, because it didn't matter to him. He spun around the doorjamb with the Roadblocker at hip height.

Four men stood in the hallway, armed with automatic weapons. One of them knelt behind a pile of sandbags, two stood half in and half out of doorways on either side of the corridor, while the fourth had no cover, and he was the closest.

Lyons fired before any of them could get off a shot. Two feet of flame belched from the Roadblocker's muzzle. The closest man took a center-chest hit that blew him off his feet and sent his vitals spraying out his back. Through-and-through .31-caliber steel balls whined down the corridor. Lyons rode the recoil wave as the semiauto cycled out the empty hull and chambered a live round. He rode it up and over to the man in the doorway on the right. A second boom shook the hallway. The doorjamb, the man's upraised gun, his arm and half his head blurred in a red cloud of mingled wood and bone chips.

Finally the militiamen in the hallway got it together

and returned fire. From the door on the left and the sandbags straight ahead, machine pistols chattered. Lyons dropped to a knee. As he did, he raised the 10-gauge's stock to his shoulder. He put two shots into the doorway. The first cut a ragged hole in the wall, which caused the gunman to step into view. Lyons's second shot practically tore him in half.

The guy down the hall had to raise himself above the sandbags in order to sight down on Lyons. When he did so, Lyons also rose and fired. The militiaman's arms flew out as he took a torso hit. His weapon clattered against the wall, and he landed, thrashing, on his back. Lyons couldn't hear his screams because of the earplugs, but he could see the man's wide-open mouth and pain-twisted face.

As Lyons approached the downed Patriot, he reached for the butt of the Colt Python he wore in shoulder leather. By the time he got up to the man, his legs had stopped kicking and there was no need for a mercy bullet.

Lyons moved down the hallway, checking rooms. He didn't find anything else until he reached the next-to-last room in the corridor. He had just finished sweeping the walk-in closet and was turning to make his exit when the wall in front of him started to disintegrate. A string of 9 mm holes stitched through the drywall from right to left. The slugs crashed into the closet's sliding doors behind him.

Lyons didn't have to think about the shooter on the other side of the wall, didn't have to wonder which end of the room he was in, which end of the line of holes he was standing at. He already knew.

The 10-gauge slammed his shoulder. It did worse things to the wall, blowing a foot-wide hole in it. The man on the other side was dusted with plaster and shredded by steel buckshot.

Lyons looked out of the doorway at the end of the hall. It opened onto the ranch's kitchen. A service counter was on his right, on the other side of that, the refrigerator, stove and sink.

As he stepped into the room, a man popped up from behind the kitchen counter. The M-16 in his hands flashed and spewed full-auto lead. Lyons touched off the Roadblocker, blasting a hole in the front of the counter. The impact of a storm of .31-caliber steel pellets sent the man crashing back into the refrigerator.

Lyons stripped live 10-gauge shells from his harness and thumbed them into the semiauto's tubular magazine. He looked around the counter to make sure the guy was dead. He was. He lay on his back in the middle of a pile of trashed food—milk cartons, eggs, lettuce, fruit. There were a couple of metal refrigerator shelf racks by his head.

Lyons removed one of the earplugs, so he could tell how the others were doing.

"Ironman!" a familiar voice shouted. "We're clear on this side."

"Right," he replied, taking out the other earplug. "Clear here, too."

McCarter, Schwarz and Blancanales stepped in from the dining room. They dumped half-empty mags on the floor and reloaded.

A sound overhead made them all freeze.

"Goddamn, that plane's coming in for a landing!" Blancanales said.

"That's not our problem," McCarter stated. "Bolan's team'll handle it. Our job is to secure the entrance to the bunker.''

"Something two guys could do," Lyons said. "I'm out of here. I'm going to stop that plane."

He didn't wait to hear any argument from the Brit. There was no argument. He was right.

Lyons hit the walkway between the main house and the remains of the bunkhouse at the same time as Bolan. Lyons took in the wet clothes and hair, the plaster-dusted M-60 and cartridge belt looped over his shoulder, and smiled. The Executioner had been busy.

There wasn't time for conversation. They could see the Beechcraft turning in the distance, preparing to land at the left end of the runway. On the right end, five figures stood huddled, waiting for their ride out of the killing ground.

"We've got no shot from here," Bolan said. He ran around the side of the bunkhouse, over the broken earth of the minefield and back out through the hole in the fence.

Lyons followed him in easy, loping strides.

As the Beech began its landing approach, they were still four hundred yards from the runway.

"I can hit it from here," Bolan said, setting the machine gun's bipod on the flat top of a boulder. He flipped the end of the cartridge belt to Lyons, took hold of the pistol grip and jacked a live 7.62 mm round under the hammer.

As he dropped the M-60's safety, the runway and compound lights went out.

A second later, the plane's landing and running lights winked out, too.

"Son of a gun!" Bolan said as his target vanished.

The Beechcraft glided in like a night owl, a hunter in the dark.

LES JOHNSON HAD FLOWN into Old Glory Ranch so many times that if he couldn't do it blindfolded, at least he could do it with the windows blacked out. He had already lined up for his landing and was beginning his descent when the runway lights went out.

That surprised him a little.

It was always a shock to see the ground disappear.

He didn't pull up and abort. He continued his downward glide, calmly reaching over to the dash and shutting off all the aircraft's running lights.

He started humming a little tune as he watched the red glow of his altimeter. The needle dropped to 4500 feet, then 4450. Another indicator dial told him the wings were level. 4425, 4420. He brought up the nose of the plane and cut the power.

The last ten feet were the longest.

As the Beechcraft fell through the dark, he couldn't know for sure whether he was still lined up with the runway. He was coming in at one hundred miles per hour. If the wheels hit sagebrush instead of asphalt, he was going to be a fireball in a big hurry.

With a jolt and a squeal, the tires hit tarmac.

He had pancaked it a bit, but he was down safe. Through the windshield, he could just make out the white line that marked the center of the airstrip. When he came to the warning lines painted at the far end, he braked to a stop and started his 180-degree turn.

The moment he stopped again, the passenger's door opened and Carmody and the other four men piled in. Rick Link was the last, and he took the copilot's seat.

Before Link had got the door closed, Johnson was

accelerating back the way he had come. He pounded down the throttle, dividing his attention between the white line in front of them and the rising needle on his speed indicator. He had made it in without getting nicked. It looked like he might make it out the same way.

As he lifted off, the Beechcraft shuddered from multiple bullet impacts. Heavy-caliber slugs punched through the middle of the cabin. To the left, the chatter of machine-gun fire was audible over the twin engines' roar.

Instead of pulling back on the stick and climbing, Johnson flew fast and low, maybe fifty feet off the ground. He knew the terrain, he knew that there were no obstacles between him and the mountains. He banked to put the tail of the aircraft toward the machine gun, presenting it with the smallest possible target.

Only when he was well out of M-60 range did he bank back to his original course and start to climb to cruising altitude. The wind whistled shrilly through the bullet holes in the fuselage. Johnson turned on the cabin and outside running lights and did a quick damage assessment.

The Beech was okay.

The worst damage had been done to the man sitting in the seat beside him.

"Rick! Jesus, Oz, he's been hit," said Peterson.

The assistant gunner slumped forward, held up only by his safety belt. Blood pooled on the floor under his seat. His mouth hung open, his face ashen.

Billy Ray Ransom reached over and felt for a pulse in Link's throat. "He's bought it."

"Open the door and dump him," Carmody ordered.

Ransom and Peterson unbuckled the seat belt and, as Johnson dipped the wing, pitched the warm corpse out into the night.

THE INVISIBLE AIRPLANE droned off toward the mountains.

"Did you hit it?" Lyons asked the Executioner.

"Who knows? I only had a good angle on it for a second. That pilot knew his stuff."

Behind them, the house lights came on, then the runway lights returned. Schwarz had probably restored the power, Bolan thought.

"How'd those guys get out of the ranch house?" Lyons demanded. "We had all the exits covered. We should've seen them."

"I was wondering the same thing. Remember that straight line in the aerial photo leading away from the compound? McCarter pointed out how the vegetation was messed up."

"The utility pipe?"

"I don't think it was a utility pipe. I think it's an underground escape tunnel."

"Got to be."

"Then we've got to close it off."

"How're we going to find it in the dark?"

"We're not going to be able to find the runway end of it, but we know that it crosses under the perimeter fence. And from the aerial photo, we know about where."

They returned to the edge of the compound and ran along the outside of the wire until Bolan noticed a slight rise in the ground in about the right spot. To verify, he sighted along the rise. It ran in a straight line in the direction of the runway. The Executioner dropped to his knees and started digging with his bare hands. Lyons got down on the ground and helped him.

After a minute or two, their fingers scraped corrugated metal. The pipe wasn't deeply buried outside the wire. They quickly uncovered a three-foot section.

"It slopes that way," Lyons said, "down into the bunker."

"What've you got over there, mates?" McCarter called from across the compound.

Bolan didn't answer, but just waved. What he had to say, he didn't want to shout. He and Lyons joined McCarter and Manning at the walkway entrance to the main house.

"The situation is a stalemate," McCarter told them. "The surviving militiamen are sealed in the bunker. We can't get at them through the flooded passage, and the passage under the barn is too hot to try. Manning and Gadgets can blow the door leading down, but if we go through it to get to them, they'll chew us to pieces."

"They'll rip us the same way if we try to go in through the escape tunnel," Bolan said.

McCarter frowned, so Bolan explained to him what they had found.

While he was doing this, Carl Lyons was looking up at the water tower, then at the hurricane fence, estimating the distances and angles with his eyes. "I've got an idea," he said. "If that tank's full, it might work."

Bolan got the picture at once. "They tried to drown

us," he said. "Turnabout's fair play. Manning, can you drop that water tower onto the fence?"

"No sweat."

"Can you drop it right where I tell you to?"

"Piece of cake, Striker."

Lyons and Bolan returned to the partially exposed pipe and stood there while Manning lined up the drop. Then Manning and McCarter attached C-4 charges to the girders that supported the water tower. When they were done, they waved for Bolan and Lyons to get out of the way and ducked around the corner of the building.

The sequential explosions at the base of the water tank's legs were small and precise; they severed the structure's supports like scalpel cuts. The far legs crumpled first, then as the tower began to tilt toward the fence, the near legs blew. With a shriek of tortured metal, the tall tower fell across the compound. The globe of the water tank crushed the fence flat, and the tower's support posts detonated dozens of mines as they crashed to earth.

As soon as the dust cleared, Bolan and Lyons started excavating the pipe in front of the tank's domed top. Manning joined them and slapped a small C-4 charge on the corrugated steel they had exposed. They all ducked and covered as he detonated it.

The result was just what they were looking for: the pipe was breached by a ragged, open maw, two feet in diameter.

"I can blow the tank, too," Manning said.

"Stand back," Bolan told him. The Executioner emptied a 30-round mag into the top of the tank, punching a tight ring of 9 mm holes in it. A torrent began to pour out of the ring of holes, into the shallow pit and the open pipe. The pit quickly filled, and the pipe started throwing up huge bubbles of air. Water rushed down the sloping tunnel, under the minefield and into the bunker below.

JAMES, ENCIZO AND Blancanales stood in the small bedroom near the trapdoor leading down to the command bunker. Through the armored floor, they heard the militiamen yelling as water rushed into the sealed room, panicking when they realized what was going to happen to them. Then somebody must've taken charge because the yelling stopped. They were getting themselves reorganized.

The Sawtooth Patriots only had one way out of the bunker, and that was up through the main house. James, Encizo and Blancanales were set up to ambush them as they came out. But they didn't come out.

From below came the sounds of single gunshots, a flurry of them, popping off all at once.

"The bastards are pulling a Waco on us," Encizo said.

When the gunfire stopped, there were no more human noises, only the sound of flowing water. It took Gadgets and Manning less than three minutes to mine and blow the steel door.

When the smoke cleared, they edged closer to the opening. There were still no sounds from below.

James armed a pair of concussion grenades and dropped them into the bunker. They clanged on the metal steps, then exploded one right after the other, raising a cloud of dust from the bedroom floor.

James went down first, followed by Encizo and McCarter.

"What a mess," Encizo said.

The bunker and all its occupants were history. The corpses of fifteen men lay sprawled in the ankle-deep water. Every head had a little entry hole in its face and a huge exit hole at the back of the skull. All four walls were spattered and dripping with blood and brains.

"Gadgets," McCarter called up the stairs, "we need you down here."

When Schwarz joined them, McCarter had him deactivate all the minefields. Then the Phoenix Force leader said, "We've got to do something about shutting off the water. It's going to make it hard to work down here if it gets much higher."

"I think I can fix that," Gadgets said.

As Schwarz hurried back up the stairs, McCarter addressed the men in the bunker and those waiting on the floor above. "Let's get on with it, gentlemen," he said. "We all know what we're looking for."

As CARL LYONS PASSED through the kitchen again, he paused in front of the refrigerator. The blood from the dead guy on the floor was puddled under him and smeared on the refrigerator door. Some of the doubleaught buck had gone right through him. Four tightly grouped holes marked the refrigerator door above the handle. Then Lyons noticed the blood seeping under the door's lower gasket. He reached for the handle and opened it.

The little light came on.

"Goddamn," he said.

Bolan came up behind him and looked over his shoulder.

The inside of the refrigerator was packed with humanity, a single specimen of humanity. The grossly fat man had evidently emptied the refrigerator of food, shelf racks and storage boxes, then he had wedged himself into the tight space in a fetal position. He had taken four steel marbles to the brain.

"Look," Lyons said in amazement, "he died sucking his thumb."

Bolan stepped over the body of the man on the floor and resumed the room-by-room search.

A few minutes later, he and Lyons came upon Carmody's study and the worktable. In silence, both men examined the documents spread out before them.

Lyons tapped the red circle on the street map, the circle decorated with a death's-head. "From this, it looks like we've located their target, if nothing else."

"Yeah, looks like," Bolan said. "Time to call home."

CHAPTER FIFTEEN

Stony Man Farm
7:04 a.m. EDT

Hal Brognola held up his hand for silence in the computer center. "Striker, please repeat," he said into the speakerphone. "Did you say there was no nuke?"

"No nuke, no cannon," Bolan replied via the scrambled link.

"Damn!" Brognola said.

"We covered all the ground inside the compound with Geiger counters," the Executioner continued. "We checked the underground passages, too. We haven't come up with any of the hardware we're looking for. Of course, they could've buried the nuke shell, the 155 howitzer and the truck somewhere out on the plain."

"Negative, Striker," Barbara Price said. "A detailed analysis of the aerial photos has turned up no evidence of that."

"From the maps and overlays we've uncovered at the ranch," Bolan said, "it looks like the intended target is the Internal Revenue Service processing center at Ogden, Utah."

"A symbolic target," Wethers commented.

"It does fit their 'get Big Brother off our backs' rhetoric," Tokaido agreed, looking up from his monitor. "What better way to remove big government from the American wallet than by nuking its number crunchers into the Stone Age? Maybe the militiamen even think they'll get some sympathy from choosing that as a target."

"In some quarters, they probably will," Wethers replied.

"The sick bastards," Delahunt said in disgust.

"Do we have a timetable?" Brognola asked Bolan.

"No, but I think we can assume they'll wait until the workers arrive before taking the shot."

"At the earliest," Kurtzman said, "that would be about five hours from now."

"We can assume they'll use the weapon as soon as possible," Brognola said. "They've got to know the longer they wait, the better our odds of stopping them."

"Do we know their firing position from the document you've recovered?" Price asked.

"Roughly," Bolan answered. "There's a mark on a map here that covers quite a bit of the area. You'll see what I mean when I fax it to you. I'm also sending a list of the titles of all the publications we found with it. If the militiamen have moved the weapon out of the truck and into a building, it could take some time to conduct a proper search."

"It's imperative that we take these guys out before they get into firing position," Brognola said, "otherwise, the risk to innocent people increases dramatically. We know the gun team can shoot quickly, and accurately. They proved that in Chocolate Canyon. I don't want them to sneak off a shot while we're kicking down the door."

"There's a phone number written on the edge of the map," Bolan said. "I don't know if it means anything. Can we get a location on it?"

"Let's have it," Delahunt said.

Bolan rattled off the number.

"I'm on it."

"There's something else I want to say."

"Go ahead, Striker," Price said.

"There's a good chance the evidence we're working on here may be a false trail, meant to distract us from the real attack."

"What makes you think that?" Kurtzman asked.

"The militiamen could have easily destroyed all this incriminating material before we took the ranch house. They had the time and the means. What I'm saying is, this looks almost too good to be true, especially the phone number."

"Are you telling us this isn't the real target?" Brognola said.

"I'm telling you I don't know whether it is or isn't. We know there are two gun teams. The one that stole the cannon in California and tested it in Utah and the other team that the informant said was drilling at the ranch with an artillery trainer. We don't know if each team has its own howitzer and nuke. If they do, maybe both teams are going to unload on the IRS. Or maybe there's more than one target. Or maybe one is just a decoy."

"I get the drift," Brognola said grimly.

"Do we have any idea where our boy Carmody went?" Bolan asked. "He wasn't among the dead, so it's a safe guess that he was one of the men who escaped.''

Kurtzman answered. ''Charles Krick's Learjet logged a flight plan from Cody to Newark. They've been in the air about fifteen minutes. My bet is they'll change destinations once they cross the Jersey state line, but they're definitely headed east. Their ETA is around noon, our time.''

''What about the Beechcraft?'' Bolan said.

''No sign of it yet,'' Brognola said. ''It wasn't at the airport. SAC Parker is still searching around Cody.''

''So we can't tie the five men I saw getting into the Beech to the Lear's departure.''

''Not yet.''

There was a long silence.

''Look,'' Bolan said finally, ''it'll be daylight in another half hour out here. I need to look over the test range they've been using. Maybe that'll clear things up. I'll call you back in an hour.''

''Talk to you then,'' Brognola said, and broke the connection.

''What Striker's saying is possible,'' Katz said. ''The Ogden hit might just be a ruse.''

''Sure,'' Kurtzman agreed, ''but the question is, how do we prove it, and quickly?''

Brognola shook his head. Every part of him was exhausted; he looked as if he'd been pounded with mallets. ''The bottom line here is we don't have containment. We still don't know where the nuke or the howitzer are, but we do know that somewhere out there we have a pair of gun teams willing and able to use them. We think we know what one of the targets is, but the other could be anywhere on the East

Coast. We know that the odds are one or both teams will fire their weapon sometime in the next five to eight hours. People, we're about to lose the handle on this one, and the stakes are too damned high to let that happen."

"What more can we do?" Kurtzman asked.

"Goddammit, Aaron, that's the point. If there is another target and it's a major city on the East Coast, we aren't going to be able to do the job by ourselves. There's too much ground to cover in the time we have. We're going to need serious backup before we're through, not just investigative manpower, but hard-strike capability. I'm going to call the Man right now, and let him know where things stand. Get him primed to take the jump when the time comes."

"Military assistance?" Katz said.

"Official-type," Brognola answered as he headed for the door, "the whole foggin' ball of wax."

"Bingo on that number," Delahunt said.

Brognola paused in the doorway.

"It's a pay phone at a highway rest area outside of Ogden."

"Well," Wethers said, "at least that fits."

"Carmen," Kurtzman directed, "let's get an immediate phone tap on that line. It may be their communication link." He turned to the youngest member of the Stony Man computer crew. "Akira, we need transportation for nine men and weapons from Old Glory to Ogden."

"Already started on it, Bear. I'll have a pickup plane in the air in ten minutes."

Brognola went into a private office to make the call. As he sat down at the desk, he reached into his shirt pocket and took out a white plastic pill bottle.

He popped the top and poured a bunch of white tablets into his palm. The antacids were double strength, and the big Fed ate twice the recommended dose, crunching them up and swallowing the gritty powder. He had a bad feeling about Ogden. What Striker had said made sense to him. If it hadn't, he wouldn't have been on the verge of interrupting the most powerful man in the most powerful nation on earth. He picked up the scrambled phone and hit the autodialer.

The hard part was, he already knew what the President was going to say.

He was going to say, "No."

Old Glory Ranch
6:30 a.m. MDT

AS SOON AS IT WAS LIGHT enough, Bolan and McCarter took a jeep from the compound and drove it out to the area the informant had sketched as the test range. It wasn't hard to find. It was a well-traveled path and they just followed the tire ruts. Bolan stopped the jeep at a place where the wheel tracks were all jumbled and crisscrossed and the sparse vegetation had been scuffed away by two-legged traffic.

McCarter knelt down and looked at the trampled earth and said, "They fired the trainer in this area. See all the holes in the ground where they staked down the tripod?"

Bolan nodded. "Yeah, this is the place, all right."

"Now all we've got to do is figure out what they were shooting at." McCarter took a compass from his jacket pocket. "Good thing that informant took a bearing for us. This is too big a country to play find-the-bloody-pickle in."

The Brit sighted in on a mountain in the near distance. "It's that way," he said, pointing at the summit.

Bolan followed the well-worn ruts and drove at high speed up the gradual incline to the base of the mountain. He stopped there, and they both got out of the jeep.

McCarter stretched out the kinks in his back as he surveyed the landscape above them. The hillside rising from the plain was a mix of thin soil and loose shards that had fallen away from the bedrock of the summit.

"We're going to have a hell of time collecting any hard evidence here," he said. "Even with a hundred men, all armed with metal detectors, every one of them lucky as bleeding hell, the chances of finding a spent trainer round on that slope is next to nil. If we can't find the evidence, Striker, then we can't verify that this hillside was in fact the test-range target. Without a clearly identified target, we can't even begin to guess what this artillery test range was designed to represent."

"Let's have another look at the aerial map," Bolan said. He unfolded it on the jeep's hood and found their position. "Look, there's a lake on the other side of the ridge we're facing. It's in a bowl between the peak and the side of the higher mountain above it." The Executioner checked the topo map for the height of the ridge.

"My guess is there aren't any trainer rounds in that mountainside," Bolan said. "I think they're all in the lake."

McCarter looked up at the ridge. "That means the

second team is drilling in preparation for an indirect-fire mission.''

''Right. They're practicing shooting a cannon over an obstacle and letting the round fall on the target. Sounds to me like they're planning to fire over a city skyline.''

''That's kind of a leap in logic, isn't it?'' McCarter said. ''Isn't it just as possible that the obstacle they're shooting over is exactly the same? More mountains, not skyscrapers. The second fire team could still be targeting the IRS at Ogden.''

''Not if they're on their way to New Jersey.''

The sound of an approaching aircraft made both men turn toward the runway.

McCarter scratched the stubble on his chin and said, ''Something tells me that's for us.''

Highway 15 Rest Area
Ogden, Utah
6:35 a.m. MDT

ED KELSO WALKED along the edge of the pavement, past the other semis parked in the truck section of the rest stop. Off to his right, the ground dropped away sharply. When he stepped over to the stone barrier of the lookout, he could see the river twisting through the narrow canyon below. It glistened like a greasy, green snake.

He closed his eyes.

He was standing on the edge of a towering cliff, but not this one.

He was about to jump off into space, but not this space.

The precipice he faced was inside his head. There

was no bottom to the canyon he visualized; its sheer walls were smooth as glass.

Once the numbers started falling, it would be easier, he told himself. There wouldn't be time to think. Just to act, to follow the drill.

He shivered. The morning was dry cold. Under his windbreaker, the MAC-10 hanging on a lanyard from his neck felt like a two-ton weight, bending his spine, dragging him down. He hadn't slept a wink.

All night long, every time he shut his eyes, he kept seeing the mushroom cloud. Like a hulking, dirty gray beast rising over the plain that led to the Salt Lake. And every time it rose, he thought, I did that. It was an event that would be photographed and videotaped from every conceivable angle, the images shown and reshown around the world for as long as there were human beings left to view it.

Every time the footage ran he could say: I did that.

All the sheeple thinking: Kelso did that.

The event would live forever, and so would he.

It made him want to puke over the lookout wall, not because he had any second thoughts about the terrible carnage he was about to inflict, but because he didn't know if he was truly worthy of such an honor. That kind of immortal fame belonged to the great conquerors and despots of history: Alexander III of Macedon, Augustus Caesar, Genghis Khan. Men who had changed the world by bending it to their will.

Kelso opened his eyes and looked down at the river. He shook off the nausea by telling himself that *worthy* didn't figure into it at all, that Fate now, as always, had done all the choosing. In which case he, like Alexander, like Caesar, was merely its instrument. As was the nuke shell and the cannon.

He walked across the parking lot to the rear of the militia's truck. Mallone was standing guard there. He wore a hooded parka that concealed the automatic weapon he carried.

"Anything going on?" Kelso said.

"Nope. I haven't seen anything suspicious. Everybody's still asleep around here, everybody but us."

"I'll send Ringman out to spell you."

Kelso walked along the trailer and climbed into the passenger's side of the truck. Speck was sitting behind the wheel. The curtain in front of the cab's sleeping area was drawn back, and Wiley and Ringman were lying down on the bunks. They looked relaxed, if not rested. At dawn, Kelso had told the gun crew what their target was. He wanted to give them plenty of time to get the whooping and hollering out of their systems. They had to be settled in, comfortable with the idea when H-hour came.

"How much longer until the call?" Speck asked.

Kelso looked at his watch. "We should hear in another hour and a half. Some time after eight."

"The call" was critical to the full success of their mission. According to plan, prior to his receiving full payment for the Soviet artillery shell, the nuclear middleman had shipped the goods to Salt Lake City in a heavy-duty washing-machine box. Still according to plan, he was withholding the PAL code until Carmody reached New York and transferred the rest of the money. Carmody was supposed to call them when he had been given the nuke's arming and firing sequence.

"Let's open the damned crate now," Speck said.

"We can close it up again after we have a peek," Wiley said.

Kelso was anxious to see the puppy, too, but he had his standing orders and they made perfect sense. Do not uncrate the shell until you are at the firing site. If something unexpected happens, if you get into a traffic accident, or if there's a skirmish with the law, you have a better chance of moving the weapon from the scene without raising an alarm if it's still in the washing-machine box. The National Guard howitzer could and would be abandoned because it was replaceable; the nuke was not. Those were the priorities.

"We don't touch it until we're in position," Kelso said.

Stony Man Farm
8:15 a.m. EDT

BROGNOLA HAD TO WAIT more than an hour for the President to return his call. When they were connected via the scrambler, he laid out the case for unprecedented action. The longer he talked, the stonier became the silence at the other end of the line. When the President finally responded, he gave it to Brognola with both barrels.

"Hal, do you seriously think that I want to go down in history as the first Chief Executive since the Civil War to order the use of full military ordnance against American citizens on American soil?"

"Sir, with all due respect, if we don't take decisive, large-scale action very soon, you may go down in history as the first guy at the helm when the nukes hit the fan."

"From what you've told me, you don't know that. In fact, you have no way of knowing at this point. But you're asking me to commit unspecified weapons of war, unselective, broad-impact weapons of war, for use in heavily populated areas. The potential collateral casualties and collateral damage to property are unimaginable. Unthinkable."

"Sir, if a nuclear weapon is detonated in a major East Coast city, the destruction and loss of life will be far worse. We're looking at damage control here."

"Only if the threat you outline is real."

"In my opinion, it is."

"You need to take care of business, Hal," the President said. "I understand the time factor in mobilizing sufficient force to do the job, but I categorically reject a military alert at this stage of the game. You haven't convinced me that the tactical situation warrants it. For all you know, your people may be able to contain the business in Utah this morning. If they do, this whole thing will go away like it never happened. I need solid proof before I will even consider authorizing such an operation. If I proceed without proof and the threat fails to materialize over your supposed East Coast target, I could have a nationwide panic on my hands."

"I understand, sir."

"Like I said, Hal, take care of business."

Brognola put down the phone. He had failed to get his point across that overwhelming lethal force had to be on standby, ready to defuse the situation if circumstances dictated. The Man wouldn't commit because there was too much jeopardy, political and social. The fallout wouldn't just be over Salt Lake City or Boston. Brognola had planted the idea, though. That was all he could do at this stage.

"The ball remains in our court," Brognola said to Kurtzman and Price as he returned to the computer center. "We're in sole charge of the operation until the Ogden attack is neutralized."

"He doesn't want to consider an East Coast primary target?" Price said.

Brognola shook his head.

"He's not alone there," Wethers said. "That would make for a real nightmare scenario. We could probably evacuate Ogden if we had to, but we couldn't possibly deal with Boston, D.C. or New York."

"Where are we?" Brognola said.

"Striker called back while you were waiting on the phone," Kurtzman told him. "The combined Stony Man teams are airborne via military jet. ETA the rest area by 08:30."

"And the test range?"

"He says it represents a separate target," Price replied, "not Ogden. Probably a big city. They practiced firing over a high obstacle to hit a lower-elevation target. From the scale of the test range, Striker estimates the range to the actual target is under four miles."

"That would give the gun crew a chance to escape the effects of the blast," Katz said, "but just barely."

"It fits into the high-angle-of-fire theory, though," Price said. "Tall buildings could absorb and block some of the blast effects, which would make a close-in shot less risky."

"It could be New York, Hal," Katz warned.

Brognola didn't respond. "Do we have any idea what their preferred targets are likely to be?"

"We're in the middle of running a word search of all the Sawtooth Patriot communications Justice has logged," Dr. Wethers said. "We're looking for frequency of usage and context in order to get a list of their priority targets. Then we can try to match the locations and the ranges with what we know about the trainer shots.''

''Sounds shaky as hell,'' Brognola said.

''At this point,'' Kurtzman explained, ''we've got nothing else to go on.''

''Assuming the worst,'' Brognola went on, ''that the East Coast is in imminent danger, I need a multipronged contingency plan that the President will agree to. Weapons, tactics, transport, personnel. With an emphasis on minimizing collateral damage and death.''

''Let's hope they find the nuke in Utah,'' Barbara Price said.

CHAPTER SIXTEEN

Highway 15 Rest Area
Salt Lake City, Utah
7:32 a.m. MDT

David McCarter sat in the driver's seat of an un-marked, cream-colored half-ton van. He was parked about 150 feet from the rest-room peninsula that jut-ted into the broad expanse of asphalt. Behind the rest-room building were some vending machines and a grassy area, and beyond that, the overlook to the can-yon and river.

From his position, the Phoenix Force leader could see all the other vehicles involved in the operation. To his right, nosed into the space at the tip of the peninsula, was the light blue utility van manned by Hawkins and Encizo. A little farther around the pe-rimeter, also in a nose-in space, Bolan and Manning sat in a white van. To his left, parked in the desig-nated truck and RV area, was a sixty-foot motor home driven by James. The RV also held Lyons and Blan-canales. The RV was the team's hole card in case the suspect vehicle tried to make for the highway en-trance at the other end of the parking lot. Depending on his angle when the critical moment came, James would either ram the truck or block its path to keep it from reaching the highway.

The suspect vehicle, a red Kenworth tractor towing a silver trailer, was parked almost directly in front of McCarter. They had identified the semitruck by matching the tread patterns on its tires with photos of the tire tracks taken at the Chocolate Canyon location. McCarter's view of the truck—and its view of him— was partially blocked by another semi that was parked between them. He could see the edge of the right rear of the trailer and the man in the long overcoat leaning against it.

Earlier in the morning, McCarter had done a walk-by himself. Only someone who knew what to look for would've noticed anything out of the ordinary. The cuts in the roof weren't visible from the street. The gun crew had washed the trailer down pretty thoroughly, but they had missed some burned propellant on the outside of the rear-door hinges. The clincher, though, was what the gun blast had done to the trailer itself. Its walls were no longer true, but bulged in the middle where half the rivets were missing.

McCarter could also see the pay phone from where he was parked. Two men stood beside it. Gadgets Schwarz had already taken their pictures. He had also photographed the three other men who had entered and exited the suspect truck in the past hour. At that very moment, all the photos were being compared against Justice Department computer banks in an attempt to get positive IDs on the men involved. A check of the license plates on the truck and trailer turned up nothing; if the vehicle had been stolen, the theft hadn't been reported yet.

The two guys by the phone were obviously waiting for an incoming call. They had even taped a phony Out Of Order sign on the coin box to keep the line free.

Were they waiting for the go-ahead from Oswald Carmody to hit the IRS processing center, or were they waiting for the PAL code so they could detonate the weapon on the target?

The Stony Man team didn't know, but, when and if the call came through, they were in a position to get the answers because the pay-phone line was tapped. In the back of McCarter's van, Schwarz was set up and ready to record and monitor the conversation, which would also be routed directly to Stony Man's computer lab.

The combined Phoenix and Able offensive had been postponed in the hope that a call would come through for the howitzer team, that it could be traced and that it would lead back to the other gun crew. After what had happened at Old Glory Ranch, McCarter was grateful for the slight delay. There had been a lot of people at the rest stop when they had first taken up their positions—rows of truckers still asleep in their cabs after a long night on the road, RVers on vacation getting a late start on the day. The situation was somewhat less dangerous to bystanders now, as most of the truckers and RVers were gone. There was still the very real possibility that the bad guys would go down fighting or would kill themselves. McCarter needed at least one of them alive, in case the nuke wasn't in the trailer and the phone didn't ring.

He heard Schwarz rustling around in the back of the van, which was packed with commandeered phone equipment and a computer with a modem and fax. The curtain that separated the driver from the cargo compartment opened a crack.

"We've got an incoming from the Farm," Schwarz said.

He passed McCarter the scrambler-equipped cellular phone.

"McCarter here."

"This is the Bear. How's it going?"

"Our friends at the pay phone are getting very nervous. One guy's been to the bathroom twice in the last twenty minutes. I think the call they're expecting is way overdue."

"Maybe it isn't coming," Kurtzman said. "Krick's Learjet never made it to Newark. At the last minute, it diverted to a private strip near Paterson. We couldn't get Bureau personnel on-site before the plane took off again. According to the airstrip's field crew, six men exited the plane and got into a waiting minivan. That was over an hour ago. If they were going to call the pay phone, they've had plenty of time to do it."

"We can't afford to wait any longer," Barbara Price cut in, "not if we want to have any margin for error at this end. We have to assume the Ogden team has been stood up by their pals. We're all agreed that you should take them down now, before they decide to make a move."

"Do it as quickly and gently as you can," Kurtzman cautioned. "We not only need survivors, but we need them to be in good enough shape to answer questions."

"We'll do our best," McCarter said, and signed off.

He used the cellular phone to call each of the other vehicles and inform them of the change in plans and the new parameters. When he was done, he picked up the Colt Woodsman .22 from the passenger's seat and checked to make sure there was a hollowpoint round in the chamber. The autopistol's two-inch barrel was extended by another five inches by a Kissinger-designed silencer. Coupled with the subsonic ammo, it made about as much noise as a worm's sneeze.

The Phoenix Force leader picked up a newspaper from the dashboard and pretended to read it while he kept an eye on the two men by the pay phone. The way one of the guys was powering down the vending-machine coffee, McCarter figured it wouldn't be long before he made another pit stop.

It wasn't. When McCarter saw the guy head for the rest room, he bailed out of the van. As he did, he put on his sunglasses. It was the signal for the attack to begin. He crossed the asphalt with the Woodsman concealed under the folded newspaper.

The blue van's engine started up, and Hawkins began to back it out of the parking space at the end of the peninsula.

When the suspect entered the rest room, the white van's doors opened and Bolan and Manning hopped out. In one hand, Manning carried a yellow plastic Closed For Cleaning sign. He placed it on the concrete outside the men's room, then followed Bolan through the door.

As McCarter stepped up on the curb, behind him, across the parking lot, the doors of the motor home popped open and Lyons and Blancanales jumped out. They closed in on the Kenworth truck and trailer, as McCarter closed in on the pay phone.

It rang when he was thirty feet from it. The sudden sound surprised the guy leaning against it and made him flinch.

At about the same time the phone rang, Hawkins drove the blue van along the front of the rest room and stopped against the curb, blocking the gun crew's view of the phone and the lavatory entrance.

McCarter was ten feet away when the man beside the pay phone turned, ducked under the privacy hood and picked up the handset. He put a finger in his left ear so he could hear better over the sound of the highway traffic.

Whatever Gadgets Schwarz said to him, it must've been very upsetting because the man dropped the phone and whirled around.

If his intention was to run back to the truck, he realized, as he looked up into a pair of hard green eyes, that he was going to have to go through David McCarter to get there. He started to reach into his open jacket.

"Don't," McCarter said, letting him see the silencer's fat blue-black muzzle sandwiched between the folds of newspaper. He tried his best to sound convincing, earnest, concerned. "You don't have to die here, mate. You have a choice."

The expression on the man's face said he surrendered. The guy let his hand fall away from his jacket. As he did so, he shook a long, thin-bladed knife from his sleeve and, in a blinding rush, thrust it at the front of the Phoenix Force leader's throat. When McCarter managed to draw back enough so the strike came up short, the man tried to gut him, whipping the knife straight down, slicing through the front of his shirt from collarbone to navel.

McCarter shot him once, center chest. The sound of the silenced .22 pistol was lost in the highway's racket. As the man slumped back against the phone hood, the Briton surged forward, catching him under the armpits. He manhandled the guy over to the sliding door on the side of the light blue van just as Encizo opened it from the inside. McCarter dumped the man through the open doorway, and Encizo helped to roll him onto the floor.

"The only way we're going to get any information out of this guy," Encizo said as he reached for a tarp, "is if we hold a seance."

"That bloody sod left me no choice," McCarter said. "Let's hope we have better luck with the others."

Then he turned back for the rest room.

As THEY WALKED down the aisle between the rows of parked semis, Lyons's and Blancanales's view of what was going on at the pay phone was blocked by the light blue van. Their immediate concern was the man standing guard at the rear of the suspect trailer. If he shouted a warning, the men in the truck cab could get the big rig rolling and make everything real messy in a hurry. The rear guard had to fall first.

They could see the man was worried about the position of the blue van. He didn't like not being able to maintain eye contact with his pals. As the Able Team Warriors closed on his position, they saw him step away from the trailer, his long overcoat flapping around his knees, his cowboy boots clunking on the tarmac as he tried for a better look.

Lyons and Blancanales got within twenty-five feet of him before he sensed their approach. His reactions were cat quick. As he spun on them, out from under the long coat came a silenced blue-steel machine pistol.

Blancanales had rehearsed in his head all the things he was going to say to the guy to convince him to give up without a fight. He was going to tell him that no one at Old Glory Ranch had survived, that the militia movement was dead, that he had to think about himself, about his own survival. That under the circumstances, there was no shame in that, and a man had to make his own peace with the world. Pol was going to ask him about his family. Ask him if there weren't people he loved who would miss him when he was dead. He was going to tell him that a prison term wasn't the end of the world. That he could do his time and get out before he was too old to enjoy himself.

All the things Pol had rehearsed went out the window as the MAC-10's muzzle moved from the vertical to the horizontal.

Blancanales and Lyons had danced to this tune before.

They each stepped wide and fired almost simultaneously. Their silenced machine pistols spit 9 mm lead into the man's chest. The mushrooming bullets crisscrossed through the space that held a beating human heart.

It beat no more.

The Patriot's gun hand dropped, convulsing as he died, and sending a dozen rounds of parabellum lead into the ground at his feet, digging shallow little pits in the asphalt.

"Let's get him under the trailer," Blancanales said, bending down and grabbing the man by his boots.

With Lyons's help, it only took a minute to hide the corpse. They straightened up and surveyed the scene. Apparently no one had seen what had happened. There were no shouts of alarm. A flock of birds tweeted at the trash receptacle along the walk, and from the open window of a nearby fifth-wheeler, a family squabble was in progress.

Lyons and Blancanales split up, moving along opposite sides of the suspect rig. Lyons slipped up on the driver's door. Noiselessly he climbed from the gas tank to the footstep. The driver wasn't looking when Lyons suddenly appeared outside the window. To get his attention, Lyons tapped on the glass with the barrel of his weapon.

The guy must've had a subgun in his lap because holes started popping through the outside of the red door.

Lyons let go of the hand grip and let himself fall away from the cab. A salvo of slugs sailed over him, thwacking into the trailer of the next rig in the row. He fired as he dropped, sending half a clip into the door. He had a split-second glimpse of the driver's head shuddering from the impacts, then he hit the ground hard on his tailbone and elbows.

On the other side of the cab, the passenger bailed out. Lyons saw his feet hit the pavement.

"Hold it," Blancanales said.

The guy didn't hold it. He took off running.

Lyons rolled to his feet and braced his weapon against the truck's front fender. He had no shot because of the bystanders. The guy had ducked around some tourists walking back along the canyon-side path and he kept on running down the path. If the guy was armed, he wasn't showing a weapon yet.

Blancanales hid his own gun and took off after the militiaman. Lyons followed in easy strides.

They both thought they had him. The guy had no-where to run. The canyon cut off all escape.

Well, perhaps not quite all.

Lyons and Blancanales couldn't do anything but watch as he jumped the low wall and ran off into space. His legs were still pumping as he dropped out of sight.

He didn't scream. In fact, he didn't make a sound.

The two members of Able Team ran back to the truck. While Lyons checked on the condition of the driver, Blancanales opened the trailer's side door. He did this cautiously, with his weapon out, even though they didn't think there was anyone left inside.

Lyons joined him and said, "The driver is iced, too."

"So we went zero-for-three," Blancanales said. "That sucks. We'd better see what we've got inside."

When they climbed into the trailer, the first thing they saw was the gun.

"The California Guard will be glad to get this baby back," Blancanales said, patting the carriage of the M-198 howitzer. While he walked along the wall to the front of the cannon and looked under the barrel, Lyons examined the 155 mm HE shells secured to the front inside wall.

"If we add in the four rounds we know they fired at Chocolate Canyon," Lyons said, "this totals up to all the conventional ordnance that was reported stolen from the armory."

"So where's the nuke?" Blancanales said. "There's nothing at this end of the trailer."

"We've got one thing left up here," Lyons said.

When his partner joined him, he indicated the wood-reinforced cardboard box that had Washing Machine written all over it. "It's got to be in here."

"It's about the right size," Blancanales said. "Let's have a look."

Using his commando dagger, Lyons pried off the top of the box and set it aside. He had to remove the interior packing to expose the box's contents.

Blancanales looked in and said, "What the hell is going on here? Is this supposed to be some kind of joke?"

"If it is, it isn't funny."

KELSO PLUGGED MORE CHANGE into the vending machine, punched the button and waited while the paper cup filled with black coffee. It would be his last cup for a while, he told himself, since he was starting to get jittery. Carmody was an hour late in making the call. Something real bad could've happened at the New Jersey end. They could've been arrested, or the middleman could've pulled a no-show, leaving them without a PAL code and stuck with a worthless nuke. Maybe the guy never had the code to begin with...maybe it was all a scam.

It didn't occur to him that he and Speck and the others might have been the ones suckered. He still thought he was going to write his name in dirty gray smoke across the pages of the history books.

He picked up the coffee and took a sip. It went down his throat like battery acid. The day had turned out bright and clear. A few sheeple filtered by him, moving to and from the rest rooms and candy machines, exercising their miniature schnauzers and cameras on the scenic walkway. He didn't make eye contact with any of them. Under his jacket, the machine pistol rode uncomfortably against his chest; the bottom of the magazine felt as though it was wearing a hole in his shirt. He took the coffee with him back to the pay phone where Speck stood waiting.

"What are we going to do?" Speck said. He had a worried look that Kelso didn't remember ever seeing before.

"We wait a while longer."

"And if the call still doesn't come? What are we going to do then?"

Kelso had been thinking about their options for the past fifteen minutes. "We can always walk away from the gun and the nuke," he said. "Hitch a ride down into town and from there split up and go our separate ways. Or we can stash the gun and the nuke somewhere until we find out what happened to Carmody and the PAL code. Drive to a safe place, dump the trailer and the tractor."

"The third possibility," Speck said, "is to just suck it up and do the dirty deed."

"If we don't arm it, it won't explode."

"But it'll break when it hits. The plutonium'll go all over the place. It'd take a major cleanup effort to make the building safe again."

"That's a minor inconvenience compared to what we could do with an armed weapon. I say, if we don't hear in the next few minutes, we get the hell out of here. Then we sit on the tools until we can use them in the way we planned."

"Yeah," Speck said, "I guess that makes the most sense."

"I've got to use the head again," Kelso told him. "I'll be back in a minute."

THE TWO MEN WHO FOLLOWED Kelso into the rest room both had weapons drawn. Mack Bolan held a silenced Beretta 93-R, and Gary Manning wielded a silenced MP-5. They checked under the doors of the other stalls to make sure they were unoccupied.

Through the crack between the stall door and the metal wall, Gary Manning could see Kelso adjusting his machine pistol. He nodded to Mack Bolan, who started to move for one of the unoccupied stalls.

Manning aimed through the crack and took the shot with his 9 mm. The H&K coughed, spitting a puff of smoke and ejecting a bright casing onto the concrete floor. The jacketed hollowpoint hit Kelso high in the right shoulder, shattering the joint.

KELSO GROANED and his knees started to buckle, but he caught himself against the wall with his left arm. His right arm hung useless at his side. Turning, he struggled to find the grip of the MAC-10 with his clumsy, nondominant hand.

Then a guy dropped down on top of him from the top of the stall wall at his back. Two hundred pounds landed on his shoulders. Pain screamed through his broken joint, and he collapsed.

When he opened his eyes, Kelso was looking into the silencer of a Beretta 93-R.

"We're going to walk out of here," the black-haired man with the Beretta told him as he reached over and unlocked the stall door. "You're not going to make a fuss. We're going to get into the light blue van at the curb. Do you understand?"

The barrel-chested guy opened the stall, then picked up a spent shell casing from the floor and put it into his pocket.

The black-haired guy pushed him out of the stall, then the two men bracketed him out of the rest room and walked him toward the blue van. Clutching his shoulder, Kelso looked over at the pay phone.

Speck wasn't there, but the handset hanging down on its metal-armored cable was still swinging. A stocky guy with green eyes picked it up and put it back on the hook. Then he retrieved the Closed For Cleaning sign and swung into step beside them.

"Closed for business is what you are," he said to Kelso. He had a British accent.

The other two men hurried him into the waiting van. They pushed him onto the floor beside a tarp. There was a long, still form underneath the canvas. When they all got in and shut the door, it was crowded in the back of the van. He counted four men plus himself.

"He's bleeding pretty bad," the man who had shot him said.

"Has he said anything?" the Briton asked.

"Not even ouch," the black-haired guy replied.

Then the van started to move. The driver took it around the parking lot and slipped in beside the red Kenworth. The Briton opened the sliding door.

"What do you think of that?" he said, nodding toward the truck.

The panel on the driver's door was riddled with bullet holes—some exits, but mostly entries.

"We got the truck, the howitzer and all your friends," the Latin-looking man said. He flipped back the edge of the tarp to reveal Speck's corpse. "Don't you think it's time you started talking to us?"

Under Kelso's fingers, blood was oozing forth

steadily. It had already soaked through his sleeve and into the lining of the windbreaker.

"Carmody stiffed you, huh?" the black-haired man said. "He left you holding the bag."

"I want a lawyer," Kelso said.

The British guy laughed at him. "We're not cops," he said. "You're not under arrest."

"You're in much deeper shit than that," the man who'd shot him warned.

"Aren't you a bit puzzled by all this?" the black-haired guy asked him. "I mean, how we got on to you so quickly? Sure you are, it's eating you up inside. And we don't want that."

Kelso glared at him.

"The reason we found you so easily is because your commander in chief left us a trail a mile wide that led right here." He waved the maps in Kelso's face. "As you can see, the number of the pay phone is written in the margin of the map that shows your firing position and the intended target. A careful guy like Carmody doesn't make a mistake like that without meaning to. It explains why he never called you, doesn't it? Face it, you're the patsy in this. The all-day sucker."

"He played you like he played everybody else," the barrel-chested man continued. "Fake reports and fake verifications of troop movements, of black helicopters, of Soviet trucks on freight trains. All of it, from beginning to end, has been one big lie. In the last eight hours, a lot of people have died on account of this asshole. He didn't care what happened to the men at the ranch and he doesn't care what happens to you. To him, you're just a means to an end."

"We want to know where Carmody is," the Briton

said. "We want the location of the real nuclear target. If you help us, it'll go a whole lot easier on you."

"No way," Kelso said. His head was suddenly spinning. What did the Briton mean by "real nuclear target?" They had to have found the weapon in the truck by now. Unless Mallone or Ringman had somehow managed to make off with it. Oh, wouldn't that be choice! Despite his pain, he wanted to laugh out loud.

"We've got something to show you," the black-haired man said.

They pulled him out of the van and dragged him around to the side of the trailer. There were two guys inside. They helped to jerk him up and in.

The second Kelso saw the washing-machine box standing there, he knew it was all over. The lid was off the crate, and the packing was dumped on the floor.

They shoved him over to the box and forced him to look inside.

"Son of a bitch," Kelso said.

"What the bloody hell were you going to do with that?" the Brit asked him. "Clean up the government one load at a time?"

PART THREE

OPERATION FIRESTORM

CHAPTER SEVENTEEN

Union City, New Jersey
10:14 a.m. EDT

Captain Andrei Sarnov dropped the magazine of the Valmet M-76F and checked the 7.62 mm round on top of the stack. It had a black tip, which meant it was U.S.-manufactured M-61. Armor-piercing. He slapped the mag back into the Finnish knockoff of the Soviet AK-47 assault rifle and made sure the fire-selector switch was set on Safe.

"You did well, Tasha," he said.

"Thank the embassy's Intel people. They scrounged up all the gear. I just put in the order."

He looked at her. Her face alarmed him, but he was stretched so thin on this mission there was nothing he could do about it.

"You must be tired," he said. "I wish I could relieve you, but you know the situation."

"I'm okay," Beloc said. "I've felt worse and still done my job."

"I know you have." He took a set of car keys from the slash pocket of his leather bomber jacket and set them down on the roof beside the walkie-talkie he had brought for her. "Those are the keys to the sedan parked at the foot of the fire escape," he said.

"Fine."

Sarnov raised himself from a sitting position and looked over the edge of the derelict factory's roof. He scanned the warehouse opposite with a pair of compact binoculars. Ten minutes earlier, shortly after he, Ferdishenko and Turgenev had arrived on the scene, all of the regular workers at the International Scrap Metal warehouse had exited the building carrying their coats and lunch boxes. They had all driven away with smiles on their faces. Apparently their boss had given them the rest of the day off, with pay. The only car left in the parking area was Sergio Ishmael Eshamani's stretch limousine. The only people who remained on the premises had machine pistols under their coats.

Three men in gray suits and silk T-shirts stood in front of the building; three more were at the sliding doors on its right side. They looked like the same brand of thug that had escorted Eshamani in Riga and had guarded his London residence. According to Beloc, there were at least three more of the hired guns inside.

Four against nine wasn't impossible odds, especially with Beloc behind the German-made sniper rifle, but Sarnov had already decided against a confrontation at the warehouse. With all the sentries milling around outside, the Spetsnaz team couldn't get close enough to the warehouse to be able to tell if the *starookha* was actually there. Based on the morning's activity, it looked like it had to be, but they had no way of knowing for sure. If they attacked and it wasn't there, they would have shown their hand to

Eshamani, which would leave them no alternative but to torture him until he gave it up. If the *starookha* was there and it was hidden in the cargo containers that Beloc had described to him, they would need time to find it. Lots of time. If they got into a firefight, the battle was bound to be prolonged since the Sicilians could easily retreat inside the building to defend it. A prolonged firefight, even in a fairly deserted area like this, would certainly bring the police, who would surround them. The weapon would be discovered by the American authorities, and the Russian government would be publicly embarrassed and humiliated.

Under the circumstances, Sarnov had decided that he wouldn't try to take the weapon out of the warehouse. Tactically the best thing for him to do was to wait until the nuclear shell was transferred to the buyer and the buyer left the building with it. If they attacked the transporting vehicle on the street, they could kill all the opposition in a single fusillade of AP rounds, take the shell and be gone before anything could be done about it by Sicilians or the New Jersey police. To that end, Sarnov had appropriated three embassy vehicles—a step van and two late-model sedans. Ferdishenko and Turgenev were already in position in the van at the north end of the block, but they were, as yet, unarmed. He had to do something about that, and quickly.

It only took him a moment to return the Valmet back into the three-gun carrying case. He picked it up, patted Beloc on the shoulder and, in a crouch, slipped back from the front of the roof.

He took the fire escape down to the street. Keeping close to the factory's high wall, he ran past the car he'd brought for Beloc, then hurried around the corner where his own vehicle was parked. He opened the rear door of the sedan and put the gun case on the back seat. After transferring one of the Valmets and a pair of extra magazines to the front seat, he drove around the block to where the step van was parked.

As he pulled in behind it, Ferdishenko opened the back doors from the inside. He gave his captain the thumbs-up sign as he accepted the gun case from him.

Sarnov pulled a U-turn and returned the way he'd come. He parked near the intersection of a cross street a block south of the warehouse. Although he was well back from the corner, he could still see the building. Grabbing the Valmet by its pistol grip, he drew the select-fire weapon into his lap. He worked the actuator handle once, putting a live 7.62 mm round under the hammer. After rechecking the safety, he set the weapon on the seat and rolled down the passenger's window.

The walkie-talkie sitting between the front seats chirped. It was Beloc.

"A vehicle's coming toward the warehouse from the south."

"Got it," Sarnov said, looking to his right. He broke the connection.

The gray Dodge minivan had six men in it. It sped past his position and turned into the International Scrap Metal driveway. As it parked next to the limo, the Sicilians deserted their posts at the side and front of the building and moved into firing stances all around it.

For the first time since his arrival in the States, Sarnov felt a surge of confidence. He had already chosen the north and south ambush sites, and they were perfect. No matter which way the transporting vehicle turned, the Spetsnaz team was ready to take it out. At one hundred yards, the armor-piercing rounds in their Valmets would penetrate a half inch of steel plate.

To reach the highway with the *starookha* would take nothing less than an M-1 tank.

AS HE DROVE the minivan down from Paterson with Skel Peterson and the gun crew in the back and Charles Krick in the shotgun seat, Oswald Carmody wasn't thinking about the men he'd left behind at Old Glory, the men under his command who had surely died. And he wasn't thinking about the gun team that he had sacrificed in order to confound his enemies and buy him the time to work. There hadn't been any news about Old Glory or Ogden on the TV in the Learjet, and five hours later, there was none on the car radio, either. It was as if nothing had happened. But he had expected that, the power of big government to conceal was enormous, especially when it was playing catch-up.

What kept running through Carmody's mind as he followed Krick's directions to the warehouse was what a perfect target the United Nations made. Because it was located on the eastern shore of the East River, there were no tall buildings to block observation of the registration shells. The spotter could do his work from the west side of the river. They had considered firing the cannon from the Long Island side, shooting the nuke straight across the river, but had decided against it because they felt it was too close to ground zero. Not only would they have been exposed to more fire-blast, but the weapon location would have been easier to pinpoint.

If the UN's physical location made it a good

choice, what it represented in the rhetoric of the militia movement made it ideal. It was more than merely symbolic of the concept of one-world government that the Sawtooth Patriots were up in arms about. The land the UN was on was no longer a part of the U.S.; it had been ceded to the world body. It was an island of invasion—literally an encroachment by a consortium of foreign powers, something that would've made the blood of the founding fathers boil. What better way to start a war for freedom than to obliterate that island? And if a quarter-square-mile of Manhattan went up along with it, if half of New York City was made uninhabitable for decades, so much the better. The idea was to create a rallying point for the millions of disaffected, disenfranchised citizens. Then all the elements would be in place for revolution: a simplistic ideology, a well-defined enemy, a charismatic leader and the final, perfect spark.

Carmody thought about Charles Krick, too. He was surprised that the man hadn't remained on his private jet. Evidently he had underestimated the depth of Krick's anger and commitment. Krick had a serious bone to pick with the status quo. It was so serious that he didn't just want to be the banker on Operation Firestorm; it wasn't enough for him that through his contacts, they had arranged to purchase the nuke and the cannon to fire it. Krick wanted to get some gun grease under his manicured fingernails.

And why not? Big government had taken everything from him. The fruit of the labors of most of his adult life. And with the ever tightening noose of environmental laws, government was making sure that he could never earn his fortune back again. The Feds were simultaneously robbing and hobbling him. Even if Krick did earn it all back, what was there to stop them from robbing him of it all over again? Krick felt that the time to strike was now and he wanted to be a part of it.

That was fine with Carmody. They were one short on the gun crew with the loss of Rick Link, anyway.

When Carmody pulled the Dodge minivan into the driveway of International Scrap Metals, Eshamani's hired hands came running. Four of them stepped up to the front of the vehicle, two more to the side—keeping their firing lanes clear. The miniUzis they carried were very short, even with the attached silencers. Carmody didn't much like going eyeball-to-eyeball with almost two hundred rounds of ammunition.

Neither did the other Sawtooth Patriots.

"Who are the greaseballs?" Skel Peterson said as he unfastened his seat belt.

"And why are they pointing all those fucking guns at us?" Billy Ray Ransom asked.

"They're just taking care of business," Charles Krick told them. When he got out of the van, he did so with both hands in the air. "We're expected," he said to the gunmen.

Before he'd advanced three feet, he was grabbed, turned and flung up against the van's stubby hood. The Sicilians roughly frisked him for weapons.

"Do know who I am?" Krick said. "Call your boss. Call him right now!"

"Stop that, Tonio," Eshamani said from the warehouse doorway. "Let him go."

His capo looked disappointed. It had been a very boring morning so far.

"I'm sorry, Mr. Krick. The boys are a little on edge

today. Come on inside, all of you. Let them pass, Tonio.''

Krick came empty-handed, but the rest of the gun crew left the minivan carrying heavy tool bags, backpacks and tubular cardboard map cases. They filed through the warehouse's front door and into the small, dingy office area. The Sicilian soldiers remained outside. The slack was picked up by a trio of armed mafiosi inside the doorway.

Eshamani continued to apologize to Krick for the rudeness of his men. "The problem was I told the boys to expect four semis, one for each of the cargo containers. When they saw the little van, they didn't know who you were. Will the trucks be arriving shortly?''

"Yes," Krick said, "but before they do, we need to examine all the goods.''

Carmody noted the surprise on Eshamani's face. The arms merchant was not the least bit pleased by the request.

"Examine?" Eshamani said. "But everything is packed in the cargo containers. I don't mind telling you that I have gone to a great deal of trouble and expense to conceal it from a customs search. I assumed that you would want to keep it that way for transport inside the U.S.''

Krick shook his head. "Before we turn the rest of the funds over to you, we want to take it out. I'm afraid our demand is not negotiable.''

"But…" Eshamani caught himself.

Carmody knew then that they had him. The sleazy, bald-headed little bastard was ready to do cartwheels to get the nuke out of his warehouse. They were going to oblige him, but not quite in the way he expected.

"All right," Eshamani said, turning for the warehouse. "Let's get on with it."

As they walked into the huge storage space lined with containers, Krick said, "We want to look at the howitzer first."

Eshamani took them over to a group of four cargo containers that had been separated from the rest. "The cannon is in the three containers on the right. It's been broken down into barrel, carriage, wheels and suspension."

He used a pair of bolt cutters to break the seal on the first container door. When, at his direction, one of the Sicilians slid back the door, Carmody saw what the arms merchant was talking about. The inside of the container was packed floor to ceiling with pieces of scrap steel.

The gun crew donned heavy leather gloves from their tool bags and began unloading the scrap. They piled it up on the warehouse planking.

"Do you see now how long this will take?" Eshamani asked Krick.

"We've got all day," he replied. "If you're in such a hurry, why don't you tell your shooters to give them a hand?"

Eshamani nodded. "Go ahead," he told his men. "Put on gloves and help them. Do something to earn your pay."

The Sicilians took off their suit jackets, and neatly folded them before they pitched in.

It did take a while to clear the gun carriage from the tons of steel that had been so carefully packed in around it. Once the carriage was free, Peterson and Gabhart used the warehouse's ceiling crane to drag it out onto the wooden plank flooring.

Next, they started work on the container that held the 152 mm howitzer's wheels and suspension, and bags of small parts. When that, too, sat out on the deck, Peterson and the others took a break, mopping the sweat from their faces and necks.

Carmody opened one of the backpacks and took out a military manual they had painstakingly translated from the original Russian. He flipped the armorer's guide to the D-20 open to the section on parts and assembly of the cannon's support and elevation systems.

"What are they doing now?" Eshamani demanded as Carmody and Peterson started laying out the small parts in groups. Ransom and Gabhart began wrestling the larger pieces of the suspension into position.

"They're putting the gun together," Krick said, amused by the arms merchant's consternation. "How else are we going to know if all the parts are here? When I pay this much for an item, I don't expect to have to run to the hardware store for some missing bolts."

"You're going to take it all apart again after you assemble it?" Eshamani said. "And then pack the pieces back into the containers? My God, that could take days."

"No, it'll go right into the trailer we've already customized."

Carmody looked up from his nut-counting in time to see Eshamani's reaction to the lie.

The arms merchant seemed much relieved.

CHAPTER EIGHTEEN

Stony Man Farm
11:55 a.m. EDT

Barbara Price picked a glass bottle from the bin at the back of the computer center, twisted off the top and took a long swallow of apple juice. The cold liquid soothed her parched throat. She'd been talking almost nonstop for the past two hours. Talking and analyzing. She was pleased with the result. The Stony Man operations crew had made an amazing amount of progress since McCarter had called in with the report from the successful assault in the highway rest area in Utah. Though she was never one to toot her own horn in public, she knew that their productivity was due in some measure to her organizational skills. From the moment she'd realized that the Ogden howitzer team might be a decoy, she'd begun delegating and compartmentalizing the team's efforts to cover all the contingencies, as she and Kurtzman had broken them down.

The first thing she'd done had been to set the Farm's tactical adviser, Yakov Katzenelenbogen, to work identifying in detail all the military countermeasures that could isolate and destroy the militiamen's howitzer, no matter where it was sited. From this range of options, she reasoned, they could quickly select a response that would fit the actual circumstances of the impending attack and still be acceptable to the President.

At her request, Akira Tokaido had continued his computerized word-frequency search of the Justice Department's compilation of Sawtooth Patriot documents and recorded conversations.

In anticipation of the target being identified prior to H-hour, she had set both Carmen Delahunt and Dr. Huntington Wethers working on the ground-search parameters for the weapon. Specifically they had the critical task of finding the keys to identifying the most-likely firing positions, given the information they'd already received from Old Glory Ranch. With the limited manpower and time they had to resolve the situation, they could only mount a highly concentrated search. They had to be able to squeeze the most out of that effort.

At 7:48 a.m. Mountain Daylight Time, when McCarter had told them that the lone surviving militiaman had confirmed the existence of a second howitzer and given up the location of its East Coast target, Price had her people ready to take the information and run with it.

Immediately things had begun to fall into place.

The target that the survivor had identified fit perfectly with Tokaido's data. In terms of the frequency of mention and the hostility of language, the United Nations was at the top of the Sawtooth Patriots' hate list. The survivor's explanation for why the Old Glory gun team had been forced to use an artillery trainer instead of a real weapon also made sense. He had told

McCarter that they intended to fire a 152 mm Soviet nuke shell through a Soviet 152 mm cannon, both of which were being kept at a secret East Coast location. McCarter had presumed, and Katz and Price had agreed, that the howitzer was most likely in firing position, if not already sighted in on the target.

The moment the target was named, Brognola had gotten on the horn with the President. After the chief executive was made aware of the developments, he gave Brognola authorization to contact the UN headquarters security force and arrange a discreet evacuation of the building.

By the time Brognola had finished arranging for that, Katz had come up with a military option that he felt was feasible and did not unnecessarily endanger a large segment of the civilian population. His plan looked good to everyone in the computer center.

When Brognola had rung the President back, the first thing he had told him was that they were on the speakerphone at Stony Man, that time considerations dictated that all parties at the Farm had to be instantly available to answer his questions about the plan they had in mind. Before going through the particulars of the operation, Brognola had explained that they were proceeding on a series of logical assumptions that were based on the known facts. According to the survivor in Utah, the militia's howitzer team had never fired the gun with which they intended to deliver the nuke. They knew the gun team had only fired a trainer at Old Glory. This virtually guaranteed that they would have to shoot several marking or registration rounds to get the nuke on target in New York. Brognola explained that that narrow window of time, between the first and the final shot, was perhaps all the wiggle room they had.

"Let's hear the plan, Hal," the President had said.

"First we have to close down the airspace over Manhattan Island and the surrounding waterways," the big Fed had told him. "Only an extremely limited number of authorized aircraft will be allowed in the area. Intruders will be subject to challenge and if they do not withdraw, lethal force."

"Okay, so far."

"We commit a pair of AN/TPQ-31 weapons-locating radar units and crews to a site near or on the UN grounds. They will be able to identify and track the first registration round back to the gun that fired it and give us its position."

"Fine."

"We put Able Team and Phoenix Force aboard a pair of Blackhawk helicopters and start them on a grid search of the most likely firing positions. By the time the strike teams arrive from Utah, we'll have compiled a potential target list for them. Even if they don't uncover the gun before H-hour, this should put them in good shape to close in on it once the AN/TPQ-31s spit out their coordinates."

"What is this 'time window' you mentioned?"

"Four or five minutes, tops."

"Not much wiggle room there."

"Which is why we need to deploy something more," Brognola had told the President.

At that point, everyone in the room had held their breath. They all knew that this was the hardest part, the request that a bona fide weapon of war be employed on American soil, against American citizens.

"Under certain limited conditions of engagement,"

Brognola said, "we feel that a Hercules AC-130E gunship could make the difference between success and unthinkable disaster."

"Under precisely what conditions do you propose using the Spectre?"

"We would commit the Hercules gunship to battle only if the hostile weapon was discovered to be sited in a sparsely populated area, only if it was clear that the Blackhawks could not intervene in time to do the job before the nuke round was fired and only if the collateral damage to other structures was within acceptable limits."

In the end, the President had only asked one question. "Will it work?"

"Given what we're up against, it's our only shot," Brognola had answered.

"Then take it."

The effort after they had received the President's okay had been, if anything, even more frantic than what had gone before. They had a plan, and the authorization to implement it, but it was all just words. They had to make the nuts and bolts of it real before they could make it happen. The next hour had been spent chasing down the necessary matériel and personnel, and arranging for everything to be transported from where it was stored or stationed to where it could do some good.

Now that everything was finally in motion, all the disparate pieces sliding into position, Price took a moment to sip cold juice and let the tension drain from her neck and shoulders. It was only a moment; she couldn't give herself more. The mission demanded that she wade in again. The lives of tens of thousands of people hung in the balance. Now that Stony Man was fully committed to the operation, among the potential victims were nine men that she deeply admired, nine brave, dedicated men who depended on her. She walked up the ramp and stood beside Kurtzman's wheelchair. With him, she watched the wall screens that displayed Delahunt's and Wethers's work.

Using the gun-to-target distance from the Old Glory test range, they had drawn a circle around the UN complex. Somewhere within the ring, give or take a few blocks, was the probable firing position of the cannon. After excluding the edges of the ring that were impossible because of topography and shot angle, they examined superdetailed satellite photos of the area to identify unlikely firing positions within the zone. These they also chopped out of the picture.

The result was a hodgepodge of widely spaced potential targets, most of which were in a corridor along either side of the Hudson River. Everyone agreed that there was still way too much ground to cover. At present, with Tokaido's help, they were trying to further narrow the scope by identifying the best firing positions from the areas that were left, the ones that could lay the weapon on target, and provide the gunners with blast protection and escape routes.

It was slow going.

Price checked the clock. Striker and the others would be touching down in Newark in about three hours. Brognola would arrive at McGuire AFB half an hour before they touched down.

She prayed they had that much time.

CHAPTER NINETEEN

Union City, New Jersey
2:15 p.m. EDT

Sergio Eshamani watched the crumpled-up paper bags from their hasty fast-food lunch blow lightly across the warehouse floor. Lunch, such as it was, sat anything but lightly on his stomach. Eshamani had the feeling that the greasy, tasteless burger had re-formed in his belly, the individual bites coalescing back into its original, burger form. Of course, the burger was only half of his indigestion problem.

For almost four hours, the potential buyers of his merchandise had been at work assembling the Soviet D-20. The equilibrator had taken a good deal of time to get operational, as it had been slightly damaged in transit. It was the balancing gear that allowed the hand wheel to smoothly and easily raise and lower the barrel. The weapon's sights had also taken painstaking preparation. Now the thing was together, right down to the last turn of the torque wrench on the final bolt head.

The green-and-black camouflage-painted barrel loomed high overhead as the man called Skel spun the hand wheel, raising the barrel toward the warehouse's ceiling. With another spin of the wheel, he dropped it down again. Then he tested the right and left adjustment. Two of the other buyers opened the cannon's breech and left it that way. Inside and out, the weapon gleamed. They had removed the cosmoline protective coating from every part and rebuttered each with just the right amount of grease before assembly.

"Are you satisfied now?" the arms merchant asked Krick.

Krick looked at Carmody, the man with the long face. "What do you say? Does it pass muster?"

Carmody was wiping gun grease from his hands with a rag. "It looks good to us. It'll do the job."

The overhand knot in Eshamani's stomach loosened a little. "Then you'll be calling for the truck to transport it out of here?" he said.

"Sure," Carmody said. "I'll make the call right now, while you guys start unloading the last container."

They had barely gotten started when the long-faced man returned.

"How long until the truck gets here?" Eshamani asked him.

"It'll arrive in about thirty minutes," Carmody said. "We should be done with everything by then."

"Yeah," Peterson said. "We'll be done."

The arms merchant nodded. Another half hour was a pain in the ass, but as long as he knew it was going to be over soon, he could deal with it. From what he had seen so far, unpacking scrap steel and assembling a howitzer was neither a spectator nor a participant sport. The three Sicilians were drenched in sweat and, despite their precautions, had managed to get black grease from the scrap metal on their shirts, pants and faces. From the way they were moving, it looked like their backs and legs were starting to stiffen up. Eshamani was tired, too, tired of standing around. He wanted his money and he wanted the military contraband out of his warehouse. He wanted to be on his way.

It was nearly a quarter to three by the time they removed the *starookha* and six HE 152 mm shells from the last cargo container.

There was still no truck in sight.

Like the artillery shells on the *Varuskya Liset*, the nuke had in its own, solidly built wooden crate. Carmody briefly examined the outside of the box, then said, "Go ahead and tear down the crate."

Eshamani started to say something about saving the box for transport, but before he could get the words out, Krick and the other three men applied their crowbars to the sides of the crate, splintering the wooden panels free.

The Sicilians pulled the remaining fragments out of the way, and the *starookha* stood there on the warehouse planking in its steel, double-locked security jacket.

Carmody bent over the shell. In a plastic bag taped to the front of the jacket was the shell's keypad and connecting cord. He ripped the bag free and took out the keypad. "Time for you to show us how to use this," he told Eshamani.

"We need the PAL code," Krick said.

"Of course," Eshamani said, "but first I need to see the balance of the purchase price."

Nobody moved. Nobody said anything.

The knot in the arms merchant's stomach retightened, big time.

"I think I've been very patient with you up until now," Eshamani said. "Perhaps too patient. You've wasted most of my day. I need to see the color of your money, gentlemen."

"Get it," Krick told Carmody.

Carmody turned and walked over to the warehouse wall, where he'd put down the backpack he'd carried in. As he picked up the pack, Krick and the three other men stepped back from the nuke, leaving the Sicilians to gawk at it as they mopped their faces with handkerchiefs. Krick moved somewhat farther away than the others and watched as Carmody returned.

"It's all in here," Carmody said, setting the backpack down on the floor. From the main compartment, he took out a silenced MAC-10. As he pointed the weapon in Eshamani's face, two of his friends swung their crowbars at the backs of the closest Sicilians' heads. For hours, the warehouse had been ringing with the harsh sounds of steel on steel. Steel on skull produced a mellower tone, a thwack instead of a clang. The thwacks knocked the stuffing out of the mafiosi; they dropped to the planking as if their strings had been cut.

The third Sicilian just stood there, his mouth hanging open in shock and disbelief. If he hadn't been so exhausted, he might have made a dive for his weapon, which hung on the front of a nearby container. He might have even reached it.

But as it was, Carmody deftly switched his point of aim and shot him once through the head. The man crumpled in a twitching heap beside his comrades.

"What's this?" Eshamani demanded, even though

he knew precisely what it was. He was trying to buy a little time to think.

"Would it surprise you to hear there isn't any more money?" Krick said. "I'm tapped out. The stinking Feds have either seized or frozen every dime I ever earned."

"Do you really think you can get away with this?" Eshamani said. "All I have to do is yell and..." He tilted his head toward the double side doors, on the other side of which his armed security force stood guard.

"You'll get shot," Carmody said, putting the hot muzzle against the base of his skull. "Dead."

"You'll never get the PAL code out of me, then."

"And you'll never get to spend the money we've paid you so far," Krick told him. "We can always find another nuke—you'll have a harder time finding a new brain to replace the one Carmody's going to splatter all over the floor."

Eshamani had to concede the point. "What guarantee do I have that you won't kill me after I give you the code?"

"You have my word," Krick said. Then he smiled. "Although I don't suppose that carries quite as much weight now as it did a few minutes ago."

"Skel," Carmody said, "let's get the gun moved into position."

With the help of the other two men in the gun crew, Peterson hooked the howitzer to the ceiling crane and started towing it to the river end of the warehouse.

Suddenly it all became clear to Eshamani. Not only wasn't there going to be any more money in it for him, but there wasn't any truck coming, either. The nuke shell was leaving the premises, and probably very soon, but the howitzer wasn't.

"You're going to nuke Manhattan from here," Eshamani said. "You crazy bastards are going to nuke Manhattan from my warehouse."

Carmody didn't bother to reply. He shoved the arms merchant over to the *starookha* and put the keypad into his hand. "Show us how to program the weapon."

"I have the coding sequence in my inside coat pocket."

Carmody aimed the MAC-10 at his heart. "Get it out, slowly."

Eshamani took out the loose pages. He handed them to Carmody, who flipped through them, then handed them back.

"They don't make any sense to me," Carmody told Krick. "They're just rows of numbers. I can't tell what the six-digit sequences actually do. Our middleman here is going to have to run us through it."

"Better yet," Krick said, "have him program the weapon for us. Tell him what we want and have him input the right codes."

Carmody prodded Eshamani in the chest with the muzzle of the MAC-10. "Get to work."

With no other option, the arms merchant had to obey. He pulled a number from the top page and tapped it into the security lock's built-in keypad. The bolts sprang back with an audible clack. "Help me get the jacket off," he said.

Krick and Carmody used the lifting handles to remove the jacket.

Eshamani connected the separate keypad to the warhead, then referred to the loose pages again.

"What are you doing?" Carmody asked.

"The first set of numbers is the handshake," Eshamani said, punching in the sequence. He showed the LCD readout to Carmody. The row of little red asterisks appeared on the readout, blinked twice, then disappeared.

Krick was also watching over his shoulder. "That's supposed to happen?"

"That's the confirmation that the codes have been accepted," Eshamani said. "Now we can fuse the warhead using these sets of tables. I need to know the distance and flight time, and whether you want an air or ground-burst."

"Definitely ground-burst," Krick said.

"Got the rest of it right here," Carmody said, digging out a scrap of paper from his shirt pocket.

The performance of the D-20 howitzer with a specific charge and payload was public record, so Eshamani wasn't surprised that they already had all the targeting numbers crunched.

When Carmody gave him the necessary information, Eshamani plugged it into the correct table, got the adjusted value and input it into the warhead's computer.

Eshamani showed Carmody the LCD. Again the row of stars blinked and disappeared.

"Now arm it," Krick said.

Eshamani hesitated, not because he gave a damn about New York City, but because he didn't like being lied to in a business deal. Nor did he like being robbed at gunpoint. He figured that when the whole thing came down, it would turn out he'd been robbed *and* murdered. Why would they leave him alive to tell the tale, to point the finger at them? He didn't have a chance in hell. The hopeless, humiliating situation cried out to his Iranian Italian blood. It cried out for vengeance of some kind.

"Go ahead," Carmody said, grinding the muzzle of the MAC-10 against his closely shaved skull.

Eshamani looked Krick in the eye, a deadpan expression on his face, and punched in the last six numbers. He held the keypad's blinking LCD screen up and said, "That means it's ready to fire."

At the other end of the warehouse, the gun crew had unloaded their map cases and backpacks and maps and charts were spread out on the warehouse floor. Peterson was using a hand-held GPS unit to locate their position and the position of the target. After lining up the barrel and target horizontally, he raised the howitzer's muzzle toward the ceiling.

They weren't going to move the cannon outside to fire it.

"You're out of your damned minds," Eshamani said.

"We're crazy like foxes," Carmody said. He lifted back the lapel of the arms merchant's Armani suit, reached into the inside pocket and took out Eshamani's fat wallet and his passport.

Eshamani stood there while the man rifled through the money, credit cards and other ID.

"Hey," Carmody said, "this stuff says he's a Mr. Walter Bertrand Combs from Texas."

"He's a slippery customer, all right," Krick said. "We'll have to tie him up extratight."

Carmody pocketed the documents, credit cards and money. Then he took duct tape and cord from his backpack. With Krick's help, he trussed up Eshamani, shoving a greasy rag into his mouth before wrapping his head tightly with tape. The arms merchant didn't struggle as he was dragged over to one of the emptied cargo containers. They pitched him inside and then dumped the dead Sicilian and his unconscious comrades in on top of him.

The steel door slid shut with a clank.

It was dark inside and hot, and there was very little air. Buried under bodies, Eshamani felt wetness oozing onto his face. Wetness that belonged in an abattoir or in a sewer. Gagging into the rag, he managed to wriggle out from under the Sicilians. He crawled away from them, scuttling across the container floor on his side. He sat, breathing heavily through his nose, at one end of the sealed box, listening to the groans of his men as they slipped in and out of consciousness. He had seen the wounds inflicted by the crowbars. The backs of their skulls were caved in, shards of bone driven into their brains.

They were alive, but not for long. As was he.

TASHA BELOC WAS beginning to wonder if anything was ever going to happen at the warehouse across the street. The excitement of the first few minutes had quickly vanished as the stakeout dragged on into the afternoon. The most interesting thing that had happened so far was when the Sicilians had sent out for lunch. She had no idea what was taking so long, and from their discussions, neither did Sarnov. Could Eshamani and the buyers be negotiating over the price, haggling for hours over a few hundred thousand? It seemed unlikely to her that the price wouldn't have already been set, agreed to long before this.

Maybe there wasn't any nuke inside and there weren't any buyers.

It was as frustrating as it was unfathomable, but the Spetsnaz team couldn't move until the artillery shell did.

Sudden activity at the front of the warehouse sent a jolt of adrenaline through Beloc's body. She hit the transmit button of her walkie-talkie a second after she saw one of the men from the Dodge Caravan step out the door. "Looks like one of them might be leaving," she said into the mike. She peered through her binoculars.

"I can see him," Sarnov replied. "He isn't carrying anything but a backpack. We know he couldn't have the *starookha* tucked away in there."

Beloc watched as the man walked past the Sicilian guards and over to the minivan. He opened its rear hatch and took out a black nylon travel bag.

"He could have that bag stuffed with cash," she said. "It could be the payoff."

"Right you are," Sarnov said. "Vlad, Uri, stay on your toes now. They may be finally closing the deal."

Instead of returning to the warehouse by the front door, the man with the backpack and travel bag walked around the right-hand corner of the building and along its side, past the double sliding doors.

"Where's he going?" Sarnov said. "I can't see him anymore."

Beloc zoomed in on the retreating figure. "He's climbing down the stairs at the back of the dock. They lead down to the water. Wait…"

She heard the drone of a single-engine airplane. It was approaching from the west, behind her, and to the north, to her left. As she turned, she saw a red-

and-white float plane coming in low about five hundred yards away. It banked sharply over the water and lined up with the shoreline.

"A pontoon plane," she said. "Approaching the back of the building."

She caught a glimpse of the Cessna as it prepared for a landing, then it disappeared behind the warehouse.

"It's stopping to pick up the man with the bags," she said. "He's getting away."

"Let him go," Sarnov said. "As long as he didn't take the *starookha* with him, it doesn't matter. We can't show our hand, yet."

Behind the building, the airplane's engine roared, and it sped off on its pontoons. Beloc caught the flash of its upper fuselage as it moved between the warehouses. She picked up the MSG-90 and with its scope tracked along the rooftops of the buildings along the river, following what she presumed to be the aircraft's path. The float plane didn't lift into the air until it was more than one hundred yards down the shore. With the tail facing her like that, she didn't have a shot anyway.

She lowered her weapon. One thing was clear, the man with the bag wasn't carrying the payoff to Eshamani. There was still no explanation for the delay in moving the nuke.

"HOW MUCH LONGER?" the capo asked Carmody as he breezed past the guards at the front of the warehouse.

"We've still got another twenty or thirty minutes and we're done. Then you guys can go somewhere and put your dogs up, maybe grab a cold one."

"A cold six," the capo said. "It's been a hot day."

His colleagues grunted in agreement. They were thinking in terms of cases.

Carmody opened the back of the van and took out the bag that contained a quarter million in traveling money. His traveling money. He waved at the capo as he turned around the corner of the warehouse. The Sicilians standing watch on the double doors did their thing the second he stepped into view: hands dipped under suit jackets, bodies dropped into bent-knee shooting stances. None of them drew down on him, though. They recognized him from earlier in the day.

They asked him the same question. How much longer? He gave them the same answer. They accepted it, if sullenly.

As Carmody walked by, he checked the narrow crack between the two-story-high, double sliding doors. The cargo containers that had held the cannon and nuke completely blocked the view. If they hadn't been in the way, the Sicilians could have seen what had gone down in the warehouse. In which case, Carmody had no doubt, the Sawtooth Patriots would have been the ones locked inside a steel box, dead or slowly dying in agony.

He walked past the end of the warehouse. As he did, he heard the sound of a small plane approaching. The dock the building stood on extended another one hundred feet before it ended at the river. Carmody stepped to the ladder that led from the dock to the water and started down. Directly below the ladder, abutting and moored to the pier's pilings, was a small floating dock.

Les Johnson's timing was perfect. No sooner had Carmody set foot on the dock than the float plane appeared from the north, dipping down and skimming over the water. The Cessna's nose came up, and it landed on the river. The drag of the water on the pontoons slowed the aircraft to a crawl in a matter of yards.

Johnson motored the plane forward, swinging the Cessna 180's pontoon into the dock. As it bumped to a stop, he reached over and opened the passenger door.

Carmody stepped up and shoved his bag and backpack on the floor in front of the copilot's seat, then got into the cabin.

Johnson didn't wait for him to buckle up. The grizzled pilot shoved the throttle forward, and the plane quickly began to pick up speed.

"We've got a problem," he said to his passenger over the engine noise.

"What's that?"

"The Feds have shut down the airspace you want me to fly in. I get the feeling they know something's up." He looked over at Carmody. "They might even know *what's* up. If they catch us in the no-fly zone, we could be shot down. If we land in the no-fly zone, they could blow us out of the water."

Johnson pulled back on the controls, and the plane lifted off the river. Instead of turning to the left and heading southeast, across the island as they had planned, he veered slightly inland and paralleled the Jersey shore.

"If you want more money..."

"It isn't money," Johnson said "It's living long enough to spend what you've already paid me. This 180 isn't exactly a combat aircraft. It's more like a sitting duck with a bull's-eye painted on its butt."

Carmody pulled the backpack up into his lap and took out the MAC-10.

"Give me a break," Johnson said when he saw the machine pistol.

"You're going to do what I tell you."

"Like hell," Johnson said. He trimmed back the throttle and steered the Cessna over the water.

"Hey! What are you doing?" Carmody said as the plane began its descent for another landing.

The instant the pontoons hit, Johnson unbuckled his seat belt and reached for the door handle. "I don't have to do squat," he said, opening the door.

Carmody took aim at his temple.

"Go ahead," Johnson said. "Whether you shoot me or not, you're going to have to fly this plane yourself. Somehow I don't think you're up to that."

Carmody didn't waver.

"What kind of a numbnuts do you think you're dealing with? We both know that if I don't take you to your observation point, this mission is finished. Put the damn piece down. I can get you there, if I take the long way around, but I'm not staying while you do your dirty business. I'm dropping you off. You're on your own."

Carmody lowered the machine pistol. The original plan had been for Johnson to fly him to an OP on the East River and to wait there until the registration rounds were marked. Then they would take off to the north and keep low over the water. When they were past Roosevelt Island, Carmody would give the "fire for effect" command.

Carmody had crafted the plan to ensure his own safety after the nuclear detonation.

All that was out the window now.

He couldn't force the pilot to do anything but die, and his dying wouldn't solve the immediate problem. Carmody had to get into position to call in the attack. There was no going back, no waiting until another day, no moving the gear out of the warehouse. They were committed.

"How much longer will it take to go around?" he asked Johnson.

"An extra fifteen or twenty minutes."

"All right, do it," Carmody said. "Get us out of here."

Then he called Skel Peterson on the cellular phone to tell him that H-hour would be slightly but unavoidably delayed.

CHAPTER TWENTY

McGuire Air Force Base, New Jersey
2:50 p.m. EDT

Hal Brognola ducked his head as he hopped out of the Justice Department's Sikorsky. The helicopter's rotors whipped grit into his face, making him squint. On the other side of the landing pad, standing next to a Humvee, was a ramrod-straight Air Force lieutenant colonel.

"Welcome to McGuire, Mr. Brognola," she greeted, extending a slim hand.

"Thanks," he said. The strength of her grip amazed him. He had to squeeze back hard, out of self-defense.

"I'm Deanne Kite," she went on. "I'll be escorting you over to the Spectre. It's ready to fly."

Brognola got in the passenger's side of the vehicle, and Colonel Kite climbed behind the wheel.

"We've got an exercise for the Jersey Air National Guard on today," she said as she whipped a sharp 180-degree turn. "The AC-130E was scheduled to participate in a firepower demonstration later this afternoon. She was going to play demolition derby with some armor that was scheduled to be chopped up for scrap. So she's fully manned and armed, as requested.''

Kite glanced over at Brognola. "I don't suppose you're free to tell me what's going on?" she said. "It's not every day that a combat-ready gunship gets jerked out of an air show. In fact, it's not something that has ever happened, as far as I know."

"No, I'm sorry. I can't talk about it."

"Like I said, I figured you couldn't. Not if the mission is half as important as it looks." She paused and then said, "Whatever job you're on, you should know that you've got an experienced crew on board the aircraft. Captain Nowlin and Senior Master Sergeant Huggins flew a Spectre in the Panama raid. They were part of the night attack on the Panama City police headquarters. They reduced the entire complex to rubble and dust."

"I'm glad to hear that, Colonel," Brognola said. His answer was suitably lawyerlike and vague. It didn't confirm or deny that the full battlefield capabilities of the gunship would be used in the matter at hand. He didn't let on that he already knew the war records of the crew.

Kite pointed out the AC-130E on the concrete apron dead ahead. Its four engines were already up and running, the propellers spinning. It looked like a regular Hercules except for the cannon muzzles sticking out of the left side of the fuselage; they belonged to a 105 mm howitzer and 20 mm electrically driven Gatling guns.

"She ain't sexy, but she's a beast and a half in an air-to-ground firefight," Kite said admiringly.

As they got out of the Hummer and approached the plane, the pilot waved at them from the cabin.

"I'm putting you in good hands," Kite announced at the stairs. "Have a safe and successful flight."

She shook Brognola's hand again, but this time he was prepared and met fire with fire. He climbed up into the aircraft and was immediately waved to a seat by the pilot.

Captain Nowlin apologized and said, "I'm afraid it's kind of cramped in here. You're going to have to take the jump seat behind me. My copilot, Lieutenant Marquez, will get you plugged in to the communications system."

The lieutenant handed Brognola a headset and mike. "Put that on," Marquez said, "and you'll be connected intership and radio."

As Brognola did so, a man in his early forties poked his head in and smiled. His prematurely graying hair was cut supershort. From the rank on his sleeve, Brognola guessed it had to be Huggins.

"Mr. Brognola," Nowlin said, "this is Senior Master Sergeant Huggins, or 'Huggy.' He and his boys keep the cannons fed and watered."

Brognola nodded, then buckled up his seat belt.

"As I understand it, this is a scramble," Nowlin said, "so as soon as you're comfortable, we'll get out of here."

"Let's go," Brognola said.

Captain Nowlin got his clearance and advanced the aircraft to the takeoff point. When the engines reached the critical rpm, he released the brakes and down the runway they went.

As soon as they cleared the field, Nowlin banked a lazy turn and said, "Where to, Mr. Brognola?"

"Put us on intership communications only." When that was done, Brognola explained the nature of the mission to the gunship's crew. "We're going to over-fly New York City," he said. "We have a credible threat of a nuclear attack there."

"Bomb?" Marquez asked.

"No, a howitzer shooting a nuke shell," the big Fed explained.

A new voice crackled in Brognola's headset. It was Huggy. "Hezbollah?" he speculated.

"Unfortunately," Brognola replied, "these guys are all homegrown, red-blooded Americans. Maybe a better way of putting it is they were born here."

"What are they aiming at?" Nowlin asked.

"We're pretty sure they're after the UN."

"Jesus," Lieutenant Marquez said. For good measure, he added, "Mary and Joseph."

"At this moment," Brognola said, "a weapons-locating radar system is being set up at the UN. If a cannon is fired at the complex, it'll give us the location of the gun. In advance of the actual attack, we'll also have helicopter crews searching for the firing position. They'll direct us to the gun if they can find it."

"How big is our target going to be?" Huggy asked.

"We won't know until the call comes through and we get a look at it," Brognola said. "From what we know of the group, it might be on a truck-and-trailer rig. It could also be inside some kind of structure. If it's on a truck, the Blackhawks can handle the job. If it's inside a building or hardsite, it's up to us to get the job done."

"What about innocent people inside the building?" Marquez asked.

"We don't think they'll put the howitzer in a populated area. It's too easily seen. We think it'll be in a factory or warehouse, or something similar, probably along one side or the other of the Hudson.''

"Makes sense," Nowlin said.

"We're hoping to get lucky and have the helicopters interdict the gun before it starts shooting," Brognola said, "but we're not counting on it, though.''

"How are we going to stop them from firing?'' Huggy asked.

"We think they'll shoot at least two registration rounds of HE before they unload the nuke. Our time window is very narrow.''

"I suggest we circle the city at ten thousand feet until we get the call," Nowlin said. "We can close the distance to any target in the area you're talking about in about a minute. Depending on the size of the target, our firing altitude will be around four thousand feet.''

"You do understand how this gunship operates?'' Marquez asked.

"I understand you can direct withering firepower into a small area," Brognola replied.

"You got it. How we do it is, we bank a constant turn and fly in perfect circles around the target, which keeps the cannons aimed at it the whole time. We circle and we direct the cannonfire electronically from up front.''

"If we're actually ordered in to do this job," Nowlin said, "you understand that the Spectre isn't a smart bomb. We shoot a lot of rounds into a fairly confined space, but we can still miss the target. We did in Panama City.''

"But that was in the dark," Huggy qualified.

"True.''

"We can do a whole lot better in broad daylight," Marquez added.

"Smart bombs aren't smart one hundred percent of the time," Brognola said. "When one misses, it does a hell of a lot more damage than a howitzer round. The odds of containing the destruction are better with you guys. In the best of all possible scenarios, we would knock out the howitzer with one shot."

"Cannon versus cannon," Huggy said. "I like it."

"That's about it," Brognola concluded. "Until we have confirmation, we circle and hold our breath."

"We'll be over NYC airspace in about fifteen minutes," Nowlin said. "I understand there's a restriction in place."

"Right," Brognola confirmed. "Except for us and the Blackhawks, the airspace over NYC is closed to all traffic."

Marquez turned toward Brognola. "Incoming scramble call for you, sir," he said.

It was the Bear.

He informed Brognola that the National Guard weapons-locating radar was in position, up and operational. Then he patched the guardsmen manning the units into the mission communications grid.

"TAKE US DOWN a bit lower," David McCarter said.

The pilot of the Blackhawk dropped the helicopter another seventy-five feet. The garbage barge loomed large beneath them. Their rotor wash whipped the crests of the trash heaps and sent a flock of gulls wheeling up from their never ending feast. The birds flew over the shabby little trailer that the sanitation workers used to get out of the elements. All of the birds landed on the sloping mound behind the trailer, and immediately resumed their feeding.

"Bloody rats with wings," McCarter said.

Beside him in the doorway, Encizo lowered his binoculars. "I hate to tell you, but that trailer house is too small to hold a Soviet 152," he said. "Even if it was rigged for travel, it wouldn't fit in there."

"I was actually more concerned about the big trash drift sitting behind it," the Phoenix Force team leader said. "The one the bleeding gulls are sitting on. It's tall enough to hide a howitzer. Someone could take that bulldozer sitting down there and bury a cannon under a few tons of garbage in a few minutes. When the time came to shoot, just uncover it again."

"Except for the way the barge is swinging around in the current," James said. "If anybody tried to use it for a shooting platform, there's no way they could zero in on a target almost four miles away. Man, they'd be marking hits all up and down the island."

"You're right," McCarter said. "Good thinking. They'd have to run the damned barge aground to stabilize it. As it stands, it's a pretty poor platform."

Hawkins gave the "take her up" sign to the pilot, and the Blackhawk chopper climbed and turned away from the barge.

"Target Bravo Delta Four is a definite negative," McCarter said into his mike. "Papa Team is moving to Bravo Delta Five."

"Roger, Papa," Stony Man's Barbara Price said. "Moving to Bravo Delta Five."

The Blackhawk dropped low over the river and headed north. The men inside the cargo bay continued to scan the buildings along the waterfront, looking for anything suspicious.

On the New York side of the river, Able Team and Striker were doing the same thing, getting as close as they could to potential firing positions and trying to shake something loose.

So far, nothing was shaking.

On the flight in from Utah, McCarter had known that this part of the mission was going to be difficult. But now that he was on-site, doing the job, he realized how bloody slim their chances were, even within the limited search area. There were too many structures they couldn't see into—structures that could easily contain the cannon. Around most of them, there was no place to set the Blackhawk down, so a foot search was out of the question. On top of that, he knew that Stony Man Intel had, quite rightly, excluded a huge portion of the area—any part of which might, in fact, hold the gun.

Through the ship-to-ship scrambler, he heard Striker's voice. "This is Alpha Team," Bolan said. "Targets Zulu George Seven through Nine are all negative. Moving on to Target Tango."

"Roger, Alpha," Price said. "Moving to Tango."

The best of British luck, big guy, McCarter thought.

The Blackhawk wheeled right and paused, hovering beside a row of double-wide trailers in a fenced-in compound. McCarter again raised his binoculars.

CHAPTER TWENTY-ONE

"Hey, Captain, what do you make of that?" Lieutenant Marquez said. He pointed at the Long Island side of the East River shoreline.

Captain Nowlin dipped the left wing a little lower for a better look. "In every crowd, there's always a clown," he said. "Considering where we are, I'm surprised we've only had the one."

Brognola turned in his seat. "What is it? What are you guys looking at?"

"Oh, we've got a single-engine Cessna skirting the edge of the no-fly zone," Nowlin said. "Maybe it's nothing, maybe it's something. Watch him as we come around again, Pete."

"Affirmative," Marquez said.

The Spectre completed another lazy circle at ten thousand feet.

"Something's hinky, Cap," the lieutenant said. "He's setting the plane down some place he shouldn't. A definite no-no."

Brognola looked out the window. As he did, he caught the glint of the float plane's white wing and tail. Behind it, he could see two white wakes. The aircraft had landed on the Long Island side of the water, directly across the river from the UN plaza.

"It could be the observer," Huggins offered. "He's in a good position to do the spotting."

The plane only sat on the water for fifteen seconds before it took off again, heading northeast, angling sharply out of the restricted airspace.

"Guess he didn't like the view," Nowlin said.

"Or he dumped a guy off," Marquez suggested.

"Alpha Team, this is Big Bird," Brognola said into his headset mike. "The OP may be getting into position along the Long Island shoreline about a mile south of the Queensboro Bridge. Break off your grid search immediately and cross the island over the target. We'll relay the exact location of the possible OP while you're en route."

"Roger, Big Bird," Striker said. "We're on our way."

"Papa Team, you keep up the search on the Jersey side," Brognola ordered. "We'll keep you informed on the OP. If turns out to be the real article and we nail it, it might give us the howitzer's position."

"Roger, Big Bird," McCarter said. "At the very least, knocking out the OP will buy us some more time to find the buggers with the gun."

CARMODY WAS STANDING on the Cessna 180's right pontoon when Johnson swung the tail of the aircraft around. He stepped off onto a low dock that was connected to the beach by a long ramp. He didn't turn and wave goodbye to the pilot-for-hire. Even if he'd had the inclination, he wasn't given the opportunity. Prop wash whipped Carmody's back as Johnson accelerated away.

After shrugging into the straps of his backpack and

shouldering his money bag, Carmody ran up to the top of the ramp. Only then did he look back.

He was excited. Across the water, on the opposite shore, he could see the cluster of buildings he was about to vaporize. He was on the verge of making real his prophecy of a world police state. Of bringing on the repression that would unify the forces of rebellion, of blowing life into the lie he had so carefully spread.

There would be a New World Order, all right. His world. By his order.

Carmody could have stood there all afternoon, holding inside the secret knowledge of his power, watching the city swarming full of people, happy in their antlike ignorance of what was to come. As much as he would've liked to wallow in his gloating, though, he knew there wasn't time for it. He turned away from the distant skyline and faced the waterfront on his shore.

This was the general area from which he'd planned to do his spotting, but he'd intended to do it from the Cessna. He had to improvise now. He picked a grim, three-story factory about a half block away that would give him an elevated, and therefore better, view of the target.

As he jogged up to the building, he saw that a set of dark letters had bled through the top coat of gray paint. In a broad scroll they read Margee's Junior Miss Fashions, Est. 1958. Carmody turned down the side of the factory and found the fire escape.

As he climbed it, he looked into the multipaned, cantilevered, industrial windows at the landings. Margee's Fashions had been subdivided and converted into artists' lofts, probably to beat the high prices of similar digs on the other side of the river.

One of the artists-in-residence on the third floor saw him on the fire escape. The guy had paint in his frizzy gray ponytail and on his arms and pants. He was in the middle of splatter-painting a huge canvas on the floor. He stopped what he was doing and blinked up at Carmody.

Carmody waved at him and kept on climbing to the top.

The factory roof was very broad and slightly domed in the middle. Carmody trotted past the air ducts shaped like little turrets and knelt down beside the wall that faced the water. He removed his back-pack and took out his MAC-10 and set it close to hand. Then he pulled out his binoculars with the artillery reticle and a hand-held GPS unit. He fired up the GPS and found his current position.

Then he called New Jersey on his cellular phone.

Skel Peterson answered before the second ring. "Yo," he said.

"I'm in position," Carmody said. He gave Peterson the exact coordinates.

"Got it," Peterson said after he'd plugged them in to his own GPS unit. "We got a live one up the pipe over here. What do you say?"

"Let's rock," Carmody told him.

The commander in chief of the Sawtooth Patriots put down the phone without breaking the connection and picked up the binoculars. They had a special scale built in. The horizontal axis was divided into ten-millimeter increments for the side-to-side adjustment of fire. On the left side of the reticle, a series of individual bars showed five-millimeter increments for adjusting the height of the burst. Carmody wasn't concerned with the altitude scale.

After adjusting the binoculars's focus, he found his aim point on the opposite bank. It was the statue entitled *Let Us Beat the Swords into Plowshares,* which stood at the edge of the river side of the UN plaza.

Good name for an aim point, he thought.

Something crunched on the roof gravel behind him. Carmody lowered the binoculars and reached for the machine pistol.

"GET ALL the sliding doors open," Peterson said. "We're going to shoot this thing."

Ransom, Krick and Gabhart ran to the rear doors and rolled them apart. Then they did the same to the side doors of the warehouse, which caused the Sicilian gunmen to look in.

"What the hell's going on?" one of them asked.

The three security men stared in disbelief at the cannon pointed up at the ceiling.

"Wait and see," Peterson said as he pulled on his ear protectors. Uncoiling the lanyard, he stepped into the open cargo container where Krick, Ransom and Gabhart had already retreated.

Then he yanked the cord.

If the sliding doors had been closed, the force of the blast would've blown them off. It would also have maimed or killed the gun crew, but because the doors were open, the pressure created by the cannon's firing had somewhere to go.

The HE shell that shot out the barrel acted like a clearing round, blasting a great, raggedy hole in the ceiling of the warehouse. As the D-20 jolted on its suspension, the end of the roof disappeared and boiling clouds of dirt and smoke gusted out the open doors. The unprepared Sicilians were blinded and deafened by the cannon shot. They staggered back from the building, choking on the corrosive fumes.

No sooner was the round away and the larger hunks of debris had stopped falling, than Peterson, Gabhart and Ransom jumped out of the container and raced back to the gun. Gabhart and Ransom ejected the spent shell. As it rolled across the planking, they dropped another HE 152 mm shell onto the loading tray. After they rammed the shell home and slammed the breech closed, Ransom tipped back Peterson's ear protectors and said, "Ready to fire, sir!"

SERGIO ESHAMANI could hear the gun crew talking outside the cargo container that was his prison. He knew that the howitzer was about to be fired. Even so, he wasn't prepared for what happened when the cannon went off in the enclosed space. His whole dark, nasty-smelling world took a sudden, agonizing upward jump. The container actually hopped on the deck from the shock wave. The sound of the cannon filled his head until he thought it would burst. Then the choking gases began to filter down into the container.

His lungs burned.

His eyes burned.

His skin burned.

He was being cauterized inside and out. He screamed around the gag, trying to equalize the pressure in his skull. He screamed until his lungs were empty. Then he gasped for air, no longer caring how much it hurt.

Why hadn't he screamed before, when he'd had the

chance? Why hadn't he risked bringing his gunmen into play? Not because he didn't think they were up to the job. He knew they would've responded with ruthless brutality; it was what they specialized in. Maybe it was because he thought he could barter with these cowboy bastards. If that was it, he'd been a fool. If he'd yelled, he might've won; either way, he would've missed what he was now enduring.

A bullet to the head wasn't a bad way to die.

This was a bad way to die.

CHAPTER TWENTY-TWO

Sarnov's mind was wandering when the roof of the warehouse came off. He was so far gone he didn't even see the side doors of the building slide open prior to the blast. A lapse in concentration was to be expected after so many hours of sitting there and watching nothing happen. Sarnov had set his wrist-watch alarm for five-minute intervals, and every time it went off, he checked in with Ferdishenko and Tasha Beloc, making sure that they were at least as on track as he was.

When the back of the building erupted in a huge ball of fire and smoke, the Spetsnaz captain was thinking about his first wife, Rita, replaying the few happy memories he had of their brief, tempestuous marriage.

He blinked at the spectacle before him, not believing his eyes, not understanding what had happened. Was the explosion internal? Had something blown up inside the building? Or was it external? Had someone targeted the warehouse with a rocket?

"Captain!" Beloc shouted through the walkie-talkie. Its tiny speaker turned her excited voice to a high-pitched buzz.

"Yes, yes, of course I see it," Sarnov told her. "Give me a minute to think."

He sat there in the embassy car, watching the larger chunks of the roof pelt the river and street, trying to puzzle it out.

There was no visible source for an air-to-ground attack. No source for a ground-to-ground attack, either.

Then he saw the Sicilians come stumbling out the side doors, through the dark smoke.

Open doors?

He looked through his binoculars. As the smoke and dust cleared a bit, he could see into the warehouse. What he saw made him curse aloud. At the back of the building, under the newly made hole in the roof, he saw a long, dark shape that he recognized.

A D-20 howitzer.

"It's a cannon!" Sarnov shouted into his walkie-talkie. "They've got a cannon in there! Get them! Close in on them!" He threw down the communication device, stomped the gas pedal, and twisted the sedan's ignition key. The starter whined. He had flooded the engine.

"Damn it!" Sarnov turned the key again, but the engine still refused to catch. He could smell the gasoline that was choking the carburetor. "Shit!" he said, pounding the dash with his fist.

He forced himself to wait a few seconds, to let the excess gas drain away. He had really screwed things up. It had never occurred to him that Eshamani would have a cannon inside the warehouse. Both cannon and nuke shell at the same location. It was so obvious. But what wasn't obvious, what he could never have guessed, was that they would fire the gun from inside the building. That Eshamani would allow it, that he would be on the premises when they started shooting at Manhattan. He had judged the man to be a criminal of the most despicable sort, but never a terrorist.

The smoke had lifted enough so that even without binoculars Sarnov could see activity around the base of the howitzer. They were reloading it for another shot.

When he cranked the key the third time, the engine started. He dropped the car into gear and peeled away from the curb. He skidded a left turn through the intersection and barreled down the street toward the warehouse.

The Sicilians at the side of the building were still out of commission. Two of them were on their knees, doubled up in coughing or vomiting fits. He didn't have to worry much about them. The men in the front of the warehouse, on the other hand, were not hit by the gun blast and they were on high alert.

Sarnov steered with his left hand and reached for the Valmet with his right. He dropped the safety and propped the assault rifle's muzzle on the top of the dash so he could fire it through the windshield.

"HEY, BUDDY, what the hell are you doing on my roof?" the ponytailed artist said to Carmody, who turned to face him.

The artist winced as a high-pitched noise split the air. It sounded like a freight train bearing down on them. A freight train from hell.

Over Carmody's right shoulder, a water spout erupted in the middle of the East River, accompanied by a thundering explosion.

The artist's mouth dropped open. When he glanced

back at Carmody, the silenced MAC-10 was already in his hands. Carmody cut loose with a savage burst, stitching the man from crotch to throat with 9 mm slugs. The impact flung the artist onto his back on the roof. He landed hard and his body bounced, rubbery limp. It didn't move again.

Carmody picked up the cellular phone and said, "Skel?"

"Right here," came the reply.

Carmody didn't need the binoculars to make the first adjustment.

"Over, line," he said. Which meant the shot was long, but in line with the target.

Peterson repeated the call back to him, then said, "Number two coming up."

A few seconds later, another HE shell screamed over the horizon at Carmody. A plume of water erupted well to the north of the aim point. It was, however, closer to the target side of the river. Close, but not close enough. Their nuke was small and dirty. To get the maximum blast and firestorm effect, it needed to practically fall down the chimney of the General Assembly.

Carmody viewed the impact point through his binoculars, then gave Peterson the correction. "Over. Right, four hundred."

"Coming at you," Peterson said.

Carmody held his breath, listening for the scream of the shell. He only had to wait a few seconds. The shell exploded in the river, right under the noses of the residents of the Waterside Apartments, which was down Franklin D. Roosevelt Drive, south of the UN plaza.

Peterson had bracketed the target, and had walked

the impacts back toward the Manhattan shoreline.

He was close, but still no cigar.

Carmody called in the spot, then added his correction. He was looking at the target through the binoculars when he saw something skim over the top of the Secretariat building.

Something black and fast, and heading straight for him.

"I've got company on the way, Skel," he said.

"WE HAVE A CONFIRMED radar track," Lieutenant Marquez declared. He did a quick course plot to the coordinates the guardsmen had given him, then rattled it off to the captain.

"Got it!" Nowlin banked the Hercules toward New Jersey and pounded down the throttles. "We're on their raggedy asses now."

Brognola held on to the bottom of the jump seat as the gut-wrenching turn was followed by a high-speed descent.

"A second mark, Captain," Marquez said. "They've fired two. The location is verified."

Brognola would've liked to have turned and seen where they were going, but the G-force kept him glued to his seat. He also had other, more important things to do. "Papa Team," he said into his headset mike. "Do you copy the gun coordinates? Do you have a visual on it yet?"

"Roger, Big Bird," McCarter said. "We can see the firing position and are closing on it. It's in a large warehouse over the water. If it's well defended, I don't think we can stop them quickly enough."

"Then stand down," Captain Nowlin said. "We'll do the job."

The AC-130E's descent suddenly slowed, and Brognola's stomach lurched up into his throat.

"We're at firing altitude, Cap."

"We should be seeing the place ourselves by now," Nowlin said.

Brognola twisted around in his seat so he could look out the front windshield.

"There!" Nowlin jabbed a finger at the shoreline. "They've blown the damned roof off."

From the near end of the warehouse, orange flame blossomed through the roof, followed by a plume of black smoke.

Something big and mean screamed over the Hercules.

"That's three rounds fired," the lieutenant said.

"Big Bird, this is Alpha Team," Striker said. "We're taking incoming on this side. A shell just hit in the river to the north of the plaza. We're over the UN grounds, now. Estimate contact with the suspected spotter position in two minutes."

"You got another one on the way, Alpha," Brognola said.

"Roger that, Big Bird."

Captain Nowlin started to bank the left turn that would put the warehouse in the middle of the Spectre's zone of death.

"When will you be ready to shoot back?" the big Fed asked.

"As soon as we get our target locked into the fire-control system's electronics," Nowlin said. "Another couple of seconds is all we need. How're we doing, Pete?"

"You're on the money."

"Huggins, are you ready?"

"Locked and loaded, sir."

Brognola released his seat belt and leaned forward so he could see the target out of the left side of the aircraft. The rear end of the warehouse roof was burning around the hole made by the howitzer. A quick scan of the surrounding area showed no police or fire presence. There were a few human targets scattered around the building, but he had to assume that they were unfriendlies.

The conditions of engagement he had discussed with the President were all met.

"Permission to fire, Mr. Brognola?" Captain Nowlin said.

As Brognola opened his mouth, another blast ripped the air and a fourth round sailed away toward Manhattan. Not the nuke, he thought. Please don't let it be the nuke.

"Sir?"

"Don't fool around with these people," Brognola said. "Give 'em the works."

"Glad to oblige."

CHAPTER TWENTY-THREE

Oswald Carmody hung tough, even though the hounds of hell were bearing down on him.

Through his binoculars, he could see the black helicopter drop down over the front of the Secretariat, dip low over the river and make a beeline for the warehouse he was currently occupying. Because there was no visible insignia on the aircraft, there was no way of telling which of the alphabet soup of government agencies it belonged to. Not that it mattered in the least who had sent it. The standing orders to the hit squad the Blackhawk carried would be the same: terminate with extreme prejudice, show no mercy.

Carmody hung in until the fourth HE shell arced over Manhattan's skyline and crashed to earth.

Behind the chopper, north of the General Assembly, something flashed bright in the pocket park, followed by white smoke and a thundering bang as the conventional warhead's detonation rolled across the water.

That was all he needed to see. Peterson had more than found the target; he'd squarely nailed it.

"Fire for effect," Carmody said into the cellular phone.

"You'd better believe it," Peterson replied.

Carmody broke the connection and threw the phone down on the roof. He didn't need it anymore. He grabbed the money bag and his machine pistol, and sprinted for the fire escape, cutting a path around the dead splatter-artist, who lay in a pool of his own splattered blood.

There was only one thing on Carmody's mind as he hustled down the ladder. He had to put some cover between himself and the nuclear blast that was only seconds away. He dashed down the fire-escape stairs and threw himself off the last landing and into an overflowing Dumpster. The bulging black plastic bags broke his fall.

As he hopped down to the pavement, he could hear the *whup-whup-whup* of the helicopter as it swept in from the river. Too bad for the guys in black, he thought as he raced for the front of the building. A little thermonuclear shock wave was about to spoil the rest of their lives. As he reached the front of the building, the fifth and final shell howled over the horizon. With the building between himself and the nuclear explosion, he had a chance of surviving. He ducked and covered against the bottom of the wall.

As the Blackhawk that carried Bolan, Lyons, Blancanales and Schwarz swept down on the UN tower from the northwest, the third HE round whacked a huge circle of wave and froth in the river to their right.

"Big Bird, this is Alpha," Mack Bolan said "Round three just hit in the water off to the south of the complex. It landed much tighter to the west shore than the first two. It won't take many more tries for these guys to bring the gun on target."

"Somebody's moving on the rooftop of our suspect building," Schwarz said, lowering his binoculars. "It's the gray one facing us end-on."

"Did you see that?" Blancanales asked.

"Yeah," Schwarz said. "Sun-flash on optics. Whoever it is, they're looking our way."

"Big Bird, this is Alpha," Bolan stated. "We have a subject in sight on the roof of the suspect building. He looks like an excellent candidate for the OP."

Behind them, a thunderclap rocked the air.

Lyons hung his head out the Blackhawk's open doorway and looked back toward the UN.

"Trouble," he said. "They laid the last round on the park. Hit it dead in the middle."

"Big Bird, this is Alpha again," Bolan said. "They just scored a direct hit on the grounds. The next shot will most likely be the nuke."

"Look!" Blancanales said. "The spotter's up and running."

"Big Bird, our spotter is hightailing it. They've definitely got the range on the target. Don't let them fire the next round."

"Goose this sucker," Lyons told the chopper pilot. "That son of a bitch is getting away."

The Blackhawk was fast, but not fast enough to reach the far shore before the man disappeared down the fire escape.

"Damn," Lyons said. "Dammit to hell." He started stripping off his battle gear. He dumped his combat harness and shoulder holster on the deck, then ripped off his black long-sleeved shirt.

"What are you doing?" Blancanales asked.

Lyons didn't answer. He yanked off his boots and

replaced them with the ballistic nylon fighting shoes he'd worn on the flight from Utah.

As they flew over the low dock that Carmody had landed on a few minutes before, above the roar of the Blackhawk's rotors, they all heard the howl of the fifth shell in the distance.

The noise was growing louder and louder.

As CAPTAIN SARNOV braked to make a hard, screeching right turn into the warehouse driveway, the second howitzer round went off. A cloud of black smoke puffed from the building's roof and rolled out the open doors and fractured windows. The sedan bounded up and over the driveway, landing on all four wheels in the parking lot. Sarnov hit the brakes again, squashing the pedal to the floorboards. The car's nose dipped, his Sicilian targets scattered and he opened fire. The front windshield shattered around 7.62 mm holes as the folding-stock Valmet rattled in his right fist.

He got one of the guards; he was sure of that.

The first burst flattened the guy up against the front of the limousine. The hail of AP bullets held him there for an instant, shuddering like a tree branch caught in a river current, as his blood and bone sprayed over the long, sleek hood.

By then, Sarnov was taking answering fire from three machine pistols that had retreated to the street entrance to the warehouse. Nine millimeter slugs sailed through the windshield at him and slammed into the car's grillwork. He realized at once that it was no longer possible for him to sit inside the sedan and survive. He wrenched open the driver's door and rolled out, dragging the Valmet and the extra mags with him. Bullets smacked the asphalt at his heels as he rounded the back of the car and crouched there.

He turned when the embassy's step van pulled up behind him. As he looked up, a hail of bullets swept over his head. They turned the two panes of the van's front windshield into ragged, frosted spikes. The machine-pistol slugs shook the truck's chassis, and the radiator drained from a half-dozen holes.

Sarnov skirted the front of the truck and rounded its far side. Ferdishenko and Turgenev were there waiting for him, safe, armed and ready to fight.

"What now?" Turgenev asked.

"Do we charge the building?" Ferdishenko said.

The whine of a heavy rifle slug over their heads answered both questions. It came from atop the abandoned factory across the street.

They would wait for Beloc to do her part.

As they knelt behind the step van, another howitzer boom shook the air.

TASHA BELOC DREW a bead on the Sicilian standing at the edge of the doorway, then swung her cross hairs over a bit, into the middle of the opening. When the gunman stepped out to fire on the step van, she tightened down on the MSG-90's precision trigger. The gun bucked hard into her shoulder. The powerful recoil wave made her lose the target in the scope field. By the time she regained it, the target was no longer standing. He was lying across the threshold with a gaping hole where his heart should have been.

The two men who remained in the front entryway of the warehouse suddenly grew very cautious and no longer showed themselves in the doorway.

Beloc raised her eye from the Leupold scope and scanned the scene across the street.

It was then that she noticed the silhouette of the Blackhawk helicopter, hovering over the river about a mile away. An instant later, she saw the much larger, fixed-wing aircraft circling overhead.

Beloc knew a Spectre gunship when she saw one. She also knew the indiscriminate and total havoc it could wreak on a stationary target.

"Captain, get out of there!" she shouted into her walkie-talkie.

She didn't wait for a response. She didn't dare. She abandoned her long gun and ran for the fire escape.

GABHART AND RANSOM carried the *starookha* in a cradle they made of their linked arms. Both men were smudged black with propellant soot, and both choked back the urge to cough and clear their lungs of the poisons they'd been inhaling. They very carefully set the Soviet nuke down on the D-20's loading tray, then pushed it into the cannon's breech. As they locked down the shell, Charles Krick put a hand on Peterson's shoulder.

"I want to pull the lanyard," he said hoarsely.

Peterson grimaced.

"I paid for this party," Krick reminded him.

It did only seem fair. Peterson handed him the end of the cord, and they all retired to the open cargo container.

"This one's from Charlie," Krick said.

The greeting was not intended for public consumption. He was the only one who could hear it. They all had their ear protectors on.

Krick yanked the cord.

As the cannon boomed and the *starookha* sailed away toward Manhattan, something different happened. The inside of the warehouse lit up white orange and there was a second bang. Sharper, overwhelming. It slammed the container so hard it sent the gun crew crashing down on their faces.

It was just a tiny taste of what was to come.

IN THE INSTANT before the Spectre opened fire, the hole in the end of the warehouse roof flashed orange. Brognola was as sure of it as he was of his own mother's name.

They had gotten off the nuke shell.

It was too late for last-minute heroics, too late for anything but all-out vengeance.

Captain Nowlin and Senior Master Sergeant Huggins sent a single aimed round of 105 mm HE through the rear of the warehouse roof. It looked like it landed right on top of the Soviet D-20. The explosion sprayed out through the open doorways and the emptied window frames, the shrapnel chopping down the men standing outside.

Then the 20 mm Gatlings opened up, and the gunship vibrated from their continuous thunder.

The electrically driven cannons whipped the warehouse and its perimeter into a foaming sea of dust. A dust puff rose with every hit, and there were thousands of shell strikes concentrated in the narrow target area. In seconds, the roof of the building vanished under the pounding of 20 mm hail, as did the parking lot and dock.

Brognola looked up from the withering onslaught, across the Hudson to the New York skyline. It should've been hit by now, he thought. A dirty gray mushroom cloud should've been rising over the city. A wave of renewed hope rushed over him.

"Alpha," he said, shouting to be heard over the rattle of high-speed cannonfire, "did you mark the fall of the fifth round?"

"Negative, Big Bird," Striker said. "We heard it incoming, but it didn't explode."

"Thank God for that."

"Yeah," Bolan said. "Alpha Team would've been toast, along with a few hundred thousand other people. We're making a move on the observer. I gotta sign off."

"Roger, that," Brognola said.

The Spectre continued to fly its lazy circle, all the while pouring fire down onto the target. A dozen more 105 mm shells, thousands of rounds of 20 mm.

The zone of fire wavered slightly, spreading out over the street and then over the river, but Captain Nowlin didn't let it slip any farther than that.

Four minutes into the barrage, the walls of the building began to collapse, then the roof toppled down onto the interior. They could see the twisted wreckage of the Soviet howitzer sticking up out of the rubble.

Brognola pulled the plug on the firepower display. "Good work," he told the Spectre's crew. Then he said, "Papa Team, Big Bird is through up here. It's your turn."

"Roger, Big Bird," McCarter said. "We're going in."

LIKE THE GUN CREW, Sergio Eshamani was protected by the cargo container from the first shot of 105 mm HE that ripped through the warehouse roof. Though he had been deafened by the previous blasts, he knew right away that this one was not the same. Its shock wave lifted the facing edge of the container off the deck. As it crashed down, big chunks of steel smashed into the sides of the cargo box, gouging rents high in the walls.

Shafts of light penetrated the darkness that surrounded him. From the direction of the blast and its force, he guessed that it had hit and incapacitated the Soviet howitzer.

For a second, the arms merchant thought he was going to be rescued.

That idea vanished as dozens of holes ripped through the roof of the container and red-hot lead slammed through the narrow space and into the floor all around him. Eshamani couldn't hear the impacts, but he could feel them in every nerve of his body. The world was shaking apart as more and more shafts of light speared through the roof of the chamber. Fragments of exploding steel cut him to ribbons. In a matter of seconds, he suffered thousands of wounds, until a direct hit by a single 20 mm shell put him out of his misery. His final thought, the instant before the huge slug took off his head at the shoulders, was that he had had the last laugh.

In the other cargo container, Krick, Gabhart and Ransom fell to pieces, as well. They died without ever hearing the punchline of Eshamani's joke.

Which was, of course, no sound at all.

TASHA BELOC'S WARNING through Ferdishenko's walkie-talkie and the drone of the Spectre's four engines overhead registered on Sarnov's consciousness at the same moment. He shoved Turgenev and Ferdishenko away from the step van. "Across the street," he shouted at their backs. "Run! Don't look back!"

Above them, something screamed to earth. The explosion rocked the ground and sent them to their knees.

"Cover," Sarnov told his men, "we've got to find cover."

As they scrambled to their feet and crossed to the front of the deserted factory, 20 mm rounds began thrashing the warehouse to splinters and churning the earth into powder.

There was no cover.

The building's facade acted like a backstop, absorbing the fragments of cannon round and concrete as the shells shattered on the pavement. Bits of razor-sharp steel smacked into the bricks above their heads and shattered the glass out of the windows high in the wall.

"Keep moving," Sarnov said, pushing his team members ahead of him, along the front of the building.

When they neared the padlocked truck entrance where Sarnov had left Beloc's car, the fusillade stopped. The roar of gunfire behind them was replaced by the sound of a lone helicopter approaching.

Sarnov rounded the corner of the building and saw the car was no longer there, under the fire escape.

It was nowhere in sight.

"BIG BIRD DIDN'T LEAVE very much for us to mop up," Encizo said as the Blackhawk angled in on the smoking ruin of the warehouse.

"Fine with me," McCarter said, "as long as they got the bloody gun."

The helicopter touched down in the middle of the cratered street, and Phoenix Force hopped out.

Manning and Encizo cut right and took what remained of the far side of the building. James, Hawkins and McCarter took the front entrance, which was still standing.

On the side of the warehouse, Manning and Encizo found all the hostiles down and out. Three men in expensive suits lay on their faces on the planking. They were dusted all over with black soot. The black stuff was even inside their ears. They had all taken grievous and obviously mortal shrapnel wounds to the back.

James, Hawkins and McCarter approached the limo, which had been virtually crushed by concentrated cannonfire. The shards of glass left in the slit of a windshield were washed pink with the driver's blood. As they rounded the limo, two men jumped out of the collapsed front of the warehouse and rushed them with machine pistols stuttering.

Whether they were panicked beyond reason by the fury of the Spectre's attack, or truly brave and seeking revenge for the deaths of their comrades, the result was suicide.

Hawkins returned fire with his H&K subgun. He chopped down both men down with multiple chest and head hits, sending them crashing to the ground.

There were no other apparent survivors at International Scrap Metal, but to make absolutely sure, they would have to call in a crane and search-and-rescue dogs.

SARNOV WAS greatly relieved to see Beloc's car pull a U-turn at an intersection and come down the street toward them. She crossed the center line and pulled up in front of the truck driveway on the wrong side of the street. Then she scooted over into the passenger's seat so Sarnov could drive. Ferdishenko and Turgenev piled into the back.

"Why did you turn the car around?" Sarnov asked her.

"Because I wanted a closer look at the men in the Blackhawk."

"That may not be such a good idea," he said.

"We're traveling on diplomatic passports," she said. "They can't do anything to us."

"Nothing but kill us," Ferdishenko said.

"Not without a reason," Beloc responded.

As Sarnov drove around the helicopter, she sized up the men decked out in full-assault black. She recognized the youngest one at once from Riga. He'd been the sniper on the trawler moored across from the *Varuskya Liset*. Beloc never forgot a man she'd had in her sights.

HAWKINS LOOKED UP from his weapon as the sedan crept past. The blonde in the passenger's seat caught his eye, then pointed her index finger at him. Crooking back her thumb, she made a pretend pistol out of her hand, then pretended to take a potshot at him.

Hawkins turned and watched the car until it disappeared around a corner.

"Who was that?" McCarter asked him.

"I don't know, but I'd like to," Hawkins said. "She was drop-dead gorgeous."

"Ships in the night, Hawk."

"Yeah, I guess so."

CHAPTER TWENTY-FOUR

As the Blackhawk descended over the roof of the gray building where they'd spotted the suspect, Carl Lyons pulled his Colt Python from its shoulder holster and tucked it into the waistband of his pants at the small of his back. He pulled the tail of his khaki T-shirt down over the gun butt.

"This is the only way we can get this bastard," he said to Bolan. "You keep a close watch on him from the air, tell me where he goes." Lyons picked up a two-way radio and pushed it into a front pants pocket. Then he stepped out of the open doorway.

The drop was fifteen feet. Lyons landed in a crouch, then ran for the fire escape. As he started down the ladder, the Blackhawk wheeled away and climbed.

"He's running east," Bolan's voice crackled through the radio's speaker, "heading down the street in front of the gray building. He's white. Sandy blond hair. Tall and wiry. He's wearing no hat, and has on a dark blue T-shirt and jeans. He's carrying a black travel bag on a shoulder sling. You'd better hotfoot it, Ironman. He's really traveling."

Lyons jumped from the fire escape into the Dumpster. He hit the pavement running. He was determined not to lose the guy. But when he rounded the front of the building, his suspect was nowhere to be seen.

He keyed the two-way radio. "Where is he?"

"Straight ahead," Bolan said. "I'll tell you when to turn."

Lyons shifted into wind-sprint mode. He emptied his mind and concentrated on making everything smooth. On making the energy flow from his center. He turned when Bolan told him to.

"It looks like he's heading for the subway." the Executioner said. "If he gets on a train, we can forget it."

Lyons didn't answer. Sweat was starting to ooze down the sides of his face and the middle of his back. It cooled him off and gave him a second wind.

ALL OF OSWALD CARMODY'S plans evaporated when the nuke didn't detonate.

Crouching there like a halfwit fool in the lee of the building, he knew the black chopper was streaking in on him. He took off as fast as he could. There wasn't anyplace for the helicopter to set down between where he was and the Vernon-Jackson Street subway stop.

He didn't look behind him after the first fifty yards or so. He figured that if they hadn't dumped off foot pursuit by then, they weren't going to. And he didn't look up while he was running; he didn't have to. He could hear the helicopter hovering above, dogging him. They hadn't fired on him yet, but he wasn't counting on things staying so friendly. He cut back and forth from one side of the street to the other, doing his best to throw off any sniper's aim.

It was the scum-sucking arms merchant who'd

screwed things up. Either he'd sold them a bogus nuke or he'd fudged them on the PAL code. Maybe he'd never ever really had the PAL code. The upshot was, the game was over for now.

Not forever.

Just for now.

He had a quarter of a million in cash in the bag. He could rent a car with Eshamani's credit card, drive into Canada, then return to the U.S. into a militia-friendly northern state. Hell, as an outlaw, he might be even more successful at making converts to the cause.

Only when Carmody ducked into the subway entrance did he stop running.

He stopped running because he was home free.

LYONS REACHED the subway less than a minute after Carmody. Unlike Carmody, he kept on running. He vaulted the turnstile and ran to the platform entrance. There was a crowd stacked up, waiting for the next train. Lots of moms and kids and a few old people. And in the middle of the crowd, a tall guy in a blue T-shirt carrying an overstuffed black bag.

The station PA system announced that the next train would be arriving in one minute. Lyons stayed right where he was. There was no way the guy with the bag would miss him coming; Lyons towered over the other people on the platform. He had to wait until the very last second to make his move. He reached under the back of his shirt and adjusted the hang of the Python, freeing the butt for a quick grab.

When the train's brakes squealed out of sight down the track, Lyons moved quickly up the platform. The guy had his back turned, so Lyons moved faster, closing the distance between them.

He realized then that he couldn't use the Python. There were too many bystanders.

The bad guy wasn't so fussy. When Carmody looked over his shoulder and made eye contact, the militiaman knew who Lyons was, and what he wanted. Carmody rammed his hand into the open top of the money bag.

Lyons caught a glimpse of blue steel as the Sawtooth Patriot leader started to haul out his machine pistol. In a blur, Lyons hurled himself forward, arms windmilling, then tucking tight to his torso as he built up momentum for the kill strike. There was only one thing in his mind. The target—Oswald Carmody's center chest.

As the train roared into the subway stop, Lyons lashed out with his right leg, making solid contact with the ball of his foot. Something crunched. Something went "Oooof!" The kick sent Carmody hurtling backward off the platform and into the path of the onrushing train.

He didn't make a sound as he fell. He couldn't scream because all the air had been forced from his lungs. The train hit him before the wheels ground him up. It hit the black bag, too. Green bills burst into the air like a startled flock of birds. They fluttered down over the astounded people on the platform.

Then the frenzy set in.

Nobody gave a damn about the dead guy under the wheels.

People who'd been on the train jumped out onto the platform and helped themselves. Everybody yelling, grabbing for what they could get.

Almost everybody. Lyons caught a few bills out of the air and handed them to a kid too little and too timid to join the fray. Only one person on the platform noticed as he left, and she was smiling.

Stony Man Farm
6:35 p.m. EDT

Kurtzman clinked glasses with Barbara Price. "Here's to you," he said. "The best in the business."

Price sipped her Scotch on the rocks. They were alone in the computer center. Everyone else had called it a day and crept off for some long-postponed sleep. Maybe because it was just the two of them, she didn't say anything modest, didn't deny the truth of the compliment right away. She gave herself a moment to savor it.

Then she said, "We had some uncommon good luck on this one, too. If the shell hadn't hit the park lawn, if instead it had hit in the middle of Roosevelt Drive or First Avenue, even if it hadn't exploded, the warhead could have shattered and sent plutonium dust drifting all over town."

"If it hadn't hit the lawn on an almost perfect, nose-down trajectory, it might have broken apart, too," Kurtzman said.

"Face it, we just barely dodged it this time, Bear."

"A miss is as good as a mile."

Price found it hard to be jubilant. "Next time,"

she said, "our would-be overnight nuclear power might be some nutcase who's raided a hospital radiation lab for its cesium. And then wrapped it around a stick of good old-fashioned dynamite. We won't get five chances to stop the bad guys then. We won't even get one."

Kurtzman rattled the ice in his glass. "You're right. The genie's out of the box. Out of control a thousand different ways, and all of them deadly. We both know the war is never going to be won in our lifetimes. But it's okay for us to celebrate a victory, even if the fight goes on."

"To victory," Price said.

"And vigilance," Kurtzman added.

The Camorra takes on the Mafia on America's streets....

DON PENDLETON's

MACK BOLAN®

BLOOD FEUD

A blood feud erupts between the Camorra and the Mafia, as Antonio Scarlotti takes the Camorra clan into a new era by killing his father. Soon a series of hits against top American Mafia men shocks the country, as families and innocent bystanders are brought into the fray. Brognola entrusts Bolan with the mission of shutting down this turf war and stopping the driving force behind it.

Available in August 1998 at your favorite retail outlet.

Or order your copy now by sending your name, address, zip or postal code, along with a check or money order (please do not send cash) for $5.99 for each book ordered ($6.99 in Canada), plus 75¢ postage and handling ($1.00 in Canada), payable to Gold Eagle Books, to:

In the U.S.	In Canada
Gold Eagle Books	Gold Eagle Books
3010 Walden Avenue	P.O. Box 636
P.O. Box 9077	Fort Erie, Ontario
Buffalo, NY 14269-9077	L2A 5X3

Please specify book title with your order.
Canadian residents add applicable federal and provincial taxes.

GSB61

TAKE 'EM FREE

2 action-packed novels plus a mystery bonus

NO RISK
NO OBLIGATION TO BUY

SPECIAL LIMITED-TIME OFFER

Mail to: Gold Eagle Reader Service
            3010 Walden Ave.
            P.O. Box 1394
            Buffalo, NY 14240-1394

YEAH! Rush me 2 FREE Gold Eagle novels and my FREE mystery bonus. Then send me 4 brand-new novels every other month as they come off the presses. Bill me at the low price of just $16.80* for each shipment. There is NO extra charge for postage and handling! There is no minimum number of books I must buy. I can always cancel at any time simply by returning a shipment at your cost or by returning any shipping statement marked "cancel." Even if I never buy another book from Gold Eagle, the 2 free books and mystery bonus are mine to keep forever.

164 AEN CH7Q

Name   (PLEASE PRINT)

Address   Apt. No.

City   State   Zip

Signature (if under 18, parent or guardian must sign)

* Terms and prices subject to change without notice. Sales tax applicable in N.Y. This offer is limited to one order per household and not valid to present subscribers. Offer not available in Canada.

GE-98

James Axler

OUTLANDERS™

DOOMSTAR RELIC

Kane and his companions find themselves pitted
against an ambitious rebel named Barch, who finds a
way to activate a long-silent computer security
network and use it to assassinate the local baron.
Barch plans to use the security system to take over
the ville, but he doesn't realize he is starting a
Doomsday program that could destroy the world.

Kane and friends must stop Barch, the virtual assassin
and the Doomsday program to preserve the future....

One man's quest for power unleashes a cataclysm
in America's wastelands.

Available in September 1998 at your favorite retail outlet. Or order your copy now by
sending your name, address, zip or postal code, along with a check or money order
(please do not send cash) for $5.99 for each book ordered ($6.99 in Canada),
plus 75¢ postage and handling ($1.00 in Canada), payable to Gold Eagle Books, to:

In the U.S.	In Canada
Gold Eagle Books	Gold Eagle Books
3010 Walden Ave.	P.O. Box 636
P.O. Box 9077	Fort Erie, Ontario
Buffalo, NY 14269-9077	L2A 5X3

GOLD
EAGLE ®

Please specify book title with order.
Canadian residents add applicable federal and provincial taxes.

GOUT6

**After the ashes of the great Reckoning, the
warrior survivalists live by one primal instinct**

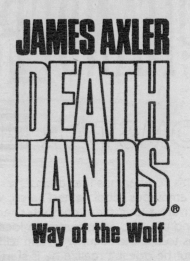

JAMES AXLER

DEATH LANDS®

Way of the Wolf

Unexpectedly dropped into a bleak Arctic landscape by a
mat-trans jump, Ryan Cawdor and his companions find
themselves the new bounty in a struggle for dominance
between a group of Neanderthals and descendants of
a military garrison stranded generations ago.

Available in July 1998 at your favorite retail outlet. Or order your copy now by
sending your name, address, zip or postal code, along with a check or money order
(please do not send cash) for $5.50 for each book ordered ($6.50 in Canada),
plus 75¢ postage and handling ($1.00 in Canada), payable to Gold Eagle Books, to:

In the U.S.	In Canada
Gold Eagle Books	Gold Eagle Books
3010 Walden Ave.	P.O. Box 636
P.O. Box 9077	Fort Erie, Ontario
Buffalo, NY 14269-9077	L2A 5X3

GDL42

Please specify book title with order.
Canadian residents add applicable federal and provincial taxes.